Born and raised in southern Oregon farm country, Ellie Spaneker flees her home and abusive husband, her trail dogged by a brutal ex-cop in the hire of her vengeful father-in-law.

In Portland, retired homicide detective Skin Kadash fills his idle days drinking coffee and searching for Eager Gillespie, a teen runaway of special interest as the only witness in a troublesome and long unsolved murder.

Eager, meanwhile, is on his own, grifting and working the angles in the homeless underground, oblivious to the unfolding events which will force him to face the consequences of a crime, and a longing, which has haunted him for years.

These disparate trails converge at a bloody standoff, the harrowing end of a string of violence that stretches from the high desert to the streets of Portland—committed by a perpetrator known only as Shadow.

Also by Bill Cameron
Chasing Smoke
Lost Dog

PART ONE

THE TRUTH HAS A WAY OF ELUDING CAPTURE

The Idiot With the Pistol

Eager Gillespie once told me he'd be more likely to shit a diamond than live to see his twenty-first birthday. I dumped his beer anyway and he wandered off, shaking his head at the cruel injustice of it all. It will be almost a year before I see him again, in the street out front of my house—still years shy of drinking age but just in time to catch a bullet with his face.

The police have surrounded the house across from mine, established a temporary command center in my living room. Doesn't bother me, being a once-upon-a-time cop myself, though it might have been nice if they'd used the magic word before hijacking my Sumatra Mandheling and high-speed internet connection. Inside the target house huddles the man who'd fired the shot that scattered his family like a flock of juncos shadowed by a hawk. The police have emptied the adjacent homes, pushed onlookers out of the tactical sight lines. A cluster of press vans are double-parked a block away. The blades of the news chopper circling above beat out a staccato background music that seems tuned to the cadence of my heart.

Watching through my dining room window, I first catch sight of Eager among the crowd straining against the barricades the cops have erected. Near me, the negotiator speaks calmly into a captive cell phone whose mate has been tossed through the open front door across the street. The man with the gun—my neighbor for chrissakes, fellow named Mitch Bronstein—doesn't have much to say. No one knows what set him off. His wife Luellen, a fifteen-years younger corn-fed trophy from down south is no use. She seems to be in shock. Aside from answering a question about their little boy— "he's with his grandfather now" —she's got nothing to say. I can't tell if she's pleased about Grandpa or not. The older boy, a sweaty eighteen-year-old with a video gamer's sullen detachment, identifies the gun as some kind of revolver. "Something big." Spoken with cold self-possession. "Maybe an S&W 500." No other guns in sight. So the cops figure best case is four hammer-blow rounds in the cylinder, assuming the kid knows a Model 500 from his left nut. Next best is Mitch topped off after his wife and son fled. But maybe he has something tucked in his waistband too. Worst case could be pretty bad when you spun out the potential scenarios—gun shows make anything possible. Thus the captive phone, the command team in my living room, the calm-voiced negotiator.

Except Mitch appears at his front door. For a moment he seems baffled by the tactical tableau before him, but then his eyes find focus and his gun hand rises. Half a dozen cops or more open fire. Mitch gets the one shot off. It's then I realize Eager has slipped through the barrier, somehow managed to get down among the clot of uniforms. No one is sure in the confusion, but it appears Eager is in the path of Mitch's bullet. I hear Luellen scream as Mitch sits down in the doorway, peers at his bloody chest and prods one of the bullet holes like he's investigating dry rot. I follow the cops out into the street. Eager looks like he's weeping blood. He opens his mouth, but only gibberish comes out, something about Jesus. I've never heard him mention Jesus. Someone rushes over to him but he insists he's fine, maybe a little headache is all. Still bleeding, a slow trickle—the eyeball bulging and red but otherwise intact. He sits on the fender of a patrol car and waves off the EMTs. Eager never cared for doctors, or anyone with half an ounce of authority—maybe why he likes me. From the porch, Mitch calls out, asks for a glass of water. He's got five bullets in him. Eager has just the one, a .22 from what turns out to be a single-shot long-barreled pistol, a pup's gun. Ten minutes later Eager has vanished, no one knows where or how, and Mitch still wants his glass of water. He has to settle for an IV as the EMTs pack his wounds.

Mitch will claim he found the pistol in his older son's bedroom. Jase is the kid's name, from Mitch's first marriage. The initial discharge, the one that sent Jase and Luellen scrambling, was supposedly an accident. He'd barged into the kitchen to confront his son, fired a shot without meaning to. Anger and a too-tight grip is his story. When the others ran and the cops showed, he panicked, replaced the bullet with one he'd found in a box under Jase's pillow. Ashamed he was such a poor parent he didn't know his son even had a weapon, he couldn't stand the thought of what that meant about who he was. The second bullet was for himself. Then the phone bounced through the door and the calm voice talked to him. *Just come to me, friend, and we'll work this out.* And so he'd come walking through the doorway and lifted the gun to offer it to the calm voice. When the cops all started shooting he'd fired again. Another mistake, a reflexive clench. Bang. He never meant to hurt anyone. Just wanted to know where his son got a goddamn gun.

No one would be buying Mitch's bullshit. His wife has a darkening bruise on her cheek she claims she got on the way out the door, but everyone knows it's from the back of a man's hand. Even worse, a kid took a bullet in the face. He's a dipshit stray maybe, but one you couldn't help but like the way you like any puppy anxious to please. Half the cops present have rousted or arrested Eager at one time or another. No one is gonna believe the idiot with the pistol. Especially when they get inside the house and find a bullet hole in the kitchen wall big enough to shove your fist through and blood spatter like a spilled jar of paint trailing out the back door.

But Mitch isn't my concern. I'm more interested in what brought Eager Gillespie to my street this morning out of so many, and where he's gone so fast with a bullet in his head. Jesus. And I can't help but recall Eager had once complained to me that some asshole stole his piece, a single-shot .22 he carried for protection, right out of his bindle as he slept under the Burnside Bridge.

November 11

Silly, Silly Shadow

Shadow. That's what he was. A shadow, cold and fluid. He moved like darkness sliding under the eaves at dusk. Like runoff pooling at the foot of a bluff. Like the chill that arrives a step ahead of bad news. It was who he was, though if you asked him about it he'd look through you like a man trying to read a sign in fog.

Shadow.

He loved the word, loved it like he loved his own name. It *was* his name, a word he could say, a sound half-breath, half-song. He rocked on his heels and gazed at the convenience store shelves around him, so many shapes and colors, like being lost in a box of crayons.

An old man came out of the back room and took up a spot behind the counter, fixed him with a cloudy gaze. A voice argued with itself from a radio on the counter. "How can I help you, son?"

"S-s-s-shadow …"

The old man's gaze flicked to the cloth wrapped around Shadow's head and he frowned, puzzled. "Come again?"

"S-s-s-singing … S-s-s-shadow."

The old man seemed to deliberate for a moment. A cigarette smoldered in an ashtray between the cash register and the need-a-penny-take-a-penny dish. The old man reached for it, took a long drag. Coughed up a moist pillow of smoke. His eyes gleamed as though he'd figured something out. When he spoke again, his voice was quiet.

"Where you from, son—the clinic? You got any family?"

He rolled his head ... not a shake, not a nod. He didn't know how to answer the question.

"No one?" Flesh hung from the old man's neck like a curtain and fluttered when he spoke, a streamer in a soft breeze.

"S-s-s-soft."

The old man leaned back, eyes troubled. He seemed to come to a decision. "Soft all right." His words were more breath than voice now. "Soft in the head." He chuckled, weary, and started to turn away, to reach for the phone on the wall at his back.

Shadow didn't think. Maybe couldn't think. His hand shot forward, swift as a snake. The old man's larynx popped like an apple under a boot heel. A moment later, Shadow was behind the counter, singing over the fallen body. "S-s-s-silly, silly ..."

Three Years, Three Months Before

Grass Fed and Pasture Raised

Elizabeth Spaneker, Ellie to her friend and Lizzie to most everyone else, sat on the bus stop bench at 41st and Hawthorne, August something, Year of Our Lord … Year One, as far as she was concerned. Day One. Her head rested against the blank brick wall at her back, her eyes on the building across the street. She didn't feel like herself. A spattering rain fell, off and on, but she hardly noticed. She was thinking back to a day at Givern Valley Regional High School. Sixth period health class, ninth grade. A different Ellie sat next to little Stuart Spaneker—the boy from whom she would later get both her last name and the stiffness in her neck on cold, damp days. At the front of the room, the teacher gestured with smooth, long-fingered hands. "Listen to me, people. Are you listening? This is serious stuff here, information that could save your lives." No one was listening. Whispered conversations hissed on all sides. Ellie was more interested in the rain outside, hoping it would stop before school let out. At the front of the room the teacher frowned, lips tight, as if to say, "Please don't make this any harder than it already is." The skin of her face seemed dry and brittle. She was giving the condom lecture, a breathless flood of information she offered every

April in a bid to mitigate the impact of hormones and spring fever, for all the good it did. In time, the lecture would get her fired as the increasingly lurid presentation collided with community standards, but Ellie would be graduated by then.

Stuart had leaned over to Ellie's desk and dropped a half-sheet of folded notebook paper. She opened the note, face front as though she was listening to the condom lecture. *Hey, Ellie. Do you prefer smooth, or ribbed for her pleasure?* He'd signed it, *Stu Baby.*

Ellie crumpled the note. "Pervert." She focused on the anxious teacher—Ellie, sitting at the bus stop, could no longer remember the woman's name—but out of the corner of her eye she saw Stuart wink and make a smoochy face. He'd claim later it was in that health class that he'd set his sights on her, and Stuart had inherited the relentless drive and sense of entitlement that made the Spanekers first family of Givern Valley, Oregon.

"Everyone is talking about you and Stuart," Luellen told her later. "They're saying you two make a cute couple."

Ellie thought about Stuart's short, stocky form and ragged chestnut hair. "I don't mate outside my species."

"I think he's kinda cute." Luellen's eyes gleamed. "He'll spend money on you. His dad is rich." She'd been Stuart's target before Ellie, and seemed to enjoy the attention—and Stuart's willingness to spend Hiram Spaneker's money. Ellie gave her a look.

"Lu, please don't tell me you're jealous."

"I'm just saying you might as well enjoy it."

"Forget it. He's a troll doll."

Years later, a different Ellie would make excuses for abandoning her instinctive loathing of Stuart. She'd tell herself she'd been dazzled by the Spaneker money, which flowed like snowmelt when Stuart wanted to impress, or by the shaggy bangs that hung loose on his forehead, by the excess of confidence in his round, shiny eyes. Or maybe it was his sudden charm whenever she seemed primed to tell him to kiss off. But by the time she began to question her capitulation, it was too late; they were married and Stuart had knocked a baby from her womb.

A woman appeared out of the rain and dropped heavily onto the bus stop bench. She shook her umbrella, spraying Ellie with fine droplets. "Goodness! It's been so rainy lately." The woman looked away as she spoke, as if the comment was meant for someone else. There was no else. Half a block up Hawthorne a boy wheeled around on a skateboard, his t-shirt pasted to his shoulders by rain. Back in Givern, rainfall like this so late in August could make the difference between bankruptcy and a solvent winter for many families.

Ellie slid to the side to make room for the woman's spongy hips and overstuffed canvas tote.

"It's been wet this year, don't you think?"

"I wouldn't know." The sky hung dark and heavy. The weathered blue awning above the bench offered little in the way of shelter. She'd lost the umbrella Pastor Sanders had given her. Yet one more small thing left behind, like so much else.

"You're not from around here?"

Ellie brushed her hair off her face. The woman looked at her. Ellie stared back, her eyes tracing the caked and flaking boundary of foundation makeup that ran along the woman's chin and up the back edge of her cheek. Her grey, wiry hair seemed to want to fly off in all directions, a well-used scrub brush. The woman leaned back on the bench and clasped her hands across her bosom. Her fingers were long and thin, the skin smooth on the backs of her hands, younger than the crazy hair and pancake makeup suggested. Suddenly, Ellie could almost smell her health teacher's perfume. Miss Layton, that had been her name. Lady Latex behind her back.

"Are you going downtown?"

"Just getting out of the rain."

"Ah." The woman hesitated. "There's a nice café up the way."

Ellie fixed her gaze across the street at the white lap-sided building hugging the opposite corner, the wide glass windows adorned with posters advertising color copies for 79¢, overnight shipping with FedEx, UPS, or DHL, and private mail boxes for rent. The Ship Shop. Not the destination she'd imagined when she fled Givern two days before. "Are you trying to get rid of me?"

The woman stiffened. "I just thought you might be more comfortable."

Ellie had seen the café earlier. Hot tea would be nice, but she hesitated to spend the money until she knew how things would work out. And in any case, she needed to keep an eye on the Ship Shop, needed to see if Luellen arrived to pick up her mail.

"I'm fine right here." None of the previous Ellies would have been so blunt to a stranger. Not Givern Ellie, no. But now she was different. Not herself—a new self. Bus Stop Ellie. Ship Shop Ellie. Waiting and Watching Ellie.

Hard to believe a week before she'd been someone's wife.

The bus arrived, groaned to a stop. The woman threw Ellie a sour look and climbed aboard. Ellie pressed herself against the bench as the rain began to fall harder. She'd sent a letter to Luellen from Klamath Falls, but she had no way of knowing if Luellen had received it and no other way of getting in touch with her. There was no Luellen Granger in the phone book.

Earlier, when she'd first arrived at the Ship Shop, the boy behind the counter had cleared his throat and fiddled with a silver hoop that hung from his eyebrow. "I dunno ... I'm not supposed to ... you know."

Ellie didn't know. "I'm just trying to get in touch with my friend. Can't you tell me how to reach her?"

The kid seemed to be only a teenager. He wore a green polyester vest over a wrinkled white dress shirt, his name DYMO-taped to a tag on his chest. RAAJIT. Ellie didn't want to guess how to pronounce that. His dull brown hair, matted into long ropes, hung down past his shoulders and tattoos snaked up his neck from under his shirt collar. She caught a whiff of nutmeg and cedar shavings.

"You see, the thing is …" He looked past her, eyes blank as if he'd just awakened from a long sleep inside the shop. Rip Van Raajit. "That's the thing, you see."

"I don't understand what you're trying to say."

"My manager will be here soon."

Yet when the manager arrived, he was even less helpful. "We don't give out personal information about our customers." His manner was as focused as Raajit's was vague. He fixed Ellie with a hard stare from behind metal-framed glasses and adjusted his tie. No green vest or name tag for him. Ellie felt self-conscious about her own appearance. She'd arrived in Portland the previous evening after a long, anxious day on the bus. Armed with a Tri-Met transit map, she'd made her way across the river, found a cheap motel on East Burnside. She might have done better to sleep under a bridge. The motel, a decaying concrete and pressboard box called the Travel-Inn, tended to noisy shouting matches in the parking lot and frequent sex broadcast through the thin walls. She got almost no sleep, and the lukewarm shower in the morning did little to refresh her. Someone had stolen her duffel bag when she dozed off on the bus. This made the third day running in the same clothes. Luellen, she hoped, would have something clean she could wear.

"Maybe you could call her and let her know her friend Ellie is here from out of town."

"I can neither confirm nor deny that your friend has a personal mailbox here. Customer information is private."

"I don't have to know what number you call."

"I can't help you."

"Would you at least put a note in her box?"

"Only regular mail or deliveries from shipping services go in the rental boxes."

"I'll buy a stamp."

"And you can put your note in the mail pickup bin. It'll get back here tomorrow or the next day, when it can be properly sorted and delivered."

Ellie looked away. There were no benches. Just a row of self-service copy machines and a couple of counters. Staplers and paper cutters. The rental mailboxes lined the side wall. Nowhere to sit, but Ellie could stand until Luellen showed up. She'd stand all day if necessary. She moved toward the corner, took up a position next to a rack of office supplies.

The manager turned to the kid. "I'm going to get a latte."

"Okay, Mister Blount."

"I want her gone by the time I get back."

Out of the corner of her eye, Ellie saw the boy squirm. The manager glowered at her as he pushed through the door. Ellie turned to Raajit, pressure building in her chest.

"Ma'am, I'm sorry—" Ma'am. She was only a few years older than he was.

"It's been over a year since I've seen her."

"You can't stay here."

"I don't know how else to reach her."

The boy looked out the window, watched until his boss was out of sight. "Okay. Give me the note. But you can't wait around here. Most folks don't come in every day to check their mail." And so Ellie made her way out to the bench, to sit in the rain, to dodge offhand conversation, to wait and to watch.

The bus pulled away, carrying off the woman and her thick makeup. Across the street, Ellie saw a man in front the Ship Shop. He looked back at her, hands at his sides, a settled quality to his stance as though he'd been there all along. Big fellow with a round head propped atop his barrel trunk, sun-bleached crew cut capping his wide face. He wore jeans and a canvas jacket, stood tall and indifferent to the rain. *Grass fed and pasture raised,* so the stolid, pious folks back home might say of him, seeing the devout and steadfast in his obvious resolve. Ellie knew better. As she met his stare, she felt her face go slack with fear. The man belonged to Hiram Spaneker.

November 9

Local Farmer Found Dead

WESTBANK, OR: Local police in Westbank report the discovery of the body of Immanuel Kern, a Givern Valley farmer, in his home Friday night. Cause of death has not been determined, pending the post mortem examination. Responding officers, however, report no evidence of foul play. Kern was 64.

Get Yourself Some Sandpaper

In over twenty-five years as a cop, I only shot one person. Mitch Bronstein was angling hard to be number two—and my first fatality. Shortly before seven o'clock on a Friday morning my doorbell rang and I knew it would be him. Since I retired, no one else would dare.

I opened the door in a sleeveless t-shirt and boxers, cup of coffee in my hand.

"Kadash, I got a problem."

"So do I. Standing on my porch at the crack of fucking dawn."

"Someone painted my house."

I sipped my coffee. Ruby Jane had given me a French press a few weeks before, a birthday present months before my birthday. I was still figuring it out, still getting the grind and portioning right. Even short of perfect, the coffee was pretty damn good. "So what happened? Painter overcharge you?"

He threw up his hands. "No. Jesus." He turned and waved toward his place. "I mean, like, graffiti. My goddamn front door might be ruined."

"Sorry to hear it, Mitch." Mount Tabor isn't Felony Flats, isn't Eastside Industrial or Portsmouth, but we get our share of taggers, especially in the summer when too many kids have too much time on their hands. Hell, my own house has been tagged once or twice over the years. As the ancient philosopher suggests, paint happens.

"The thing is, I was hoping you could help me out."

"I'm not much of a handy man."

"No, not like that. I mean, help me find the guy who did it."

I knew what he was going to ask as soon as he mentioned graffiti, but I'd hoped my attempt at willful witlessness would derail his intent before I had to tell him to blow me. "Sorry, Mitch. Can't help you."

"You're a cop though. Aren't you?"

"I'm retired, Mitch." He looked at me. From his expression I might as well have been speaking Klingon. "I don't work for the police bureau anymore."

"What's that got to do with anything?"

"Well, what you want is a cop. I'm not a cop."

"I just thought—"

"Listen. What do you do for a living?"

"What difference does that make?"

"Indulge me."

"You know what I do, Kadash." True. "I'm a marketing consultant. I develop campaigns, do some creative direction and copy writing. Media, you know."

I nodded. "Sure. Makes sense."

"What's that supposed to mean?"

"I bet you have a half-finished novel or screenplay tucked away on your hard drive. You work on it weekends, or when Lu takes the kids out for ice cream. But you've got this busy life keeping you from giving it your all. Am I right? So you tell yourself when you retire you'll finally dedicate yourself to who you really are. Not just copywriter, but author with a capital A."

He regarded me for a moment, his expression a mix of bewilderment and restiveness. I guessed I'd hit pretty close to the mark. Mitch wasn't a bad-looking guy. Early forties, fit. He kept his dark hair cut short and combed back. He'd obviously been up a while, was coifed and dressed for casual Friday at the office: white polo shirt and tan Dockers. "What's your point?"

"It doesn't work that way for guys like me. I was a cop. Being retired means not having to be a cop anymore. If I wanted to still be a cop, I'd still be a cop. But I'm not. I sit on my deck. I watch the birds. I read vampire novels and rent movies."

"But—"

"Mitch, listen to me. I'm not sitting over here itching to investigate your shitty little vandalism. Do you hear what I'm saying?"

From the moment he moved in, Mitch exuded a hail-fellow, well-met bonhomie I had little patience for. He might show up at any time, invite himself in for a beer or try to drag me over to see his latest toy. Stainless steel gas grill, high def television, margarita blender. I tried to be polite, but the extent to which Mitch and I knew each other was mostly dependent on his own need to be seen and heard.

"What am I supposed to do?" The hurt added a wobble to his voice.

I sighed. "Go back home, pick up the phone, and dial the Southeast Precinct non-emergency line. They'll take your report right over the phone. Hell, I'll give you the number if you like."

"Kadash—"

I stuck up my free hand. "Your graffiti problem is not a novel on my hard drive. My hard drive is for Audubon Society newsletters and internet porn, okay? You want someone to do something about your door, you do what I told you. In a week or a month, an actual cop might stop by. Or not. Just in case, take a picture of the tag before you clean it off so they can add it to the file if someone ever shows up."

"What're you, Kadash, fifty-something? Fifty-five, tops? That's too young to go limp, man."

I imagined his polo shirt drenched in coffee. Ruby Jane would decry the waste of a good cuppa joe. "Mitch, I'm retired."

"But, Jesus, man. Look at the front of my house. You're the neighborhood cop."

No one would blame me if I shot him. Goddamn seven o'clock in the morning over some spray paint. The fact I was up and fiddling with the French press was beside the point. A man needed boundaries. But then Mitch turned and flung his arm out, like he was pointing at a heap of bodies. I looked across the street. His place was bigger than mine, a nice two-story faux Victorian with a wide front porch. When he and his cute little wife moved in a few years before, they'd painted the joint an overly lemon yellow with blue and white trim, had the yard landscaped. Pulled out the rusted chain link fence and installed cedar pickets.

The tagger had hit the oversized oak front door: the black symbol stark against the blond wood and inset stained glass. A deft touch with a spray paint can.

"What the hell am I supposed to do about that?"

"Get yourself some sandpaper."

"I thought you were a police officer."

I was talking to a houseplant.

"I mean, you still know people. Right? You know how to do this. I sure as hell can't do it. What the hell do I know about tracking down a criminal?"

"Southeast Precinct. Non-emergency line. Report." I waved ta-ta with my cup, took a step back, started to close the door.

Mitch stuck a Topsider across my door jamb and stood before me, arms crossed, lips pressed out. I sighed, shook my head. My coffee was getting cold, but Mitch was oblivious. I suppose I could have told him I already knew who did it; I recognized Eager's tag. I didn't know he was back in town. He was supposed to be living with his mother in Spokane. And while I didn't want Mitch to know it, I had to admit I was a wee bit curious why he chose the Bronstein door as a spot to plant his flag.

None of Your Concern

Just before sundown, a man showed up on the front porch of the duplex, hollering and banging. He appeared during summer evening twilight, front windows open to let some air in. Eager had just got his sisters into the tub. They'd laughed at his dumb joke about how you could grow tomatoes in the dirt caked on their fingers, something he'd heard some granny say in Fred Meyer. He left them splashing in the bubbles and was sitting in front of his mother's TV flipping between *Spongebob* and *Scrubs* when he heard the voice boom through the house. "Charm! Hey! Open up!" Eager looked down the stairs and caught a glimpse of the man's bulk in silhouette through the narrow window beside the front door.

"Who is that?" Eager tried to talk to his mother as she swept through the hallway from the kitchen.

"You're supposed to be getting your sisters ready for bed."

"They're taking a bath."

"Mmm." Charm Gillespie forgot Eager in an instant, went to the door and flipped the porch light switch.

Eager crouched on the stairs. Charm had her chef's knife in one hand, a cigarette in the other. She called through the front door.

"Who's there?"

"Hey, baby. How you doing?" The man's voice echoed.

"Big Ed?" She opened the door as far as the chain would allow, peered through the gap. "For chrissakes, what the hell are you doing here?"

"Come on, baby. Open the door. I came to see you."

The girls appeared at Eager's back, their skin soapy and slick. He raised a finger to his lips, then started sliding down the stairs, butt cheeks bumping one step at a time. Gem and Jewel, wrapped in towels, pressed their faces between the uprights of the banister and dripped onto the worn carpet. Below, Charm had one foot jammed against the base of the door as if she expected the man to pop the chain. She was slapping the knife blade against her thigh, the gesture increasingly wayward. Eager hoped she didn't slice through the shiny denim and open a vein. He'd have to clean the blood up.

"You got no business here. Get lost."

"Don't be that way, baby."

She dragged deep on her cigarette. "Drop dead, and when you do, make sure it's not on my fucking porch."

"Jesus, Charm. You're so dramatic. I happened to be in town and wanted to see you and the kids."

"Ever think I don't want to see you? As for the kids, I doubt you could pick 'em out in a room full of monkeys."

"They're that wild, huh?" The big man's laughter rattled the window frames.

"No, asshole, you're that stupid."

"Aww, come on. I thought we could spend some time together." He reached through the opening, grappled her breast with his meaty hand.

She swung the knife up so quickly the big man barely yanked his hand clear in time. "You are out of your fucking mind if you think I'm letting you or your septic cock anywhere near me." She brandished the blade. "Grab my tit one more time and you'll wake up in a body bag."

Eager reached the bottom of the stairs and slipped up behind his mother. "Who's that?" He caught a glimpse of the man's big face and crew cut through the open door.

"Nobody." Charm spat smoke through the gap in the door. "Fuck off, asshole. I squared my debt with you and Hiram ages ago." She pushed the door shut in his face, flipped the deadbolt as he shouted out on the porch.

"Charm, goddamn you! Open the door, you skanky bitch!"

She swept into the front room and closed the windows, muffling the shouts of the big man on the porch. Eager followed her through the dining room into the kitchen. The air in the house seemed to condense behind her.

"How come he wanted to see us kids?"

"Shut the hell up." She grabbed the phone off the charger and punched the number pad like she was trying to poke out someone's eyes. "Police, yes, goddammit." She looked like she wanted to swallow the handset. "There's a goddamn psycho screaming on my porch and I want to know what the hell you're gonna do about it."

The guy beat feet long before the cops arrived.

Next day, Eager asked his mother about him while she drank her coffee at the kitchen table. "Just some crazy asshole who overreacted to a misunderstanding a long time ago. None of your concern."

"Why was he yelling like that?"

"What did I tell you? I'll kick your balls up into your belly you don't shut up about it."

He shrugged and munched cereal. Charm was a big talker; he got worse from bullies at school. The girls came down, poured cereal and spilled orange juice on the kitchen table. They started flicking Cheerios at each other. Charm ignored them. She sat haloed in smoke and stared into her coffee cup until her cigarette burned down to the filter. Then she dropped the butt into her cup and got up.

"Eddie, Gem, Jewel, I expect you all to get this shit hole cleaned up while I'm at work. And don't you dare leave this house."

The girls stopped playing with their cereal and looked at Eager. He rolled his eyes. Charm didn't seem to notice. She left her cup on the table. Ten minutes later, Eager was out the door and skating down to Hawthorne to scare up some spending money. Beg, borrow, or steal, only there'd be no borrowing and little enough begging. The girls were on their own, digging holes in the yard or setting fires or whatever it was they did all day.

The last thing he expected was to see the big man from the porch again, this time in the auto repair parking lot next to the coffee shop, with his hand clasped around some woman's throat.

November 11

Disturbance At Area Clinic

MERRILL, OR: County police were called in to help control a disturbance at the Upper Basin Center for Cognitive Medicine outside Merrill last night. Staff at the private clinic report a female visitor became agitated with a patient. When asked to calm down, she responded with verbal abuse and threats of violence toward staff members. The woman fled before police could arrive, but in the ensuing confusion a number of patients left the facility.

County sheriffs are currently searching for the missing patients, who suffer from a variety of cognitive impairments. Deputy Raelene Suggins of the Klamath County Sheriff's Office asks area residents to report anyone seen wandering or suffering apparent disorientation or confusion.

Roaming Eye Rolls

I'm not part of this. This electronic buzz, this steadfast authority. Cops move from here to there in the street out front of my house, pre-programmed automatons following invisible tracks. Some enter Mitch's; others come out. A few stand at the crowd control barricades, shaking their heads and repeating the phrase, "We'll have this cleared up as soon as we can, sir and/or ma'am." Others work the street, knocking on doors or interviewing neighbors. On his porch, the EMTs crawl over Mitch like ants scaling a picnic lunch. Everyone has a job. Each knows exactly what to do.

I have no idea what's going on anymore.

A typical November drizzle falls, too thin to send gathered onlookers looking for umbrellas. I feel it in my shoes. I ask a few people about Eager, but no one has seen him. The EMTs are focused on Mitch and don't have time for me. I'm only allowed inside the barricade out of deference to my status as a former one-of-us—a pity lay. Or maybe it's the fact they still have command of my house. I'm talking to one of my neighbors, a woman with two daughters in pre-school, when Mitch goes into cardiac arrest.

"What an awful thing." She's watching the EMTs. Her name is Helen, and this is the most we've spoken since she and her husband moved in three years before. "Right here on our street."

It can happen anywhere, I tell her. "A street full of manicured lawns and well-maintained minivans sure as hell didn't stop Mitch from going off the rails, did it?" She looks troubled, mutters about her daughters stuck inside with her mother. They need to get going. Everyone is late for everything: work, day care, bridge club. Helen flinches when, up the street, a television news van backs up under a birch tree and catches a branch with a satellite dish raised up on its telescopic armature. The branch snaps with a sound like a gunshot. Helen trots toward her house, hands gripping her upper arms, cotton-swathed thighs swishing. No doubt I'll see a For Sale sign in her yard in the next couple of weeks, she and her husband convinced life is more certain out in Forest Grove or Happy Valley.

I move back to my front lawn. The EMTs have got Mitch on an IV now, oxygen mask over his nose and mouth. His face is bone white and the way his head flops side-to-side makes me wonder if I'll ever see him again. A hand grasps my elbow. I turn and there's Susan, my former partner in Homicide. Lieutenant Mulvaney now. She's running the investigative side of this circus, coordinating with tactical from my living room. I've known Susan for a long time.

"Skin, do you have a cigarette?"

"You're smoking again?"

She squeezes her lips together. "If I was smoking again don't you think I'd have my own cigarettes?"

"I dunno. Maybe you've become a mooch in your old age."

"Do you have a cigarette or not?"

"I quit."

Susan is tall and slender, with dusty blond hair wrapped up in a loose bun under her hat. She's in uniform this morning, a look I'm not used to. Her green eyes appear dull in the watery light, and her hair sports more grey than I remember. She breathes through her nose. There was a time when I could read her every expression, but things have changed between us. "You're sticking with it then."

"Sometimes it's easy, sometimes not so much. You know how it is."

"I had Eric and Leah to keep me honest."

I'm not sure if she's tossing a jab my way or not—she knows enough of my own disastrous romantic history to be aware of my shortage of anyone to keep me honest. But with Susan it isn't always easy to tell, especially since I retired and she got her promotion. Like a marriage falling apart, the collapse of our partnership had been driven by both bitterness and regret. To say our relationship is amicable these days is perhaps overstating the case. But at the same time, I'd still like to believe I can trust her when my nuts are in a vice.

"How long has it been?"

"A year and a half."

She nods. "That long." The skin under her eyes is dark. I can tell she has something else on her mind, but I'm not sure if she's come out here to share with me or is taking a break from all the clanking brass furrowing their brows in my living room. I myself had fled at least two captains and a commander, and hell, even the Man herself, Chief Rosie Sizer, who solemnly shook my hand, thanked me, and apologized for my trouble before handing me off to some spit-polished sergeant who wanted to know where he could plug in a tangle of cell phone chargers. I can't blame Susan for slipping away. She's been juggling a lot all morning, and I almost feel bad about adding to her troubles.

"So. Who you got looking for Eager?"

Her posture goes taut. "Eager Gillespie? Why should I have anyone looking for him?"

"You didn't see it? When Mitch got the shot off?"

"What are you saying?"

"Eager took the bullet in the eye."

She doesn't answer right away. "No one informed me." I can tell she's not pleased, but her only outward concession to an emotional response is to blink a couple of times. "Where is he now?"

I turn over my hands. "That's what I'd like to know. The paramedics checked him out, but he got pissy the way he does and they turned their attention to Mitch. Next thing I know, he's outa here. No one knows where."

"You must not have seen it right." I'm sure that's what she'd prefer. If he wasn't shot, he's not her problem. She also won't have to deal with the fact she wasn't informed of another victim of this morning's fiasco.

"I was looking right at him when the gun went off, Susan."

Her tongue probes the inside of her cheek. She's staring across the street at Mitch's porch, but I don't think she sees anything. "Maybe he's all right."

"Has Eager ever been all right?"

She drops her gaze and tilts her head, conceding the point. We encountered Eager the first time together after he was discovered at the scene of a homicide. Young woman shot to death, murder weapon never recovered. Eager the only witness—a useless witness, as it happened.

"I don't know what to tell you, Skin."

"Don't you think it's interesting he was here this morning?"

"I don't know. Should it be interesting?"

"Well, we're a short stroll from the scene of an unsolved murder he was part of and now he appears again the morning a straight goes Virginia Tech on his own family. I find that interesting."

"You think Eager has something to do with this?"

"I think it's pretty damn convenient he happened to show up this morning. Here."

"Hmmm." She's wishing my interest in Eager would burn off like the morning fog. All Eager can do at this point is make her life more difficult, particularly if Mitch's errant bullet is in back of his eyeball. "Skin, here's the thing: Luellen Bronstein and the kid, Mitch Bronstein's son?"

"What about them?"

"What do you know about them?"

"Only what anyone knows about his neighbors. They've only lived here a few years." Susan cocks her head at me. For some people, that's enough time to get written into the will.

"You've never talked to her?"

"Luellen? Sure. Mostly to say hi, lousy weather we're having. Why?"

"What do you know about the kids?"

"Their names."

"Jason and Danny."

"Right." I'm being more reticent than necessary, but I'm annoyed Susan isn't concerned about Eager. I don't want to tell her I've watched the little one for Luellen more times than I can count. Good boy, calls me Mister Skin. Beyond that, I know Jase has been in and out of trouble ever since his mother left Mitch when the kid was fourteen. But I also know if I tell Susan all this she'll want to interrogate me, and I have no interest in becoming a part of her investigation.

I've also never been able to match Susan's patience. "Jase is from Mitch's first marriage."

"He doesn't get along with Luellen. I could see it in their body language."

"Near as I can tell, Jase doesn't like anyone."

"This morning when the first patrol cars responded to the 9-1-1, they caught him running one direction, Luellen another. When we talked to them, she was upset, anxious. Like you'd expect. He acted like we were keeping him from something more important."

I turn my hands over. "Susan, he wouldn't piss on you if you were fire."

"How about Danny?"

"What about him? He's four years old." I study her face, but as usual she's a stone. "Susan, what's this about?"

"The Bronsteins were married three years ago. According to one of his colleagues at work they only met a few months before they were married."

"Okay. Danny isn't his kid. So what?"

"Danny wasn't there this morning."

"Damn good thing too."

"At least, that's what she told us. 'He's with his grandfather now.'" She pulled at her lower lip. "*Now*. Don't you think that's an odd way to put it?"

Susan doesn't talk just to hear the sound of her own voice. I know from long experience she's trying to fit the pieces together, looking for what connects to what. Mitch, Danny and his grandfather, the .22, the blood in the kitchen, the bullet hole in the wall. I'd be doing the same thing if I was still on the job. And, in a way, maybe I am. But I have my own interest.

"Have they recovered the bullet?" I'd rather Susan answer my questions than the other way around.

"From the kitchen wall?" She nods, pensive. "There was tissue and blood present. Justin Marcille says it's most likely a .357 or .38, but he won't know for sure until he gets it processed."

"It went through somebody."

Another nod.

"And definitely not from Mitch's gun."

"Not the one he had on him, no."

"And you don't believe any of that shit Mitch jabbered at the EMTs."

"We'll check it out."

"What does Luellen have to say?"

Her lips squeeze together again and she raises her hand to her face. It shakes a little as she rubs one eye. Susan isn't easily troubled, and I feel a chill run through me. Or maybe it's the rain dribbling down inside my collar.

"Luellen and Jason are gone."

"What do you mean? Gone where?"

"I left them in my car to catch their breath while I talked to Bronstein's boss. They'd had a rough morning, you know?" She's breathing through her nose again. "The officer I asked to keep an eye on them got distracted by an argument, one of your neighbors unhappy his car was inside the perimeter. When the officer got back to my car, they were gone. No one saw them leave."

She's losing witnesses left and right. "Whose blood is it? In the kitchen."

"We're pretty sure it's not Bronstein's. His wounds all appear to be from the exchange on the porch, and the trail goes out the back door, not toward the front of the house. It's definitely not Luellen or Jason's. They were both uninjured."

Who does that leave? Susan doesn't ask and I don't answer, but we're both thinking the same thing. Someone else was there. Grandpa maybe. Packing heat, whoever it was. But who got shot, and who did the shooting? Neither of us want to contemplate little Danny in that kitchen.

"Susan." I'm trying to duck the obvious. "This isn't the first time Eager's appeared at a scene involving a missing gun."

"Okay." But then she shakes her head. "It's not his blood either. I don't know why he was here this morning, but a teenager making an appearance in his old neighborhood is hardly cause for a press conference."

"He's supposed to be in Spokane with his mother."

"So now we're surprised Eager Gillespie isn't where he's supposed to be?" She gives me a sad little smile. "Skin, I know you like him. A lot of us like him. But that doesn't change the fact he's a poster child for mandatory minimum sentencing. I don't have time to deal with him and all his crap right now."

I feel a tickle in my throat, the beginning of a cigarette craving. *Thanks, Susan, for waking that up again.* This would be the time to tell her about Eager's tag appearing on Mitch's door a few months back, but instead I shake my head and turn away. "Sorry for troubling you." I try to keep the edge out of my voice, but don't think I pull it off. I'm fuming, because I hate the feeling that a year into retirement, I rate no better than some guy down on Pioneer Courthouse Square selling Scientology or 9/11 conspiracies.

"Skin, wait." She grabs my forearm before I can walk off. "Listen, if he's hurt, he'll turn up in an ER sooner or later. I'll put the word out, make sure I'm flagged. Okay?"

"Sure. Fine."

"I've got to go. We'll be out of your place soon." She lets go of my arm, turns toward the house.

"Susan, do me one favor at least." She looks back at me. "Check the bullet from the kitchen against the one they pulled out of that girl."

"Skin—"

"Just do it. Might get a surprise."

She heads back up my walk. Sun breaks through from the east, but the rain is still falling. I glance around. The chaos continues. So many vehicles are idling, cop cars, news vans, I feel light-headed from the exhaust. Reporters hound my neighbors, some on camera, some on tape. I can hear the voices but can't make out the words. Uniforms are talking to others, making notes. Detectives will do more detailed interviews later. Thankfully not me.

I decide it's time to get the hell out of there. Come back when things are back to normal. But before I can lift a foot, I catch sight of a figure standing at the barricade. For a second I think it's Eager. But only for a second, because the size and shape of their frames are the only things this fellow and Eager have in common. I almost turn away, thinking about coffee, but then I give him another look. Something about him. He's short, half past five, and narrow at the waist but thick at the neck and forearms, dressed in what appear to be dusty scrubs under a denim jacket. His head is wrapped in dirty white cloth, a scarf of some kind, an imperfect turban. He stares at Mitch and Luellen's house, watches as Mitch is attended by the EMTs. When they hoist Mitch onto the gurney, he turns my way, and for a moment our eyes meet—his are dark and round and unfocused, and one, the left, rolls loose and independent of the other.

I don't interest him, though, and after only a brief pause his head keeps turning and rising until it stops, abruptly fixed. I follow his gaze up and over my shoulder to the summit of Mount Tabor behind me. When I look back, he's still staring. Then, arms stiff at his sides, his hands flex open and his roaming eye rolls into place. *Flex, fists, flex, fists.* I can almost see the recognition in his face. But of what, I wonder. I know what I think of whenever I look that direction. Three years before, we found Eager Gillespie up there on the summit weeping beside the body of a dead young woman.

I blink, and the man is gone.

Thinking the Devil's Thoughts

Ellie was born on a simmering June night, an event she'd recall years later with almost as much clarity as supper the day before. It didn't occur to her there was anything odd about such a memory. She remembered the sound of her mother's cries, and strange lateral motions and choking pressure. The first piercing sensation of light. "I'm glad I don't have to go through that again," she mused one morning over scrambled eggs and sliced tomatoes. Age nine. Ellie's mother, a hard-eyed woman with forearms like canned hams, asked what possessed her little Lizzie to say such a thing. Unconscious of the sharp edge to her mother's voice, Ellie described the pain of being turned in the womb, her sudden awareness of cold and moisture, of being smothered by her birth caul. Her mother flinched at mention of the caul and started clearing the breakfast dishes, her movements brisk.

"What's the matter, Mommy?" Her father and brothers were already up and out, her sister still in bed. Ellie didn't often get to be alone with her mother.

"Finish your eggs." Spoken to the window over the kitchen sink.

"I didn't think I was alone in there, but I guess I musta been, huh?"

Her mother turned and slapped her, a blow so powerful it spun Ellie around in her chair. She held onto her tears, but ran from the kitchen and never mentioned the memory to her mother again. The only other people she ever told were Stuart and Luellen. The admission to Stuart came in a moment of foolish weakness after Rob, her oldest brother, revealed during her mother's funeral reception that Ellie had had a twin. It was a boy, half-developed and stillborn, buried as Aiden Kern in the children's plot behind the adult graves. Ellie had seen the stone, but it included no dates and for her it had always been just one among many. The Kerns had been in Givern Valley for a long time, longer even than the Spanekers.

Stuart loved gossiping almost as much as talking about himself. The story of Ellie's recollection spilled from his mouth into the ears of Pastor Wilburn and others at the Little Liver Creek Victory Chapel during Men's Breakfast the following Saturday. The same afternoon the old man took it upon himself to drive out to the house to tell Ellie she should forget such nonsense.

When she heard why Wilburn was there, she refused to make coffee. They sat in the front room of Ellie and Stuart's little house on the secondhand couch passed down from her grandparents.

"I don't see what the big deal is." She could hear Stuart in the kitchen, fridge door opening and closing, drawers slamming. No doubt making a mess as he eavesdropped.

"It's dangerous to be thinking the devil's thoughts."

She pointed her chin at Wilburn. "It's just a memory."

It had been raining, and the old man's hair was wet and slick against his scalp. "But it's a false memory, Elizabeth. No one can remember being born." He rubbed liver-spotted hands together. At least he didn't call her Lizzie, the hated nickname she'd been saddled with when Myra, as a toddler, had mangled Elizabeth. "Satan is trying to lure you into his fold. He wants you to remember the caul—to desire the power it promises you."

She almost laughed out loud, but the conviction in the old pastor's eyes stopped her. *The man watches football on a big screen television,* she thought. She looked past his ear and sighed.

Wilburn suggested some Bible passages she should read. Ellie didn't bother to tell him the house Bible was tucked under the broken back leg of the couch he was sitting on. "It's the influence of that Jewish girl," she heard him tell Stuart on his way out. "They're all atheists, you know. The Jews." After the old man left, Stuart had a few choice words for Ellie's careless tongue and Luellen's unwholesome influence. Ellie listened with the stoicism reserved for all complaints about her friend.

She'd read that once upon a time a birth caul had been viewed as a sign of imminent good fortune. Ellie was still waiting. She grew up a rustic, dark-haired girl in a family of honey blondes. One of Ellie's aunts claimed the dark hair came from an Eastern European many-great grandmother—a witch who'd also been born with a caul—but Ellie didn't much care where she had gotten it. She loved her hair. She brushed it until it shined and refused to have it cut. "It's my clothes," she announced another morning at breakfast—age eleven—having spent the night before poring through Bullfinch's *Mythology*. All she had on were a pair of white cotton panties. Her family stared at her for a long moment, then her brother Brett started laughing. "Hey, Lizzie, I can see your nips." Her mother smacked her with a spatula and sent her running right back up stairs to get some clothes on this second, and to put her hair up in a proper bun. The Bullfinch vanished from her room while she was at school that day. From then on her mother insisted on approving all reading material in advance.

At a church picnic the following summer, Brett drew laughs recounting the story of the hair. A group of boys sat together at a table under the birch trees at the back of the churchyard. Ellie saw them from her own place, quiet and alone among a clump of chattering girls. She could feel the boys ogling her, an experience more and more common in recent months. She went to her mother. "Tell Brett to stop talking about me."

"Don't be ridiculous, Lizzie." Her mother was sitting with a group of other moms. From the tightness in her jaw Ellie could tell she didn't appreciate being interrupted.

"I'm not being ridiculous. Make them stop."

Her mother closed her eyes, then stood and walked over to the boys' table, arms heavy at her sides. They quieted at her approach. Ellie watched as her mother spoke with them, then returned. "Stay away from those boys."

"I wasn't anywhere near them."

"Then how do you know they were talking about you?"

"I just know."

Her mother's mouth went hard and she looked away. "That girl was born with a caul, you know." An anonymous whisper. Ellie's mother clenched her teeth. "Lizzie, go find a seat and finish your dinner. I don't want to hear another word out of you."

Ellie still had a pile of Jello salad and a chicken leg. Most folks were done eating and sat talking, or had started to peel off for home. Half the tables were empty. Ellie dragged a folding chair off to the far side of the lawn, as far from the boys as she could go without getting yelled at, and sat down, back to the picnic, face to the sun. She spooned salad into her mouth without tasting it. Something to do. Around her she could hear conversation and laughter: her uncle complaining about the signal on his satellite dish; who was gonna apply at Jeld-Wen; endless discussions about irrigation and prospects for new water certificates. After a little while, she felt them gather behind her and to either side. The boys. Brett's friends. They smelled like sweat and grape Kool-Aid.

"What the hell's your problem?" Brett always came looking for a fight.

"Leave me alone or I'll tell Mom you're swearing."

"Whatever, bitch. I'll tell her you're a liar."

They both knew how that would work out. "Just go away."

"Hey, Lizzie." One of the boys pressed against her from behind. "Show me your tits."

She swallowed Jello and tried to imagine she was alone.

"Come on, you showed Brett."

"Yeah, Jesus, your own brother." Laughter. "You gotta show everyone now. Ain't that right, Brett?"

Brett moved around to face her and grinned, his eyes black points. "It's only fair, Lizzie. Unless you want me to tell Ma *you* was swearing."

She looked down at the soggy paper plate in her lap, the chicken leg and half-eaten Jello, remnants of baked beans and potato salad. The sight turned her stomach.

"How'd you know Brett was even talking about you anyway?"

"Yeah, you some kind of freak?"

"Leave me alone." Teeth together.

The boys snickered behind her. She saw movement at the edge of her vision, boys crowding in around her. A wall of backs to the adults lingering over coffee. "God fucking damn, Brett, even if she is your sister you gotta admit she's got some nice toots."

"You can tell right through her shirt."

"They're bigger than my sister's and she's going to college."

"Hot."

Ellie's cheeks burned, and her vision swam. She gripped the spoon so tight her knuckles turned white.

"No wonder she wanted to show them off. Take four hands to manage all that pudding."

As if that were some kind of signal, a hand snaked in from behind and gripped her breast. For an instant she didn't move, stunned by the unexpected contact. Then the hand squeezed and Ellie surged to her feet. Her plate fell onto the grass. A second hand clawed at her other breast, accompanied by hoots and laughter. Ellie heard a sound like an insect buzzing and her vision went dark. Her mother later claimed she started howling as she threw herself at the boy, that she'd become some kind of animal, possessed, clawing and shrieking. When her father got to her, dragged her off the screaming kid, she had a bloody clump of his hair in one hand and the spoon in the other. Two knuckles of his right middle finger in her mouth. She spit the finger out, stumbled away from her father's grip. She saw red crescent bruises on the boy's cheeks, evidence of her attempt to scoop out his eyes. Only then did she even recognize him, George Quinn, Brett's best friend. A well-liked boy. But to Ellie, in that moment, he was little more than eyes and fingers. *Eyes that stare, fingers that grab.* All around her, white faces gaped. George sobbed on the grass, his Vacation Bible School t-shirt smeared with blood and Jello salad.

Her sister, Myra, two years younger, came up. "Are you a witch, Lizzie?"

Ellie fled, ignoring her mother's shouts for her to stop. She ran across the fields behind the church and through stony pastureland to her house, four miles distant, where there was a place she knew no one would find her. A giant honeysuckle bush behind the equipment barn with a hollow inside, a smooth spot in the dirt where she could sit. Filtered sunlight dappled through the leaves. She still had the spoon. The distorted reflection she saw in its curved surface could only be the face of a girl with big toots and a dark soul. *All that pudding.* She dug a hole and buried the spoon between the honeysuckle roots.

After a while, she heard the pickup come up the driveway, and then her father walking through the yard. "Ellie, come on, honey.

We can fix this. Just come out." He went into the equipment barn, then across to the tack shed, calling over and over. She wanted to go to him, but she knew her mother would be somewhere behind. Waiting. He might try to comfort her, to fix this, but her mother would have her own ideas. So she waited him out in silence, biting her lip to keep from making a sound. Finally he returned the way he came.

When the sun began to set and it started to get cold, she crept out of her hiding place and never went back. She imagined the spoon there in the dirt, slowly corroding, and she decided that was where she would leave her self, buried in the ground to rot. Skin shed, a new Ellie emerged. Her mother dragged her to church to say prayers for weeks afterward, made her read her Bible every day and stand up in front of the congregation on Sunday morning to confess. Show repentance and beg forgiveness, particularly of George Quinn. "For rebellion is as the sin of witchcraft, and stubbornness is as idolatry." Ellie heard, but only she would know she had not prayed at all during that time, hadn't given a damn about forgiveness, particularly Pudding Boy's. She was glad they hadn't been able to reattach his finger. But she also knew that she could never win against her mother. Shortly afterward, at school, Ellie asked Luellen to cut her hair off. That seemed to provide her mother at least some measure of satisfaction.

Afterward, Ellie did what was expected of her. She took down her posters of rainbows and unicorns, smiled when her brothers made idiot jokes around the supper table, looked after her brat sister without complaint. She went to church, to school, to the relatives for family gatherings. But only because she had to. She became known as a quiet, solitary girl; but pretty in her strange, dark way. Maybe a little dangerous. Later, when Stuart took an interest in Ellie, her mother didn't even try to hide her relief. A Spaneker. They owned half the valley. She believed Ellie would find a grounding in

Stuart, and a chance to make a good home. Ellie was more inclined to agree with her father, who called Stuart a champion beer drinker but a barely competent farmer. She told Luellen, the only person in whom she could confide, that as far as she was concerned, Stuart was a blockheaded pig fucker with more brains between his legs than above his shoulders. Luellen collapsed into giggles. She had dark hair as well, but her family was notably dark, not farmers but professional types, insurance agents and bankers and software developers. Ellie believed she had originally been attracted to Luellen because she hadn't been of a farming family, though later the friendship ran deeper than that. Ellie's mother complained that she was involving herself too much with material folk, with Jews, not the kind of people a Christian girl should associate with. Ellie didn't bother to tell her mother Luellen's family wasn't Jewish but Lutheran, mostly German with a little Eastern European like Ellie's infamous great-great grandmother. Her mother believed what she wanted to believe. A dark-haired doctor or lawyer was a Jew, and that was that. So when confronted about her friendship, Ellie observed there was a little good in everyone. Didn't the Lord command us to reach out to those not in His sight?

Her mother let it stand at that—so long as Ellie stayed out of trouble she was allowed to continue associating with the Jew. But years later, when one of Luellen's cousins, a credit union officer, initiated foreclosure on Brett's farm, Stuart forbade her to see Luellen again. He told her to make friends among the church women—as if he gave a damn about the life of the Little Liver Creek Victory Chapel. Ellie didn't argue with him. She'd learned long before to hide the things important to her.

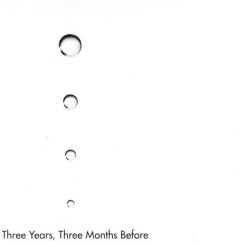

Three Years, Three Months Before

He Was a Cop

The responding officer reported two bodies at the scene. It was clear at a glance at least one of them was dead. A bullet had entered the young woman's head through the nasal cavity and tore through her right frontal and parietal lobes before exiting above the occipital bone. She lay at the edge of the summit drive at the top of Mount Tabor, her feet pointing toward the Harvey Scott statue. The second body was in the road, a figure who ran headlong into the patrol car, then collapsed. When the officer, fellow named Michael Masliah, put his hand on the figure's shoulder to check for signs of life, it unwound with a jerk and cried out, "He was a cop!" A boy, twelve or thirteen, and a mess: drenched, muddy, and slick with vomit, lower lip split and left eye socket swollen and dark. Hair buzzing atop his head like he'd stuck his tongue in a light socket. He'd been in the thick of some shit. Masliah bent down. "Damn, kid, are you all right?" The boy looked up into Masliah's eyes, then down at his badge. "Aww, fuck." He didn't speak again for the duration of his time in custody.

Susan and I took the call-out, our second in two days. The first involved a Franklin High basketball player who had been showing off for his teammates by shooting an arrow straight up into the air with a hunting bow and then trying to catch it on the way down again. After a series of failed attempts he finally succeeded—with his forehead. Dead on the thirty-five-yard line of the Franklin football field. The high school and attached park is near my place, and I sometimes walk down there on summer evenings to watch recreational league softball or soccer. If I'd been down there that day I might have saved his life, something his friends seemed to have only a passing concern with. "I told him he was an idiot, but he did it anyway." A typical response. No doubt the fence around the football field would get covered in ephemeral memorial objects over the coming days, photos and handmade, WE MISS YOU signs. "I told him he was an idiot," would be the real epitaph. Death-by-misadventure ruled an understaffed DA's office with no interest in filing charges. So we ended up back at the top of the call-out list just in time to catch this kid and a homicide cop's nemesis, Jane Doe.

The crime scene was a disaster. Pouring rain had obliterated most of the physical evidence. Susan and I left it to the crime scene team, but we didn't expect much. We counted ourselves lucky they found the .357 round in the mud downslope from where the girl lay. Otherwise, the kid was all we had. After the EMTs checked him out and declared him bruised but otherwise unhurt, we took him to the Justice Center. I set him up at Susan's desk with a mug of Swiss Miss and a towel, figuring an interview room would be too much for him. He stared at me, ignoring his cocoa, and I guessed I was too much for him too. I was born with a red patch of skin on my neck the shape and color of a mound of ground meat, and my face is none too pretty either. I left it to Susan to do the talking.

He wouldn't provide his name or the name of someone to call—mom, dad, anybody. Too young for a driver's license, but he'd written E. GILLESPIE in black permanent marker on the white rubber toes of his Chucky Ts. Armed with that it didn't take us too long to learn he was registered at Mount Tabor Middle School, an incoming eighth grader. E for Edgar. He had a juvie record, nothing serious. Shoplifting, some panhandling scams, chronic truancy. He lived with his mother and two sisters in a duplex on Southeast 53rd—not too far from my own place. We left him in the care of a case worker from Child Protective Services and went by the house.

No one was home, but we found a neighbor who told us the mother, Charm Gillespie, worked as a marketing associate for a commercial real estate firm in the Wells-Fargo building downtown. According to the neighbor, Mom called the kid Little Eddie, but everyone else called him Eager. His sisters—Gem and Jewel—were nowhere to be found. Word from the neighbor was the three kids ran wild all day while their mother worked; the girls could be anywhere. No other known family in the area. School records didn't mention the father.

Back at the Justice Center, we tried talking to the kid again.

"Eager? Is that your name?"

No response.

"Was someone there with you and the girl?"

Nothing.

"Did you see the gun? Do you know what happened to it?"

Silence.

"What's her name, Eager? Do you at least know her name?"

I'd interrogated career bangers who couldn't shut up. Not Eager Gillespie. The kid was a rock. When the CASA advocate arrived, called by the case worker, she shut down our feckless attempts to mine him, at least until we could find Eager's mother and get consent for further questioning. Turned out she was in Eugene for the day with her broker and wouldn't return to Portland until evening. She wasn't answering her cell phone, which didn't surprise her co-workers. Without prodding, the receptionist at the real estate firm, a catty slip of a thing with hair the color of buttermilk, volunteered that everyone knew Charm was screwing her broker. They'd probably pulled over for some afternoon delight after their sales presentation. We left messages on her voice mail and a patrol car at her house, and finally Charm Gillespie swept in like a storm front.

"Who are you people? Why are you harassing us? When can I take my kid and get the hell out of here?" There was more along those lines. She was hard to keep up with, waving her hands as she spoke and refusing to make eye contact with anyone. Tall and thickset, not unattractive under a dense clot of metallic hair and heavy, exaggerated make-up. Agitated and uncommunicative, suggesting she had something to hide.

Which it turned out she did. The night before she'd made a 9-1-1 call, someone trying to get into her house, her ex-husband. Now she didn't want to talk about it. I couldn't tell if she was scared or naturally belligerent. Maybe a little of both.

"When was the last time you saw your husband, Mrs. Gillespie?"

"First, he's not my husband. I divorced that piece of shit ten years ago."

"Okay. So when did you last see him?"

"Last night. But you already know that."

"What did he want?"

"A blow job, more than likely. He's lucky I wasn't in the mood. I'd have bit his dick off."

"What about the kids? Did they talk to him?"

"I wasn't about to let him near my kids."

"And he didn't tell you why he was in town?"

"I couldn't care less."

"So all he wanted was …"

"Jesus. How the hell do I know?" She tried to light a cigarette, but she was no Sharon Stone and Susan made her snuff it. "Listen, he just showed up pretending to be a human being. I figured he wanted to get laid and maybe a free place to sleep, though why he thought I was offering either I can't tell you." She blew air through her over-dyed bangs. "He also pretended he wanted to see the kids, but I wasn't buying that bullshit. He hasn't seen the kids or paid child support since we split."

"Did he mention anything about a woman, maybe someone he was traveling with? A name, anything?"

"A woman would have to have the brains of a dog turd to take up with Big Ed Gillespie."

The prosecutor, a buzz cut from Astoria named Witt Deiter, urged us to keep working on Eager and Charm. Eager held his silent ground while Charm screamed lawsuit and demanded a smoke. Eventually Deiter let them go. The word to us was to keep digging. CPS would be spending some time with the Gillespie clan, so if we did turn something up, we'd know where to find him.

Deiter was a recent transfer to Multnomah County anxious to make a name for himself. "I like the little brat for it." He had a rep for drawing his dialog from television cop dramas—not the good ones on cable either.

Susan pointed out the obvious. "If he shot her, where's the gun?"

"It's there. Find it, or get him to talk. I don't care which. He did it, or knows who did."

I was thinking about Charm. "He's just a kid."

"He's a thug in training. Make the case."

But there was no case to be made. The dearth of evidence left us with only the thinnest of working theories.

Theory one: Eager shot the girl. Simple enough, for what it was worth, but we had no weapon and Eager's lone statement suggested someone else had been at the scene. Until he started talking, we could only guess who. The paraffin test of his hands for gunshot residue might have cleared some things up, but with the help of the CASA rep, Charm tied us up long enough to ensure the test came back inconclusive.

Theory two: Eager came across an argument, a husband or boyfriend and the woman. This unknown subject shot the woman and fled the scene with the gun. Eager saw it, for some reason thought the shooter was a cop. Which, hell, maybe he was, though it wasn't a popular notion in the Homicide pit.

Theory three? Who the fuck could guess? We took a number of runs at Eager, especially after we learned Big Ed Gillespie had been a cop himself once upon a time. A few years earlier he'd voluntarily separated from the Klamath County Sheriff's Department rather than face an investigation into questionable activities on the job. We didn't learn much, but the thrust was that he was linked to a protection racket in some remote corner of the county. Since he'd left of his own accord, the investigation was dropped. No doubt the department down there was glad to get clear of a problem with minimal ruckus.

But even that piece of info failed to break Charm's resolve, or Eager's. He'd been in enough trouble during his short life that Charm knew the system, countered us at every turn. She had a way about her, a kind of reptilian ruthlessness. She didn't display maternal instincts so much as a dogged combativeness toward all who challenged her.

Three years later, we still don't know who the woman is. Jane Doe. Sister of John, daughter of mystery, mother of frustration. She was buried on the county tab, what little evidence we had stored in paper bags. Susan and I kept digging, and we found a few candidates among the Missing Persons files, both local and statewide. Female, early- to-mid-twenties, dark hair, fair skin, full figure. One by one we ruled them out, either through dental records or because the missing turned up again. Her prints weren't in the regional AFIS, her DNA profile wasn't in CODIS. No criminal record, no government service, no first responder or job requiring a background check. The woman was vapor until someone showed up to claim her.

After three years, you gotta figure no one will.

November 12

Gas Station Owner Found Beaten To Death

MERRILL, OR: Oregon State Police in cooperation with the Klamath County Sheriff's Department are investigating the beating death of Teller Bowes, owner of the Union 76 Qwik Mart on Klamath Falls-Malin Highway just north of Merrill. The victim was found late Monday evening by a store customer.

Investigators initially suspected robbery, but the day's receipts remained in the cash register and there was no evidence anything was stolen. Police are considering other motives for the killing.

Anyone with information pertaining to this investigation is asked to contact the Klamath County Sheriff's Department.

No More Fucking

It was hot for so early in the morning so late in the year. Sweat shot off the flanks of the horse beneath her like spray off a waterfall, but Ellie didn't let up. She drove the horse along the path between a hedgerow and a gully overgrown with weeds, jumped cut banks and outcrops of rotted blueschist. A shoulder of sun shone over the round hills behind her. The smell of pig hung thick in the air, the stink clinging to her like an oily rag. She found a gap in the hedge, headed downhill with the heedless speed of a fugitive. Only when the horse leapt the stream at the foot of the hill and stumbled did she rein in. Far enough, for now. She slipped off of the weary animal. Her feet were bare and the soft mud at stream's edge oozed between her long toes.

She looked up the path behind her. The house was there, at the far end of the gully hidden from view by the trees. And Stuart. She looked away, ran her fingers through her hair. Allowed the dress to slide off her shoulders and drop around her feet, heedless of the mud. Felt the pig-sodden air on her bare skin. No underwear. She'd only had time to grab the dress, quickly, before Stuart knew she was leaving. He'd have stopped her if he'd known, maybe even stood watch over her while she did her morning chores, just to make sure she didn't go anywhere. He'd caught her in the Cup 'n' Saucer with Luellen the day before.

The horse snorted behind her and she turned. "Thank you, Jack." She patted the animal's long, wet neck. "Go ahead and drink. You did good." She kicked her dress into the bushes. Jack led her along the stream, dipping his head and gently nuzzling the water. She entered downstream from the horse. She didn't want to muddy water he was so careful not to muddy himself. She moved with care across rocks slimy on the bottoms of her feet. In the blistering heat, the cold water offered the only indication winter would soon be upon her. Last season's finisher hogs had been sold. Only the gilts, sows, and boars remained in her father's barn. Work around the farm would slow down. Stuart would have more energy.

He'll want to fuck all the time now. She gazed down at her body, at the round smoothness of her stomach, at her heavy breasts, at the tangle of pubic hair below her navel. "You got more hair down there than a gorilla." Stuart had offered this keen observation a week before the wedding. He'd demanded an inspection, insisted they try things out, "just so we know the plumbing works for the big night." Romantic. She didn't think she'd ever forget her first glimpse of his long, thin penis. Twisting, purple veins stretched along its length like a disease, a violent worm. She had seen other penises, her brothers' penises. They had seemed smooth and healthy in contrast, not so cruel and thin. Of course, she'd seen her brothers' under the most harmless circumstances: down at Little Liver Creek swimming, in the bath at night. Stuart's penis strained tall while she and he lay on a blanket under the moon outside her house, and it wanted inside her. All it wanted was inside.

"I don't think we should, Stuart."

"What do you mean? Come on." He moaned and slid up closer to her, stroked her hair, ran a hand over her breasts. She caught it, pinned it to her side.

"Wait till we're married." She cast a furtive glance over her shoulder at the house.

"It's just a stupid ceremony. This is the real stuff. Come on."

The penis gleamed in the moonlight, almost seemed to stare at her. She wanted to turn her head away. "I can't. Not yet."

"You like Luellen better than me." He sat up. "You're not a lezzie, are you?"

His eyes lost their gleam, and she moved away from him. "I have to go." She tried to climb to her feet, but he reached out and grabbed her.

"Wait. I'm sorry." He gripped her hand, but she twisted away from him and ran into the house. Later that night she made her way to Luellen's and told her about her decision not to marry Stuart after all. Luellen was supportive, but the next morning at breakfast Ellie's mother had little sympathy.

"You shouldn't have led him on."

"I didn't lead him anywhere. Stuart finds his own way."

Her father chuckled from behind his cup of coffee, but her mother frowned at him.

"Immanuel, you're too indulgent of this girl."

"Hiram thinks I'm more likely to sell if we're in-laws. Maybe just as well if—"

"Don't interfere." She turned her frown on Ellie. "What were you doing out late at night when you're not even married then?"

Ellie had no response. She sat with her hands in her lap, quiet and brooding, glancing only at her father in time to catch his tight-lipped submission before he pushed away from the table and left. Her mother ignored her, accustomed to her silences. Finally Ellie spoke up. "I'm not going to let you force me into this." She stalked off, secure in her decision.

It didn't last. Over the next few days the whispers started: strange goings-on between Ellie and that friend of hers, Jewellen. Ellie walked into the church kitchen during Wednesday soup supper just in time to hear the pastor's wife tell her mother, "It must be so hard having a child so willful. No one blames you, of course." The words knocked the air out of her, and in that moment she knew it would never end. These people, these fine church folk—her mother included—would never free her from the cage of words they'd conjured to confine her. *Bad girl. Lizzie the lezzie.* Somehow her sister Myra's sins, the smoking and drinking that started in middle school, the endless string of boys, were never discussed. But Myra had always been an afterthought—an accident according to Rob and Brett—yet fair like the rest of the Kerns. Ellie stood out, dark-haired and large-breasted. Different.

She considered running, leaving the valley for good. But she knew there was nowhere she could go. Even Klamath Falls, only forty miles down a winding county road, seemed a world away. When Luellen left for Southern Oregon University in the fall, an option never even considered for her, Ellie would be alone. Helpless. And so, come Saturday, her father escorted her down the aisle in the Victory Chapel sanctuary, pausing only to squeeze her arm and sigh before moving to his seat in the front row. It took all she had to hold back her tears as she and Stuart spoke their vows. That night the worm found its home.

Ellie sat in the brook, allowed the water to fill the smooth valley between her legs and draw away the heat. A sense of chilly calm crept up her back. The wedding had been two years before, a lifetime ago. A sharp boundary between Ellie Kern and Lizzie Spaneker, two different girls. After the wedding, she and Stuart moved onto a small farm, a joint gift from the Spanekers and the Kerns. The water rights were restricted, but adequate to run a small crop of field corn and another of barley. Ellie cared for the house while Stuart split time working on her family's hog ranch and for his old man. In time, Stuart hoped his efforts on behalf of the Kerns might earn him a portion of the plentiful Kern water. Another foot or two per acre would enable him to plant mint or peas or potatoes, real cash crops.

Until then, the long hours kept Stuart busy and tired—a blessing for Ellie. He'd come in late at night, eat, and fall right to sleep. Every so often he awoke in the night. "I want some of the sweet stuff." A compliant wife, she'd spread her legs. Sometimes she bled, but her mother told her bleeding was common for new brides. Ellie wasn't so sure—Lady Latex had never mentioned it—but she kept her mouth shut. Stuart gave her money for expenses and she worked around their little farm. There were some chickens and rabbits, the garden to keep up. Housework. She stayed busy. Stuart was tired often enough that when he wasn't she could deal with the worm.

But now it was the end of the season. Field corn laid up, barley sold. Stuart was around more, wanted sex more often. The worm remained long and thin and always stretched out tight like a steel spring.

"I'd leave him." Luellen was home from college for a visit. "That, or make him do some reading on the concept of foreplay. They have books with pictures and everything."

"You're from another world."

Luellen had no response.

As autumn settled onto the valley, Stuart came to a decision. "Let's make us a son." He'd barged into the house full of energy after a slow day doing equipment maintenance with his father. *Just last night,* Ellie thought, the waters of the brook trailing ripples from her dipped fingers. For herself, Ellie hoped for a daughter. Someone who could grow up in the house with her while Stuart was working, someone she could talk to and teach to be a woman. But when she said as much to Stuart, he scoffed.

"Someone you can lezzie with, Lizzie?" He laughed as though he'd made a joke and pressed her into the wall, kissed her hard.

Then he picked her up with one arm around her waist. He carried her into their bedroom and dropped her on the bed. "Remember when everyone thought you were a witch?"

She sighed. "I'd rather forget."

"Aw, come on. It's kinda funny when you think about it." He laughed again and dropped his pants. The worm looked up at her. "If you were, you could make sure it was a boy. Cast a little spell." He giggled, amused with himself. She hiked up her skirt and pulled off her underwear. He spit on his fingers and rubbed her, cursory circles against her pelvic bone, then without warning thrust into her. She held her breath, but almost immediately she felt him shudder and ejaculate, hardly enough time for her to wonder would it be like to have the kind of lover—attentive, even playful—Luellen sometimes described. Stuart collapsed, lay panting into the depression where her shoulder met her neck. She turned her head, but couldn't escape the smell of sweat and machine oil. "You like this?" She couldn't tell if he was murmuring to her, or to himself. "It's the sweet stuff, isn't it?" After a while he rolled to the side. She tried to creep from the bed but he grabbed her. "Stay here." He pawed her breasts through the fabric of her blouse. "Give your witchy spell a chance to work." After a while, he entered her again. She'd loosened up from the first time, was still moist from his semen, so she barely felt it. He fell asleep with his thumb inside her, a cork in a bottle.

When early morning came she eluded his grasp. Maybe he'd remember his joke and tell himself she cast a spell to escape, but she knew she'd simply slipped away as he slept. She had no influence over Stuart or his hand, even less over the fluid processes deep within herself. Still, Stuart might be right—his seed might take. With that thought arose a fear long quiet. "Witches," someone had once said, "can only bear more witches." She left the house and escaped into the countryside.

The cool stream lapped her sore vulva. Behind her, Jack began to make a fuss, eager for another run after his drink. She could sense his brisk energy, his desire to gallop again. "Witches like to do it with animals," was one of Myra's favorite pronouncements to the younger girls at church. Ellie eyed Jack's hanging penis with a clinical eye. She thought it looked more wholesome than Stuart's straining member. She shook out her shoulders, remembering the days when her hair had been long enough to hide them.

"Jack!" She clapped her hands over her head. "Go! Go home!" She wanted to be alone. The horse rolled one great eye and shook his head. "Go!" After a moment's further hesitation, Jack stepped across the brook and trotted back toward the house. She watched him with a satisfied gaze. A tickle ran through her stomach and she wondered if she'd tapped into some primal power. The notion was ridiculous, yet strangely pleasing. She smiled into the breeze, alone and content. The last warm day, perhaps, before winter.

Jack left a muddy trail in the water as he crossed. The murk made its way down the stream bed and roiled around her. She lost sight of her legs under the floating silt. The water was cool and soothing. Thin strands of mist rose from the stream. She sat, eyes half closed, sun warm on her face and breasts. After a while, she heard the crackle of brush and looked up the gully toward the house, gasped when she saw it wasn't the horse returning.

"Stuart—"

"What the hell are you doing?" He hurtled toward her down the slope. "You're washing me out of you, aren't you?" He looked terrified.

She recoiled at his approach. "I was just resting—"

"You're lying!" She tried to scramble away, but her bare feet slipped on the slick rocks in the stream bed. "Trying to kill my son! I know it!" He caught her by the hair with one hand, wrenched her neck around. She fell onto her hands and knees in the water. Stunned. He slammed his balled fist into her cheek, then into back of her head, and she dropped onto her elbows, breasts contracting against the touch of frigid water. As she hung there, gasping, he took her from behind. "You never," he grunted, "wanted me ... never *wanted* ... my *son* ... only care about ... *that Jew bitch!*" When he finished, he stood and buckled his pants. "That'll take." His voice quavered in the heavy air. "That'll take no matter what you try to do." He ducked his head, wiped one trembling hand across his mouth. The fear was still there, a shadow in his wet eyes. "Now find your clothes and get your ass back up to the house."

Time passed. The next day and the next month. Winter came, creeping up and settling on her hard shoulders like a shroud. The breeding sows on her dad's farm got sick and a quarter of them died. She gazed out of the shroud at her husband. "You been witching, Lizzie?" Stuart was jolly with a baby on the way. He laughed, because everyone was so pleased. His folks were pleased and her mother was pleased and her brothers were pleased. Even her father seemed a little bit pleased. And Stuart, he especially was pleased, convinced he'd fathered a boy. When he didn't know she was nearby he'd mutter under his breath. "A son, a son. My son." But with the sows sick and dying so artlessly in her father's barns, Ellie visited the obstetrician. UltraSound revealed the girl growing in her womb. Ellie told Stuart there was nothing she could do. There was no magic. The caul had given her no power over her fate, or good fortune.

He didn't believe her. He screamed, accused her of casting a spell and making it a girl. He pushed her to the floor and kicked her. She vomited. Within the hour, a pint of blood flushed the dead fetus into the toilet.

Winter stayed on hard that year. Ellie wrapped herself in a blanket and moved through the house like a ghost. She shivered as Stuart worked. He fed the surviving pigs and trucked in oil for the furnace, even collected the eggs. On her best days, her torpor made supper hours late. More often there was no supper at all. And though there wasn't much heat in the house, even with the furnace firing around the clock, Ellie refused to share what little warmth remained in her. *There will be no more fucking,* she told Stuart. As her snowy shroud trickled out of the dark sky he looked into her eyes, and he believed her. He knew what she said was true.

November 19 — 10:02 am

Between Him and His Right Hand

I can't blame Susan. At best, Eager is just another complication in a day already fucked beyond reason. Another charge to hang on Mitch when there's no dearth of charges. Maybe a witness at trial, assuming the case ever comes to trial. Assuming Eager survives the bullet behind his eyeball.

But Mitch isn't going to trial. Assuming *he* survives. A couple dozen cops saw him draw down, and at least one eye in the sky above recorded it. He'll plead out. As far as Susan is concerned, Eager represents little more than another stack of paper. She has her own problems; Eager is all mine. Unease plays across my belly like a charged wire.

I don't know what to do with myself, so I start walking. I need to get away from all the boiling motion, the staring onlookers, the earnest cops. I don't bother to go back to the house for my keys. The cops in my living room could very well still be there tomorrow. But before I move a dozen paces, I knock up against someone. He turns, face sour until he recognizes me. Michael Masliah. He'd been on district patrol when I was still in Homicide, but he's moved over to the Neighborhood Response Team. I haven't seen him since I started working on my tan full time.

"Michael."

"Hey, Skin. What's going on?"

"Wondering if I'll ever get my house back."

"That's right, they moved in. I heard even the chief was up there." He shakes his head. "Crazy morning, huh?"

"You said a mouthful." I laugh, though I'm not sure where the joke is. Sometimes I feel like I hung up my ability to trade banter with other cops with my dress blues.

"What are you up to these days?"

It's the kind of question I don't like answering, but I figure Michael isn't interested in an actual response. "As little as possible."

"I heard you were working at that coffee shop where you used to hang out."

I feel my cheeks ignite and I look away. Outside of Susan, I didn't realize anyone was keeping track of me. "I do a little insurance investigating, but otherwise ..." He's looking at me sideways. I shrug, realizing it's a stupid thing to lie about. I'm hardly the first ex-cop to pick up honest work after retirement. "The coffee thing, it's ... well, yeah, different shop, but the same owner."

"She's a cutie, if I remember right."

Tell me about it. But I keep my mouth shut and lift my shoulders like it's something I never think about. But the comment shifts my thoughts to my part-time job at Uncommon Cup. From cop to barista had never been the plan. Some cops are in it to do some good for others, some to do good for themselves. For me, it was about making a living off my one half-assed aptitude: teasing a plausible, admissible narrative out of available evidence. It was a job I did pretty well, and we all need a job. Until the job doesn't need us anymore. Now it's hard to look a working cop in the eye and talk about pulling espresso shots for tips and a gnat's hair more than minimum wage. Or, if I'm lucky, spend a day or two a month snapping long lens photos of some nitwit bricking retail shop windows and so he can file a phony insurance claim.

Michael doesn't help by being decent about the whole thing. "Hell, Skin, I don't blame you. If there's one thing citizen hate more than paying our salaries, it's paying our pensions after we've busted our humps for twenty-five years. You gotta make ends meet."

"Yeah, I guess."

"Thanks for stopping by to cheer me up, man."

I smile, in spite of myself. "Ah, you know me. Far as I'm concerned, the whole world's a shit hole and we're all looking up from the bottom with our mouths hanging open."

"Then shut your fucking mouth, Skin. Jesus." He slaps me on the shoulder. "So what happened here, man? Guy was your neighbor, right?"

"I'm as shocked as everyone else." If I'd have picked anyone in that house to go off the rails, it would have been Jase, but even he would have been a long shot. Just a pissed-at-the-universe teenager, like there aren't a million of those. I don't want to get into another post-mortem of Mitch on the porch, but it occurs to me that while Susan might be dodging my bullets, Masliah may be able to help with my real concern. "You remember that kid, Eager Gillespie?"

"From Mount Tabor, sure. What about him?"

"He was here this morning. He got hit by the round our friend on the porch got off."

"Jesus, you're kidding. Is he all right?"

"You didn't see it?"

"I've been tied up since I got here. Talking to the neighborhood association folks and trying to get people back in their houses. Dealing with all this." Beyond him, citizen press against the barricades as uniforms work to maintain some semblance of order.

"Sure. So you don't know where he went."

"Where he went? Are you saying he swallowed a pill and then just walked away?"

"I don't know. The paramedics tried to check him out, but then they got busy with Mitch and no one's seen him since."

"Well, I don't know what I can do, but if I see him—I mean, Jesus, where'd he get hit?"

"Eye, looked like to me."

Masliah whistles under his breath.

"That was my thought."

"What did the lieutenant say?"

To mind my own business. "She's got enough on her plate, Michael."

His lips tighten, and I can tell what he's thinking. In his spot, I'd be thinking the same thing. He answers to a chain of command, and I ain't a part of it. "You know if he took a bullet in the head, we'll probably find his body somewhere, an hour or a day from now."

I don't like admitting that, but I know he's right. I'm sure I'm wearing the denial on my face, but Michael has other things to worry about. I can feel him pulling away, but he throws me one last bone.

"Where would he go if he is still on his feet?"

There is one place where I might find, if not Eager, then someone who knows him. Trick'll be getting them to answer my questions. But my car is still inside the perimeter.

"Michael, you got anyone heading downtown, maybe I could hitch a ride?"

He thinks, and then smiles indulgently. "Give me a minute." It takes him two, but then Masliah connects me with a taciturn sergeant named Kuhl who could give a lesson to a cucumber. He's on his way back to Central Precinct and agrees to drop me on the way. I try to make small talk, but his responses are monosyllabic. Then, when I mention I used to be on the job, he lets me have it.

"Yeah, I know what you *used* to be, Kadash. And I know you also stood by and let a suspect pop one of your own. So how about you shut your yap, unless you'd rather get out and walk."

So that's it. He's a friend of Richard Owen, a former colleague, former boss—a man I'd never gotten along with. It's true enough that I'd let a citizen hit Owen and done nothing, but the fellow in question wasn't a suspect and Owen more than deserved it. His retirement, at my encouragement, made room for Susan to move up to commander of Person Crimes. The encouragement hadn't been friendly, and clearly Owen wasn't the only one who knew it. I shut my yap.

Kuhl doesn't speak again until he drops me at the corner of Burnside and MLK. I walk to Ankeny, then a couple of blocks down to 2nd through a brief spit of rain followed by a sudden sun break that threatens warmth. My destination is tucked under the Burnside Bridge. To a certain kind of person, the place is world famous, a destination feared by the skittish and admired by the recklessly skilled. To the rest of us, it's a strange landscape of curves and ramps sculpted of discarded fill and smooth-skimmed concrete.

The Burnside Skatepark came about as a result of a little organized anarchy, such as it was, when a group of determined skaters started building banks and transitions under the east end of the bridge back in the early 90s. Squatters, but squatters with their shit together. The early work was good, and with time and growing commitment the later work got better and better. A trash-filled vacant lot under the bridge grew into one of the premier skateparks in the world. Eventually the city sanctioned the park, and improvements are ongoing. I've been here when as many as two hundred skaters sparred for space and status in a kind of Brownian alpha skirmish. Master of the board, a position coveted by a species of stringy, agile creature, male and female alike, who don't give a fuck about anything except not being anybody's bitch.

In my age range, there are three kinds of men who linger at the margins of a place like the Burnside Skatepark. You got the man with a few dollars in his pocket and a taste for the young, taut skin hinted at beneath the hoodies and baggie shorts. Then there's the man with a mission, salvation on his mind, hoping to peel off a soul or two from among skate punks for whom the only real danger is wiping out on a monster tranny or getting hassled by some asshole straight who can't mind his own fucking business. And then there's the cops, but they stick their heads in no more than necessary to make sure there's no obvious dealing or hooking. They're too busy, the guys on patrol, to waste time tracking every street kid with authority issues and a skateboard. And at Burnside, the skaters know they have something good; they police themselves well enough.

Finally there's me. No one confuses me with the first type, and I've made it clear I'm not interested in lost souls or any misdemeanors and minor felonies that might go down in the shadows on the far side of the bridge wall. Some of the guys know me, nod when I show up to stand at the fence and watch the action. Some only offer the barest acknowledgment, letting me know we got nothing in common, but we got no beef either.

There's not a whole lot of action when I arrive this morning. A dozen guys, a few girls, standing board-ready at the top of the banks or staring through the chain-link fence on the north side of park. Only a few are skating. I take up a spot behind the street-side bank and watch the skaters work their lines. My usual habit. After a few minutes a fellow I know skates up the ramp and skids to a stop, stares down at me. He's tall and thin, buzzed hair under an orange knit skullcap. No clue if he's fifteen or twenty-five, if he has a job or a home or a just cardboard box to sleep in. But he's always here and he talks to me. Goes by Push.

"You're looking more raggedy than usual, old man." He taps his neck with the first two fingers of his right hand. His knuckles are tattooed with little red stars.

"Your mother name you Push, or is that what she wants to do when she runs into you on a busy street corner?"

"I hatched from an egg, man." He grins and kicks off the bank, rides across to the big hip opposite and performs a perfect, unconscious ollie, then swerves back among other skaters and rejoins me. Can't stand still for long.

"So what's the word?"

"No word. Just need a laugh and thought I'd come watch you amateurs fall on your asses for a while."

"If you weren't such a pussy, I'd let you give my board a try. But I hate to see someone's granny cry."

I chuckle and he starts to kick off again. "Hey, you seen Eager Gillespie lately?"

Push's smirk is made sinister by a pattern of black filigree tattooed around his eyes and across his cheekbones. "He steal your social security check?"

"Something like that."

He tugs at his cap, thinks for a moment. "Ain't seen Eager in I don't know how long. I heard he moved."

"He's back. You know anyone he hangs out with, maybe someone who knows where he's staying?"

"You should ask Jase."

"Jase Bronstein? Is he here?"

Push laughs now, picking up on my obvious interest. He points toward the fence opening where a clump of skaters are smoking and jawing. Among them I see Jase's beefy figure. "Maybe you catch him, he don't see you coming first." Then he rolls off.

I move along the back of the bank, head down. Push skates over to a group sitting at the top of the bridge wall bank. After a moment they all hop onto their boards and skate in different directions. I don't know why he's giving me cover. Maybe he likes the fact I'm an old guy who doesn't mind being fucked with. I round the bridge support at the northeast corner of the park, my footsteps masked by the skirr of wheels echoing under the bridge. Jase stands with his back to me, hands waving as he talks to some other kids. His plaid boxers bulge with ass between his sagging pants and a black Raider's jacket at least one size too small. I hunch my shoulders and move along like I have no interest in anything, just a fellow walking from here to there, maybe a guy heading to work at Pacific Fruit the next block up. No one pays me any mind until I'm standing behind the cluster of boys.

"Jason." He turns his head my way, but doesn't respond. Then his eyes pop. He starts to back away and I raise my hands, palms out. "No one is with me, no cops, nothing. No one knows I'm even here."

"Fuck off."

"Not until we have a chat."

His friends have already scattered. He turns, ready to bolt, then sees Push at the top of the bank above us. Push stands with his arms folded across his chest, chin down. He shakes his head and Jase surrenders. He drops his board. It rolls to a forlorn stop against the park wall. "What do you want?" Over Jase's shoulder, I see Eager's tag on the wall, an EG® the size of my palm, faded and partly obscured by other graffiti, drawn with a fat black marker.

"I was hoping you could clear something up for me."

"Don't know nothing about what happened this morning. Dad flips out, bang bang, and I run. That's it."

"I'm more interested in Eager."

His face goes carefully blank. "Eager."

"Yeah. Eager."

"I don't know what to tell you."

"He was there this morning."

"So were like a million other people."

"I'm only interested in one. What was he doing there?"

"Like I give two shits what Eager does."

"How many shits you give when he tagged your house a few months ago?"

That catches him off guard, but he recovers quickly. "That was my dad's thing, not mine." Then he smirks. "He thought you were gonna go all *Magnum, PI* for him."

"He didn't need me. He had you."

Jase looks back toward Push, who is skating in lazy circles close by and not paying obvious attention to anything.

"Why didn't you tell your father that was Eager's tag?"

"If he's so out of it he can't figure out EGR, why should I care? Not my problem."

"Wasn't it you out there scrubbing it off?"

A shadow passes over his eyes. "So fucking what?"

"What did Luellen say about it?"

"Nothing. I don't know."

"Then what did Eager say about it?"

"The dude moved away."

"His mother may have moved, but he stuck around. Which you know. I've seen you two running around together since she left."

He throws his hands out, shifts his weight from one foot to the other. Eyes twitching, refusing to look back at me. I'm boring him, or making him nervous. I try a new tack.

"Didn't you two try out for that Gus Van Sant movie together, the one they filmed here at the park? That was after his mom left."

"My dad wouldn't let me, even though it was just extras. Skaters. I don't know if Eager tried out, but it wouldn't matter anyway. He's not that good."

"He seems pretty good to me."

"He's a poser. Got no business skating here, that's for sure."

"But I guess he's good enough when you want to scam money at the off-ramp."

He shakes his head. "That was a long time ago, man. We were never friends or anything. He just hung around."

"Why did he hang around if you were such not-friends?"

"I don't know, man. Maybe because he has a thing for my stepmom."

"A thing?" I try to keep the sudden interest out of my voice.

"I guess it makes sense. She's hot enough to give a squeaker like Eager wood."

It unnerves me a bit to hear Jase speak of his stepmother like this. To me, Luellen is the mom of the little boy who calls me Mister Skin, whose plants I've watered during Bronstein family excursions. Still, she possesses a beguiling self-assurance; I can see why Eager would be drawn to her. Her country-girl loveliness and finely turned figure are only a part of it.

"Did she reciprocate?"

"You mean, does she like him back?"

"Yeah."

"She was nice to him, but she's nice to everyone."

"Is that why he tagged your house? Because of how he felt about Luellen?"

"How should I know? We never talked about stuff like that. Whatever he thought about Lu was between him and his right hand."

The resonating whir of skateboard wheels under the bridge seems to increase in pitch. Jase takes a half step back, finds himself up against the fence. His eyes tell me he thinks I'm going to hit him. I'm tempted. Probably get my ass kicked for my trouble though, if not by Jase then by the other skaters. Burnside Skatepark is not a place that tolerates shit from outsiders, and I doubt I can count on Push to help me if the situation blows up. He might enjoy playing the tough for me with a sloppy tub of attitude like Jase Bronstein, but no more than that. Still, I lower my brow, move a step in on

Jase and ball my fists at my side. There's more I want to know, and I figure I might as well press while I've got him off-balance.

"You know, Jase, I'm not sure why you think it's a good idea to give me attitude. The cops are looking for you. Cops who are my friends. You can't run from a crime scene like that."

"She did."

"Luellen?"

"She left first. Cop turned his back and she zaps. I wasn't gonna stick after that."

"Jase, you were in that house this morning. You saw what happened, and a lot of people wanna know about it. You tell me now, maybe I can keep them off your back."

"I told you, my dad freaked out and we ran. That's it." He's blinking now, head swinging side to side. I can smell his sweat, vinegar tinted with nicotine. I'm on the edge of something, but he doesn't want to give it to me. "I got nothing to do with any of this. Never have."

"What about Danny? Luellen said he was with his grandfather. Do you know who that is? I can't help you if you won't talk to me."

"You don't give a fat fuck about helping me." Suddenly he draws himself up, kicks the tail of his board. It pops up into the air and he grabs it with one hand, thrusts it toward me like a spear. I jump back in time to avoid taking a jab in the batteries. "This is what I know about, man. This." The bottom of the board is covered with scratched and faded stickers: band names I don't recognize, skateboard logos I do. Element, Black Label. "Fuck my father, fuck Luellen, and fuck Eager. I ain't taking a bullet for bullshit's got nothing to do with me."

At that, he turns and sprints under the bridge down 2nd. I let him go; couldn't catch him if I wanted to. But I can't help but wonder about the darkening bruise I saw on the back of his neck as he spun away from me.

Push skates up to the fence.

"Everything cool, man?"

"Yeah. No worries."

But it's not cool. Jase knows a lot more than he's telling, not the least why he said his dad was packing heavy metal when all Mitch had was a peashooter. I wave to Push, head in the direction Jase ran. There is no sign of him, just the old brick buildings of Eastside Industrial, the scent of wet asphalt, delivery trucks belching exhaust. I pull out my phone, dial Susan's cell. She doesn't answer, but I leave a message telling her I saw Jase at Burnside, summarize our chat. If she wants to send a car down to look for him, she can. As I head up to the bus stop on MLK, I think about how part of me didn't want to reach out to Susan, considering her attitude toward me earlier. But all the cop hasn't been burned out of me yet. She's the lieutenant, after all, and it's just a phone call.

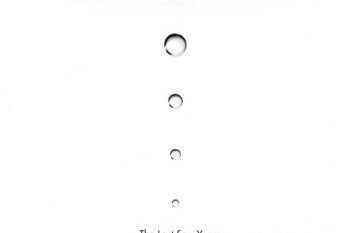

Stay Away From the Kid

She was officially Jane, but I called her the Tabor Doe, as if she was a disoriented deer that wandered into a hunter's bullet in the middle of town. She was hardly my only open file left after more than six years in Homicide.

There were the gang shootings, drive-bys where you have a pretty good idea who pulled the trigger, but the evidence is too thin to make an arrest. Much as such cases rankled, you had to figure justice would be served in the end, most likely bloody street justice. So be it.

Harder for me to take was the six-year-old girl found beaten to an unrecognizable pulp in her basement, two parents baffled and heart-broken upstairs. Portland's own Jon Benet Ramsey, perhaps, but one who didn't make national headlines because she was neither pretty enough nor her mother and father wealthy enough to merit the attention of anyone but me and Susan and a gaggle of crime scene examiners. Maybe there was a little frowny-faced coverage on local news—it's been a while. We turned up nothing on her behalf. Susan and I agreed the father did it, but we could never build a proper case. Nothing probative, just a lot of murk in his piece of shit alibi—fly fishing with a brother whose girlfriend never heard about no goddamn fishing trip—and a wife who assured us that, *no, oh no,* she couldn't say what happened but she knew it couldn't be him—he was a good father. He loved his little girl so. His credit card statements and browser history indicated he loved barely legal porn too, the kind where the girls look like they're fourteen even if the fine print claims they're all voting age.

Sure.

No other leads ever developed, but a year or so later mom shoved a fondue fork through dad's eye after she caught him surfing porn again, this time on her laptop. The fork didn't kill him, but did damage not unlike a massive stroke—maybe worse than dying. He's in a chair now, unable to hold his head up on his own or control his bowels. His wife got a good lawyer and skated on the assault charge, then divorced him. Moved to Bend, left him living in an assisted care facility out in East County.

No trial, no conviction. Eats through a straw, I hear. Sometimes you take what you can get.

The Tabor Doe was different. We never identified her, sure. But the real pisser is we have a window into the events of that day, a window forever fogged over. Eager Gillespie knew what happened, but between his mother and her lawyer, the fog would only thicken with the passage of time. Since we couldn't get past Mother Cerberus, we focused on, "He was a cop!" And there was only one likely candidate.

In the early days of the investigation, when we weren't reading missing persons reports, we pieced together the bits and pieces of Big Ed Gillespie's background. During his sworn days, he'd served as a deputy in the sheriff's sub-station in Givern Valley, an out-of-the-way district in southeastern Klamath County. The sub-station rated only two full-time deputies, their primary duty dealing with DUIs and domestic violence in the unincorporated areas of the valley. Westbank, the valley's only town, had its own police force: four officers, two part-time staffers, and a chief. Most of the time the deputies deferred to the townies.

Armed with the broad strokes of Ed Gillespie's history, Witt Deiter dragged Susan and I along for a visit to Charm, tried to convince her to let Eager talk to us.

"Mrs. Gillespie, you understand Eager made a statement at the scene, don't you?"

"You call that a statement?"

"He mentioned a cop. As you're well aware—"

"Yeah, yeah. Big Ed used to be a cop a million years ago. What the fuck of it?"

"By your own account, he was in town the day before the murder."

"What … the fuck … *of it?*" Charm had little patience for Deiter. I was inclined to side with her in that regard, if little else.

"I'm sure you can see why this information is of interest to us."

"Eager has nothing to say."

"Mrs. Gillespie, if you're worried about what your ex-husband might do if—"

That brought out barking laughter. "I am not afraid of Big Ed Gillespie." She firmed her chin and stared Deiter down. "I know how you sick pukes work. Anything Eager says, you'll figure out a way to turn it around and make it his fault. So here's the way it is. Eager didn't see nothing, he doesn't know nothing, and there's nothing you can say or do to change that. You hear what I'm saying, fuckwit?"

Witt bristled at what I'm sure he thought was a shot at his name, but ended the interview without incident. On the drive back to the Justice Center, he announced a new strategy: catch Eager in the act of committing some petty larceny or vandalism and play a little carrot-and-stick to compel him to talk. All well and good, but

Susan and I had enough to do without spending our time chasing juvenile misdemeanors. Lieutenant Hauser backed us up; the Tabor Doe wasn't our only case. Deiter had to settle for flagging Eager's jacket at the DA's office and hoping the kid got caught doing something serious enough to provide leverage. Susan and I went back to reviewing missing persons files and working cases with a future. Meantime, I put Eager out of my mind.

He had other plans.

I'd have to dig out my notes to remember exactly when it started. Late October, or thereabouts. I came home from work one day and saw Eager gliding down the middle of my street on a battered skateboard. He wore a brown DC hoodie and a dark blue knit hat pulled down to his eyebrows. His ears stuck out under his hat through long, feathery hair. His low-slung jeans bunched on his ankles above checkerboard Vans. He didn't seem to notice me, but I could see his head bouncing from house to house. I got the sense he was looking for something. Or someone. I waited until he rolled out of sight before I parked and went inside.

A few days later, he caught me dragging the recycling bin to the curb. "Hey, Detective Kadash! This your place?"

"What are you doing here, Eager?"

"Just skating. You know how it is. A man can't never get enough board time."

Deiter wouldn't be thrilled if he knew I was talking to Eager without benefit of counsel. But that's not the first thing that popped into my mind. A person of interest in an open homicide now knew where I lived. The thought generated a little fillip of anxiety as Eager rolled to a stop at my curb.

"I guess I can see your point."

"Fucking hell, yeah." He jumped the board up onto the parking strip, then kicked it up into his hand. "I only live a few blocks away."

I swallowed. "I know."

"Your street has too many cars on it."

"Tell me about it."

"Wanna see some shreds?"

"Maybe some other time." I told myself he was just a nitwit skate punk. It's not like my address was classified information.

"Okay. Whatever." With that he was off, scraping down the street and bouncing between parked cars. I had to give him credit. He knew some shreds. Near as I could tell, anyway. I'm not big on the X Games.

He started showing up more and more often, usually on his board, sometimes without. He didn't care if it was raining, sunny, hot or cold. If he wanted to skate, he'd skate. If he wanted to visit, he'd visit. Sometimes I'd hear about some trouble he got into, small-time stuff usually. Shoplifting, maybe a car prowl. He was always scheming, but it was never enough to trip Deiter's Eager Meter. Never enough to lever him into talking about the Tabor Doe.

I can't say why I never told Deiter what was going on. Maybe I just didn't like him. Maybe it was other things, my slow descent into senescence. When Eager's visits started, I was a year and a half away from a cancer diagnosis that would eventually lead to my retirement, but I was still working cases with Susan.

I knew it was a dangerous game. If we ever got enough of a break to open Eager up about that day on Mount Tabor, our "casual" encounters could taint the case. Maybe I was already planning my exit without realizing it, though in a weakly rationalized gesture to professionalism I decided to steer clear of any discussion of Big Ed. I told myself if I remained aloof but not unfriendly, perhaps I'd establish a bit of rapport with the little pissant.

Over the next few weeks, I would learn more than I ever wanted to know about skateboard decks, truck geometry, wheels and bearings. Eager endlessly described his deck—a carbon fiber/

birch composite with kicktails at both ends—and his trucks, a half dozen sets that he swapped out depending on how he wanted to roll. Ceramic bearings for speed runs, steel for when he was just messing around. I could make little sense of any of it, but it all sounded expensive. But when I said as much one day he abruptly decided to head over to the park to practice some bluntslides and kickflips and shit. I didn't see him for a week. Then he was back again, jabbering about grinds and aerials like I had a clue what the hell he was talking about.

It all seemed benign, almost to the point that I found myself questioning our official suspicion toward him. Then, shortly before Christmas, I caught a glimpse of the flip side of Eager Gillespie. The older couple across the street put their house on the market and moved to Panama. Eager displayed an interest in the place. I caught him more than once on the porch, looking in the windows, or poking around in the yard.

"Eager, don't get any ideas about that house."

"What the fuck hell you talking about, Skin?" I have no idea how he found out people called me Skin.

"I know the kind of stuff you get into. Just because we're friendly, don't think I won't bust your ass if I catch you in that house."

"I'm not gonna do nothing." His indignation threw a snap into his tone.

"I'm telling you up front so there's no misunderstanding."

"You don't know what you're talking about." As he skated away, he showed me both middle fingers. "Asshole!"

I wouldn't see him again for months. Mitch and Luellen moved in to the house some time after the first of the year, along with little Danny and Jase and a mountain of Kitchen Kaboodle boxes, Hive Modern furniture, and Video Only's finest brushed-aluminum crap. I figured at that point, the security of the house was their problem.

The next time I saw Eager he was wrapped in a blanket and sitting in a wheelchair at the end of the off-ramp from I-205 at Division. He'd propped a sheet of cardboard in front of the chair, a poorly lettered plea:

Hungary, Outdors, anthing helps. 'God' bless!

I pulled off onto the shoulder and got out of my car. Eager jumped out of the chair and bolted away under the 205 overpass. I let him run. Someone else was with him, another kid, broad-backed, dark-haired and losing his pants as he fled. I collapsed the wheelchair and hefted it into the trunk of my car.

Two days later I arrived home to find Eager sitting on my porch, skateboard across his lap. I couldn't tell if he was rolling on ceramic or steel. His expression was guarded but also a bit hopeful. "What can I do for you, Eager?" I sat down on the top step next to him. It was a warm March day, a dry respite between two long rainy stretches.

He didn't want to make eye contact, dropped his chin and mumbled something into his shoulder.

"What's that? You missing something, you say?"

I inspected the crabgrass in the lawn as I waited him out.

"Ain't my chair." He looked up, and I felt myself soften under the ache in his eyes.

"Whose is it?"

He pointed across the street. I turned and looked, but all I saw was Mitch and Luellen's place. "What are you saying?"

"Jase got it from his grandmother's house. She doesn't know because she only uses it if her scooter gets fucked up. But I guess she's talking about selling it. I need to get it back to him."

I didn't realize Jase and Eager knew each other. The Bronsteins hadn't lived there long, though Mitch had already started his campaign to annoy the living shit out of me. I'd met Jase in passing, one of those encounters that featured the teenager grunting monosyllabically as his father badgered him about being polite. I wasn't insulted by the kid's manner, but Mitch had his own ideas about the way the world worked. Reason enough for me to make friends with Luellen and little Danny instead.

I suppose Jase and Eager met at school, and I guess I could see what brought them together. Close enough in age, isolated, troubled boys. But as I gazed at the slight form beside me on the stoop, it occurred to me Eager and Jase may not be friends. Eager seemed anxious. Jase was a lot bigger than he was, a gangsta-wannabe type in sagging pants and football jerseys. The kid looked like a phony to me, but perhaps to Eager he exuded a kind of attractive menace, a street strength Eager craved for himself.

"I wouldn't have thought Jase would be your style."

"Have you seen the shit he packs? I mean, damn."

Yeah, I'd seen the iPod, the two-hundred-dollar shoes. Mitch loved his toys, and he wasn't stingy about sharing the wealth with his kid.

"I mean, seriously, man. He's got an Xbox *and* a PS2. MacBook— supposedly for homework, hah! But the serious rig is his Alienware. Man, that fucker can play WoW with full pixel-shaders, nineteen-twenty by twelve-hundred and pin the gauge. Like, a hundred-and-ten plus framerate."

"Wow?"

"World of Warcraft?" He stared, shocked, at my blank face. "Man, you *are* out of it. Even my mom knows what WoW is."

"If it doesn't involve a hex map or doubling down on an ace, I don't play."

He looked at me like I was speaking Swahili. What can I say? The feeling was mutual.

"Tell you what, Eager. You come help me get the chair out of the trunk of my car, maybe we can talk about a few things." It was a risky move, but there had been no movement on the Tabor Doe and I figured if Eager told me something of significance, I'd work out a way to use it later.

"I'm not supposed to talk to you."

"So I've been told. But it's not like you ever do anything else Charm tells you."

That earned me a quick smile, but no talk. We walked down to my car. I popped the trunk and together we hoisted the folded wheelchair out onto the sidewalk. Eager relaxed at the sight. He nodded and smiled and tugged at his ear, then pushed off.

But before he got too far, he stopped, looked back at me. His face was screwed up again, and I knew he was chewing on something. Then he spat it out. "I saw his badge, that's all."

"Portland Police badge?"

"No, somewhere else. It was a star, but it looked old." He paused. "Maybe it was fake."

I nodded. "Was it your dad, Eager?"

He thought some more, tongue working his cheek. "I got no fucking dad." Then he turned and was off, rolling the chair down the street with his skateboard on the seat. I didn't know where Jase's grandmother lived, but I don't imagine Jase wanted Eager rolling the wheelchair right up to his own front door.

Two days later, he and Jase were back at it, wheelchair, sign, blanket, at the end of the off-ramp from I-205 at Division. I didn't bother to stop a second time.

Based on the badge and the non-denial *I got no fucking dad* amounted to, I came clean to Susan about my encounters with Eager. Her reaction was better than I expected.

"He's looking for a father figure."

I almost made a snotty comment, but she was right. On some level. Why else would he spend so much time showing off and bragging about his kickflips and road rash?

"I suppose I should tell Deiter."

"He'll need to know."

Deiter told me to stay away from the kid, but in a way that made it clear he understood if Eager showed up at my door of his own accord, I couldn't be blamed. So I went back to listening to Eager's incomprehensible antics, waiting for an opportunity to delve a little deeper into the badge, the cop. His father. He had nothing for me. Sometimes I'd see him with Jase, and when I did he pointedly ignored me. The rest of the time it was all pop shove-its or some fucking crazy downhill stunt he pulled up on Mount Tabor. Wipeouts and rail grinds. Dude.

A year and a half after the Tabor Doe I stepped out onto my porch early one morning for a smoke only to find Eager standing on the sidewalk in front of the house, gazing at me with an expression reminiscent of the look he'd given me the day he'd declared he had no fucking dad. It was early. No teenage boy I've ever known would be willingly awake at such an hour.

"My mom's moving to Spokane."

"You going with her?" I meant the comment as a joke, but Eager didn't laugh.

"Fuck no. I'm staying here."

"I'm not following you." I knew the Gillespies had no family in Portland.

"She's whack. I'd rather sleep under a bridge than live with her. Besides, she's got a new boyfriend."

I was supposed to be at work. But I sat down on my top step, motioned for Eager to join me. He dropped his skateboard in the grass and came and swung off the wooden porch railing. "So she dumped her broker?"

"More like he dumped her. Or maybe his wife did."

Eager's understanding of his mother's activities always astonished me. "How do you feel about that?"

"What the fucking shit're you talking like a brain cracker for?"

I laughed, a bit ruefully. Somewhere inside I thought that maybe I should tell him to watch the language, but I had more important things to worry about than the inexpert profanity of a fifteen-year-old. "You can't live on your own."

"Sure I can. I know people."

"Who do you know?"

He shrugged, kept swinging, his face turned away from me.

"Not your father."

"Who?"

Susan and I still hadn't tracked Big Ed down. Last known was years out of date. We tried to get some help from the Klamath County Sheriff, but while they promised to have their Givern Valley sub-station people do some checking around, nothing ever came of it. The State Police weren't much more help, though I think they tried harder. Big Ed had just dropped off the map. Rumors were that he'd hung around Westbank for years after leaving the sheriff's department, but no one knew what he did to stay afloat. He hadn't filed a tax return since he quit, and near as we could tell hadn't drawn a paycheck either. If Charm hadn't called the cops on him the day before the Tabor Doe, we'd have no reason to believe he was even alive.

But whenever I hinted about Big Ed to Eager, his stare would go long and he'd clam up. "Who?" he asked again. I was convinced Big Ed was the cop Eager saw on Mount Tabor that day, and Susan admitted the possibility. But we had no other witnesses, no physical evidence, and no trace of the big man himself.

"Hey, Skin. Check out this three-sixty, man!"

"Did your old man take the gun with him, Eager?"

"Who?" Kickflip, crash. What else could Susan and I do but move on to other things?

Couple of Years Back

Sunlight in His Eyes

When the cop grabbed him on Tabor summit, words spilled out like falling water. Four lousy words, look at the damage. Eager refused to speak of the man on the hill again. But in his dreams, his voice couldn't be silenced. In his dreams, Eager shouted as loud as mountains cracking open. Up from the depths clambered the big man, a shriek gushing with purple blood from his open throat. The shriek would rise like a wave and toss Eager weeping from sleep, his flesh clammy and cold, fearful of his voice in the dark. No one else ever heard. Awake, he remained silent, allowed his silence to drive the big man away. In silence, he found, the hilltop empties, the body dissolves. The awful specter of mud and blood and pouring rain washes away into nothingness.

Gone …

   … poof …

      … forever …

Except, deep down, Eager knew it wasn't that simple.

So a month later, two months later, as the heat died down and Charm quit watching his every move, as she got back into her own groove, sneaking off with her boss and pretending it would make their lives better, Eager took to trolling the neighborhood. He knew he had to keep a low profile, cut back on his work. He couldn't afford to get caught with his hand in someone's purse, or pulling a stereo out of a car. A little panhandling, that was it. The prosecutor guy, fuckwit—Jesus, Charm could crack him up sometimes—talked about using his work against him. To make him talk. Like that was gonna happen.

He didn't suppose he could afford to get caught skipping school any more than he could afford getting caught busting the glass on some overloaded Hummer. Bullshit. What the hell did he care about the Boston Tea Party, storm formation, means and medians? But school was only six hours, plus maybe a half hour of Charm bitching about how he was gonna be held back if he didn't start doing his homework. Rest of the time, he hit the pavement. Searching, but for what?

Hard to say. Different things. When his dreams were loudest, he looked for the man from the hill, always over his shoulder and half on edge. Awake, he knew the guy had to be miles away. Maybe in a hole. But maybe around the next corner. Eager knew it wasn't too bright to show himself out in the world. Asking for change, skating, searching. What would Charm say? Fucking brain-dead, that's what. He could get snatched off the street and Charm would never know what happened. Whatever.

Lu kept her head down. Looked after the baby, made nice with that slob she met at Common Grounds. Working her own deal. Couldn't blame her for that. But she didn't like Eager being so public, so soon. One month, two months. Too soon.

Still.

Day after day, Eager rolled along, 50th to 60th, Hawthorne to Division. Familiar ground, little different street to street. Closer to Division, the houses were smaller, maybe. Duplexes like the one he lived in were the exception, but that wasn't the sort of thing Eager noticed. He was looking for something specific, just didn't know what. So he skated, up and down, back and forth, dodging traffic on Lincoln, grinding retaining walls until old ladies shouted him off.

Luellen was more cautious. Sometimes he went weeks without seeing her. Look in the coffee house window, no sign of her—roll.

Halloween, that was the day. Kadash. Eager remembered a lot from his afternoon sitting at the woman cop's desk drinking shitty cocoa and exercising his right to remain silent. Skin. Shaggy grey hair and that neck, Jesus. The ugly fuck was hauling a yellow recycling bin full of empty cans and newspapers down to the curb. Their eyes met, cop's surprised, Eager's not. Eager knew he'd find him, even if he hadn't known he was looking.

He waved, put on the face he wore for adults. "Hey, Detective Kadash! This your place?"

The detective didn't answer right away. "What are you doing here, Eager?" He set the bin down and stood up, one hand on his back. Face was screwed up in a knot like his tongue was made of lemons.

"Just skating. You know how it is. A man can't never get enough board time."

"I guess I can see your point."

"Fucking hell, yeah." Eager ollied up onto the parking strip. "I only live a few blocks away." He waved in some direction, no matter if his house was that way or not. Skin didn't look anyway.

"I know."

"Your street has too many cars on it."

"Tell me about it."

Eager laughed. He liked the old guy's voice, gravelly from cigarettes, tempered by amusement. "Wanna see some shreds?"

"Maybe some other time."

Eager waved again and continued on. Didn't look back. He could tell Skin was watching him. At the next corner, he turned toward the park. Now he knew where the cop lived, time for some serious skating. He grinned, not recognizing the relief he felt as relief. Just glad he could find the cop when he needed to.

That night, in his dreams, the man on the hill stayed quiet. Eager woke up with sunlight in his eyes.

A few days later he skated past again. Kadash's house was different from the rest on the block, older, smaller. A bit more run down. Eager possessed no awareness of architectural nuance, couldn't tell the difference between an Old Portland and a Craftsman. But he had an eye for nice, and Kadash's house wasn't nice. It was average: one story, sagging porch. The grass had been cut, but aside from that, the yard looked like a whole lot of nothing. A few box hedges under the windows beside the porch, crabgrass and moss in the lawn.

About what you'd expect for a crunchy old cop.

The houses to either side and across the street were another story. They showed off fresh coats of paint, new windows and hanging plants. Security company signs. Eager didn't bother with house prowls, but if he had, these were the kinds of joints he'd consider. Nice, but not too nice, with a *Protected By* sign tucked under the azaleas next to the front steps. Eager didn't worry about security systems. He knew the score. People set them off all the time, false alarms. But he knew a nice neighborhood full of those signs meant a lot of taxpayers with shit to protect. Police kept an eye out for such types, people with more than a jar full of change and a stack of CDs and DVDs to sell at Everyday Music. Include a cop, no matter how good or bad his house looked, and the street was everything he hoped to find. Even if he hadn't known he was looking.

Eager made a mental note, satisfied. Skated. Later, he ran into Skin again. Jawed a little, talked about his deck, his wheels, his trucks. Eager, rarely a talker, found himself describing the transitions at Burnside and O'Bryant Square. Skin sat on the top step of his porch and listened, maybe even a little interested. Eager liked him.

And the way he figured it, it was good to have a friend who was a cop. Especially once the house across the street went up for sale. Perfect house, safe house, even if Skin didn't understand Eager's interest. Luellen would love it, once she convinced that slob she had on the hook that he needed to buy it for her.

November 13

Police Investigate Two Deaths in Rural Klamath County

MIDLAND, OR: Police are investigating the deaths of Gene and Sue Ann Famke, discovered Tuesday at their home six miles northwest of Midland after dispatchers received a 9-1-1 call from a neighbor reporting screams and possible gun fire.

The couple appeared to be victims of a deadly assault, said Deputy Raelene Suggins of the Klamath County Sheriff's Office. Gene Famke, 43, was found on the front lawn. A recently fired .38 caliber revolver registered to Famke was recovered from the driveway nearby. Inside the residence, a double-wide manufactured home, police found the body of Sue Ann Famke, 41.

Anyone with information about this case is urged to contact the Klamath County Sheriff's Department.

PART TWO

GUTTA CAVAT LAPIDEM, NON VI, SED SAEPE CADENDO
(A drop of water hollows a stone, not by force, but by continuously dripping)

—Ovid, Epistulae Ex Ponto, Book 3, no. 10, 1. 5

November 19 — 6:04 am

Whole Family Is Made of Butter

Big Ed Gillespie preferred the direct approach. But he wasn't the boss, and if the boss said stay off the radar, that's the way he would play it. He wasn't going to fuck this up. Not this time.

He awoke early the morning after he found the Bronsteins and took a shower, then left his motel room before anyone nearby was up and moving. Still dark out. He'd paid cash for the room and done nothing memorable during his brief stay, though a man big as a mule deer who spoke with an electronic larynx would likely stick in the mind no matter what he did. That couldn't be helped, but his actions could. He'd selected a motel near the highway, a place that catered to nobodies passing through. He'd also insisted Myra stay somewhere else. Anywhere else, he didn't care. He didn't want anyone to be able to say, yeah, some dude with a fucked up throat was running around with a bony, hot-tempered tweaker.

He stopped to eat at the Jubitz truck stop on I-5, just another big, beefy man shucking off the night over a plate of eggs and sausage links. After breakfast he drove into town with the first gasp of morning rush hour, wipers set to the slowest interval. He got off at the Rose Quarter exit, followed MLK down to the Inn at the

Convention Center. Hiram Spaneker was waiting for him on the corner at Holladay Street.

"Good flight?" One hand on the wheel, the other pressing the electrolarynx to his throat. He'd gotten good at doing things one-handed when he wanted to carry on a conversation.

Hiram dropped a nylon bag onto the back seat and slid into the passenger seat. "I suppose. I felt like a fucking sardine, but at least they gave me a bag of pretzels the size of my nut sack to keep me occupied."

"What's in the bag?"

"Stuff to occupy the boy."

Big Ed wheezed in response. He continued down MLK and followed the loop under 99E onto Division. Easier than Hawthorne, especially this time of day. That much he'd learned in the three days since he got to town.

"Did ya see her?"

Big Ed nodded. From a distance, but she entered the right house.

"And the boy?"

"Mmm-hmmm."

"What about the others? A man and an older kid too, right? That's what Myra said."

"Whole family is made of butter."

"That ain't no family." But Hiram smiled grimly and leaned back in his seat. Ten minutes more, and Big Ed parked in the upper lot in Mount Tabor Park, a location that appealed to some primitive desire for symmetry. Too dark and too cold for anyone else to be around; he expected to be gone again before the sun rose. He opened his glove box, hefted the piece: A brushed chrome Desert Eagle chambered for .44 Magnum. He'd taken it off a Yreka meth cooker who'd crossed Hiram, one of many firearms he'd acquired from the less deserving over the years. Probably used in a dozen drugstore holdups, so if the cops ever got their hands on it, it would be tied to some NoCal shit.

But as he checked the magazine, Hiram's face went red.

"Are you fucking nuts?"

"Just in case. I do not expect to need it."

"That's why you'll be leaving it here, numbnuts." Hiram's cheeks twitched as he spoke. "I don't want no one to have cause to come looking like before. No goddamn bodies. You got that?"

"Seems to me like you would want at least one body."

"Not today, I don't." Big Ed looked at Hiram, saw the dark glint in his eye. "I'm a patient man, if you're not."

Big Ed didn't want to argue with Hiram Spaneker, not after Hiram had announced his intention to offer Ed a second chance. He knew the rules, understood them better perhaps than Hiram realized. Back in Givern, bodies weren't a problem. Local cops were a wholly owned subsidiary of Spaneker Enterprises, and the county guys knew to stay out of the way. But this wasn't Givern. Hiram was out of his element. Big Ed could sense the old man's discomfort in the city. Didn't surprise him—didn't disquiet him either. Big Ed was uncomfortable everywhere now, but three years on the run had provided a stern education in finding his way. His last trip to Portland, he'd come in big and cocky, looking for trouble. Found it, too. Took a bullet, almost lost his life. He was a different man now, no longer a man on fire.

He slid the gun under the front seat.

They locked the Suburban, then he and Hiram walked down into the neighborhood until he saw what he wanted parked on the street, a late-80s Accord, four doors with a battered left front quarter panel. He slim-jimmed the door and punched the ignition with his Leatherman. Hiram scowled as he climbed into the passenger seat; not as much leg room as the Suburban.

Daylight Savings had fallen back a couple of weeks before, but the sky was still dark when he turned off 60th into the girl's neighborhood. A few short blocks, a right and a left. He drove past the house once, saw lights and movement through the window.

They were up already. Folks with jobs and kids to get off to school were gonna be early risers on a weekday morning. He continued up the block until he found an empty space.

Mitch Bronstein was some kind of ad fellow, worked at a snooty agency downtown. Probably a queer. Loafers and cotton shirts. Big Ed planned to go in quiet and strong, do what they had to do quick. He told Hiram they'd be back in the Suburban and rolling south by the time the sun cleared the shoulder of Mount Hood. Drive straight through to Givern, sleep in their own beds tonight. Hiram promised Big Ed a big sack of money to use for a pillow if everything worked out. Big Ed smiled. Been a long time since he owned a pillow.

"Are you ready?"

"You gotta ask?" The old man cracked his knuckles. "What kinda car does this bastard drive?"

"BMW. Let me get up on the porch before you come up."

The street was quiet. A few houses showed lights, like the Bronstein place, but no one was outside. Making coffee, yelling at their damn kids to get outa bed already. Big Ed tucked the larynx into his belt, then crept up onto the porch, quiet as his bulk would allow. The front door was half glass, the foyer beyond dark and empty. He pressed himself against the wall to the right of the door, then gestured to Hiram waiting down on the walk. Hiram went straight to the door and knocked. Put a pleasant look on his sun-baked face, much as possible. Slouched a bit. A moment later, light spilled through the glass pane in the door, then a shadow.

Hiram cracked an unctuous smile. "Mister Bronstein, sir, sorry to bother you so early."

Bronstein didn't open the door. "Do I know you?" His voice wary.

"It's Dave. I just moved in a couple houses up. We met the other day."

Big Ed could almost picture Bronstein's confused expression, but Hiram's bullshit flowed thick. He heard the door open a crack. "We did?" Big Ed tried to make himself even flatter against the wall.

Hiram kept smiling. "You were getting out of your car. The Beamer?"

"If you say so. What can I do for you, Dave? It's damned early for a social call."

Hiram looked back over his shoulder, then down at his feet. "Well, it's about your car. I'm afraid I ran into it parking, and put a dent in the left front quarter panel." Big Ed thought of the Accord and had to fight down a chuckle about that little detail. *Nice touch, Hiram.*

"What?" Bronstein yanked the door open and took a step onto the porch, his face searching. "When the hell did—"

Big Ed slid sideways past Hiram and grabbed Bronstein by the throat, one-handed. Mitch's eyes bulged and he clawed at the meat clamp on his windpipe. Big Ed spun around to face him and Bronstein stumbled. Ed pushed him through the doorway, hand still on his throat.

"Who is it, honey?" The girl, calling from another room. He could hear a note of Givern Valley in her voice. "It's awfully early for someone to be knocking on the door." Bronstein tried to speak, but Big Ed's grip was too strong. "Jase, sweetie, go see who it is."

"I'm eating." The older kid. The one Myra mentioned.

"Come on, Jase. Help me out here. I still need to get Danny up."

Big Ed walked Bronstein backward and cracked his head hard against the wooden trim around the front closet door. Bronstein crumpled, but continued to struggle. Big Ed cracked his head again then pushed him down onto his ass, head slumped against his shoulder. Dazed, but conscious. He pressed his face into Bronstein's and stuck the larynx against his own throat. Spoke in as much of a whisper as the device would allow. "Be quiet and you and your family might live through this."

An idle threat, but Bronstein didn't know that. His hands went to his throat. "What … you … what do you …" A coffee-laced gasp.

"We are here for the boy."

Bronstein's eyes rolled. Big Ed stood, looked to either side, assessing. Fingers curled around the black cylinder of the larynx. The living room at his left opened onto the dining room. To his right, a hallway led past the stairs into the back. Both routes must connect to the kitchen. He heard a sound, the scrape of a chair across the floor. A muttered curse, then footsteps. A door opened, flooded the hallway with light. The door swung shut again as the tall, overweight kid appeared in the hallway next to the stairs. It seemed to take him a moment to realize what he was looking at. "Whoa, jeezus—!" Big Ed caught his eye as he turned, tried to flee. One quick step, then his arm locked around the kid's neck. He yanked the kid backwards off his feet, slammed him into the floor. He kneeled down on the boy's chest, looked him in the eye. The terror on the kid's face was clear as reading a newspaper headline.

Jase, the woman had called him.

Hiram Spaneker stepped in through the open front door. "Think you're making enough noise?" The old man looked down at Bronstein, then Jase, with obvious disdain. "I bet folks could hear your goddamn ruckus halfway to Salem."

"It went as planned."

"I don't doubt it, if stampeding cattle was the fucking plan."

Footsteps. "Jase, honey, what's going on? What was that noise?" The swinging door in the hallway started to open.

"You go find the boy." Hiram slapped him on the shoulder. Big Ed nodded, headed up the stairs. Out of the corner of his eye he saw Hiram slip around through the living room as the woman pushed through the kitchen door into the hall.

Her scream followed Big Ed up the stairs. He hit the second floor landing at a run and moved down a dark hallway, four doors, two on each side, and what looked like another stairway leading down at the far end. The two nearer doors stood open. He looked into a bedroom, empty, the bed heaped with rumpled blankets and sheets. Clock radio the only light. An adult room. No one home. The other open door led into the bathroom, dimly lit by a night light over the sink. Big Ed moved down the hall and pushed open the first closed door. Had to be the older kid's bedroom. The walls were covered with posters of rappers and oily girls in bikinis. A computer sat on the desk next to a small flat-screen television. Video game console, stacks of game cases and DVDs. Big Ed pulled the door shut and turned.

The boy stood behind him, one hand on the doorknob of the room opposite. No more than four years old, chestnut hair and big eyes.

"What's your name?" The kid's voice was hardly louder than a breath. As he spoke, he studied the scars on Big Ed's throat, but he showed no fear.

Big Ed leaned down. He could hear sounds downstairs, movement, rough banging. But the screaming had stopped. The kid didn't seem to notice.

"What's your name?"

Big Ed didn't plan on getting into that. He put his hand to his neck, trying to hide the larynx in his big paw. "Hey, kid. You got some shoes? Pants?"

"Where's my mommy?"

"She told me to come help you get dressed. We are going on a trip."

"Where's my mommy?"

Big Ed stood, slipped around him into his bedroom. It was small and neat, toys organized in stacked cubbies in one corner. Cookie

Monster wallpaper and a Transformers lamp. A pair of shoes on the floor in front of the small dresser.

"Where are your diapers?"

The little boy parked his hands on his hips and lowered his eyebrows, stern and ridiculous. "I wear big boy pull-ups."

Big Ed saw the package of pull-ups on the dresser top and decided to grab a couple, just in case. He yanked open the dresser drawers until he found pants, turned around to find the kid standing behind him, bare-ass naked, pull-up in his hand.

"I made pee-pee."

Big Ed hadn't thought about this part. He planned to grab the kid and go. Diapers and pants, what was he supposed to do? He's wasn't some kind of nanny.

"Here, put these on." He thrust the clean pull-ups at him, but the kid just looked at him.

"What's your name?"

"Call me Joe." As good a name as any.

"I made pee-pee, Joe."

"Okay. Good boy."

"You talk funny."

Big Ed could feel himself getting frustrated. He tried to smile. "Let me help get you dressed."

"I can put my own pants on."

Big Ed bowed his head. *Thank you.* The kid wriggled into one of the pairs of pull-ups. He looked at the pants Big Ed held and apparently rejected them, went to the dresser and got out a different pair, blue corduroy overalls. He flopped onto his butt, struggled with the pant legs. Downstairs, Big Ed heard a crash, door slam, something. Didn't sound good. Maybe a voice. "No—!" The kid looked up at the sound, concerned.

"Where's my mommy?"

"She is fine." Big Ed grabbed the overalls by the suspenders and lifted, allowing the boy to plunk down into the pant legs. Then he hooked the suspenders and pushed the boy's sneakers onto his little feet without socks. He thought briefly about rooting around for a shirt, decided the pajama top would have to do.

He pointed the little boy toward the door and gave him a gentle push, one hand on his shoulder. In an instant, the boy slithered out of his grip. Before he knew what was happening, the kid darted through the door, trailing giggles behind him. Big Ed charged into the hall, saw a tuft of hair vanish into the darkness of the back stairwell. Still giggling.

Big Ed made chase, astounded by the speed with which the little monkey got away from him. He took the stairs three at a time and plunged through the doorway at the bottom just in time to hear the gun go off.

November 19 — 11:10 am

Not on the Schedule

My last conversation with Charm Gillespie had been four months earlier when I called in the aftermath of Eager's tag on Mitch and Luellen's door. It had been our first contact since she left town, though I knew Dieter still hassled her, probably on a schedule set in Outlook. I had to remind myself I wasn't doing Mitch's bidding so much as chasing my own curiosity when I called the Spokane phone number I'd browbeat out of Eager during one of his many flights back to Portland. One of the girls answered. I didn't remember much about them except their names, Gem and Jewel. Twins. No clue which one I got.

"Hey there, sweetie. Can I talk to your mother?"

"I'm not your sweetie. I don't know who you are."

"I'm sorry." I swallowed. "Is your mother there?"

"Who shall I say is calling?"

"Tell her it's about Eager."

"We're not allowed to say his name."

Blunt, this one. Got her personality from her mother.

"Would you put your mom on?"

"I'll ask her, but I bet she won't talk to you. She doesn't like Eager anymore."

I listened to the buzzes and hisses of long distance and to the sound of a television while I waited. Distantly, through the phone, I could hear the little girl's conversation with Charm.

"He says it's about *you-know-who.*" As if I'd called about Voldemort.

"It's that goddamn cop, isn't it? Tell him I'm not home."

"Mom."

"What?"

"He probably knows you're here."

"What did you say to him?"

"*No*thing."

"Jesus Christ, you told him I was here, didn't you?"

"Mo-*ommm.*"

"Give me the goddamn phone."

I heard a clatter and a sigh.

"Hello, Mrs. Gillespie."

"It's Mrs. Hutchison now."

"Sure. Mrs. Hutchison."

"What do you want?"

"I was wondering if you know where Eager is."

"What makes you think I'd want to?"

"He's your son. He's supposed to be living with you."

"Spare me." She knew even better than I did how hard it had been to keep Eager in Spokane.

"So I take it you don't know."

She went quiet, though I could hear her breathing against a *Dr. Phil* backdrop.

"Mrs. Hutchison … Charm—" Maybe pretending we were on a first name basis would warm her up.

"I don't have to talk to you. We established that a long time ago."

She had me there. I waited, hoping to draw her out with my own silence. She almost outlasted me, but then she sighed.

"He was here a few weeks ago."

"Really? How long did he stay?"

"About as long as it took him to ask for money and for my husband to say no."

"Did you say no too, Mrs. Hutchison?"

"Is that all, Detective?"

"Did he mention where he might be heading?"

"We didn't chit-chat."

"Apparently he's been down this way recently. Do you know anything about that?"

"I'm hanging up."

I've always enjoyed my little chats with Charm. But I never have a fucking clue what they amount to.

Now I need to call her again, a prospect with all the appeal of a colonoscopy. Hard to guess if this morning's events in front of Mitch's house will mean anything to her. Still, even Charm Gillespie might get a little misty when she hears her kid took a bullet in the face.

The number 14 bus drops me at Hawthorne and SE 47th, and a fleeting rain chases me the last half block to the door of Uncommon Cup II. It's been my home away from home since retirement—Ruby Jane's second location in her growing empire of coffee. I hesitate before going in. When RJ offered me hours a few months earlier, my gut response was to decline. I'd been a cop so long the thought of serving lattes seemed on a par with auditioning for the ballet. Standing behind a counter, asking customer after customer what they'll have. Saying "thank you" and "come again," all while smiling and looking them in the eye.

A year ago I'd have sworn I'd come to terms with my neck. But suddenly I found myself self-conscious for the first time in years.

You come into contact with plenty of folks investigating homicides, but a little disfigurement isn't as much of a problem for a cop. If anything, it gave me an edge, generated disquiet, put people off their game. In interviews, with Susan working the warm, sympathetic lady cop angle, I'd lead with my neck. But behind a coffee counter? One gander at me and the *come agains* were sure to suffer a serious drop-off.

I said I was too busy not finishing the *Times* crossword to get a job. Ruby Jane told me to shut the hell up and come learn to pull shots. She should have listened to me. Hell, *I* should have listened to me.

Inside, I take a moment to inhale the aromas of coffee and milk steam. The old Armenian who looks like Saddam Hussein in witness protection is in his usual spot near the window, and a couple of unremarkable specimens hog the couch. Marcy is working the counter. I'm not on the schedule, won't be for the rest of the week. I'd asked for the time off, and Ruby Jane agreed it was a good idea. By email.

"What's going on, Skin?"

"Not much. Is RJ coming in?" Time spent with Ruby Jane inevitably consumes all my energy, which makes me wonder why I'm even here. Not that I wonder for long. I know exactly why.

Marcy's cheeks color, as if she's surprised I've got the nerve to mention RJ's name. But Ruby Jane wouldn't have told her what happened. "She went over to the Hollywood shop."

"I need to make a phone call, thought I would use the back room."

"No one's back there right now."

I make my way through the kitchen to the doorless nook behind the dish sanitizer. It's not quite an office, just an out-of-the-way spot where Ruby Jane has put a small desk and file cabinet, chair, and a bulletin board with the weekly schedule. It's not much, but it provides a measure of privacy. I sit down, pull out my cell phone. Charm's number is saved in my contacts list.

A man answers after half a dozen rings. "Hello, Hutchisons."

"May I speak to Mrs. Hutchison, please?"

"Who's this?"

"I'm calling about Eager."

"The detective."

"Kadash, yes."

"She won't talk to you, Detective Kadash." His voice isn't unfriendly.

"Are you Mister Hutchison?"

"Yes." In the background, I can hear the murmur of a weather report; I'm grateful it isn't *Dr. Phil.* "What do you want?"

"I have some news about Eager."

"Is he dead?"

Preternatural. Or maybe they'd both been expecting a call like this for a while now. "I'm afraid I can't say for sure. He turned up this morning, but he got hurt and now he's missing again."

"He's not here."

"I didn't think he was." He'd need rocket boots to get to Spokane in the couple of hours since I'd seen him. "I'm just trying to figure out where he might have got to. I was hoping someone there could tell me where he might be staying here in Portland."

"Have you checked under all the bridges?"

"You think he's living outside?"

"I don't know, but that would fit."

"Does he have any friends or other family down here?"

"Listen, Detective. I don't know what to tell you. Eager hasn't been here in I don't know how long. He shows up every so often, usually to beg for money and upset my wife. Then he disappears again for months at a time. We've reported him as a runaway for all the good that does. We just don't know what he's up to."

"He was shot this morning."

There's a long silence. Spokane's high will be forty-two today. "That's ... unfortunate."

"You don't sound too upset."

"Listen, I hardly know him."

"You and Charm got married when she moved to Spokane, what, two years ago?"

"I see where you're going with this, but it won't fly. Yes, I'm his stepfather, but my focus is on the kids who actually live here."

"So not upset then."

He sighs. "Charm will be upset enough for the two of us." I find that hard to believe, but I keep my thoughts to myself.

"May I speak to your wife?"

"She's at work."

"Not you?"

"Christ. Charm was right about you."

"Mister Hutchison, I didn't mean—" He hangs up.

I fold my phone, weigh it in my hand along with my limited options. I suppose I could check all the bridges and overpasses in the city. Maybe the other skate parks, though I don't think Eager will be doing any ollies with a bullet behind his eyeball. But finding Eager is a job I'm no longer in a position to do. I have no access to resources, can't issue a BOLO, or even ask friendly uniforms to keep an eye out for him. If he ends up in a hospital, the gunshot wound will mean a call to the cops, but no one will tell me about it.

I push myself to my feet, move into the kitchen and all but knock Ruby Jane on her ass.

She backs up into the opening between the kitchen and the counter area up front, hands clasped at her waist. The shoulders of her jacket are spotted with rain.

"Jesus, Skin, you scared the hell out of me."

"That's what all the girls say."

I can smell her shampoo, the crisp scent of apples. Ruby Jane has been letting her hair grow out, and it hangs loose over her shoulders. With some surprise I notice a few strands of grey at her temples, a dash of salt with the cayenne.

"I'm going to make some tea. You want something? Maybe we can talk." She won't make eye contact. I'm not used to that. Ruby Jane has never been one who let discomfort unsettle her. "If you want."

A knot forms in my stomach, and I half wish I'd found somewhere else to make my call. Yet even as the thought blossoms, I know this awkward collision is exactly what I'd hoped for by coming here this morning.

"Sure." I nod and manage an awkward smile. "Back here? Or—"

"Go grab a table up front. I'll join you in a minute."

She doesn't want to be alone with me. I can't blame her.

Four Years, Seven Months Before

When It's Safe

Stuart hadn't come home, or if he had he'd slept on the couch and was up and gone again before she woke. Not that Ellie cared. She was content to sleep alone. But with Stuart out she was stuck with the farm pickup. No heater, rust eating through the floorboards, and winter hanging on into April like a tick on a yard dog. It was anybody's guess if the truck would even start. The carburetor had been rebuilt so many times the walls of the float bowl were thin as paper. And her with an eight mile drive into Westbank.

It couldn't be helped. Ellie needed to see Luellen. Stuart would be no use to her. She almost laughed imagining his reaction to the news.

"My father called, Stuart. Brett is dead."

"I thought you didn't like Brett."

"That's not the point. He's my brother."

"Well, what did the dumb ass think was going to happen, enlisting in the middle of a war?"

These last few years, Kerns had been dying off like pigs with swine fever. First her mother, eaten alive by bone cancer. Rob followed, stabbed in the parking lot of the Kla-Mo-Ya Casino in

Chiloquin. No one even knew why he'd gone up there, though dark rumors of drug deals and gambling debts filtered back to Givern Valley. Ellie didn't know what to believe. Myra alone was proof enough being a Kern was no guarantee of clear thinking or virtue. Not long after Rob's death, on the very day his farm went up for bank auction, Brett joined the Marines—an act he admitted was born of a need to feel like a man again. Now a man in a flag-draped box. Of the Givern Kerns, once a large and sprawling clan, only her father survived from her parents' generation. Among her own generation, siblings and cousins alike, just Ellie and Myra lingered, though Myra hardly counted anymore—for her, the valley served only as a layover between broke and desperate.

For the time being, her father was on his feet, active and busy, if weighed down by the deaths of so many he cared for. Instead of her brothers to act as hands he hired locals, but he still ran the farm, still drove the combine in the spring and the harvester in the fall, still hauled the water trailer out to the pigs at pasture. But he wasn't getting any younger. With Rob and Brett dead and Myra off chasing crystal meth, Ellie alone remained to care for Immanuel Kern in his failing years. The task of planning Brett's memorial service would fall to her.

She layered up against the cold, scarf tight around her aching neck, then made her way to the equipment shed to get the battery off the charger. Lugged it to truck port and dropped it under the hood. Couple squirts of ether into the air intake. Her breath was like smoke as she climbed behind the wheel and turned the key. Out past the plowed fields she could see snow on the rocky uplands.

The truck was a blocky F-150 older than she was—on its second engine, its third transmission, and she didn't know how many sets of gaskets and rings. The cab still smelled of Lucky Strikes three years after Hiram bequeathed the truck to Ellie and Stuart. When she turned the key the starter growled and fought, but then the engine caught. The transmission was sloppy and as she pulled out across the frost-rimmed gravel driveway a cold draft rose between her feet. But the truck ran. She had a quarter tank of gas. On the way in she could check a few likely spots, the Cup 'n' Saucer or Hiram's card room at the Big I Motor Inn. If she found the Tahoe, she'd take it and leave the pickup for Stuart. Serve him right if the damned thing broke down halfway up Little Liver Road.

Ellie had last seen Luellen just after Christmas, a couple of weeks before the miscarriage. Luellen's attempts to go to school took her away from Westbank for months at a time. She didn't say much, but from what Ellie could glean there was a boyfriend, someone who presented nicer than he turned out to be. Luellen hadn't returned to Ashland for winter term. With help from her parents, she'd rented a little apartment above a hair salon in town.

Ellie didn't see anyone else on the road until she came to the feed store at Four Mile Crossing. No sign of the Tahoe, though she saw Hiram's Suburban in the lot among a half dozen other trucks and SUVs. No doubt Hiram was inside holding forth, the Givern Valley patriarch never shy about sharing an opinion if he could pin down an audience. She didn't stop. A few miles farther the fields and rocky hills gave way to clusters of ranch-style houses and mobile home parks. Town was quiet, the streets devoid of traffic. She continued to Westbank Center, a dozen or so square blocks consisting of struggling businesses and local government buildings. Every third or fourth window along High Street featured a For Lease or For Sale sign. *Good terms, motivated seller.* A buyer's market, fresh out of buyers. Twelve years before, the locals had passed a referendum to rename the town in the hope Westbank would be more palatable to outside investment than Little Liver. A pointless gesture. Whatever it was called, the town was too far from good slopes to attract skiers, too far from timber to support a mill, too far from Klamath Falls or the interstates to support manufacturing. The silver and copper mines had played out before her grandfather was born. For the most part, the rocky soil of the valley gave up only short season field corn and a little barley. Half the billboards along the county highway warned against the perils of domestic abuse, alcohol, or gambling. The rest advertised beer and Indian casinos. The growth industry in recent years was *get-the-hell-out.* For those who lingered, the choice was to try to pick up a rare county job or commute forty miles each way to K-Falls. Much of the good land was owned by the Spanekers, and they worked to buy the rest when they could. Even Brett's farm had ended up in Hiram's hands, picked up at auction after the foreclosure. Hiram offered to hire Brett as foreman, have him continue to work the land on salary, but Brett had already made his choice.

Ellie parked in front of the salon. Closed. After Luellen chopped it off so many years before, her mother had insisted on cutting her hair and did so until she died. Since then Ellie hadn't thought about it much. Her hair had grown out some now, enough to brush her shoulders. Not that anyone noticed. Stuart paid little enough attention, and when she went out, to church or to the store, she bound it up in a knot on top of her head. The last time she'd been to a hairdresser was for her wedding.

An unmarked door between the salon and a locksmith led to the apartments above. Ellie entered the narrow foyer. The stairway was dark. There'd been a light at the top of the stairs when she'd come before. She hesitated, and found herself scanning the names written on torn strips of masking tape affixed to the vertical mailboxes on the wall inside the door. Luellen's wasn't among them. *Had it been here at Christmas?* She couldn't remember.

A shadow fell across the doorway and she heard heavy footsteps come to a stop. She turned, felt her breath catch in her throat. Stuart peered in from the sidewalk. He was wearing his work clothes, canvas coat and coveralls, and stood with his hands in his pockets, shoulders up around his ears. "Hey." He looked past her up the dark stairway. She felt herself shrink away from him.

"What are you doing here?"

He gestured vaguely with one hunched shoulder. "I saw the truck. Figured you were here to see your friend." Voice quiet, a little tired. She listened for a trace of anger, surprised she couldn't detect one.

"How did you know about this place? She's only lived here a few months."

"I don't know. You hear stuff." His weight shifted from one foot to the other. "It's a small town."

"Oh." Dead air seemed to hang between them. Ellie felt off-balance, bewildered at Stuart's uncharacteristic unease. "I know you don't like me seeing Luellen. I just wanted—"

"Don't worry about it." She blinked at him. "Listen, I know how I've been. I also know you like her. It's probably not fair for me to tell you who you can be friends with."

He might as well have said he was running away to join the circus. "What's going on, Stuart?"

"You don't know."

"Know what?"

He licked his lips, looked away. "I guess she's gone."

"What are you talking about?"

"She left. Moved away, something. A couple days ago."

"How do you know that?"

"I told you. I hear things."

Ellie turned and climbed the stairs to the second floor, the darkness of the stairwell forgotten. Luellen's door was first on the right. She knocked. An echo sounded from within. She tried the knob, but the door was locked.

Stuart stepped into the foyer, looked up at her from the foot of the stairs. "I told you. She's gone."

Ellie pressed her forehead against Luellen's door, worried her legs wouldn't support the growing heaviness behind her breastbone. "How long have you known?"

"I don't know. I'd have thought she'd call you or something. I never figured I'd have to be the one to tell you."

Luellen had called, more than once in the days after Ellie lost the baby. But she'd never mentioned plans to leave Westbank. And they hadn't spoken even by phone since the middle of February. It was the way things went since their lives diverged after Ellie and Stuart were married.

Ellie knocked again, the sound forlorn in the darkness. She didn't want to cry in front of Stuart, but she feared she might not be able to stop herself. Perhaps she could wait him out, stay up here in the dark hallway until he left. But Stuart didn't leave. "She's really gone." Ellie drew a sharp breath, then turned and came back down the stairs. *Why didn't Luellen tell her? A phone call, a note. Anything.* The back of her eyes felt hot.

"I'm sorry. I should have told you."

She tried to push past him, but he put a hand on her arm. "Let go of me."

"I need to say something first."

She refused to look at him, afraid if he could see her eyes she wouldn't be able to hold back the tears any longer. "What do you want, Stuart?"

"Listen, I know it was bad, what happened with the baby and all—"

"Let me go."

"Ellie, come on." He never called her Ellie, not since high school. Always Lizzie. She squeezed her eyes shut. "Listen, I know I've done you wrong. I understand that. It's just that my father, he—"

"Your father what?"

Stuart shrank away from the acid in her tone. She didn't want him blaming his father for his own actions, though part of her knew Hiram Spaneker loomed behind so many ills in the valley. Stuart licked his lips. After a moment he let out a long breath. "There's just so much pressure. You don't know what it's like. But I've been trying to figure things out. I want to make things better between us."

"Stuart—"

"What if I said I was sorry? What if I said I want to change?" His voice now pleaded. "I don't like how things have been. You so cold and upset all the time, and me, well—Ellie, it's been lonely."

She wished there was some way she could dig down inside herself, find a way to laugh in his face. But all she could do was press her lips together and stare at the backs of her eyelids.

"Remember when we were in high school? You used to let me take care of you." He released her arm and moved away from her. She stole a glance his way, saw him jam his hands back into his coat pockets. "You used to like me."

She was afraid he'd bring up Quentin Quinn, toss the name out as if it was a free pass for too many wrongs too long committed. But Quentin was no more excuse than Hiram. "That was a long time ago." Or maybe it just felt like a long time. The burden of a lifetime bound up in a few short years.

"Give me another chance. I know I don't deserve it. I know I've mistreated you. But I promise it'll never happen again."

She had nothing to say to him.

"Ellie? I promise."

"I need to find out what happened to Luellen."

She stumbled past him. Outside, snow had started to fall, dry crystals that seemed to evaporate before they hit the ground. The hair salon was still dark, the street as empty as her heart. Through a halo of tears she recognized the Tahoe parked up the block and headed for it, chin pinned to her chest—though against the cold or as a buttress against her own confusion she couldn't say. All she could allow herself to think about was finding her friend.

She yanked open the door of the Tahoe, felt in her coat pocket for her keys. Stuart stood gazing at her from the apartment doorway. Grim-faced, his shoulders still hunched. He lifted one hand, a faltering half-wave. She slammed the Tahoe door, circled around to the pickup. He could keep the damned Tahoe. But that was all. It was too late for anything else. No words, no promises, could ever make up for her child dead in the toilet.

Yet she already knew how it would play out. Stuart would start talking to people, telling folks of his change of heart. About how he'd seen the error of his ways, how he now yearned to be a good husband. And people would work on her. Hiram Spaneker and his batty wife, Rose. The women at church. "Give him a chance. He's a Spaneker, for pity's sake." Maybe even her father, though he'd never shown any fondness for Stuart. The cage would tighten around her, choking off her resolve. Luellen might serve as a lone voice of dissent, if only she hadn't left Ellie alone, and without explanation. Ellie didn't have Luellen's options.

At the Granger house, Luellen's mother said she'd gone away the week before, leaving a note on the kitchen counter and a stack of boxes in the basement. *Mom and Dad, I need to get away from here. Please store my things. I'll be in touch when I can.* No one knew where she'd gone. No one knew why. Mrs. Granger hoped Ellie might have some news. But she already knew more than Ellie; she, at least, had gotten a note.

Ellie returned to the farm, loose and adrift. When Stuart came in that evening he washed up without having to be asked, then waited for her to notice him. She served his supper, salad and a bowl of chili, then sat with him while he ate. She nibbled cornbread, ate a flavorless slice of under-ripe tomato. He tried to keep a smile on his face, made small talk. Her father's shoats were looking strong, almost fifteen hundred this year. The forecast called for a warm front to push through the following week. The creek was starting to bulge with snowmelt. Ellie listened without comment. He didn't press her. But he also didn't give up. Over the days that followed he made overtures, shared soft-spoken promises. Helped her organize Brett's memorial service. He stood solemnly beside her in his black suit at the service, then helped her father across the thawing bog of the cemetery to the Tahoe. And when they got back home, he offered her a gentle embrace where in the past she'd known only his rough clench. She didn't know how to respond, so she didn't respond at all.

Every couple of days she'd call Mrs. Granger. They shared idle conversation about nothing. Two people hoping for news that never came, each seeking a thin comfort in their shared sorrow. The day after Mrs. Granger told Ellie to stop being so formal, to call her Natalie, she and her husband died in a head-on collision with a drunk driver. They were returning from Klamath Falls where they'd met with a private investigator. Ellie asked Stuart to come to the funeral, but he made an excuse and she went alone. She had no idea if Luellen even knew what had happened.

Two months after Luellen's disappearance, a letter arrived, an envelope with a Portland postmark but no return address. The note inside was typed, laser-printed on plain white paper. Unsigned.

Dear Ellie,

I hope you can forgive me. I know I should have talked to you first, but there was no time. I had to get away.

But I want you to know I'm okay. Sometimes you just have to drop everything and go, just leave it all behind. It's such a mess. I can't explain it all right now. I'm sorry.

Please don't tell anyone about this note. I'll be in touch again when it's safe.

November 14

Police Investigating Attempted Assault

EUGENE, OR: Local police seek a suspect in an attempted assault of a University of Oregon student late Wednesday night. The suspect is described as about 5 feet, 6 inches tall, 160 pounds, wearing a dark-colored jacket, a scarf or bandana on his head, and medium blue pants. He may have a bite injury to a finger.

In a news release, police indicated the victim is female in her early twenties. She was riding her bike home at about 12:15 a.m., she told police. A man jumped out from behind bushes near the intersection of East 21st Avenue and Agate Street. She lost control of the bike and fell. In the ensuing struggle, the woman bit her assailant's hand, at which point he fled into nearby Washburn Park.

The victim was taken to Sacred Heart Medical Center, where she was treated for a sprained wrist and contusions, then released.

November 19 — 11:32 am

The Color of Hay

The fish are nervous.

Before Ruby Jane leased the space for Uncommon Cup II, the building housed a commercial aquarium supply business with a built-in showpiece fish tank in the waiting area. She liked the tank so much that when she remodeled, Ruby Jane worked it into the interior design. The aquarium takes up most of the wall across from the counter; on work days I often find myself transfixed by the glittering motion during slow spells. This morning I sit at a table next to the tank, hoping to be soothed by the complex, graceful dance of gouramis and angelfish. But the fish seem to have picked up on my mood.

I last saw Ruby Jane four days ago for our old friend Andy Suszko's funeral. After the burial, Ruby Jane and I went to the reception, an event Andy wouldn't have tolerated were he alive to object. He was never much for sentimentality, and a raft of neighborhood biddies bemoaning his demise over Waldorf salad and Swedish meatballs would have driven him off the rails. We stayed only long enough to shake a few hands and each drink a plastic wine glass overfilled with astringent merlot. Ruby Jane drove me back to my place and, before I could say anything, invited herself in. I assumed she didn't want me to spend the evening alone, brooding in the dark. More likely I'd have brooded with the lights and television on, but in any case I was grateful for her company.

She'd dropped her coat on the floor next to the front door and kicked off her shoes. Roamed the perimeter of the front room. My place is a fairly typical Old Portland bungalow, living room to the left, dining area to the right. The original built-ins anchor either end of the wide space. She inspected the place like she was seeing it for the first time, despite the fact she'd been here a hundred times. The old mirror over the fireplace seemed to occupy her attention for a long time, but I couldn't tell if she was gazing at her own shadowy reflection in the degraded silver, or at mine. I moved to the couch, flicked on the lamp on the end table. Specks of dusts floated in the stale air. Ruby Jane turned.

"What do you got to drink?"

"Not much. Water from the tap, grape juice in the fridge."

"Dude, you're living on the edge."

I blinked. "Did you just call me 'dude'?"

"Of course not." Her lips curled into a half-smile. "I think I was in shock over the grape juice."

"Alton Brown says it's good for my heart. It's got polyphenols."

"I was thinking of something more in the solvent category."

"Solvent."

"Some kind of grain distillate perhaps."

Ruby Jane was never much of a drinker, aside from a beer here and there. She noted my surprise with a shrug.

"I know, I know. Funerals just make me feel so—" She wandered over to the couch, but didn't sit down. "I don't know. Loose. Unmoored. Like I'm going to blow away afterward."

"When you put it that way, I can see why you'd want to get all liquored up."

"Skin ... *dude* ... you got any booze or not?" She tried to fix me with an impatient glare, but her dimples spoiled the effect.

I went into the kitchen and rooted through the cupboards, looking for the bottle of twelve-year-old Macallan Ed Riggins gave me as a retirement gift. "You might think I'm a cheap bastard, Skin, not springing for at least the eighteen for such an auspicious occasion, but the twelve is better. Trust me." I'd never opened it. I wasn't supposed to drink during my cancer treatment, and by the time my doc declared the cancer in remission, I'd all but forgotten Ed's gift. I found the bottle on the shelf beside a canister of flour that had been there since the Clinton administration.

I cracked the seal and poured a couple of fingers each in a pair of juice glasses. Back in the living room, Ruby Jane accepted hers with a grin and tossed it back like an accomplished drunk, then held out the glass for more. Good thing I'd brought the bottle from the kitchen. She sipped her second round, settled back with her hair pulled up off her neck and draped over the couch back.

"I don't like whisky."

I took a sip my own and joined her on the couch. The warm, heavy atmosphere around her seemed to stir a nest of bees behind my belly button. "So why are you drinking it?"

"This is good." She raised the glass and peered into the fluid. "It's the color of hay. Or shellac."

"That was fast."

"What?"

I tilted my head.

"I'm not drunk." She continued to stare at her glass, her eyes at half-mast. A faint smile danced on her lips. "Did you know shellac is made from bugs?"

"I must have missed the Discovery Channel that day."

"I want ice for my next one."

I wasn't sure she needed a next one. Her mood was weird. Talk about feeling unmoored. She'd cooked in my kitchen, watched birds on my back deck. Hogged the remote on my couch. This was the first time I'd ever felt uncomfortable around her.

"RJ, what's going on?"

She rolled her head my way. "Nothing. Want some ice?"

"I drink my whisky neat."

"I'll take that as a yes." She sprang off the couch and vanished through the door into the kitchen. I heard her banging around in the freezer, then a moment later she was back, her glass full of ice. She dropped a couple of cubes into my glass and topped me off before sitting down again. I looked at her, but she didn't return my gaze. Her eyes went back to the glass in her hand. I could hear the ice cracking in my glass.

"Ruby Jane, you're freaking me out."

She continued to smile her hazy smile. "Sorry."

"What's going on?"

"I don't know. Feeling bad about Andy, I guess. How old was he?"

"Eighty-one."

"That's right. You joked about him traveling the Oregon Trail in a covered wagon. *'You have died of dysentery.'*"

"Yeah, I was hilarious."

"He laughed about it." She sipped her whisky, her blue eyes remote. "The funeral didn't do him justice."

I have my own feelings about funerals, but I didn't want to unload them on Ruby Jane. I'd known Andy Suszko all my life, and no ceremony arranged by the little old ladies who lived on his street and spent their days trying to mother him could ever do him justice. But I knew the funeral wasn't for him, and it wasn't for people like me and Ruby Jane either. I was okay with that. Ruby Jane seemed to feel differently.

She knocked off her whisky, reached for the bottle. I put my hand on her arm and she stopped, turned her eyes to me. They were deep and unfocused, or maybe they were fixed on the space behind my own eyes. "Skin ..."

I kissed her.

I didn't plan it, didn't quite realize what was happening until the moment was upon me. For the briefest of instants, I felt her lean into me, felt the softness of her lips, tasted the woody smoke of the Macallan.

Then, abruptly, she pulled away and jumped to her feet. I looked up, couldn't read her expression. She raised a finger to her lower lip, and for a second I thought she was going to wipe her mouth. Instead she offered me a quick, embarrassed smile and looked away. "You know what? I'm opening the Hollywood shop tomorrow. Five o'clock comes early."

"Ruby Jane—"

"It's no big deal. It's not." She scooted around the coffee table, bumped it and almost knocked over the bottle. I got up to follow, but before I knew it she had her coat on, the door open.

"Do you think it's a good idea—"

"I think I could use a little walk. Don't worry. I'll call a cab or something."

Her car was still there when I stumbled to bed, hours later, the Macallan dangerously depleted. The car was gone by morning.

I've managed to avoid her for days, managed to avoid this awkward encounter beside the fish tank. I'm glad Marcy is behind the counter, working just a few feet away, that other customers sip drinks around the shop. College students, people tapping away on their laptops. Free WiFi helps keep the place middling full all day long. A couple of guys seem to run their businesses from RJ's deep couches. Dark, edgy music plays in the background, a playlist from Marcy's iPod. Ruby Jane offers me an uncertain smile from behind the counter. I don't know what's going to happen.

A deep disquiet rumbles through me. I need to leave. Quit my job, go find a new coffee shop to haunt. Create some distance and give Ruby Jane air. Drown my sorrows in a stranger's lesser latte.

Hell, Common Grounds is a few blocks down the street and I'd only have to trade in two syllables. Instead, I'm sitting here like a nervous adolescent while she makes tea. My stomach is knotted up; I don't want anything. I know she'll bring me something anyway. That it will be something I like helps explain why I created this mess. I can hear her talking to Marcy, but I can't make out the words. Shop talk, most likely, but I'm feeling paranoid. When she finally sits down, she doesn't make eye contact. Or perhaps it's me who won't make eye contact. We both look at the fish as she slides a mug across the table top. The aroma rising from the surface of the cup offers me a small measure of comfort. Coffee, black: my current poison of choice. I lift my eyes.

"RJ, listen, I just want to say—"

"You don't have to say anything. Really."

"It's just … I feel like I owe you an apology."

Her gaze bounces around, finds her tea cup. "If anyone should apologize, it's me."

I slump. It's even worse than I thought. "How do you figure?"

"I just think—" She brushes her bangs off her forehead. "It wasn't fair, what I did—"

"Ruby Jane, don't. You have been my friend. I'm the one who crossed the line."

"I don't know why you think you crossed some line. Maybe I crossed the line." She blinks, and light glitters in her eyes, silver reflections of fish. "Maybe no one did."

I feel like she's trying to somehow excuse my behavior, but the effort is only making me feel even older and more ridiculous. I sip my coffee, concentrate for a moment on the crisp warmth, the flavor of earth and cocoa. I'm trying to decide what to say, sure whatever I come up with will only sound foolish or desperate.

"Skin, we've shared a lot over the last few years. I've been closer to you than anyone else."

"What about Pete?"

She looks away from her tea, meets my gaze at last. Her eyes are moist. "You're sitting here, aren't you? Where the hell is he?"

I am only too aware of Pete's absence. Theirs had been a mercurial relationship from the start, erupting out of the hot flash of a murder investigation that ended with Ruby Jane gut-shot and half-dead, and Pete nearly so. After a long period during which my own emotional fluctuations were downright stable in comparison, he'd moved to California the previous year to work as the greenhouse manager for a plant nursery. It was supposed to be temporary, six, maybe eight months, a stop along the way to a planned transfer back to Oregon and an even bigger operation out near Woodburn. But he keeps not getting the transfer, continues to stay on in the Central Valley. As the months pass, an inertial stasis seems to have set in. Except for one thing.

"He flies up to see you fairly regularly though, right?"

Fire floods her cheeks. "You think I'm building a life around a once monthly weekend round trip from Sacramento? Even if he didn't realize he was blowing me off when he took the job, I sure as hell did." Her back goes rigid and she presses against the table top, mouth set into a hard line. I expect her to get up and walk away. But then her face softens and her hands relax, her shoulders drop. She shakes her head. "I like Pete. He's a kind of weird I can appreciate. There was a time when we might have had a chance. But that was a long time ago. He's never gonna get past himself."

I'm not a stupid man. I've puzzled out crimes as petty and simple as car prowls and as complex as multiple murders and criminal conspiracies. I've served on organized crime task forces, held my own against hot shot defense attorneys on cross. Hell, I even manage to surf the internet without handing over control of my computer to Ukrainian identity thieves. But apparently I'm too damn dumb to understand what Ruby Jane is trying to say to me. I lower my eyes, raise one hand to my neck. I try to resist scratching my red patch, but my fingertips brush the rough flesh, an involuntary reflex as old as I am.

Ruby Jane reaches across the table, snatches my hand away from my neck. I look up, meet her eyes. She's smiling, melancholy. I let her pull my hand away from my throat. "Skin, you're in your fifties and you still let that thing on your neck convince you that you don't deserve anything good." Her touch thrills me, an electric buzz in my spine. I don't want her to let go. She doesn't. "I get it. I'm smart and pretty and ambitious and young, or at least younger. But not nearly so young I can't decide for myself whether I want a crusty grump with a face like a baboon's ass to kiss me."

She studies me, the crusty grump. It's an act I find undaunting—but only from her. I see the strands of grey at her temples again, and I realize I know exactly how old she is. Her age was one of those personal details about a crime victim I'd learned in the course of the investigation into the attack that had nearly killed her. She's thirty-five, almost twenty years my junior. She's not a child. Not a girl, but a woman who can look me in the eye and not flinch.

"You may not realize it, but I haven't seen your neck since you came to check on me at the hospital the day I got shot. Remember that?" The question doesn't require a response. "You're a good, funny, smart man when you're not awash in self-pity. Okay, so you're retired. It's not a death sentence. Stop acting like it is."

Anyone else—Susan or anyone from my cop days—could tell me the same thing, use the same words, and they'd strike me as harsh or condescending. Raise my hackles and bring out the fight in me. But from Ruby Jane they're like the gentle caress of a cool, damp cloth on my fevered forehead. I feel at once embarrassed and reassured. I open my mouth, intending what, I don't know. But she isn't finished, which saves me the trouble of saying too much.

"I was as much a part of what happened as you were. I've made more than my share of bad choices, but this isn't one of them. My mistake was not being sure of what I wanted, and instead of facing it I ran away. I'm not sorry you kissed me, and I'm not sorry I kissed you back. But before we can go further with this, whatever it is, we both need to be clear about something. I know why I kissed you, Skin. But do you know why you kissed me?"

"I ... Ruby Jane, of course—"

"No. Wait. Don't just toss out an answer. Think about it. Did you kiss me because of how you feel about me, or did you kiss me because you've lost faith in who you are? I can be with the Skin who first walked into my shop two years ago and made fun of frou-frou coffee. I can't be with the Skin who fears his own imagined irrelevance." She lifts her free hand, touches my cheek. "Don't you become Pete. Okay?"

"I couldn't handle the jail time."

She laughs quietly, then turns her head to the fish tank and stares into the water. Without releasing my hand, she reaches out and runs our interlocked fingers along the cool surface of the tank. A coral gourami bumps along the glass, following our fingertips.

The shop door opens behind me, bells jangling, and the fish darts away. Ruby Jane looks past my shoulder and I turn. I don't know who I expect to see, but Susan isn't it. She oughta still be hip deep in the operation at Mitch's place. Neither Ruby Jane nor I speak as Susan crosses the café and stops at our table.

"Hello, Skin. I'm sorry to intrude. I tried calling, but you never answer your phone."

I look over at Ruby Jane, then back to Susan. "Sorry. I must not have heard it beep."

"I realize this is abrupt, but I need you to come with me. Something has come up."

I don't respond right away, and her gaze bounces between Ruby Jane and me, then down to our clasped hands. I wonder for a moment if she realizes what she's walked in on. I don't want her to even guess. When she turns her gaze back to me, RJ gently disentangles her hand from my own.

I lean back in an attempt to appear casual. "So what's up? Did you find Eager?"

"No, it's not that." Susan has known Ruby Jane as long as I have, if not as intimately, but she hesitates the way she would in front of a stranger.

"What is it then?"

"Mitch is out of surgery."

"That was quick. How's he doing?"

"They say he'll pull through."

"That's good, I guess. But what does it have to do with me?"

"He wants to make a statement."

I'm surprised he didn't lawyer up. "I still don't see what this has to do with me."

"He says it's a matter of life and death. Skin"—her fingers drum against her thighs—"he's only willing to talk to you."

A Day, A Week, Eighteen Years Earlier

You Can Call Me Hiram

Big Ed Gillespie first met Hiram Spaneker in a casino parking lot in Reno. Big Ed was twenty-two at the time, three weeks past being cut by the Oakland Raiders, dead broke and dead drunk. A decent senior year as linebacker for Southern Oregon University and a four-six forty got him invited, undrafted, to Raiders camp. His beer-drenched work ethic and inability to cope with pro blocking schemes got him sent packing again. He took his training camp pay—two weeks' worth plus a modest signing bonus—to Vegas, where he distracted himself with craps and blow jobs purchased from plasticine women he met off full-color postcards. He burned through five grand in a baker's week. When he checked out of the Barbary Coast eight days after his arrival, he couldn't buy gas for the drive back to Medford. He sat in his car in the parking lot, windows open under the hot sun, and thought about a guy he knew who went to Australia to play Aussie Rules football. Whatever that was.

A couple crossing the parking lot caught his eye. They were holding each other up, weaving as ineffectively through the parked cars as he had through the silver-and-black tackling dummies. Just another afternoon in Vegas. His first thought was they must be in the same shape he was in, broke, drunk, and short of options. Why else leave the casino in the middle of a hot afternoon? But as they neared his car he heard them laughing. Mid-fifties, overweight suburban types. Khaki and Keds, red cheeks and white arms. Big Ed got out of his car and approached.

"Do you folks know where the Lucky Duck Lounge is?" A name he made up on the spot.

The two turned as a unit and stopped, unsteady even with four feet between them. Sunlight gleamed off the woman's hair, the color of L'Oreal brass.

"Lucky who?"

"Not you." Big Ed waded in, one hand for each of them, the dregs of his last Jack-and-Coke doing his all thinking. He crushed the man's larynx with a single strike, put his knee into the woman's gut as he pulled her toward him. She gasped and started to call out, but too late. He cracked her head against the pavement while her husband clutched his throat, gagging.

They'd been happy for good reason. He pulled fifty-eight hundred bucks out of the man's pocket, a roll of crisp hundred dollar bills, fresh from the cage. He left them in the parking lot and drove straight through to Reno. No idea if the woman was alive or dead, though he guessed the man would survive. Maybe never speak again. Either case, no point in hanging around in Vegas waiting for cops to start asking questions.

In Reno, he checked in to the Peppermill, but this time he stuck to bar sluts and nickel craps. When the dice went cold, he backed away, hit the buffet or returned to his room for a nap. He gambled enough to get his room comped, won enough to maybe nurse the old couple's fifty-eight hundred bucks for weeks.

Then he met Charm Butcher.

She was practically his neighbor. Born and raised in Klamath Falls, fifty miles down the highway from Big Ed's home in Medford. Tall and blond with pillow boobs and a mouth to rival his ill-tempered conditioning coach back at S.O.U. She'd just graduated, though her alma mater was the type that advertised on late night television, and she'd come to Reno with a flock of girlfriends for a bachelorette weekend. When Charm saw Big Ed in the bar at the Peppermill, tan and fit and stretching his black Raiders t-shirt out of shape with shoulders like a pair of loin roasts, she decided he should be the one to deflower her virginal, soon-to-be-wed gal pal. And, what the hell, he could give her and the others a ride as well. He spent two hours slamming tequila shooters with the crowd of grain-fed Klamath beauties, then allowed himself to be led to a suite and straddled first by one, then another in succession. Big Ed awoke the next morning, naked and alone. When he finally collected his scattered clothing, he learned not only had the girls from Klamath Falls given him the ride of his life, rivaling even the team parties back in school, they'd left with the remains of his fifty-eight hundred dollars—more than three grand. All he had to his name was his car, a couple of changes of dirty clothes, and eighty bucks in Peppermill chips.

At first, Big Ed thought he could parlay the eighty bucks into some real cash. He'd been playing pretty well. But when he got down to the craps table, the bleat of the slot machines and the stench of the dealer's cologne seemed to settle behind his eyeballs and lay siege to his concentration. His chips didn't last through his first watered-down drink. It was noon, and he was more sober than he'd been in two weeks. He headed for the Fish Bar, the very spot where he'd met Charm and the girls the night before. He didn't figure there was anything to gain admitting that he couldn't pay for incidental charges to his room, so an hour and a half and six Blue Hawaiians later, he scrawled his name on the tab and then stumbled out into bright daylight.

In the parking lot, he caught sight of an older man climbing out of a Suburban. A good omen. Big, expensive truck, fellow coming rather than going. The way he saw it, the universe was in a giving mood again. Dude like that would have some money in his pocket. Big Ed tacked toward him, not planning anything specific, just some variation on Vegas. As he got closer, he opened his mouth. "Hey, fella—"

The old guy stopped. He wore jeans and battered cowboy boots, a tan shirt and a baseball cap. Early thirties, maybe. Ed moved toward him. The hot, still air thrummed against his eardrums. In his mind, he was thinking he needed to say something, ask for directions. Wasn't that how it worked? But he was too drunk, and still whipped from his night with the girls. He raised his hands, a lurching B-movie Frankenstein. The old guy stepped inside his reach and threw a fist hard as a hammer into Big Ed's gut. His breath rushed out of him and he plopped backward onto his ass. For a moment he looked up at the old guy, then dropped his chin and puked into his lap.

The fellow backed away from the acrid spatter. "What the hell you think you're up to, boy?"

"I'm sorry. I got, I mean …" His stomach was rolling over in the aftermath of his expulsion. Hard to talk.

"You broke?"

Big Ed nodded, ran the back of one hand across his chin.

"Okay. Not too smart, are you?"

"I graduate college."

"You do, huh. Let me guess: football scholarship."

Big Ed nodded. The motion threatened to bring up more vomit, and he leaned to one side.

"Tell you what, kid. Let's get you inside, get you cleaned up. Then maybe we can figure out what to do with you."

"You gonna call the cop?"

"Which one?"

"Huh?"

The old guy laughed, then hooked a hand under one of Big Ed's arms. "You gotta help me out, big boy. I'm not used to hauling the whole goddamn hog all by myself." The last thing Big Ed remembered was walking across the parking lot toward the hotel.

He awoke in bed, in his own room. The fellow he'd failed to rob sat in a chair near the window, looking out at the brown rise of the Sierra Nevada to the west. When Big Ed stirred, the man turned and looked at him.

"Morning there, big guy."

"Morning?" Big Ed ran his hand over his face. The inside of his mouth tasted like a sock left at the bottom of the laundry bin.

"You slept all the way through. You were seriously fucked up." The man grinned. "How do you feel?"

Like someone was cracking two stones together between his ears. "Been better, I guess."

"I'll bet."

Ed threw his legs over the edge of the bed and his stomach lurched. He was wearing a pair of unfamiliar boxer shorts. He wondered what happened to his own underwear. "What's going on here?"

"Son, it's like this. I figure you owe me, so I've got a proposition for you."

"A proposition."

"You're gonna come do for me."

"I don't care what you think was gonna happen in that parking lot. I ain't sucking your dick."

The old man kept grinning. "Ain't like that. I'm offering you a job, big boy. Come back with me, I'll get you all set up. You know Givern Valley?"

"Never heard of it."

"You and everyone else. No matter. Southeast Klamath County, tucked away, which has its advantages. And when you get stir crazy,

K-Falls is just an hour down the road. What do you say? I can use a big fellow like you."

"You don't know nothing about me."

"Sure I do. I done some checking while you were sawing logs and belching swamp gas. Linebacker in college, washed out of the pros before they had a chance to learn your name. You're strong, you're quick, but you're stupid. Strong and quick I can use, and stupid I figure I can train out of you."

Big Ed couldn't decide whether to get angry or curl up and go back to sleep. He didn't like being called stupid, but it wasn't something he hadn't heard before. He needed to piss, but he wasn't sure he was ready to attempt upright travel. He wasn't ready to answer this crazy old fuck from Butthumper, Oregon either. Then the old fellow said something that got his attention.

"I understand you spent some time with a group of young ladies. Good time had by all, if expensive."

"How the hell you know all this shit?"

"I make friends easy. You can be one of my friends too. I'll help you out, help you find the missies what walked off with all your cash."

"And in exchange I work for you."

"We take care of each other, that's the way I see it."

"And if I say no?"

The fellow turned over his hands. "Your choice. You'll have to figure out how to pay the balance on your room, though I don't figure you'll get the chance to attempt another robbery since I already talked to hotel security about you. You walk out of here with me, you won't have any trouble. You walk out alone ..."

"Jesus."

"Close enough for your purposes, but you can call me Hiram."

"What am I supposed to be doing for you?"

"Whatever I tell you to do." The old man stared at him across the room, lips curled into a grin but his eyes dark and hard. "Son, you and me, we gonna have one helluva party."

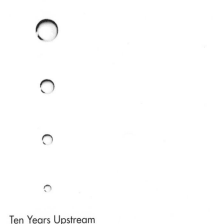

Ten Years Upstream

Stuart's Ellie

More than anything else, what Ellie most remembered from the night she surrendered to Stuart for the first time was the smell of mud and beer vomit, and the sound of the Southern-Pacific filling in the gaps between revving tractor engines. All familiar scents and sensations, every tractor pull the same: tooth-rattling racket, sickening clouds of exhaust, flying mud clots observed with open-mouthed expectation by breathless males captivated by noise and horsepower. The tractors themselves would never pull a cultivator or combine. Rob and Brett had once tossed Ellie into the manure lagoon after they caught her sitting in the saddle of their '47 John Deere Model M, restored and adored for the Classic Combined division. They claimed she'd scuffed the opalescent green paint.

Fortunately for Ellie, most of the meets featured more than just tractors dragging a variable weight sled across a field. Food stalls and vendor booths inevitably sprang up between the bleachers and the parking area, sometimes a plywood platform where one of a half dozen local country bands might perform—assuming they could be heard over the din. When the family piled out of the pickup at each event, Ellie would immediately flee the frenzy of sound and churned turf, get a funnel cake or ice cream and occupy herself with the displays of quilts, hand-thrown pottery and Klamath tribal baskets. At the larger competitions, held a couple times a year at Little Liver Dragway and as thick with Westbank townies as country folk, Luellen might make an appearance. But most of the meets were small, less carnival than church picnic with a diesel ambience.

The Victory Chapel Harvest Power Pull came round each September. Fund raiser, Rally Day kick-off for Sunday School, chance for gear heads to show off for the first time after the long summer lay off. The event was held in the field adjacent to the church. Luellen refused to come to Victory Chapel events, which left Ellie on her own to roam among the coagulating scents of fried dough and grilled sausage. Myra followed—mother's orders—but half a step behind and sullen.

Ellie ignored her as they moved from booth to booth. She looked at myrtle wood puzzle boxes, leather-bound journals, beeswax candles, glass bead earrings their mother would never let them wear.

Before long, Myra folded her arms across her chest. "I want to go watch the pull."

"Mom said I'm not supposed to leave you alone."

"This is church, Lizzie. We're not alone."

"A tractor pull is not church."

"Everyone from church is here. We parked in the church parking lot."

Ellie looked up at the darkening sky. The first stars were just appearing. The shadows beyond the tents and bleachers would be deep enough to hide whatever Myra had in mind. "You just want to go get felt up by your boyfriend."

"You're disgusting. I'm telling Mom."

"Go ahead. I'll tell her how you gave Trent a pair of your dirty underwear."

"Bitch."

Ellie smiled as Myra disappeared into the crowd gathered at the entrance to the beer tent. A while later, she saw a cluster of red sparks under the dark eaves at the back of the church and knew that's where Myra had ended up, smoking with a clot of middle school friends, Trent Adams among them. Within a year, Myra would have her accident—that's what everyone called it, the accident. As if dragging a razor across your inner thighs because your boyfriend dumped you the day after he popped your cherry was mere mishap.

Ellie could tell by the sound of the engines out in the field that the Amateur class was done, the Classic Modified finishing up. Super Modified would be next—big, souped-up machines that could haul the sixty-thousand-pound sled the distance. For these tractors, it wasn't a question of how far, but how fast. For Ellie, it was only a question of how loud. A lot of the stalls were starting to shut down as folks headed for the bleachers. The Supers always drew the big crowd. Ellie headed in the opposite direction.

She made her way past the last line of stalls and into the darkness beyond the event lights. Fall had started to assert itself, and the evening was cool but not uncomfortable. As she moved further from the action, the grinding sound of the engines grew less obtrusive. Ellie could hear the crickets between pulls. She threw her head back. The lights behind her washed out all but the brightest stars, so she continued down the sloping church lawn toward the road. She liked the sensation of the turf springing back against the bottom of her shoes with each step.

A dozen paces ahead, a figure materialized out of the dark shrubs between the lawn and the parking lot, joined quickly by a second. Ellie stopped.

"Well, if it isn't Lizzie Kern."

She recognized the voice. Quentin Quinn, a senior, two years older than Ellie. Older brother of the idiot whose finger Ellie had bitten off. He held a plastic cup in one hand. She knew the boy with him as well. Nate Lewis, also from school. Nate didn't say anything. Waiting to see what Quentin would do, maybe.

"What do you want?"

"Like you don't know." He pointed his middle finger across the cup's mouth at her. "You fucked up my brother."

Ellie suppressed a sigh. "That was a long time ago." She should have gone to watch the Supers.

"Fuck a long time ago, you stupid cow."

Nate smacked Quentin on the shoulder. "You crack me up, man."

Quentin grinned. Backlight from the bleachers gleamed on his long, densely packed teeth, a row of sugar corn kernels. He raised his cup, a mock toast, then tossed off its contents in a gulp and threw the cup at her feet. She caught a whiff of beer, likely filched from the beer tent.

"What do you got to say for yourself, psycho?" She'd wandered too far away from the crowd. Too far to run. The church was closer, thirty paces to her left. Probably locked; the windows were all dark. She was alone with Quentin and his stooge beneath the stars. She might yell, but who would hear over the roar of the tractors in the field? Myra and her boyfriend smoking under the eaves at the back of the church? They'd just laugh, if they even noticed.

A band tightened across her stomach. Fear? Anger? She wasn't sure. Part of her wondered what Quentin and Nate would do if she showed them a little bit of the crazy she'd displayed the day she bit George's finger off. But they were bigger, older, stronger. Drunk. She drew a breath. She wasn't sure she had enough crazy in her for two.

"I said I was sorry."

"Talk don't grow his finger back."

Ellie knew George Quinn now treated the missing digit as a badge of honor, waving his middle stub at opportune moments in a play for sympathy or to elicit squeals from girls on the bus. People

called him Hilarious George. He even came to the house with Brett
from time to time, usually when Ellie wasn't there. Quentin wasn't
here for his brother. She took a step back and started to turn, but
he lunged forward and grabbed her forearm.

"Not so fast, psycho."

"Let go of me."

"Maybe I want a bite of something first." She could hear the beer
in his humorless laugh. She tried to wriggle free, but Quentin only
tightened his grip.

"We all know what George wanted, don't we, psycho?"

All that pudding …

"Please, stop—"

His free hand hooked under her armpit, pulled her back toward
him. His breath smelled like half-digested bread. Off in the darkness,
Nate slapped his hands together and huffed, a breathy singsong of
anticipation. The sound filled her with a sudden terror, as if she'd
only in that moment come to understand what they intended to do
to her. Quentin thrust his forearm up under her chin, forcing her
teeth together. His free hand slapped across her chest, kneaded her
breasts like he was softening up a ball of clay. In the distance, Ellie
heard the urgent shriek of a Super blasting across the field, followed
by the cheers of spectators. "Nate, help me hold her down, man."

"How about you let her go instead, asshole?"

Not Nate's voice. Ellie twisted. Stuart Spaneker strode down the
lawn out of the darkness. The bleacher lights were at his back so she
couldn't see his face. But his posture and stature were familiar, as
was his shaggy head, even in silhouette. She'd spent much of spring
and all of summer avoiding him after the note in health class.

"Fuck off, Spaneker. No one invited you to the party."

"I don't think that's the way you want to go with this, Quinn."

Quentin released his grip on Ellie and turned to Stuart, arms
cocked at his sides. She swayed but kept to her feet, moved a step
away. Her legs felt wobbly and uncertain. She wanted to run, but

Stuart's appearance seemed to act as some kind of anchor. As he faced off against Quentin, her fear drained out of her, replaced by a strange wonder at his actions. He'd come out of nowhere.

"You may think you're hot shit, pipsqueak, but we're not afraid of you. Fucking sophomore."

"Leave her alone."

"This ain't none of your damn business."

Stuart moved between Ellie and the boys. "I'm making it my business."

"Just because your father thinks he—"

Stuart reached up and grabbed Quentin by each ear, yanked him straight down. "My father ain't here, is he? It's you and me." Quentin started hollering, at least for as long as it took for him to hit the ground. Ellie moved away from the writhing figures as Stuart jammed Quentin's face into the damp turf, then dropped one knee into the center of his back below the juncture of his neck and shoulders. Stuart lifted his head, stared down Quentin's boy. Nate faced him for only a moment, then fled, stumbling and nearly tripping over himself before vanishing into the bushes at the edge of the lawn.

Quentin sputtered, unable to lift his face out of the mud and grass. "You motherfucker!"

"There's no need for that kind of language." Stuart had a grin on his face now. Ellie had heard him use that kind of language in the hallways at school.

Quentin managed to get his hand beneath him, but was unable to gain any leverage. Stuart was anything but a large specimen, but he used his weight to advantage. Quentin rocked and kicked his legs without effect.

"Do you know what she did to my brother?"

"He got off easy, you ask me." Stuart pressed down with his knee. "Now, you gonna apologize and play nice? Because if you don't, this is the best thing gonna happen to you between now and when you wake up in a body cast."

"Get the hell off of me!"

"You didn't answer my question."

Quentin struggled, but succeeded only in grinding his face more deeply into the turf. At last he gave up. For a long moment, he didn't move. His breath bubbled through the wet grass. Then he went slack. "Whatever. You're welcome to the crazy bitch."

Stuart drove his fist into Quentin's cheek with a sound like a hammer hitting raw meat. "I'm welcome to *what,* dickweed?"

"Fine, fine! I'm sorry!"

Stuart stood up. Quentin scrambled to his feet, jeans and letter jacket caked with mud. A smear of gluey puke glazed his chin. He looked around blankly, seemed surprised Nate was gone. "Christ." He staggered off into the darkness.

Stuart turned to her. "You okay?"

Ellie could feel her heartbeat in her throat. "Why did you do that?" Her image of Stuart had never included chivalry.

"I didn't think he ought to be treating you that way."

"Maybe he should have written me a note first."

Stuart didn't say anything for a long moment. Then he shrugged. "I know I seem like a retard to you most of the time." He turned his head and his eyes gleamed in the light from the bleachers. "I shouldn't have given you that note." His expression was contrite, but she caught the hint of a wayward smile. "I like you is all."

She didn't know what to say. She wrapped her arms across her chest, listened as faint voices filtered down from the beer tent and beyond. An instant later the sound of a tractor dragging its skid downfield drowned them out. She felt cold, confused. Ellie didn't like Stuart. But she didn't like anyone. Luellen was her friend, but aside from her, who else was there? Myra was a weight around her neck, and her brothers were both jerks. Her mother was a tyrant, her father kind in his way but too busy most of the time to notice what went on around him. Everyone else she kept at arm's length or further, a distance she preferred. But as she stood there, staring back at Stuart Spaneker, thinking about his defense of her, somewhere inside she realized it felt good to have someone on her side for a change.

She took his hand and let him lead her away from the church grounds. Soon, they left behind the lights and noise of the tractor pull. They walked along the dark road back to her house, Stuart gabbing about nothing the whole way. Miles, they walked. She was quiet, letting him natter on, but she felt comfortable and strangely safe. At the house, on her porch, Stuart squeezed her hand and hesitated, and with only the slightest roll of her eyes she presented him her cheek and let him kiss it.

Soon after, her family arrived home. At first her mother was angry. "We had no idea where you were. Your sister was frantic." Myra looked at her, bored. Ellie smelled Tic Tacs and Marlboro Lights.

"Stuart walked me home. I should have told you." She didn't mention Quentin Quinn.

"Stuart Spaneker?" Her mother's voice hiked up with a note of surprised, yet obvious pleasure.

"Yes."

"Ah."

Inevitability bound up in a single syllable, if only she could have recognized it. But it was years before she came to understand that was the night she became someone new, not only in her own eyes, but in the eyes of everyone else. She'd made a deal, bought security and an ephemeral sense of belonging in exchange for a piece of who she was. Stuart's Ellie.

November 19 — 1:05 pm

Just an Afterthought

It's not the first time I've been up to OHSU to talk to a suspect, but it's the first time I've done so as a civilian. These kinds of opportunities don't come up often. Or ever. I sit quietly beside Susan as she steers the car west down Division, then cuts over to Powell on 39th. Traffic isn't too bad, midday dense. She navigates like the old pro she is, changing lanes by instinct, no signal, easing off enough to catch fresh green lights on the roll, tapping the gas in time to squirt through yellow. Once we're across the river and weaving through the arterial tangle up to Pill Hill, she's ready to explain the meaning of life to me. I'm not sure I want to hear it.

"Skin, here's the deal—"

"I'm sure I have the basic idea."

She licks her lips. "The situation is unorthodox."

Tell me about it. "So will he have a lawyer there, or what?"

"Mitch says he doesn't want one, but the DA is worried."

I'm not surprised. Mitch has gotta be swimming in morphine. Even if he's waived for now, at some point he'll have a defense attorney who will no doubt move to get whatever he says to me tossed. Given the circumstances, the motion will probably fly.

"Who's the DA?"

"Jessup is the lead, but Schrunk himself is keeping a close eye on this one."

"Jessup is the woman with the nose ring, right?"

More lip licking, and out of the corner of my eye I can see her hands flex against the steering wheel. "Skin, not everyone can be defined by a single distinguishing characteristic."

"I bet Aesop wrote a fable about that one."

"Can we talk about the interview?" Better than talking about what she observed between Ruby Jane and me. I watch the landscape roll by, thinking of the last thing Ruby Jane said. "You can call me tonight." I don't like having to wait that long. The stretch of Terwilliger up to OHSU winds through trees, too narrow for the congestion the medical complex above inevitably creates. When the aerial tram from South Waterfront up to Marquam Hill opened the year before, it was supposed to ease the traffic pressure, but based on our slow crawl I have to wonder.

"No one is thrilled about this, Skin. But if he tells us something to clear up the mess in his kitchen, maybe points us to whatever's going on with the little boy, then it'll be worth the risks."

"What am I not allowed to ask about?"

"Stay off of the front porch." No hesitation.

I nod. There's little chance Mitch will get clear of any charges stemming from the shooting, but Jessup and the others won't want anything he says to me today to muddy the waters. Still, as much as I want to know about the kitchen and about Danny, about what spilled Luellen and Jase out doors and windows in fear for their lives, I'm more interested in Eager. And Eager is all about the front porch.

"Who's going to be there?"

"Fran Stein and Moose. An ICU nurse and Bronstein's doctor will be right outside the door. Jessup will wait outside too." Jessup wouldn't want to be in the room. No DA wants to risk finding themselves a witness in their own case. But she'll stick close in case I get out of hand. Moose and Frannie Stein are Homicide, which makes their presence more surprising.

"So you think you might be investigating a murder then."

"We're not sure what we're investigating yet, Skin. Assault with a deadly weapon almost certainly. Attempted murder, maybe—a lot of blood got spilled in that kitchen. Kidnapping? Who knows until we hear what he has to say?"

"FBI?"

"Not yet."

Hopefully not at all. "What else?"

"Find out who has Danny. Name, location, anything Mitch can tell us. We need to know that he's safe."

"Definitely not with Grandpa then."

"Not that we can confirm. There's a lot we don't know."

And she's hoping Mitch can fill in the blanks. "Who's coming in with me? Moose and Frannie, or just one of them?"

She doesn't answer right away. I feel warm. Susan and I partnered for almost seven years, but when things fell apart, the partnership crumbled like dry leaves under a boot. I know cops who are more comfortable around their ex-wives than I am with Susan.

"The doctor has made it clear if Mitch shows even the slightest indication of distress the interview is over."

The interview. I want to say I don't do interviews anymore. I drink coffee and pull shots and blunder through my relationships like a hormone-addled middle schooler. But I just nod some more and listen as she runs down the rules. Keep it brief, but get him on the record. Don't press. The DA doesn't want there to be any reason to think we're bringing undue pressure to bear a mere five hours after a man ate five bullets. This is all Mitch's idea, that's the play.

"Should rank just ahead of crotch rot on the fun-o-meter."

It's another five long minutes before she turns in to the main parking garage and an Official Vehicles Only parking space. I follow her across Sam Jackson Road to the main building, through the lobby into an overlit corridor. Her pace is quick enough I have to hot-step to keep pace. I feel half-naked trotting along behind her. She's half a head taller, crisp in her uniform. Gun and radio on her hip, badge on her chest, silver bar on her collar. I'm just a guy in worn jeans, sweatshirt, and battered Rockports.

We don't speak on the elevator, or as we move down the hallway to the nurse's station at ICU. The bustling energy of the unit sets my nerves on edge. I see Moose Davisson well before anyone else. The man came by his name honestly. Frannie Stein, his partner, is with him. Standing next to her I recognize the DA, Jessup. The last time we met, she was trying to decide whether to hang me with a murder charge.

I don't remember her first name, and she doesn't enlighten me. Her brunette hair hangs in a straight bob; her makeup is artful and understated, accentuating her penetrating brown eyes. She stands only as high as my chin, but radiates a composure that fills the corridor. Riggins told me she performs in an 80s cover band on weekends, said it's pretty good. I presume that's when she wears her nose ring; the tiny hole in her nostril is unadorned now.

Jessup ignores me as Susan checks in. Then she introduces us to the doctor, fellow named Seres. Weariness tugs at his chin. He doesn't approve of the interview. I know because he says so over and over.

"I don't approve of the interview. It's far too soon."

Jessup tries to mollify him. "If we didn't think time was of the essence, I assure you we wouldn't be here."

"Mister Bronstein's condition is very serious. He's only just out of recovery."

I figure it's time to chime in. "Is he lucid?"

Seres turns his tired gaze on me. "And you are?"

Susan all but steps in front of me. "This is Mister Kadash, the man Bronstein has asked to talk to."

He scans me from my Rockports to my flyaway hair. "You're the neighbor?" He's no more impressed with my appearance than I would be.

"I watch little Danny every now and then."

Susan stares at me, surprised. I avoid her gaze, focus on Seres. Mention of Danny softens the doctor's stern countenance. "Well, Mister Bronstein is awake, but you need to understand he's only been out of surgery for two hours."

Jessup puts a hand on his arm. "We understand, Doctor. Mister Kadash will be as quick as possible, and we've already made it clear to him we want the interview to be very low key. We have nothing to gain by upsetting Bronstein or aggravating his condition."

I see a twitch in Seres' cheek, but he leads us to the doorway of Mitch's room. "I'll be right here."

The lights in the room are set low. Sheer curtains obscure the view out the two narrow windows across the roof of another building. The cream-colored walls are mostly hidden by monitors. Mitch seems small in the middle of the bed, his ordinarily substantial form shrunken. Both arms rest at his side above the blanket. An IV runs from the back of one hand, clear saline from the looks of it. His other arm is wrapped from shoulder to wrist in gauze. What little exposed skin I can see is blotched with Betadine, its antiseptic tang sharp in the air. An oxygen tube loops under Mitch's nose. Wires snake from sensors on his neck, his right middle finger, from under his hospital gown.

I move to the side of the bed. I feel Susan behind me, a hovering vulture. Mitch's red-rimmed eyes gaze out at me from dark orbital pits.

"How you doing, Mitch?"

"Jesus, Kadash, how the hell do you think I'm doing?" His voice is a hair past a whisper.

I smile, closed-lipped. "Yeah, not too good, I guess." I see the bounce of a monitor on the far side of the bed, a steady rhythm. 93 … 94 … 92. His heart rate. There's a plastic, straight-backed chair against the wall and I slide it over and sit down.

"Glad you came, Kadash."

"No problem." I pause. All I can do is to forge ahead. "But first I need to get some things out of the way. Then we can talk."

He manages the faintest of smiles and a single quarter-inch nod. The pillow under his head crackles like paper.

"Lieutenant Mulvaney here is recording our conversation, okay? She tells me you've waived your right to counsel and are willing to talk to me on the record. If that's true, I need you to say so."

"I'll talk to you. Now. Without a lawyer. But no promises once you're gone."

I look up at Susan. She nods, so I turn back to Mitch.

"Okay. So can you state your name for the record?"

"All formal, eh, Kadash? You sound like a cop." He offers another half smile. "Thought you were retired."

"Old habits, I guess." His eyes close. "Mitch, you okay?"

His eyelids roll back, slowly, and for a moment his gaze is unfocused. I wonder if we're going to have to end the interview before it even begins. But then he finds me and swallows. "Name's Mitchell Bronstein. I'm father of Jason, stepfather to Danny …" Blink. "… and helpless thrall to Luellen Granger Bronstein."

He emits a raspy little chuckle. I sit back, feel my jaw start working. Susan shuffles her feet behind me. The heart monitor speeds up for a moment, 106 … 108 …, then settles back again to the mid-90s. I swallow and lean forward. "What do you mean?"

"What do I mean. What do I mean. What do you think I mean, Kadash?"

"I'm just trying to figure out what's going on."

He licks his lips, a gesture that for a moment makes him look like Susan. "I do whatever she tells me."

"Do you know where she is?"

His eyes roll sideways, the shrug of a man fulla bullet holes. "Kadash, listen. When the cops start digging, they're going to find something out."

"What's that?"

"I'm sleeping with an account executive at work, a woman named Lynn."

Surprise, surprise. Mitch Bronstein is a dirtbag.

"Cops'll think that explains something, but they'll be wrong. They have no idea."

"No idea about what?"

"Lu's a good person, Kadash. She's better than anyone I know, and I mean that."

"And you show this by screwing some woman at work?" I'm trying to keep my tone neutral, but anger bleeds into my voice.

"You don't understand. Lu and I, we're married, but it's—"

"Open? You have an arrangement?"

"You don't understand."

"I guess not." My stomach shoves my thoughts around like a playground bully. The heart monitor picks up the pace and I feel the tension radiating off of Susan behind me. We haven't learned anything of use yet.

"I'd do anything for Lu. I love her. That's why today happened. Lynn is just … she's what I do to help me forget."

"How about we talk about something other than you trying to make excuses—"

"Skin." Susan puts a hand on my shoulder. She wants me to calm down. I'm not the right man for this and she knows it, but Mitch wasn't thinking about my credentials or interview skills when he asked to speak to me. He thought I was his friend, a fantasy he carefully constructed over the last two and a half years.

"Okay. Okay." I sit back and draw a breath. "Mitch, here's the thing. We need your help. We're trying to find Lu, and we're trying to figure out what's going on with Danny."

"You've been in the kitchen."

I nod.

"I tried to tell her."

I wait, but he doesn't add anything. "What did you try to tell her?"

"We should've called a lawyer."

"Why?"

"It was bigger than us. Couldn't control it."

"What's bigger than you?"

"I know a guy, a lawyer who works with our firm. I said we should call him." He tries to raise his hand, but a loop of IV tube tangled in the side rail restrains him. "I wanted to call him, but she wouldn't … she wouldn't let me."

He drifts off again, and this time I suspect it's for good. His chest is still, his eyes closed. I know he's still alive only by the silent hop on the heart monitor screen, a shallow rhythm in white phosphor. He seems to have gone to sleep, gone away, whatever. I'm sure Susan is disappointed, but maybe it's just as well. He didn't say anything of consequence, nothing that's likely to fuck over the DA's case. I turn to Susan, about to tell her we should go when I hear his voice again.

"She's stronger than me, Kadash. She's stronger than anyone I've ever known."

Susan nods at me. She wants me to keep going. I turn around. Mitch is staring at me now, his eyes fixed on my own. I shift in the chair.

"I want to tell you about what happened on the porch."

Stay off of the porch. I smile, turn my hands over. "The thing is,

Mitch, everyone saw what happened on the porch. What we need to know is what happened in the kitchen."

It takes him a minute. "I wasn't there."

"But you have to know—"

"Kadash, I shot the kid on purpose. I'm sorry now, but I did. That's what I wanted to tell you."

I don't know what to say. I don't even know if I believe him. I think back to the moment when Mitch stepped out the front door, the piddly little gun in his hand. He looked scared, confused, like a man who went to sleep in a feather bed and woke up in a nest of spiders. I can't believe he looked out at the scene before him, the cops, the barricades, the helicopters overhead, and even noticed Eager, let alone targeted him.

"Come on, man. Don't be ridiculous—"

"I'm not." The heart monitor is ticking up again, 105 … 109 … I can see his blood pressure fluttering too. Sweat glistens on his cheeks and forehead. "She loves him, Kadash. She doesn't love me. She loves him."

… kinda has a thing for my stepmom …

"It's always him she turns to. I'm never anything but part of her disguise. She loves that stupid kid. I'm just an afterthought." 111 … 114 … His chest starts to jump.

I hear movement at the door, and I know Seres is on his way to shut me down. I need more. Stay off the porch.

Fuck it.

"Mitch, was Eager there earlier, before everything happened?"

"Not Eager. Not at first."

"Who was there at first?"

"I don't know who they were."

"Danny's grandfather? Can you tell me who he is?"

"I don't know."

126 … 127 … 132 …

"But you've known Eager since before he tagged your door, haven't you?"

His eyes look troubled for a moment, but then he nods.

"What did you want me to do when you asked me to look for the tagger?"

"Arrest him."

I'm not a cop, I almost say. His answer is nonsense, and he knows it.

"You wanted me to scare him off, something like that?"

He doesn't answer, which is answer enough.

"Tell me about this morning." Susan is at my back, her hand on the back of my chair. "How did Eager end up there?"

"She called him."

"Luellen called him? On the phone? How?"

"On his cell."

I find myself rubbing my eyes. "Where did Eager Gillespie get a cell phone?" Though I assume he stole it.

"She never tells me anything."

Then Seres is next to me. "That'll be enough. I need you both to leave now."

I turn to him. "Wait, just a couple more questions—"

"I said now, and I mean it." 140 … 142 …

Susan pulls me away. I can hear voices out in the corridor, but I can't make them out. People in scrubs have clustered around Mitch's bed—Seres, nurses. I can hear a sound now, beeping, the beeping of Mitch's heart monitor. I'm not sure why I couldn't hear it before, maybe it had to cross some threshold. Susan leads me out through the door. I almost walk through Jessup. She glares up at me, her eyes black. Moose and Frannie are there too, but they won't look at me. "Skin, let's talk this through." Susan's voice is a question, Jessup's a reprimand. "I was rather hoping you wouldn't fuck this up, Kadash." Seres pushes through us, a nurse in his wake. Jessup plants herself in front of me, arms across her chest, hip thrown out in pose I imagine she uses on stage. She opens her mouth, but I cut her off. "I don't work for you anymore." Then I spin away from all of them, head for the elevator. Susan is right behind me, still talking, but she's little more than a buzzing in my ears. All I can hear is the beeping, 143 … 145…, and the echo of Mitch's voice. Mitch, my annoying, idiot neighbor.

She loves that stupid kid. I'm just an afterthought.

I stop at the elevator doors, punch the call button. Susan stops beside me. I look at her sideways, angry, frustrated. Feeling useless and empty. It was never about Jase, about one of those lopsided teenage relationships, younger kid looking up to the older. Jase was just an excuse, a reason for Eager to hang around. He put up with Jase so he could be near her.

I don't look at her, speak into the elevator doors. "Susan, you think maybe you can put some effort into finding Eager now?"

November 14, Overnight

Shadow Slinking

Shadow paid no attention to the sleet. It had been unseasonably warm for the whole shallow depth of his recollection, a circumstance he also failed to note. Now, the cold and wet soaked him to the skin, but he ignored the bitter itch crawling up his biceps and thighs. He walked along a road in a county he couldn't name, near a town he'd never heard of. The sky overhead was swirling and bright despite the late hour. A word came to mind, a word from the time before memory. Skyglow. Somewhere, somewhen, in a group of people whose faces eluded him a man spoke of the stars and skyglow. Skyglow hid the stars, the man's voice said from beyond a curtain of mist. Tonight the clouds hid them too, clouds illuminated by skyglow. From behind the curtain the man's voice spoke as if skyglow was something to dislike, but the sleet fell from a shiny mackerel sky, and Shadow smiled.

Skyglow, skyglow. "S-s-s …" He could say it, he knew he could say it. But he didn't need to. "S-s-s …" Skyglow came from cities, the voice told him suddenly. He could say that too. "City." A word swallowed by the sounds of sleet. The word surprised him, stumbling from his mouth so readily, but he didn't know why.

Something was different about it. "S-s-s-see … See city." He blinked and walked and hummed a sing-song tune. "City see, see city, city city skyglow."

Something.

He stopped. Stopped on the road and looked all around. The road was empty and long, with wide fields on either side. He remembered fields, fields not so flat as these. Fields of grain on rolling hills huddled below steep rises and mountain crags. Fields growing out the of mist. Far ahead, in the darkness beneath the glowing sky he saw a light. Not skyglow, not starlight. A yellow-gold gleam, a point of glowing silence in the night.

Shadow smiled and continued on his way, slogging through the sleet toward the light. His legs and arms itched. He was a moth in the night, moving toward and away from something. Sometimes the mist gave him a glimpse that meant nothing to him of where and who. A woman with dark hair. He saw her on the bike, spoke, called out of the darkness. But she shouted and snapped. Maybe she couldn't see his smile. Wasn't he smiling? He couldn't remember. He couldn't remember the woman with dark hair.

Shouting? Snapping?

The images boiled in the darkness and made no sense. But the light drew him forward until he found himself standing in front of a house. Dark house under a bright sky, small round light glowing like the sun, a teeny-tiny sun, next to a door.

He slipped through the darkness, slipped through the door. It opened under his hand as though that was what a hand was for. The room beyond was a cavern of shadow, an extension of himself. He felt his way along, surprised by warmth. Shivering; he'd been shivering but now he felt snug. The room smelled salty. He ran his hands over countertops without knowing what they were, felt metal and plastic. A single spot of orange blinked in the darkness. He put his finger over it, hid the tiny light. It came from a pot on the counter, surface warm. Not on the stove. He knew the word, stove, and this was something else. He felt with his hands, lifted the lid and heard the simmering sound. Salty steam flooded the room and his stomach spoke.

"S-s-starving." He knew the word. "Starving." He blinked. He could see, a little, here and there. Shapes formed in the shadows, extensions of himself. Canisters on the counter, a sack of bread. The pot simmering, filled with soup. "Soup." He didn't have a thought. He opened the sack and took a slice of bread, dipped it in the soup. Savored the salty broth. His stomach spoke and he smiled, swallowed stew-soaked bread. Saw the spoon, a long wooden spoon. "S-s-spoon." He stirred the soup and sipped from the spoon, scooped and swallowed. Salt pork and string beans. He ate spoonful after spoonful, swallowed until his stomach stopped speaking, swallowed until he heard the sound.

Then he stopped.

The room was brighter now as his eyes found light he hadn't noticed before. The sound came from another room, a stirring, a shuffling. He set down the spoon and followed the sound in the shadows. Sound in the mist. "Shhhh ..." Shadow, slinking in the darkness. The mist opened before him and he remembered a face, two faces. Angry, screaming faces. Shooting, shooting. Shotgun shooting. He blinked and the mist closed in again and he found himself in another room. Soft chairs and sofa. A room he remembered from a dark place beyond the mist. This room? Like this room?

The sound, the stirring. A tip-tap in the dark drew his eyes down to the floor. Two gleams gazed back. Eyes, he saw them as eyes. They were eyes, eyes gleaming out of a shadow, extension of himself. He blinked and the shadow coalesced into a shape. A short, shimmying shape. He kneeled down and the shape slipped up to him.

A dog. He didn't know the word, but he recognized the shape. Small and round with frizzy fur. It shimmied and shook and when he reached out his hand it licked his fingers. He smiled and scratched the dog's chin, then heard a sound out of the darkness as it wiggled some more. Laughter, laughing. The sound was laughter. Shadow was laughing. The dog sidled up and pressed against his cold wet leg, its body alive and aquiver. He laughed and scratched and the dog's tail wagged.

"Silly, silly ..."

Smiling Shadow, sated with soup. He didn't know the sensation, didn't recognize the simple pleasure of a quiet moment with a creature pleased with his companionship. He only knew the voices and faces that slid out of the mist. But as he scratched the dog, contented, the mist closed in and surrounded him with silence. Sweet silence he hoped would never end.

But end it did, suddenly, with screaming.

November 15

Woman Escapes Prowler By Fleeing House

AURORA, OR: Melody Palmer of Aurora escaped a prowler last night who entered her house while she slept. There was no sign of forced entry, leading police to speculate that Mrs. Palmer had left a door unlocked.

Mrs. Palmer reported being awakened by a sound she believed to be her dog, a miniature poodle prone to epileptic seizures. She went downstairs to check on the dog and encountered the intruder, whom she described as 5'6" to 5'8" with dark skin and wearing a cloth wrapped around his head, which Mrs. Palmer described as a "turban." The man reportedly threatened her and she fled through the back door. She ran to a neighbor's house, who called the police.

The intruder had fled by the time police arrived. Nothing of value was stolen, though police confirmed the presence of wet footprints in the living room and kitchen. Area residents reported seeing a stranger in the vicinity earlier that day who fit the description given by Mrs. Palmer. Police continue to investigate.

Drop Everything

Sometimes you just have to drop everything and go.

Theirs was an unlikely bond, Ellie and Luellen, two girls too different to be anything but friends, too similar to recognize the gulf between themselves. Country girl and townie, one whose future stretched no further than her own reflected gaze in the bathroom mirror, the other whose path roamed to the limits of her imagination. As the years wore on, they saw each other less and less often, but it wasn't until Luellen fled the valley that Ellie came to recognize her relationship with Luellen as a kind of sanctuary. In her friend's absence, her life grew increasingly bounded by the inescapable disquiet she felt when Stuart returned home drunk and insistent.

Two months after the first, a second note arrived from Portland, a single short paragraph:

> *I'm still finding my way. This address is for a mailing center. I've rented a box so you can write back. As I move around, I don't want to miss any of your letters.*

Ellie needed a week to gather the courage to write to Luellen about her parents' deaths. The response was so long coming Ellie feared Luellen might never write again.

> *I killed them, same as if I was driving that car myself. I waited too long to write and tell them I was okay.*

Ellie wished things were different. In dribs and laser-printed drabs, Luellen admitted she wished things were different too. Details trickled in over the subsequent months, but there was no further talk of her parents or of life back in Givern Valley. Only snatches of a new life far away. She asked Ellie to burn her notes after she read them.

> *I've moved again. Things are complicated, but I'm hoping they settle down soon.*

Then, a few weeks later …

> *I start a job this week. It's nothing much, answering phones and setting appointments for a small clinic, but it's enough to help me get by.*

The longest arrived right before Christmas.

> *I've rented a room in a house near a city park called Mount Tabor. I guess it was a volcano once, but now it's covered with trees and paths and playgrounds. I like to climb to the top and sit next to this statue of a grumpy-looking old guy. I like him. People ride their bikes and walk their dogs. The whole city is laid all around you, and on clear days you can see all the way to Mount Hood. It's beautiful. I wish you could see it.*

Ellie replied, *Maybe someday I will.* She didn't believe her own words. Yet now she was here in Portland, free of her cage at last. Until she saw Hiram's man outside the Ship Shop.

Doesn't he understand I'm not who I am? Portland Ellie, not Givern Ellie. Givern Ellie died on a railroad bridge in a dark corner of nowhere.

She couldn't quite remember the man's name. Ed something, last name started with a G. He'd been a county deputy until he was run out of the department for offenses rumored to include everything from drunk driving to assault and extortion. After that he served as one of the Hiram's hired apes. Ellie had never spoken with him, though she remembered a time when he'd pulled the pickup over. It was shortly after she and Stuart were married, and as always Stuart was driving too fast. But Deputy G didn't write a ticket. He and Stuart leaned against the tailgate and spoke in hushed tones. Ellie sat alone in the cab and wondered what the two had to talk about. All Stuart would say was what a shame it was the man's wife refused to live in Givern, and then up and left him anyway after he agreed to commute from K-Falls.

She rose from the bench and headed for the café. People would be there, city people, Portland people, people slurping milk foam from the surface of their lattes as they read the paper or surfed the internet on their laptops. Two short blocks to safety, a brief stroll on any other rainy day. She felt isolated and exposed as she moved past the windowless brick wall at her side. She glanced over her shoulder, eyes flicking up and down the street. And hesitated.

The man was gone.

Ellie reached out to the wall beside her, but found no reassurance in the cool touch of brick and mortar. She drew a breath and tried to convince herself she'd imagined things. Weariness and anxiety after a long trip and a short night had deceived her, transformed a stranger into Hiram's deputy. Then, she simply missed seeing him go. He probably had no interest in her personally, just some guy staring at her breasts. *All that pudding.* Even Reverend Wilburn—him on the downhill tumble past sixty—paid more heed to her chest than her face when he lectured her.

But what if she was wrong?

Be smart, Pastor Sanders had told her. Go quiet. The smart response was to assume he was here for her, and that meant she had to get out of sight. If Luellen came for her mail, Ellie would miss her, but that was better than being caught by Hiram's man.

She started moving again, eyes sliding up and down the empty street. Near the corner she came to a solid wooden door with worn plastic letters affixed beside the lock. MACHI E WORKS—NO S LICITING. She tried the knob, but it only vibrated under her touch. When she knocked, the sound was so hollow it threw a shiver through her. She darted through the crosswalk without waiting for an answer.

There was too little traffic, no one on foot. Ellie almost wished the woman with the spongy hips was still around. Or that boy on the skateboard. Someone to notice if Hiram's man reappeared. She passed a knickknack shop and a martial arts studio, a specialty pet supply store across the street. Used furniture. Hand thrown pottery. Wine and cheese. Doors were locked, interiors still and dark. Signs in the windows indicated business hours starting later in the day. The other direction, a couple of blocks back, there was a convenience store, but she didn't want to retrace her steps. She continued on, crossed at the next corner, then paused outside an auto shop. Through a half-open window she could hear activity: the rattle of a pneumatic wrench, the tinny whine of talk radio. She looked through the glass door, hopeful. But the face behind the counter chilled her. Blue striped shirt over a barrel chest, embroidered name Dutch over the left pocket. Razor stubble and a crew cut. Deputy G had a crew cut too.

What could she say? "Someone is following me."

"I don't see nobody." He'd probably grin and direct his voice to her pudding.

The auto shop was separated from the café by a narrow parking lot surrounded by a black, wrought iron fence. A dozen paces further, no more. She hesitated at the open gate leading into the lot, scanning for movement. A car went past on Hawthorne, moving quickly, driver's eyes fixed ahead. The lot was half full of cars and trucks with crumpled hoods, dented fenders, shattered glass. The long, cinder block wall of the coffee shop facing the lot had only a few windows of frosted industrial glass. She saw no one, continued on. Ten paces more. Six. Before she could clear the open gate, a hand clamped onto her upper arm. She gasped, twisted, dug in her heels. The grip was too strong. She looked up into Deputy G's great round face. Mountain air and growth hormone.

"Hey, now. Slow down, little lady."

He was six-six if he was a foot. Unlike Stuart's compact, wiry strength, his was a boar's power. Inexorable, rooted in its own dense gravity. With her free hand he grabbed her neck. "Let me go." Her voice sounded remote in her own ears. *I'm not who you think I am.* His fingers dug into her throat, choked off her air before she could make another sound. No one nearby, no one on the street. No one to see.

He dragged her into the lot behind a minivan with missing side panels. She was a rag doll in his hand. He spun her, slammed her against the fence with enough force to bounce fluid from her eyes. A sharp ridge of iron cut into the back of her skull. His left hand remained clamped on her throat, but he eased up enough to allow her to draw a shallow breath. Her nose wrinkled against the cloying scent of Old Spice. With his right hand, he reached up and scratched at the corner of his eye. He inspected her as though trying to memorize her face.

"I'm not who—" He choked off the words before she could finish.

"You're Elizabeth Spaneker." Not a question. "Your father-in-law is worried about you."

The air seemed to darken around her and she heard a sound like the rattle of a two-stroke engine. Maybe he was strangling her, or maybe she was being swallowed by terror. The man saw the fear in her face and smiled. An instant later, the sound resolved itself into footsteps on gravel.

"Heya—?"

Ellie twisted her head a fraction of an inch and saw the boy from earlier. He stood at the far end of the minivan, one foot on his skateboard, the other on the ground. Hands loose at his sides, shoulders still wet. Hiram's man turned his head and suddenly released her, jerked his hand back as if from an open flame.

"Fuck off, kid." His voice resounded in the narrow space between the buildings. "This isn't none of your business." Ellie thought of what Pastor Sanders told her. *Do the last thing he expects.* As Deputy G turned toward the boy, she shot her foot out, felt it connect with muscle and bone. The big man responded with a howl and eased his grip. Ellie scrambled along the fence, ducked a wild backhand slung her way. Her feet skidded on loose gravel as the boy kicked the back of his skateboard. The front end shot forward into Deputy G's gut, chopping off his howl. As Ellie fled past the minivan she caught a glimpse of the two entangled, boy on his back, big man above with one knee on the ground and his arms splayed in a spread eagle.

"You little son of a bitch—"

Ellie bolted through the open gate and up the street, then crashed through the coffee house door. Just inside, she pitched up against a round table. For a moment she hung there, hands flat on the tabletop. The shop was half-full, customers seated at tables or on couches against the walls to either side. Ellie sensed them more as abstract shapes than human forms. Her gaze fixed on an Asian man behind the counter. Next to her stood a young woman who could be the sister of Raajit, the boy from the Ship Shop. They stared at her, openmouthed.

"Someone is after me. Please."

The man hesitated for only a moment, then raised a hinged section of countertop. "This way." Ellie followed him through a doorway into the kitchen. The sound of a dishwasher filled the compact space. She could smell lemon cleanser and ground coffee. The man continued through another door into a tiny office. Desk, computer, file cabinet, bulletin board pinned with calendar pages. Somehow he'd managed to fit a straight-backed wooden chair into the corner between the desk and the door.

"Wait here. I'll call the police." Ellie moved to the chair, but didn't sit. The man studied her, sharp-eyed and concerned. Black hair shot through with silver framed his long, hard face. After a moment, his brown eyes fixed on a point below Ellie's chin. "Did he hit you?"

"I—" Ellie had no breath. A sharp pain flared from her neck to her shoulders and down her back. She nodded.

From the other room, they heard shouting. Ellie recognized Deputy G's voice, but not the words.

"Stay here. You'll be safe." The man turned and went back into the kitchen, closed the door behind him. Ellie sank onto the chair. From beyond the door, she could hear him attempt to reason with Hiram's man.

You're a smart girl, Pastor Sanders had said. What was the smart choice now? Sit here and wait for the police? That might save her from Hiram's man, but in the long run, it wouldn't save her from Hiram. Cops were the last thing she needed. They'd have questions, would make calls. They'd know how to get at the truth, even if

Hiram wanted to try to hide it.

She crept to her feet, cracked the door an inch or two.

"—don't have time for your bullshit. Now get that bitch out here, before I—"

"Sir, the police are their way. You'd be wise to keep that in mind."

The man's voice was calm. He sounded like he could handle whatever Deputy G threw at her. Ellie didn't want to stick around to see what that might be. The hinged counter wasn't much of a barrier.

Across the kitchen she saw another door, pebbled glass panes suggesting a way out. Ellie peeked through the opening to the front of the shop, saw the Asian man's back, his assistant at his side. Hiram's man loomed on the other side of the counter, hands balled at his sides. His eyes seemed to pulse with red energy. Then something caught his attention, a sound or movement behind him. As he turned Ellie dropped low, almost to her hands and knees, and scampered across the kitchen to the door. She heard new voices, but didn't wait to see who they belonged to. The doorknob stuck for a second, then turned. She tumbled out into a narrow passage between the café and the auto repair lot, and nearly flattened the kid with the skateboard. He smiled at her, a broad, boy's grin. "If you want, I'll help you get away."

The Fleshy Part of the Thigh

Doorway opened onto bright light and linoleum, the kid five steps ahead of Big Ed. The sound of the gunshot filled the kitchen, a black wall of force that compressed Big Ed's eyes and set his ears alight. It never occurred to him the girl would have a gun.

Hiram leaned against the stainless steel stove. Somehow he'd got hold of the kid, had one hand wrapped over the boy's shoulder. His right leg leaked blood. Not squirting—that was Big Ed's first clear thought. Not squirting, no arterial flow. Even so, could be bad. Thigh shot. "Oh holy hell, help me, Ed." Hiram slid to the floor, pulling the boy down with him.

"Get out, get out, *get out!*" The girl's voice sounded like stressed metal. "Let go of my son and get out!" She stood in the shadows through a doorway across the kitchen.

"Be quiet." Big Ed could hear a mechanical buzz in his ears, like he wasn't talking at all, but the girl heard him. She turned the gun on him. In two sharp strides, he crossed the kitchen and gave her his backhand. She fell and dropped the gun—a revolver. As she reached for the piece he gave it a kick and it spun clattering through the doorway. She threw herself at him, shrieking, and he punched her in the face. She fell backward through the dark doorway, voice silenced. He turned to Hiram.

"Take the boy." Hiram spoke through clenched teeth. "And help me up. We gotta go."

Lips pressed together and larynx at his side, Big Ed's raised eyebrows asked the question.

"How many people you think you can carry?" The old man's voice cracked. "Leave her. We take the boy, she'll come to us. Now help me."

Big Ed pulled a dishtowel off the refrigerator door handle, bent down next to the old man. The bullet had hit the fleshy part of the thigh, in the front, out the back. The exit hole was pretty big, but Big Ed wadded up the towel and pressed it against the wound. With his free hand, he dragged open a drawer, spilling utensils, then another and another until he found what he was looking for. More dish towels. Hiram grabbed one of the towels and wrapped it around his thigh with one hand. Big Ed tied it off. It was already soaked through.

"How does it feel, boss?"

Hiram gave him a look. "Take the … goddamn … boy."

Big Ed picked the kid up by the middle and tucked him thrashing under one arm. The ringing in his ears from the gunshot blunted the boy's high-pitched cries.

"Boss, can you carry the towels? I can carry the boy and help you to the car, but we need the towels to control the bleeding."

"Jesus Humpin' Christ, I got a fuckin' bullet in me."

"It went through."

"That's supposed to make me feel better?"

Big Ed hooked his free arm under Hiram's armpit and hoisted him up. The kid kept squirming, but he wasn't making so much noise now. They hobbled out the back door, Hiram gasping with each step. "We need someone to help with this."

Big Ed couldn't respond with a boy in one arm and an old man in the other. The larynx was in the hand pinned by Hiram's right arm. He carried the two down a short stoop to the paved walk that ran along the side of the house. The sky was brightening, salmon-streaked clouds against deep blue, but it was still more night than day. The windows of the house next door remained dark. Big Ed propped Hiram against the stoop railing, put the larynx against his neck.

"Do you think you can get to the car?"

"Sure, dancing a fucking ballet the whole way." Hiram leaned into Big Ed, gripped his forearm. Together they hobbled up the path, Big Ed half dragging Hiram. When they got out to the sidewalk, Big Ed tried to put the kid down, but his little feet started scooting the moment they touched pavement. Ed hoisted him up again, pressed on to the Accord. Any moment he expected to hear the girl screaming from her front porch, or the sound of sirens. It was supposed to go different. They were supposed to take charge of the boy and the girl, and rely on threats to keep the husband quiet. Big Ed didn't know the Bronsteins had a gun. Since when did hippies come strapped?

As they reached the Accord, the front door of the house across the street opened. Big Ed dropped Hiram and crouched down. A woman in a robe stepped out onto the porch and bent down, grabbed a newspaper. She glanced at the front page, then turned and went back into the house.

Big Ed looked at the kid, pointed at the back passenger door. "Get in." He tried to squeeze a growl into his mechanized voice. The kid ignored him, kept thrashing. He remembered his own brats, all those years ago. Tantrum machines and poop factories. He yanked the door open, tossed the kid like a sack onto the back seat. Slammed the door. Hiram moaned beside him. He opened the front door, helped the old man into his seat.

"Let's go already. Get on the phone, call Myra."

"Are you sure that is a good idea?"

"Just call the bitch. She's blown fellas from Oroville to Bellingham. She'll know someone to tap."

"I cannot use the phone and drive."

Hiram slumped against the door post. "Jesus, next time remind me not to hire the handicapped."

Big Ed reflected upon the Desert Eagle in silence. After a moment, Hiram groaned.

"Christ, what a baby. Gimme your phone, I'll call her. What's her number?"

"It's the only 503 number in the recent calls list."

"Saved under 'crack whore'?" Hiram managed a whimper-laced chuckle.

"Just the number."

Big Ed tossed Hiram his cell phone, trotted around and got behind the wheel. Hiram's breath came in gasps as he thumbed the key pad. Ed drove down 60th, then east on Division. He wanted to loop around the far side of the park, make sure they hadn't been picked up by law enforcement before they headed back to the Suburban. After a moment, Hiram snapped the phone shut.

"Problem?"

"I can't work this goddamn thing. Where the fuck is she?"

"She's at some motel on Burnside, not too far from the bridge."

"Like I'm supposed to know where the hell that is. Just get hold of her."

"We should get rid of this car. I will call her from the Suburban."

But Big Ed didn't like it. Myra was too reedy, a bomb waiting to explode. Take a city block with her when she popped. But she was the one who brought the situation to Hiram, the land swap and all the rest. She was the one who told them where the pressure points were, who revealed the secret that brought Hiram Spaneker out of

Givern. And when did that ever happen? So Big Ed nodded, found the turn that led back into the park. He slowed down as he climbed up through the trees, looked around to make sure there were no early morning joggers or dog walkers nearby. All he saw were wet trees wrapped in still air.

"Ed, what's wrong with the kid?"

"What do you mean?"

"He's damn quiet back there."

Big Ed glanced over his shoulder, but couldn't see anything. Sudden cold anxiety coiled through him. Had he thrown the boy too hard? He braked, rolled the Accord to a stop on the side of the park road. Turned, leaned over the seat back. Hiram breathed through his teeth.

The back seat was empty. No kid, not on the seat, not on the floor.

He turned, looked at Hiram. Hesitated.

"What the fuck is it, Ed? What's wrong?"

He raised the larynx to his throat. "The boy is not here."

"Not here? Jesus Christ." Hiram's voice cracked, half in anger, half in pain. He tried to twist, to look into the back seat—failed. He turned his black-eyed gaze on Big Ed. "What in fuck's sake did you do with my leverage?"

November 19 — 2:15 pm

Shared Minutes

I can't be bothered with whatever plans are being made by Susan and the others upstairs. I'm waiting down in the lobby, staring out the glass doors across the narrow street at the parking structure. Someone in the waiting area at my back is coughing—wet, ragged hacks with enough vigor to bring up organ meat. The eastbound Jackson Park bus stops and swaps passengers, but not until the bus pulls away does it occur to me I could have jumped aboard. As the coughing continues, I think maybe it's time to call a cab.

"Skin, are you ready?"

I didn't hear them come up behind me, Susan, Moose Davisson, Frannie Stein. No sign of Jessup. "For what?"

"We're going back to the Bronstein house. I want to check on the crime scene team and see if we can find Eager's cell phone number."

"You want my help?"

"I thought you could use the ride."

My gaze bounces from Moose to Frannie. Moose shrugs and looks away. Susan is willing to let me pretend to still be at least peripherally associated with the tribe, but Moose wrote me off a long time ago. Frannie Stein offers me a thin smile. She doesn't know me, but I'm sure Moose shared a few choice tidbits.

I stare at the bus stop. "I'll be fine. Thanks."

Moose moves to the door. "We'll meet you down there, Loo." Susan turns, nods. "Sure, you two go ahead." Frannie follows. Susan watches them as the automatic doors slide shut again, wait until they've crossed the street and disappeared into the parking garage. "Skin, come on. Let's go."

I try to fight my Pavlovian response to the silver bar on her collar. I don't have to follow her orders. But in the end, there's little point in resisting, and anyway I've got no enthusiasm for Tri-Met or for the cost of a cab.

I wait until we've cleared the garage and are heading down the hill. "Susan, what are you up to, anyway?"

"I'm going back to the crime scene."

"Sure, that's what Moose and Frannie are doing. What are *you* doing?"

"What do you mean? I'm doing my job."

"Hauser never followed the investigators around crime scenes. Hell, even Owen left us to do our work without his nose up our asses."

"You know major crime scenes bring the brass out."

"Sure, but they stand around at the margins being self-important, not haunting the working cops. Why are you driving me around? Why are *you* going to Mitch's house? Again. Why aren't you back in the office?"

She doesn't answer right away. I can see her chewing on it, trying to decide exactly what to say to me. "You think a lieutenant can't be a little hands-on with a case this messy?"

"Is that what you're doing? Being hands-on?"

She sighs. I'm badgering her. But I don't like feeling as though I've got a babysitter. She got stuck with me twice today—teach me to live on a street too narrow for the mobile command unit. It's always easier to deal with an ex-cop than a citizen. But setting up a command center in my living room wasn't anything compared to Mitch fixing on me for his confessional.

"You didn't used to be so angry all the time."

"Maybe if you'd taken me seriously when I told you about Eager I wouldn't have anything to be pissed about. Retirement doesn't turn people into high-functioning morons."

A silence stretches out between us and I start to feel like an ass. I sigh, stare out the window at the tree-clad hillside.

"I know that. In fact, after our talk this morning, I got to thinking and there's something I want to run by you. We've been bringing in retired homicide detectives to do open case file reviews, to help take the pressure off the cold case squad. I thought you might be interested."

"You want me to review case files." All the women in my life feel duty-bound to load me up with busy work. I can't blame them. It keeps my hands otherwise occupied.

"It's got to be done, Skin. My cold case guys are good, but they're swamped. They can't drop everything every time someone calls wanting to know if there's anything new on their dead father or husband or sister or daughter."

"So you're pulling in fogies to do the grunt work."

"That's not the way I see it. You're qualified, you've got the experience."

"The pension is what I've got."

"So hanging out in a coffee shop all day is working out for you? Doing off-the-books insurance investigations? Chasing women half your age?"

She stays informed.

"Riggins has been helping us out. We've even got a federal grant coming through. We'll be able to pay a small stipend. Simple case review, flag anything that stands out. No interviews, no testifying, just helping us stay on top of things. The detectives develop the evidence."

"Maybe I like sitting in a coffee shop all day."

"Well, think about it. Okay? You've got good eyes. You could help us out."

I grunt. I can't decide if she really wants me or is trying to do me some kind of half-assed favor. I decide to change the subject.

"Did you send someone to look for Jase?"

She seems to appreciate the change of topic. "He'd left. You should have called me first. I might have been able to get a car down there before he ran off."

"Susan, you ever been down there?"

"Of course."

"Then you know a scrotum face like me stands out. And anyway, I went looking for someone who might know Eager. It's one of his hangouts. I wasn't there to be furtive. You're lucky Jase talked to me at all."

She nods, conceding the point. "Do you think he was telling the truth?"

Nobody is ever honest with a cop, even a dried-up ex-cop. And Jase, no doubt, is an accomplished liar, which means he mixed in enough truth to avoid tripping himself up later but omitted everything important. "Maybe. I'm sure he knows more than he was telling, but where Luellen went probably isn't it."

"But beyond that ... he must know about the kitchen."

"You have to figure." And you have to figure he knows what Eager was doing there too, despite his protests to the contrary. Kids that age always know all the household secrets, and between his hints and Mitch's revelations clearly there are a lot of secrets. I know none of them. For a moment I have the eerie sensation I'm chasing a ghost. Eager's, or my own, who can say? Where I ought to be is back in Uncommon Cup. And what I ought to be doing is drinking coffee with Ruby Jane and getting past myself.

But Susan isn't done with Jase. "Not too broken up about his father, I take it."

"Shoot his Xbox, that'll draw a tear."

She chuckles and some of my tension lessens. Suddenly we've become two cops jawing about a case. Spinning out the threads, seeing what can be woven together. Been a long time since we talked to each other like colleagues.

"What all have you found out about Luellen and Danny?"

"Granger is Luellen's maiden name."

"Yeah, she's mentioned it."

"She's from a small town in southern Oregon, but moved to Portland about four-and-a-half years ago. She worked part time at the women's health clinic over on Southeast 50th until August 2004. Both her parents died in a car accident shortly after she came to Portland."

August 2004 is also when the Tabor Doe dropped, but I don't mention that. No need to wreck the mood. "I'm pretty sure Mitch's father is dead too, way back. I know his mother died last year." I think for a moment about the wheelchair I carried around in my trunk for several days.

"So whoever Danny's grandfather is, he's neither Mitch nor Luellen's father."

"Biological father?"

"So far, nothing on him. Danny's birth certificate lists the father as unknown. But we just started looking."

There's only so much you can find out in a short morning, but sometimes you can sense when you've hit a wall. "You're not going to find anything else."

"It seems unlikely."

"Mitch confirmed he's not Danny's real father."

"The math didn't add up."

"So grandpa could be the bio father's old man."

"Whoever that is."

"Luellen never struck me as someone with a lot of random sexual partners. She knows who the father is."

Susan thinks for a moment. "Unless she was raped."

It wasn't a possibility I'd considered until that moment, but Susan might on to something. If true, it could explain a lot, everything from Luellen's singular dedication to Danny to her flight from the police this morning. Hell, it might even explain the strange things Mitch said about their relationship.

"Skin, you need to come clean to me. I mean, that bit about watching Danny? Come on. What do you know about these people?"

I hesitate for only a moment. There's no reason to stick with my earlier reticence. I'm already part of the investigation; Mitch saw to that. I shrug. There's little enough to tell.

"They moved in a couple of years ago, late winter. Two and a half years, I guess."

"Did Eager ever show any interest in them?"

The question embarrasses me a little, but after what Mitch said, it's a good one. "I thought he was hanging around me."

"What do you mean?"

"You know he used to show up at my place a lot. We'd talk about nothing. He'd show me skateboard tricks and I'd patch him up when he wiped out. I'd try to draw him out about that day up on Mount Tabor."

"For all the good that did."

"Yeah."

"What else?"

"I don't know, Susan. I saw him running around with Jase a few times, but I didn't think much of it. He lived in the neighborhood."

"But Jase is older than he is."

"Yeah, by a year or two. I figured it was hero worship or whatever."

"If you say so."

"I had no idea Eager had a relationship with Luellen."

"What was that about the tagging?"

I sigh. I'm feeling like a fool, but it's not like she wasn't there. I describe my visit from Mitch a few months earlier, about seeing Eager's tag on the front of the house.

"But you didn't do anything about it."

"I told Mitch to report it to the police."

"Did he, that you know?"

"I don't know."

"But you didn't tell him you knew who did it."

"Susan, you don't have to live next to the guy. Mitch is mostly just one endless pain in the ass. I thought Eager was in some kind of dog fight with Jase, so I figured I would talk to him about it the next time I saw him. And as it happened, today was the first time I've seen him in a year."

"Did you look for him after he tagged the Bronstein house?"

"A little, here and there." A few visits to Burnside, and O'Bryant Square in addition to my fruitless call to Charm. "I didn't see the point in pushing it."

"Obviously there was a point. If Mitch is to be believed, he targeted the boy this morning."

"What do you want me to say, Susan?"

"I just think you were behaving irresponsibly." So much for collegial discourse. I suppose this is her stab at me for holding out about my sideline in childcare, but I can't read her face. It's blank.

"Oh, Jesus Christ. Are you kidding me? I had no reason to think anything was going on but a teenage spat."

"You know Eager's history."

"Better than you do, goddammit. A little spray paint on Mitch Bronstein's front porch wasn't cause for calling out the National Guard."

She knows I'm right, but I also know she's a little right too. Obviously I missed a lot playing footsie with Eager, all the while babysitting for Luellen and dodging Mitch whenever I could. Across the street, I saw unremarkable domesticity. Husband, wife, two kids. All they lacked was the dog. But what the fuck did I know?

I don't speak again until we turn on to my street.

Things have changed since this morning. The street is open, the barricades gone. Hardly any cars are parked along the street, a sight I don't expect to see repeated in my lifetime. There is a patrol car parked in front of my house, though, along with two vans belonging to the crime scene examiners. Warning tape crisscrosses the porch. Moose and Frannie are waiting on the walkway leading back to Mitch and Luellen's kitchen door when we pull up in front of the house.

"What's the plan?"

"Thanks for your help, Skin. I'm sorry things didn't go better at the hospital."

"So I'm dismissed."

She pauses, then surprises me. "You can come in with us, if you like. Perhaps you can tell us if anything seems out of place."

She's assuming I've spent enough time inside the house to know. "A lot seems out of place today." She smiles, eyes weary, and I follow her up the walk to the back door.

The kitchen isn't in too bad a shape. There are dishes in the sink and a skillet of coagulated eggs on the stove, fingerprint powder on the counters and cupboard doors. A couple of spilled drawers. Trail of dried blood on the floor, gouge in the plaster where the bullet was extracted. But not the disaster I expected. Justin Marcille, primary examiner for the state, is there boxing up his kit. He looks at me like I'm covered in my own vomit. I guess he still remembers the last time we spoke. He draws himself up, five feet, seven inches of irritable French Canadian and faces Susan.

"We're packing up, Lieutenant. We should be out of here in another ten minutes."

"Anything of interest?"

"Nothing obvious that you haven't already seen. I'll have a prelim for you tomorrow, but it's going to be a while before we process everything."

"Give me the highlights."

Justin frowns. From experience, I know he doesn't like to speculate until he's had a chance to review the evidence. But he also knows cops want to know anything they can, as soon as they can. "There are points of disturbance in the foyer, front hall, dining room and kitchen. We collected material from each location, but I have no sense yet of how much of it is relevant. A lot of latents, of course, mostly partials. Don't be in a hurry there."

"I understand. Maybe you could help us with something. We're looking for a phone number. Did you turn up an address book, anything like that?"

Marcille thinks for a moment. "Nothing like that, Lieutenant. The warrant—"

"We're working on an amendment."

"Fine." A couple of others join us from the dining room. They're PPB criminalists, but I don't recognize them. After my time, I guess.

Susan nods. "What about the computers?"

I whistle. "Computers? Who wrote that affidavit?" Then I realize they're interested in Mitch's state of mind. Emails, letters, anything that might shed light on what happened this morning. I wonder if they'll find nudie shots of his girlfriend Lynn from work.

Justin ignores me. "A couple of laptops. Password protected, so you'll have to wait till the IT guys can get at them. Won't be a problem, but you won't get anything today."

"How about a cell phone?"

"There was one charging in the study. But you're stuck there too. It's got a PIN."

Susan's lips go thin.

"Check with IT in the morning."

Time is ticking. Tomorrow morning could be too late. "Tell you what, Justin. See if you can expedite IT. We need that phone number, and the computers or the cell phone is our best bet for it, okay?"

"I'll see what I can do."

"Thank you."

She turns to us. "We might as well have a look around."

I wonder where the amended warrant is, but I don't say anything. Neither does Frannie Stein, but Moose has a question. "What are we looking for?"

"A cell phone number for Eager Gillespie." Moose's eyebrows raise a fraction of an inch. He knows Eager too. "An address book would be great, but I'm not hopeful about that." Her eyes stray to the fridge, which is a mess of photographs and coupons. Magnetized block letters, C-A-T and B-I-R-D and D-A-N-N-Y spelled out in primary colors. One of the N's is a sideways Z. "Maybe a sticky note somewhere. Or check to see if the house phones have speed dial numbers programmed."

"Frannie and I can take upstairs."

"Okay. Skin, what do you think?"

I've only ever been in the kitchen and living room, and on the rear patio. But I know Mitch has an office on the first floor overlooking the back yard, likely where Justin found the cell phone. Frannie and Moose head up stairs as I lead Susan through the dining room and down a short hallway to the office.

The crime scene team doesn't seem to have spent much time in here. No powder residue, just the ordered disarray of a room someone actually uses. The furniture is Swedish, lots of blond wood and visible fasteners. Two floor-to-ceiling bookshelves, half full of books, mostly popular fiction but also a mix of titles I suppose Mitch uses for work. *Fundamentals of User Interface Design, 21st Century Value-Added Metricity.* Someone may know what that means. The DVDs under the flat-screen television opposite the desk make more sense to me. Mitch seems to favor series television. *Lost, Buffy, The Shield.* I'd almost consider asking to borrow some of it, except that would mean talking to Mitch.

Susan isn't interested in Mitch's taste in entertainment. She starts with the desk. I move to a four-drawer file cabinet.

"Skin, any ideas on Mitch's password for IT?"

"No."

"Come on. Anything? Just a guess?"

"'ITHINKIMJESUS.' All uppercase. Maybe an exclamation point at the end."

"Can you be serious for a minute?"

"Susan, I hardly know the guy."

"What do you suggest, then?"

"Look in the desk. Maybe he writes it on a notepad or something."

"Would Mitch do that?"

"It's a stupid thing to do, so yeah, he would."

I catch myself smiling when she sighs. But I also hear her pulling open desk drawers. I open the file cabinet, flip through a row of folders that seem to be connected to his work. A bunch of company names, some I recognize. The folders have sketches and handwritten notes in them, as well as color printouts of what look like magazine ads and billboards. The second drawer has more of the same. Mitch does a lot of work for environmental groups, Nature Conservancy, 1000 Friends of Oregon. Probably thinks that makes him a radical. The third drawer is dedicated to tax records, IRS and Oregon Department of Revenue returns organized by date and going back to the late 90s. "Susan, tax records here. Maybe you can figure something out about Danny from them."

"I'll let the DA know."

The fourth drawer is bills. Comcast, Qwest, Portland General Electric. Familiar stuff. I start to close the drawer, then have an idea. I look through folder after folder, find what I want near the end. Verizon Wireless. Susan comes up behind me.

"What do you have?"

"Cell phone bills."

I open the folder and pull out the most recent bill. They're on a family plan. Four phones. I flip through the pages. "Bingo."

"What?"

"You think Danny carries a cell phone?"

"Seems like they're starting younger and younger, but age four would be a stretch."

"Not according to this. They've got four numbers on their plan, one assigned to Daniel Granger."

"That could be Eager."

I memorize the number, then hand her the bill. She writes each number in her notebook. "He doesn't use it much. He only called Luellen's cell, at least on this bill."

"Can you do anything with his number?"

"Call it."

"What if he doesn't answer?"

"I'll see what we can do about tracking it."

It's not much, but an hour ago we didn't even know Eager had a phone. Maybe she could get a line on his location. I haven't kept up with the technology since I retired. Cell phones have had GPS in them for a while now, but how accurate it is I can't say. I also don't know if it works if the phone is turned off.

"What's next?"

Susan takes a second to answer. "We're good now. Thanks for your help."

"Susan—"

"What do you want me to say, Skin?"

There's nothing she can say. I signed the papers, I took the pension. I no longer work for the Portland Police Bureau.

Unless I want to come review cold case files for a stipend.

Her attention returns to the sheaf of pages in her hand. I head for the door. "See ya around, I guess." I don't know if she hears me.

Three Years, Three Months Before

I'm Your Man

Hard to say what surprised Eager more: that the man in the parking lot was a cop, or that he was Eager's old man. Cop was bad enough. Cops had this habit of going all wiggy when you stole their shit. Anyone's shit, though Eager had met cops who'd glance left while he ran right so long as some green passed hands. Hell, one graveyard five-o let him make off with the climate control cluster from a Honda CRV for the Jackson in his pocket and half an ounce of pot.

But that asshole hadn't been his old man.

For the bulk of his thirteen and three-quarters years, he'd been only vaguely aware he even had a father. His mother rarely acknowledged the existence of Big Ed Gillespie, a name she'd mention in the same tone one might use to talk about the little man from under the basement stairs who crept out at night to spirit away naughty children. Eager couldn't remember ever seeing his father. There were no pictures of him in photo albums or on the computer. After a few wine spritzers, Eager's mother might admit a past life in southern Oregon—Eager and his sisters were all born at Sky Lakes Medical Center in Klamath Falls—and would sometimes grumble about a "leathery fuck who ruined her goddamn life over a goddamn prank." Not Eager's father, someone else, though it was never clear exactly who the leathery fuck was. The rest of the time the kids may as well have hatched from eggs for all Charm was willing to reveal. If asked direct questions about Big Ed she would only say, "I'll roll in dog shit sooner'n discuss that asshole."

But now he was here. First on the porch last night, hollering and banging, and today outside Hawthorne Auto holding the girl up by her neck.

Eager'd seen the girl earlier. First he thought maybe he could work her for some change, but something about her stopped him. A pretty girl, dark-haired and dusky, with deep shadows beneath her eyes and worry compressing her lips. She smiled thinly at him as he skated past in the rain. Rather than stop, toss out a request for spare change, he'd kept rolling. Something about the smile, about the smooth curve of her cheek and the round brown depth of her eyes grabbed hold of him in the pit of his belly. He glanced back once or twice as he rolled up the block, almost wiped out against a No Parking sign. He was pleased when the bus came and went and she was still there.

He skated to the corner, worked on ollies off the curb. It wasn't a good spot for skating. No real lift from the sidewalk and too much traffic on Hawthorne, but at least he could keep an eye on her. Not that he could say why she'd need looking after. Just seemed like the thing to do. After a bit, some frizzy-haired fat lady came and sat at the bench, then climbed heavily aboard the next bus. All the while the girl gazed across Hawthorne. Looking for something, he thought.

Or someone, maybe.

She's probably waiting for her boyfriend. A wave of doubt swept through him and he spilled out into the street. He jumped up quickly, afraid she'd seen, but she was still staring. At what? The Ship Shop?

Eager forced himself to roll up the side street. It occurred to him watching her was a little weird. Keeping him from business too. Skating off a street corner for half an hour so he could check out some girl on a bench, no matter how pretty she was, didn't put green in the pocket. He needed to get himself to a spot with more foot traffic. Outside Fred Meyer, say, where people came and went all the damn-dong day.

And if he happened to skate by her on his way down to Freddie's, well, who could say what would happen? Maybe she'd want to talk. That would be cool. He pictured the conversation, wordless in his mind, and a wave of heat swept through him. He popped a one-eighty and rolled back toward Hawthorne, in time to see her cross the street in front of him.

As she moved, she threw quick, anxious looks over her shoulder. Eager hesitated, but once she disappeared beyond the corner, he followed. Maybe she was being chased by some dirtbag, an aimless drifter with black gums and stolen shoes. Maybe Eager could find some unknown reserve of strength and power. Kick the bastard into the street, arms windmilling, there to get plowed by Tri-Met. She'd fall into his arms in relief and gratitude.

He tugged at his shirt collar as he rounded the corner, certain she'd be waiting.

"I'm in trouble. Will you help me?"

"Anything you need, I'm your man."

But she was gone.

He stopped, looked up and down Hawthorne. The print shop across the street was open, same with the art supply store. But he could see through the front windows of both joints and she wasn't in either. Between him and the auto shop on the next block, everything else was closed. He didn't see any buses. Traffic moved at a steady pace both directions. Didn't look like anyone could have stopped and picked her up.

She must have been moving faster than he realized. He rolled past the Poekoelan dojo to the next corner. Maybe she had her car in for service and went to pick it up. He crossed 43rd, looked through the window of the auto shop.

There were a couple of chairs in the small waiting area and a plant on the countertop. No girl. Some guy with big arms stood behind the counter. He gave Eager a look and went back to whatever he was doing. Farther up the block, a woman came out of Common Grounds. For a moment Eager thought it was her, blue jacket and dark hair, but when the woman glanced his way she had a pinched face and cats-eye glasses. She scurried across the street, cup of coffee in hand, and got into an Acura RL. Eager watched her drive off, thinking about how he could get eight bills for the RL's driver side air bag, six for the passenger side. It occurred to him the girl might have just burned rubber, desperate for a coffee.

But a sound from the auto shop parking lot caught his attention. A grunt, maybe a squeal. The lot was surrounded by a tall black fence with a wide open gate. At the far end, the garage door was closed. Parked inside was a beat-up minivan, a couple of Subarus beyond. The sound came from behind the van.

He stopped at the van's bumper, one foot balanced on his board over the rear truck, the other on pavement ready to push off. At first he didn't understand what he was seeing. A big man wrestling with himself, crew cut on a bowling ball for a head. Looked to Eager like the fellow was pounding his pud, the way his big shoulders rolled around inside his tan jacket. Then the man moved and Eager saw the girl. His girl. The big man held her pressed against the fence, his hand on her neck. Her face distorted as she struggled, cheeks red, eyes like twin moons.

"Your father-in-law is worried about you." Big voice, but not loud, steeped in certainty. Something in the big man's voice caused Eager's eyes to water. Gone were any fantasies of fearsome heroics, vanished into vibrating air between buildings. The windows of the auto shop were frosted and closed, the windows of the coffee house the same. They were alone, unseen, unheard, shielded by a wreck. All Eager wanted to do was slink away before anyone noticed. But the look on the girl's face, the terror and the pain, seemed to yank his voice out of him.

"Heya—?"

The big head turned, big eyes locked with Eager's. The big hand released the girl. But that only freed up those meat hooks for use on the dumbass with the skateboard. Eager's nuts seemed to crawl up inside himself.

"Fuck off, kid." The big voice rattled the windows of the coffee house behind him. "This isn't none of your business." Big hand balled into a fist. Eager pushed backward as the girl suddenly lashed out with her foot, connected with the big man's knee. Eager's foot rolled a pebble and he fell, tried to catch himself on the minivan. Popped the kicktail of his board with the heel of his other foot. The board shot into the big gut. Eager plopped onto his ass and in an instant the big man was on top of him. Big grunts. Limbs tangled. Eager drew in a breath pungent with the smell of eggs and fried fat.

"You little son of a bitch—"

The girl darted past. Eager sensed the movement, sudden shadow and light, the sound of footsteps on pavement. He'd run too if he could. He wanted to call out to her, tell her he was sorry. But the big chest pressed against his face, big knee crushed his groin. He struggled, twisted, grabbed big flesh. Tears squirted from his eyes, but the big head popped up, suddenly indifferent to Eager's squirming. He pushed himself up with his big arms. Eager wanted to stop him, but he could only dream of being a hero to a pretty girl who would never know his name. As the big man twisted free of the tangle of boy on the asphalt beneath him, Eager did the only thing he could. He lifted the fucker's wallet.

November 16

Police Seek Assailant
In Assault On Sleeping Woman

CANBY, OR: Police are looking for a man who broke into a Canby woman's home this morning and assaulted her while she slept.

The 31-year-old woman reported awaking about 6 a.m. to find a stranger in her bedroom. She screamed, at which point the man grabbed her face and neck and pressed her down on the bed, according to police.

The assailant—believed to have entered the home through an unlocked side door—fled when the woman's five-year-old son called out from the adjacent bedroom. The victim was treated at Willamette Falls Hospital for facial contusions and released. The boy was unhurt.

Pig Rode The Hot Breeze

The only reason she had supper waiting when Stuart came in was Ellie had loaded the Crock Pot before she left the house that morning. Potatoes, carrots, onions and meat. Lots of salt and pepper, celery, canned beef broth. Ordinarily she'd warm some rolls or make a salad to go with the stew, but when she got home she tossed the prescription on the counter, still in its Rexall bag, and sat down at the kitchen table. Breakfast dishes still in the sink, a rare failure to wash up. Outside, low, dark clouds gathered but the day remained hot. She listened to the stew simmer, stared at her hands. Rough farm hands. She thought she could remember a time when they'd been soft as a peeled orange. A different girl, another life. The scent of pig rode the hot breeze through the open kitchen window, mingled with the aroma from the Crock Pot. What on earth had possessed her to make stew in high summer? She wondered what that cold tomato soup she'd seen on the Food Network would taste like—what was it called? Not that it mattered. Stuart would never tolerate something so exotic on his table. She pressed her palms to her thighs, drew a long breath. All around her she saw the drab sameness of the kitchen, of her life. Chipped canisters on the counter, neat and in a row. Kerr jar full of old wooden spoons beside the stove. Her grandmother's iron skillets on their pegs on the wall. All the effort she put into keeping things clean and well-ordered now seemed so pointless.

Just after seven Stuart slammed through the kitchen door. He didn't bother to wash his hands, went straight to the refrigerator. "Hotter'n hell today. Did you think to pick up any beer?" Ellie hadn't. The long drive into town, the doctor's sterile office, the line at the pharmacy—they'd taken all her strength. She looked at the Rexall bag. A week's worth of pills that would solve the least of her troubles.

"I saw the doctor."

Stuart, bent down and staring into the fridge as though beer would appear if he wanted it badly enough, only grunted in response. Ellie knew he wouldn't be interested.

"It was a follow-up visit."

Stuart looked over his shoulder at her, fridge standing open beside him. The compressor kicked on to fight the stale kitchen heat. "What the hell does that mean? I gotta make two co-pays, is that what you're saying?"

"The doctor wanted to talk to me about my test results."

He looked over his shoulder. "What test results? I'm not paying for test results. I never said you could go to the doctor."

Ellie closed her eyes, pinched the bridge of her nose. She could hear him breathing, feel the cold from the open fridge. "They're your results as much as mine, Stuart." She spoke from behind her hand.

"Jesus, you haven't done the dishes from this morning yet?"

She wanted to shake him. "Have you been feeling funny lately? You know, down there?"

"Down where?" He swung the refrigerator door shut, moved to the Crock Pot and set the lid on the counter beside the Rexall bag. "What's in here? Stew?"

She lowered her hand and looked at him. "I have chlamydia, Stuart."

"Sounds like a personal problem." He chuckled, too witless to know half the joke was on him. With the dirt-crusted fingers of his right hand, he plucked a chunk of beef from the pot and juggled it from palm to palm.

"You have it too."

"Have what?" He blew on his hands.

"Chlamydia, Stuart. You have chlamydia."

It seemed to take a moment for her words to catch up to him. "Wait. That shit's contagious?" He dropped the piece of meat. It fell with a wet splat onto her clean kitchen floor. "What the hell did you give me?"

"I didn't give you anything, Stuart. You gave it to me."

He opened his mouth but said nothing, his defense stalled behind the flash of anxiety in his eyes. Stuart had offered her so little. Little love, rare concern, infrequent and usually guilt-driven tenderness. His fidelity was all she had, and now even that was gone. In its wake, bitterness and desolation spilled into the emptiness left behind. "I can't believe you did this to me, after the promise you made—"

He dropped his gaze. "I don't know what you're talking about."

That morning at Luellen's apartment, the kind words and pledge to change, they'd meant nothing. With Stuart, it was always just talk, meaningless words and empty promises offered up as a pretense, then forgotten once he got what he wanted. His voice now, sullen and whining, brought her bitterness to a boil. "You call infecting me *nothing*? Chlamydia's a disease you get from fucking, Stuart, and the only person who fucks me is you." Her anger seemed to give her clarity. "You might want to check in with your girlfriend. Or did you cheat on me with the pigs?"

She felt herself buoyed by unexpected pleasure at his panic, but Stuart gave her no time to enjoy her triumph. His hand snapped out from his side like a snake, a backhand clout so sharp she experienced it as sound rather than sensation. Her mouth fell open as he pulled his hand back, balled into a fist. She felt the second strike, this one to the mouth. Tasted beef fat and dirt. He hit her again and she fell onto her hip and hands next to the table, knocked one of the dinette chairs over. Blood from her nose and split lip splashed onto the linoleum. Her clean linoleum. Above her, she heard Stuart's voice, now muttering and frantic.

"Oh, holy hell. Oh, Jesus …" He stumbled through the door into the sitting room. Ellie pushed herself to her feet. She took the dish towel from the refrigerator door handle, wiped her bleeding mouth. "Jesus jesus *jesus* …" Stuart had no idea what chlamydia was. *The idiot thinks he has AIDS.* Should have paid more attention to Lady Latex.

Beyond the doorway, Stuart moved back and forth like an old boar restless with rut. The sitting room was darker than the kitchen, with lights off and clouds dense out the window. All she saw was his silhouette, his filthy hands raking his hair. "What'd that stupid skank do to me?" The sound of his voice, cracked and childish, the mention of the other woman, stoked Ellie's anger back to a white hot flare. She dropped the dish towel and threw herself through the door. Her hands connected with the flesh of his neck, caught one of his ears. She grabbed hold and yanked. She felt blood between her fingers as a yowl burst out of him. He tossed her off with a shrug. She landed hard on the worn fir floor. His eyes seemed to flash out of the shadows. The faded flower-print wallpaper on the sitting room wall framed his florid face. One hand cupped his damaged ear.

She felt her own blood and snot on her hands and knees as she tried to clamber backward away from him. Not quick enough. He kicked her in the soft cup between her neck and collarbone with enough force to lift off the floor. Her head struck the corner of the kitchen doorway and for a moment all she could see was a scatter of white light. Stuart grasped the front of her dress. "None of your damn business who I fuck." His words crackled with rage. "Or when I fuck 'em. Or what they send me home with." He dragged her across the sitting room floor, tossed her onto the braided rug his parents gave them as a wedding present. She tried to move away, but he dropped down on top of her, pressed her to the floor with his knee.

She realized with sudden sinking despair she'd uncaged the Stuart last seen that morning at the creek over a year and a half before. "Please—" Gasping, hopeless.

"Shut up!" He slapped her so hard the rug couldn't soften the blow as her head snapped around and her cheek cracked against the floor. "You telling me I got the clam dip, whatever the hell you call it? That what you're saying?" He yanked open his trousers, the zipper and the seam of his crotch ripping with the force of the effort. She could barely see, but the violent worm appeared before her. "Lick it off, bitch." He leaned over her and through the blood she smelled something like moldy bread. She reached out, struggling, searching, found the couch leg above her head. Tried to pull herself away from him, but he gripped her by the throat with one hand, cuffed her across the face with the other.

"I told you to lick it off."

Her arms flailed, beat against him uselessly. She felt him straddle her, felt the slap against her cheek. His cock, flaccid and diseased. Bile rose in her throat. She tried to turn her face away from him but he gripped her more tightly. Strangling her, slapping her again and again with the filthy worm.

"That's right. You know, don't you?"

Her arms whipped around and her eyes bulged. She could feel him moving, gripping her with one hand and himself with the other. Her cheeks crawled with each meaty slap, as if she could feel the germs leap from his flesh to hers. Then he began to beat himself off as he choked her. She tried to scream, knowing no one would hear even if she managed to force a sound past his grip. No living thing within half a mile except the pigs and horses, the rats in the grain bins, chickens in the poultry yard. Stuart couldn't hear her either, listening only to the sounds inside his own head.

Her eyes started to lose focus, but she could still see him, his face above hers, his hand on the worm. Reaching, desperate, her own hand brushed something, a basket. The basket she kept by the couch.

Stuart's head dropped, chin to chest. He moaned, a thread of saliva swinging from his bottom lip. Ellie overturned the basket, felt a pincushion, spools of thread, scattered buttons. She found the scissors just as Stuart expelled himself onto her face and neck, thrust her arm with sudden force. Buried the blades to the hinge in the right side of his head. He didn't seem to notice. Ellie stared transfixed as he continued to squeeze and stroke, a horrifying rhythm. Then, strangely, his eyes took on an almost sorrowful glimmer and his lips struggled to form words.

"S-s-s-ahhh, … s-s-s-shouldn't—"

Slowly, he slid sideways to the floor and all motion ceased.

For a long moment—a second, an hour—Ellie could only suck air through her aching throat. Then, bit by bit, she pulled herself away from Stuart's limp form. She stumbled into the kitchen, found the dishtowel, ran cold water in the sink, washed off the viscid result of his final effort. Her skin felt hot and aware, as though she could hear electrical potential in the air through the pores in her face and neck. She moved back into the sitting room, horrified yet lured by incomprehension. She looked at him, expectant, anxious. Momentarily indifferent. He didn't move. From outside, she heard a crackling pop, the sound of tires on gravel. She went to the window. Dusty white Suburban rolling up the long driveway. She stepped back and leaned against the couch, a thick sensation like hot mud in her bowel. At that moment, the sun broke through the clouds, one last blaze before dusk. A shaft of light fell through the sitting room window, glinted off the damaged ear, the scissor handles. In the orange light, Stuart's eyes stared sightlessly, one down and to the left, one upward, as though he couldn't decide which way he was going. Dead.

She was dead too. She could say anything, describe Stuart's violence, describe her terror. Hiram Spaneker, the man behind the wheel of the Suburban rolling up her driveway, wouldn't listen, and once he got hold of her, no one else would get the chance.

That Crazy Bitch'll Know Someone

S on, you and me, we gonna have one helluva party.

Big Ed was still waiting. Sure, Hiram paid well enough; kept him in booze and bitches, so long as he wasn't too picky. Big Ed had learned long ago not to order from the top shelf. And three years earlier, when he'd staggered into Westbank delirious with blood loss and fever, Hiram had done right by him. The doctor may have been a veterinarian, but at least the man's work was sound. Hiram even paid for the electrolarynx—a used, obsolete model—and spread around enough cash to misdirect the investigators from the state police who showed up to ask questions on behalf of the Portland cops. Hiram didn't like spending good money to fix a fuck-up, but he also knew Big Ed could hurt him if the OSP got hold of him.

In retrospect, the smart move might have been to sink him in a bog. Big Ed expected exactly that during the long, empty days of recovery, laid up in Hiram's attic staring at the exposed ceiling joists or watching the flies tick against the dusty window. He knew as well as anyone how easy it was to vanish a body in Givern Valley. But in the end, Hiram's pleasure in owning a man seemed greater than the satisfaction he might derive from putting Big Ed down like a broke leg mule. His life now carried a second mortgage at an interest rate that'd make a payday lender blush. He spent his days intimidating migrant workers, breaking the occasional thumb, and laying low.

This little adventure was supposed to be his redemption, the means through which he'd repurchase at least a partial share in himself. Simple enough: enter the house, grab the little boy and his mother, then out the door and gone. The negotiations would be up to Hiram, but the results were a given. Get the kid, get paid, with some respect as bonus.

No wonder everything went sideways.

All he could figure was the kid bolted from the back of the car while he helped Hiram into the front. More than likely he was back home with his mother and her fucking gun. Which meant they were genuinely screwed. "She won't call the cops, no worries about that, so long as we make the grab and go." So Hiram had insisted. But who knew what would happen now? Maybe she still wouldn't call the cops, though a whole-grain fairy like the husband might talk her in to it. Even if she didn't, the element of surprise was shot.

They abandoned the Accord in the Mount Tabor parking lot, and hobbled together to the Suburban. Hiram's bleeding had slowed to a seep, but when Big Ed changed the dish towel it was clear the wound was serious. He managed to get it wrapped tight, then helped Hiram into the passenger seat. Moved around to the driver's side and climbed in.

When he reached under the seat for the Eagle, Hiram's tendons rose in his neck. "Just leave the goddamn gun where it is. You have a call to make."

He felt a muscle twitch in his cheek as he opened his phone and dialed, tapped in Myra's room number at the motel phone system prompt. Just when he was sure it would kick into voice mail, she answered, her voice raspy and ravaged. "It isn't even daylight. What are you calling me for?"

"I did not think you ever slept."

"What's that got to do with anything?"

"We have a problem. Hiram has been hurt."

"I told you to be careful."

He didn't want to get into it. "Do you know anyone who can deal with a gunshot wound?"

"Christ. What the hell happened?"

"It does not matter."

"Is he going to die?"

"Do you know anyone or not?"

He heard her light a cigarette, cough. "I know a guy who stitches for some bikers in town. I'll call you back." She disconnected before he could respond.

"What'd she say?"

"She says she knows someone. She will call back."

"You don't sound happy. Even through that fucking dildo I can hear the gripe in your voice."

"She is calling some outlaw biker medic."

"So?"

"You cannot trust a biker, Hiram."

"I ain't gonna *trust* him. I'm gonna *buy* him. You know how the hell it works."

Ed put his phone and the electrolarynx in the center console and started the Suburban. Whoever Myra called, they'd need to meet up with her. He left the park and wound down to Burnside, then headed west. Hiram sat quiet, only wincing when the street curved through Laurelhurst, and again when Big Ed slowed abruptly for a police car that appeared at a side street. The cop turned east after the Suburban passed.

"Ed, dammit, call that crazy bitch back. I can't sit here leaking half the day." Hiram's voice was more hiss than clear vocalization. He grabbed the cell phone from the console and tossed it into Ed's lap. Big Ed couldn't drive and talk on the phone at the same time, so he tossed the phone back, then stuck the larynx to his throat.

"I need to find the boy."

"Goddamn right you need to find the boy. But you need to get this hole in my leg dealt with too."

"She said she will call back."

"Today, you think?"

"I can always take you to a hospital."

"Now you think you're a comedian."

A cell phone chirped, the sound muffled.

"About fucking time she got back to—"

"It is your phone, Hiram. Not mine."

The chirp sounded again and Hiram awkwardly fished into his pocket. "Hello? … How did you—?" His abrupt silence drew Big Ed's attention. Hiram listened for a moment, then managed to smile through his pain. "Could be we can work something out. I'll be in touch. Don't do nothing stupid." He closed the phone.

"What is it? That could not have been Myra."

"It wasn't."

Big Ed continued down Burnside, waiting Hiram out. The old man was thinking, rarely a rapid process, if sound in the end. As they neared Myra's motel, a rattletrap hellhole called the Travel-Inn, Hiram whistled softly through his teeth.

"She called the house. You believe that? Rose gave her my cell."

"Who?"

"You know the fuck who." Now Hiram was grinning. "The kid's still out there somewhere. She doesn't have him. Now if you can do something right for once in your sorry excuse for a life, maybe we can turn this shit around and get what we came for."

Three Years, Three Months Before

Back Door

Edgar Gillespie.

A familiar name, if rarely used. Edgar, Eager, Edgar, Ed. Big Ed. Big Ed Gillespie, a name spoken in the same tone used to describe the little man who lived under the basement stairs and crept out at night to spirit away naughty children.

Eager inspected the driver's license. Expired, but he didn't know what to make of that. An address in a town called Westbank. The name seemed vaguely familiar to him, perhaps a place Charm had mentioned during one of her drunken lathers. Down south. But the license was worth only a moment's attention. The badge, now that was the thing. Charm had never said anything about his old man being a cop.

What was a cop doing chasing after the girl? What was his old man doing being a cop? Eager moved out of the parking lot onto the sidewalk, edged toward the coffee house. A brief squall swept through, wet his head and back. He didn't care. Too worried about what his old man, the cop, had in mind for the girl.

Hand on the throat, girl pinned against the fence. Cops could be assholes same as anyone. Rough bastards too, kick you twice when they didn't need to kick you at all. But that scene didn't look like a cop takedown, even a dirty cop takedown. No gear, no cuffs, no radio. No backup. Just muscles and threat.

Eager peered around the corner of Common Grounds through the front window. Big Ed stood at the counter, fists balled at his sides. A man faced him from across the counter, his long face grim. Eager knew him, the manager or something, old Asian guy. He sometimes let Eager hang out when it was raining, even if he had no money to buy a drink. A few customers shrinking into their chairs, mouths agape. Big Ed's shoulders shook as he confronted the fellow. His voice buzzed against the window pane. Eager didn't see the girl. Hiding in the back maybe. The manager looked like he was standing guard. What he'd do if Big Ed decided to go through him Eager couldn't guess. Get mushed.

Maybe Eager couldn't knock a side of beef the size of Big Ed windmilling into the street, but he knew every block between 39th and 60th, between Belmont and Division like he knew his own scarred knuckles. He'd skated every inch of pavement. Every buckled sidewalk, every cul-de-sac. He could help her get away.

In the girl's place, Eager would have skipped the coffee house. Joint like that, too easy to get pinned down. But if he was gonna hide in a shop, and if he did find himself pinned, he'd head for the back door. Here it was a side exit off the kitchen, which opened onto a narrow passage between the coffee house and the parking lot, wide enough for the garbage and recycling bins. At the back end of the passage, a tall cedar fence blocked the way. Far as anyone knew, the only way out was back onto Hawthorne.

He knew different.

He grabbed his board and moved down the passage. The door was metal with frosted-glass panes. As he reached for the door knob it turned and the door popped open. The girl stumbled out, Big Ed's voice chasing after her. She pulled up when she saw him.

He grinned, pleased to realize she thought like he did, and that fast too. "If you want, I'll help you get away."

She hesitated for only a second. "Please."

"Follow me."

He led her past the garbage bins to the end of the passage. The cedar fence was weathered and grey. Eager tugged at two of the overlapping vertical boards and they parted, creating a narrow opening. "It's a squeeze." She went first, and he followed, passing his skateboard through first. They found themselves in the back corner of a yard, a shaded pocket of quiet. The lawn was patched with moss, toys lay in careless heaps in the overgrown grass. Ivy wet with the morning rain draped over the fence.

"Is this okay?"

"Nobody's around in the daytime, mostly."

They followed a narrow concrete walkway alongside the house, picking their way past rusty gardening tools and an old fiberglass truck cap. At the corner of the front yard, the tall privacy fence gave way to rusty chain-link. The house looked east from the end of a short cul-de-sac. A couple of cars were parked in front of houses across the otherwise empty street.

"Come on."

He led her up the cul-de-sac to 44th, then turned north, away from the bustle of Hawthorne. Small single-story houses hugged the sidewalks as they weaved, right turn, left. Most blocks, cars parked up both sides of the street, leaving only a single lane for traffic. It didn't matter. There was no traffic. The girl followed close beside him, checking back over her shoulder again and again. Within a few blocks, he could tell she was lost, but that was okay. There was no sign of his old man. At last he stopped beneath a gnarled hawthorn tree growing out of the parking strip in front of a yard so overgrown they couldn't see the house beyond.

"I think we're okay now."

She leaned against the tree, rubbed her side. Not used to running, he figured. It took her a moment to catch her breath. "Thank you." She raised her head, put one hand to her face. He stared back at her, eye to eye. "What's your name?"

"Eager."

"That's an interesting name."

He shrugged. "Technically it's Edgar, but no one calls me that." *Edgar, Eager, Edgar, Ed.* Charm called him Eddie.

"It's nice to meet you, Eager."

Eager waited, but she didn't add anything more. He wanted to ask her own name, but he had a feeling she wouldn't tell him. If Big Ed had been chasing him, he wouldn't have told his name either. "What'd that dude want anyway?"

She lowered her head, grasped her upper arms with her hands. "I just needed to get away."

"Hey, I hear that. Sometimes you just gotta drop everything and go."

She looked at him sharply. He ducked his head. For a moment, he thought she might run off. He tried a smile. "He was pretty scary, wasn't he?" She blinked at him, then relaxed and offered a thin smile in return.

"Yes, he was."

He wondered if she knew his old man was a cop. Was that why he was chasing her? Had she done something, stolen something? Hurt someone? He wasn't sure how old she was; not too old though. Young and pretty. Her eyes were soft and brown, and a little sad. For a moment they pulled him in, but then he felt himself blush and he dropped his gaze. Fixed on the "FFA 2000" stitched over the breast on her dark blue jacket.

"It's from high school. I don't know why I still wear it."

"What's it mean?"

"Future Farmers of America." She shook her head. "My father made me join."

"You live on a farm?"

"Yes." She looked away, and her eyes grew troubled. "I used to."

"You live in Portland now?"

"I just got here."

"You want me to show you around?"

She seemed to think for a long time. He watched her look up the street, her eyes darting back and forth. Finally she turned back to him. "Do you know about a statue at the top of Tabor park?"

"Mount Tabor?"

"Yes, that's it. Do you know where it is?"

He pointed over his shoulder at the tree-clad hilltop visible between a pair of apartment buildings. "That's Mount Tabor."

She followed the line of his gesture. Her mouth dropped open. "I've been looking at it all morning." Her tone was bemused.

"There's like a grassy area at the top with trees, and a statue at one end."

"The Harvey Scott statue?"

"I don't know. I guess. I never looked at it much. Some old guy."

"You've been up there?"

"Sure. I take my board up there all the time. There's some killer turns coming down."

She looked up at the park. It wasn't far. He could take her up there, show her the way to the top. Maybe she'd want the company. He could be like a guide, and maybe she'd want to be friends. She couldn't be that much older than him, after all. His mom fucked men twenty years older than she was, so Eager could be friends with a girl who got out of high school a few years earlier. Weirder things happened.

But she had another idea. She gazed at the green Tabor crest, pulled at her lip. "That's where I'll find her." Voice a whisper, a breath shaped like words. "Right there in front of me all along." She lowered her hand, drew herself up. Her face relaxed.

"Thank you, Eager. I know the way now." She bent and kissed him lightly on the cheek, lips soft and warm. A scent hovered around her, a strange musk accented with tea. He felt the blood rush to his face, felt another stirring further down. But she didn't seem to notice. She smiled, then turned and walked away.

She left him under the hawthorn tree, his shoulders wet with rain and eyes alight with a fire freshly ignited. He watched her dwindle until all he could see was her dark hair framed in sunlight breaking through the clouds. He gripped his skateboard, knuckles white. A damp breeze tickled his neck. He headed for the fir green hill.

November 17

Stargazers Assaulted

OREGON CITY, OR: An unknown assailant assaulted a couple at the Haggart Observatory on the campus of Clackamas Community College early Saturday.

According to the couple, they were taking a break from stargazing in their pickup truck at about 2 a.m. when a man wearing a hood or scarf over his head approached the driver's side. The assailant dragged the two from the truck and proceeded to hit and kick them, though he stopped abruptly when both curled into protective positions. He stole a wallet, purse, cell phone and car keys, then fled toward Beavercreek Road.

Witnesses differ on the sequence of events, according to Clackamas County Sheriff's Deputy Elliot Forstenberg. Another stargazer at the observatory suggests the couple may have verbally antagonized the assailant before the assault.

The keys, cell phone, wallet and purse were later recovered from where the assailant apparently dropped them near the corner of Beavercreek Road and Trails End Highway about a quarter mile from the scene of the assault. Only cash was taken.

Balls to the Wall

Myra never did call. She stood smoking in the parking lot of the Travel-Inn as Big Ed pulled in. The motel behind her was two stories of cinder block and slumping composite siding. A reek of urine hung in the air. Big Ed didn't know how Myra could sleep in such a joint, but then enough crystal had gone up her nose she probably couldn't smell urine if you pissed on her head. She looked like she'd been run through a thresher, her face blotchy and gaze dead-eyed, her orange quilted coat tattered and greasy. She wasn't alone. A bald-headed brute in biker's leathers waited next to her, fingerless gloves on his hands, ears full of metal, braided beard down to his dick. He loomed over a Harley Super Glide, late model, polished and pearl black.

Hiram didn't wait for Big Ed to stop the Suburban before he threw the door open, grimaced as he swung his bloody leg out and rested his foot on the pavement. "You the guy can get my leg fixed up?"

The smooth head dipped half an inch. "If you got the cash, I am."

"Cash ain't the problem. Time is what I'm short of."

"Ain't far."

Big Ed didn't feel particularly protective of Hiram as a human being, but he was disinclined to leave his income source in the care of a stranger, particularly not some outlaw Myra had scared up. He lifted the larynx to say as much, but Hiram cut him off with the wave of a hand.

"What's your name, fella?"

"I go by George the Flea."

"Who do you ride with?"

The biker looked down at his chest, and for a moment Big Ed thought he needed to check to make sure. But all he did was point with his chin at the crest patch on his battered leather vest. SUB ROSA MOTORCYCLE CLUB. Red gothic lettering circled a rose growing from a tangle of barbed wire.

"Don't the Free Souls run Portland?"

"They can think what they want, don't make it so."

That yanked a sharp laugh out of Hiram. "Good enough. How you feel about driving me? My associate here has an errand to run."

"Ain't leaving my bike anywhere near this 'rat hole." He glanced around the lot, at the beater cars and broken glass.

"Fine, we'll follow you, but we gotta be quick." Hiram looked at Big Ed. "After we get to the doc's, I'm keeping the Suburban."

"You will not be able to drive."

"I expect George here can find someone to drive me"— he tilted his head the Flea's way — "since I got the cash."

The Flea seemed to think for a moment, then offered another terse nod. "Sure."

"What am I supposed to drive?"

"I don't give a shit. But you get caught nicking a car, I don't know you."

"You do not know this insect either."

He'd kept his voice low, speaking only to Hiram, but the Flea heard anyway. Leather-clad shoulders suddenly squared, hands balled into fists. "You wanna step out of the truck and repeat that, robot man?"

Fucking bikers, balls to the wall all the time. Big Ed fixed George the Flea with a cold glare and set the larynx in the center console, dropped his hands between his legs.

But Hiram stuck out both hands, one toward Big Ed and the other toward the Flea. "Boys, boys, we all got monster cocks, okay? No need to be whipping them out and scaring the women folk." The Flea's eyes bounced from Hiram to Big Ed, perhaps balancing the cash Hiram promised against the pleasure of cracking Big Ed's skull. Big Ed had no plans to let it come to that. He brushed the floor mat with his fingertips, feeling for the Desert Eagle.

"Dickheads." Quiet to this point, Myra drew hard on her cigarette and exhaled a brown fog. "Ain't seen a pecker yet scared me none."

The Flea's mouth fell open and for a moment no one moved. Then Hiram busted out laughing and Big Ed found himself fighting back a smile of his own. The Flea shook his head and looked at Myra, then relaxed. "Tell you what, I'll call a guy to come meet us here. That leg don't look like it needs to be dripping all goddamn morning." He pulled a cell phone out of his vest and dialed.

"Best damn idea I heard yet." Hiram leaned back in his seat, let out a breath. Big Ed could see the pulse in Hiram's temple. "Ed, whyn't you take Myra's car? The morning's getting away from all of us."

"Nobody's driving my car."

Hiram scowled. "I wasn't asking your opinion, Myra. You know what needs to be done."

Ed picked up the larynx. "Boss—"

"I ain't asking you either." Hiram's gaze was hard, half with threat, half with the pain he must be feeling. "Grab the bag for the kid out of the back."

Big Ed nodded and looked away. "Okay, boss." He was thinking about how Hiram had no reason to trust some goddamn outlaw biker, no matter that they'd shared a laugh. But he also knew Hiram couldn't be deflected once he fixed on a decision. Big Ed could do little more than wear his misgivings on his face as George the Flea rode out ahead of the Suburban, some nameless outlaw the Flea scared up behind the wheel, taking Hiram who the hell knew where. Hiram returned his gaze, way too comfortable for a man with a hole in his leg. But all he could do was set his mind to finding the boy as quickly as possible. Sooner he got their leverage back, the sooner he could get Hiram out of the hands of outlaws and they could beat feet back to Givern Valley.

Somewhere Beyond Corn

The leaves of Stuart's field corn hung limp from the stalks, battered by the late summer thunderstorm. Ellie felt the sharp-edged leaves drag at her shirt and rake the bare skin of her arms. She didn't slow down. The rain had already soaked her to the skin. The hard drops striking her head and neck hardly registered. Somewhere off to her left beams of light bounded and flashed as Hiram Spaneker's Suburban hurtled down the track that separated the corn from the barley. The track bottomed out at creek's edge and, aside from the railroad bridge a quarter mile downstream, there was nowhere to cross for miles in either direction. The stretch of Little Liver Creek along the farm's western edge presented a difficult crossing in daylight in any but the driest years, and it had been running swift and foam-blue this summer after a deep winter snowpack and late spring. Ellie's only hope was the bridge.

But Hiram and his man would head for the bridge too once they reached the stream, unless they pinned her down in the corn first. If they reached the creek ahead of her, they'd have no difficulty driving her away from the bridge. Then, even if they couldn't flush her from the corn, Hiram would have time to call in more men.

Her only choice would be to move back toward the house. But that way offered only a bottleneck and they knew it. The rocky hills rose too steeply north of the farm for her to climb in the dark and the rain, and were too exposed to the south. Sooner or later they'd find her.

But on the far side of the creek, the county road into Westbank crossed the Southern-Pacific tracks and then curled away toward town. Westbank itself would be risky, assuming she could get that far, but the county road was dotted with farmhouses. She'd find someone to hide her from Hiram Spaneker. Down inside, she knew she couldn't escape the consequences of Stuart and the scissors, not for long. But there were consequences, and there was Spaneker justice. The local Klamath County deputies and the town cops belonged to Hiram.

Her breath caught in her throat, but she refused to slow down. The tilled earth drank in the rain as fast as it fell and congealed under her feet as sticky mud. It was easiest to follow the plowed rows, but she knew her only hope of reaching the bridge before Hiram was to cut against the grain of Stuart's furrows, to push not just downslope but downstream.

She heard a loud bang, almost a popping sound, as sharp as a shotgun blast. The headlights suddenly vanished. She hesitated, her feet sinking into mud. The rain poured from the sky like water through a hose and for a moment she lost all sense of direction. A voice shouted, but she couldn't make out the words. Another voice answered and the headlights appeared again, now beaming at an angle into the dark sky. They'd got off the track somehow, back wheels in the ditch maybe, front wheels unable to grab the slick earth. The wind carried tones of accusation and defense. She fought the temptation to turn her back on her pursuers, to put distance between them and herself. That would only take her deeper into the corn. Instead she cast about, pushed down stalks, looked for a landmark, anything. But the darkness was too deep, the pouring rain too heavy. She rubbed the back of her hand across her face, smelled blood. Stuart's blood, or her own—no way to tell. She pushed through another row, then another until she came to an oval clearing of stunted corn. The view opened up in front of her. She hesitated, muddy soil sucking at her feet. The sky above was a dark, roiling grey, but she could see a dull, mustard glow on the horizon, a thin sliver of the lingering sunset breaking under the storm clouds. The glow provided a bearing to follow. The creek was west. The bridge was west, somewhere beyond the corn.

Go.

One of the voices called out again, joined by a grinding sound. She crossed the clearing and pushed back through tall corn. In an instant she lost sight of the horizon, but knew if she continued through the rows she'd reach the creek. Arms swinging ahead of her, she lifted one heavy leg then the other, again and again and again. At some point she noticed one foot felt colder than the other, realized she'd lost a shoe. It didn't matter. She kept moving, stumbling, a thousand green blades hacking at her, raking her face and arms. She tasted blood now. Then her other shoe caught in a tangle of roots and she sprawled face forward. Liquid mud filled her mouth and nose, her eyes. She tried to push herself up, but her hands skidded across the muck and she fell again. Momentum carried her forward, sliding, slipping, falling through slime and roots and the broken corn stalks. The rain swallowed her cries. Then the corn ended and for an instant it seemed as if the earth itself vanished. She felt herself floating in a dark space made of falling rain and noise. Her head struck something hard and all around her the rain shattered, a thousand shards of flashing glass. She came to rest abruptly on her back, legs twisted beneath her. Above, through the scintillations inside her eyeballs, she saw the storm clouds falling toward her from the bottom of a deep, black well.

A heavy weight seemed to press down on her chest, rain struck her face like needles. She tried to lift a hand, to flex a leg. Nothing. A cold shudder passed through her. Somewhere over her shoulder she heard the sound of rushing water, and a dense grassy aroma overwhelmed the smell of mud in her nose. She'd reached the creek.

Then she saw a flash of light, different from the splintered radiance inside her eyeballs. The Suburban. They'd gotten free of the ditch and reached the creek. The Suburban would come no further. A broken path followed the stream, twisted among boulders and hummocks of grass and sedge. A fisherman's path, slow going on foot, risky for horses. Impossible for the truck. She still had time, but they'd be here soon. Too soon, maybe. She had to get to her feet, had to find the bridge.

A voice called out, harsh, close enough now that she understood broken words and phrases. *"—ing bitch ... soaked through—"* She tried to breathe again, tried to move. Her muscles refused to respond. She blinked against the stinging rain, then closed her eyes. An image of Stuart's blind, staring face flashed in her mind, the scissors gleaming.

Lick it off—

"No!"

She twisted onto her side, teeth clenched against the pain in her ribs, and reached out, grasped a loop of tree root, maybe the fallen branch from one of the red alders that grew at creek's edge. She pulled herself onto her hands and knees. Lifted her head, looked out across the stream. The water rolled by, silver and shouting beneath the clouds. The flood moved so fast she couldn't see the rain striking the surface, just the swift, bucking foam. Behind her, the voice shouted again. She dragged her feet beneath her, tested her weight. Shaky, uncertain. But she found her footing. Her legs held.

"—can't be too far—"

She ran.

She couldn't feel her feet. Her only thought was to reach the bridge, to get across and find the road. Find safety. Yet even as she stumbled down the path, lungs burning and legs heavy as stones, she knew that hope was remote. Across the bridge she'd find the same wet darkness, the houses that might offer sanctuary scattered and distant. Maybe she'd reach help, or maybe Hiram would find her.

Lightning flashed ahead, the sharp flare silhouetting the looming railroad bridge. Close now. Stuart often came down to the bridge to cast for trout in the deep eddies the spring flow gouged under the piers. At other times, she would ride her horse along the railroad tracks and stop at the bridge to rest and watch the water flow underneath. She liked to sit at the end of one of the deck timbers, chin resting on her arms folded across the lower rail, feet dangling in the open air. A safe place, a comfortable place. Now, as she pushed up through the tall grass on the shore, the long support beams below the deck seemed too flimsy, too widely spaced, the steel trusses brittle and forbidding. But more dangerous still were the voices behind her.

"—think I hear—"

"—keep moving … see the bridge—"

She climbed the railroad embankment, dimly aware as the sharp gravel of the footing cut into her numb feet. She was glad for the darkness and rain, which would hide her bloody tracks, which might enable her to get across the creek unrevealed. But when she stepped onto the deck her foot slid and she caught herself. The rain pooled on the creosote-treated wood to produce a surface as slick as ice. She grasped the metal rail and took another step. She could see her feet, pale against the dark wood. The deck timbers, oversized railroad ties, were spaced too close together for a full step, too far apart to allow her to move at more than a slow, mincing pace. As she eased forward, the gravel embankment dropped away and she found herself over the creek itself. She kept both hands on the rail. Her feet throbbed against the wood, step by step.

"Don't be stupid there, girl. This is no night to be playing on this damn bridge."

She froze and looked back. He stood at the end of the bridge, a long, heavy flashlight in his hand. His man waited in shadow behind him on the gravel embankment. Hiram turned and handed off the flashlight, then stepped onto the bridge, moved toward her with slow, careful steps, hand on the rail.

"I know you're scared, Lizzie, but I want you to come back with me. Everything's gonna be all right."

"I'm not stupid." She took another step, then another.

"I don't know what you think's going on here, girl." He matched her, step for step, his free hand reaching toward her, palm up. "I just want to get you safe off this bridge and out of this weather. Then we can sort things out."

"I've done all my sorting."

She heard him laugh, a guttural chuckle with no humor in it, little louder than the sound of the rushing creek below. "That I guess you did."

"He deserved it! I don't care what you think, he deserved it."

"Let's not talk about this here."

Step. "I'm not sorry."

"I don't doubt it."

She wouldn't go back with him. Whatever happened to her, it wouldn't be at Hiram Spaneker's hands. She turned, hopped across two ties and slipped, caught herself on the railing. Her feet hung between the ties. Below, the water churned and leapt between the two bridge piers. She wrapped her arms around the rail and lifted first one foot, then the other, back onto timber.

"Lizzie, stop being crazy. Come on, let's go deal with this."

She couldn't see his eyes, but she didn't need to see his eyes to guess the thoughts behind them. She shook her head, took another step. The railing pressed into her damaged ribs.

"Nothing's so bad it can't be fixed."

A dead Spaneker can't be fixed. She felt behind her, grasped the railing with both hands. There was no running now. The bridge was too slick, the gaps between the timbers just enough to snap her leg if she made a single misstep. But Hiram faced the same problem. If she could get across, she might lose herself in the fields across the county road. She turned her back on Hiram and managed a couple of lunging steps.

And stopped.

A new face appeared out of the darkness, a figure crossing from the far side of the creek. Tall and broad, dressed in dark clothes, flashlight spraying back and forth across the bridge. The only clear detail she could make out was the John Deere cap. She sagged against the rail. Hiram had made a call, gotten someone else out there after all. The far side of the bridge might be crawling with his men. No sanctuary, nowhere to hide. She turned back to see Hiram within a dozen paces, hand still extended.

"Come on, damn it! I ain't jacking off here."

"I won't go back with you."

He grimaced, close enough to reveal the tobacco stains on his teeth when the beam of the flashlight from behind splashed across his face. "Keep that damned thing out of my eyes, you stupid son of a bitch."

Ellie looked back. The John Deere cap was closing in. As it drew nearer, the features below the bill resolved, shadowed eyes and grinning mouth. He took another step, and another, and then she knew who it was. Quentin Quinn, Stuart's once upon a time nemesis, a boy with nothing but contempt for the Spanekers, now a Spaneker man.

She threw her leg over the rail, let her body trail it over.

"Holy Christ!" She couldn't tell if it was Hiram or Quentin who'd shouted. She didn't care. She wasn't going back with them. She'd rather die than face whatever Hiram had planned for her, give herself up to the water below, slide into the dark emptiness of the racing creek. The water would be cold and swift. She wouldn't feel it, just sink into the deep, rolling flow and lose herself. Safer than any county road farmhouse. No need for scissors ever again.

"Stop this, Lizzie."

She allowed her legs to drop, hung from the wet steel rail by her hands. The rain battered her. Her strength seemed to drain from her hands with the rain into the stream below.

"Get me some rope or something." She knew Hiram wouldn't want to let her go, wouldn't want to lose his chance to make her pay for what she did to his son. "We can work this out, you goddamn idiot."

She smiled. She no longer felt any fear. Hiram Spaneker's face appeared over the edge of the bridge, his eyes screwed up and dark. He reached out. "Take my hand, you stupid bitch. Just take it."

She turned her head. She wanted to see the creek below her, wanted to watch it rise up to her as she fell. But she could only hear the water, a great rushing sound as soft as down. Somewhere far off to the west she saw the last glimmer of sunset, and above her the brown egg that was Hiram's head.

"Take my hand, goddammit!"

She let go.

November 19 — 8:30 am

Follow the Babysitter

Myra's car was a beat-to-fuck Eldorado built before Big Ed grew his first pube. The interior reeked of cigarettes. The radio was AM/FM-only, with twist knobs for Christ's sake. Myra carped about his driving, but Ed had no intention of sitting in the passenger seat while a keyed-up tweaker navigated Portland streets. Even if she managed to keep the car between the lines, any cop worth his salt would pull her over at a glance. He didn't need that shit.

"How long have you known that guy?"

"What guy?" Myra smoked as he drove, burning a quarter of her cigarette with each frantic drag. Big Ed opened his window, but that did little to clear the air.

"The insect."

"He doesn't like being called an insect."

"But he is okay with being called the Flea."

"That's different."

"I am wondering why Hiram was so quick to trust him."

"He's cool. Don't sweat it." She smirked through smoke. "Robot man."

The Caddy wanted to pull left; he decided to stop talking and put both hands on the wheel. He took the most direct route he knew back to the girl's place, retracing his path east on Burnside, then 60th south alongside the park. He intended to drive right into the neighborhood. They had no time to dick around. Big Ed didn't know kids, but he figured if it was old enough to talk, it was old enough to know what its house looked like. Neighbors might recognize the little bastard, or at least realize a piss dribbler that age had no business roaming the streets alone. Fact was, the kid could end up back home again any minute.

Right before the big park reservoir, traffic came to a dead halt. Big Ed saw a helicopter hovering low enough to make out the NewsChannel 8 logo. He tried skirting the jam by turning down some nameless side street, hit another backup within a couple of blocks. But he was close now. His fingers drummed the steering wheel as the cars crept forward, enough to allow him to turn onto the Bronstein's narrow street. He made it a couple more blocks and managed to get across Hawthorne before everything stopped for good. Ahead, a crowd had gathered. Dressed in everything from winter parkas to bathrobes, they stood indiscriminately in the street, on the sidewalks, on lawns below the chopper.

Big Ed killed the engine. Myra sat up and tossed her butt out the window. "Christ, there's cops everywhere."

Shit. He only mouthed the word, larynx still in his pouch. He palmed the keys and got out.

"Where the hell you going?"

Last thing he needed was a load of freak-out from Myra, but as he absorbed the scene before him he realized he could use her help. He leaned against the hood of the car and pressed the larynx to his throat. "We have to learn what is going on."

She popped open her door and stuck her head up, one foot on pavement, one inside the car. "Are you fucking crazy? No way we get the brat away from all those cops."

He closed his eyes and breathed. "They do not have him."

"What are you talking about? Of course they got him."

"No." He moved away from the car. "They do not."

She slammed her door and slinked after him. Alarm twisted her bony, acned face. He'd seen his share of tweaker paranoia, and he had no patience for it right now.

"I need you to pull your shit together."

"My shit is fine. You're the idiot about to walk into a jail cell."

"Myra—"

"How could they not have him?" She waved wildly down the street. "Cops are fucking everywhere—"

"If they had him, the street would be quiet."

She opened her mouth, but the retort died on her lips. She surveyed the street before them, the traffic, the gathered onlookers, the patrol cars. Slowly, understanding seeped into the desiccated meatloaf she used for a brain. "Oh."

"Yes. Oh."

"So where is he?"

"I do not know yet."

"What fucking good does that do us—"

"Myra, calm the fuck down."

"I'm fine."

"Good. Now I need you to go find out what is going on."

Now she shrank away from him. "I ain't going up there." Her hands slapped an arrhythmic beat against her thighs.

"It has to be you. You can blend in." Of that, he was uncertain, but he knew he would stand out like spotlight in a mine shaft. "I cannot." People always noticed the man who talked with a machine.

"I ain't talking to no police."

Big Ed massaged the bridge of his nose, larynx tucked in his palm. He wondered where Hiram was, if George the Flea was taking care of him or robbing him blind and leaving his body in a Dumpster.

"Of course you will not speak to the police." Even a probie would recognize a raging meth addict. "Just join the crowd up there. There will be talk, and lots of rumors. I need you to listen."

"I don't know …"

"Myra, it has to be you. Walk up there and see what you can find out. You may not have to even talk to anyone if you keep your ears open."

"What are you gonna do?"

"Wait for you, and try to figure out how we find the boy."

Her lips pulled back from her yellow teeth and she folded her arms across her chest. He could tell she was retreating into herself. No idea how long it had been since she last used, but he could see the incipient signs of withdrawal. Her eyes darted from side to side from inside deep hollows, evidence of an oncoming crash if she didn't get fixed soon. The paranoia was a bonus.

"Myra. Think of the money. You can swim in crystal once we are finished."

She threw him a dark look and pulled her tatty quilted coat tight around herself, moved hesitantly up the street. Big Ed watched until she neared the crowd. Then he got back into the car. People would be less likely to give him a second look if he was just a guy stuck in the traffic jam, same as anyone else.

More police arrived on the scene. He had to start the car and edge to the side to allow a couple of patrol cars past. Cops set up barricades, pushed onlookers back. Suits gathered in clusters, uniformed brass in the mix. All very stern. Something big was going on, something that wasn't a missing boy. He found himself entertaining his own paranoid uncertainty. What if it wasn't about the kid? What if it was about a pair of pre-dawn home invaders? If so, sitting landlocked in a Caddy a block or two away from the crime scene was the last place he wanted to be.

But that didn't fit. It had been a long time since he'd served, and even longer since Hiram put him through the state police academy at Monmouth. He'd forgotten more than he could remember, and hadn't been a strong student to begin with. Still, he knew you didn't stage a manhunt in a residential neighborhood by throwing up barricades at a half-block radius and then sitting tight.

He fidgeted. The crowd never stopped moving, interrupting his line-of-sight again and again. Myra could be anywhere. Mighta given up on the whole endeavor and ran off. Or, hell, she could even be in custody. He ran his hands over his head, flexed his fists. Breathed through his mouth to minimize the effect of Myra's stench on his sinuses. It was a mistake, he decided, to send her. As the minutes ticked by, he grew increasingly convinced he should have scouted himself, taken a chance on making an impression. Hiram wondered aloud more than once why he wouldn't at least give a goddamn turtleneck a try. Sure as hell woulda come in handy now. Even without something to cover his neck, if he didn't try to speak to anyone, all he'd be was a guy with some scars on his neck. With everything else going on, no one would pay attention to him. But it was too late. Myra was up there, doing who knew the fuck what. To distract himself, he flipped on the radio and spun the tuner until he found a local talk station.

Caught a news report in progress.

Police in a stand-off near Mount Tabor ... a man holed up in his house with one or more guns ... Portland Police SERT team is at the scene ... negotiators attempting to defuse a tense situation.

He stared at the radio, willing it to give up more information. The man's name, was it Bronstein maybe?

"Police haven't released the name or names of persons involved."

Christ. Had to be them.

He leaned forward, rested his forehead against the steering wheel. Myra's speakers were shot. The news sounded like it was being broadcast from the distant past. He heard sudden pops and crackles, or was that from outside? He couldn't tell.

Onlookers gathered behind the barricades ... command unit

established at the scene. They broke away for weather and traffic, commercials, then back again. *Some indication the negotiator is making progress.* When he looked up again, Myra was returning, strolling casually down the middle of the street.

He jumped out of the car. "What the hell did you find out?"

"Lookie who's got his panties in a bunch."

"Just tell me."

Her grin revealed missing molars on both sides of her mouth.

"Myra, damn it—"

"Fine, fine." She laughed and pointed up the street. "See that guy talking to the woman cop?"

"Lower your arm."

"Jesus." She snapped her hand back to her side. "Do you see him or not?"

Big Ed looked. An older man stood talking to a female officer, a woman of rank if the silver on her collar was any indication. The man had grey, uncombed hair, wore jeans and a sweatshirt. Unremarkable at this distance, though Ed thought there was something about his neck, a bruise perhaps. He stroked his own scar tissue. He felt himself calming down again.

"What about him?"

"He's the kid's babysitter."

"What do you mean?"

"Don't you know what a babysitter is? Christ, Ed."

"I know what a babysitter is. I just—"

"Yeah, it is weird. Some random old puke in charge of a little kid." Myra licked her lips, didn't seem to care for the taste. "I guess he's the neighbor across the street. Someone was saying he watches the kid a lot."

"Did they say where the boy is?"

"With Grandpa." Myra laughed, gleeful. "You hear that? With fucking Grandpa."

"Interesting."

"Your robot tube took the word right outa my mouth."

Ed nodded, indifferent to her swipe. If they were saying the boy was with his grandfather, it meant they didn't know Hiram no longer had the boy. It also meant they weren't sending up an alarm. The Bronsteins wanted to keep the morning's events quiet, whatever was going on now. That could work in his favor, if he could only find the boy before the cops did.

"What about the man in the house? The one in the standoff. Is it Bronstein?"

"Fuck if I know. They shot him, whoever it was." She pulled out her smokes, lipped one from the pack. "I thought you only cared about the kid."

He rolled his eyes, but he knew he should be grateful for whatever he got out of Myra. And if they did shoot Bronstein, that could only help the plan. "You're right. The boy is the focus."

"So you got a plan, or what?"

He gazed at the grey-haired man. "We need to get out of this traffic."

"Okay. We get outa traffic. Then what?"

The woman cop moved away, leaving the old guy alone in the street. Big Ed watched as he thrust his hands in his pockets, shoulders hunched. The man was anxious. And able to get the ear of a senior officer in the middle of a crisis. Ex-cop, Big Ed was betting. A man who knew how to look for what was lost.

"Ed? A plan?"

"We follow the babysitter."

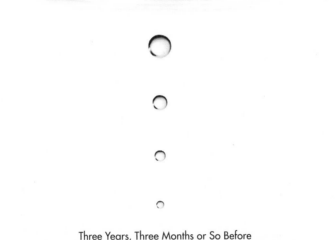

A Long Way From Long Gone

Ellie awoke to the sound of water flowing over rocks. She lay on her side beneath a white sheet. From her pillow, she could see out a tall, open window onto a silver rolling creek rimmed with rust, the flowing water a dozen feet away. A sheer white curtain obscured then revealed the view, inflated by a breeze that smelled of metal and cut grass.

She turned onto her back. The room was small, with faded lemon wallpaper and dark woodwork. A chest of drawers stood against the opposite wall next to the door, and a tall wooden chair sat below a second window. The door was open, and from elsewhere in the house she could hear the sound of movement, a rattle of tools or utensils.

"Hello? Is anyone there?"

Footsteps tapped her way. After a moment, a tall, stooped older man appeared at the door. Klamath, she guessed, but with deep blue eyes that regarded her from within a face the color of old leather. "It's good to see you awake. How are you feeling?" His voice sounded calm yet rough, as if tempered by years of filterless cigarettes. He seemed unashamed by her naked body under the sheet. She folded her arms across her breasts. Maybe he had a wife, a daughter, someone else who'd put her into bed.

"Okay. My head hurts." She felt a throbbing ache in her ribs as well, heat in her ankles, a siege of scrapes and scratches all over.

"You probably want your clothes. I washed everything and hung it outside. Should be dry by now." He paused. "I couldn't find your shoes, I'm afraid."

An image of pounding rain like falling stones flashed behind her eyes. "It's okay." She ran a trembling hand over her face and tried to push the memory of the cornfield out of her mind. When she looked up again, his blue eyes were still fixed on her.

"You were something of a mess, soaked through and muddy. Bleeding too, from that cut on your head." He dropped his gaze. "I couldn't leave you in those wet clothes."

"Thank you." Her cracked lips hurt when she spoke.

"You're Immanuel Kern's older girl."

She flinched at his recognition, but he offered her a reassuring smile. Aside from crow's feet, the skin of his face was smooth. Salt-and-pepper hair clung to his knobby scalp. His eyes seemed to almost glow against his dark skin. She'd seen him around the valley. "I should know you."

"Name's Pastor Sanders."

"Oh."

"I used to work for the senior Spaneker, back before Hiram took over and decided he ought to be the center of everything. These days I take care of my own acreage and pick up odd jobs when I can." He slipped into the room and sat on the tall chair. "Word from Hiram is you ran off to Arizona and left his boy heartbroken and locked away in your house."

She drew a sharp breath and looked through the window at a fringe of aspens on the far shore of the creek. "You talked to Hiram?"

"Not me. Couldn't help but hear him going on at the Cup 'n' Saucer yesterday morning." The Cup served as the gravitational center for valley men who'd spent their lives with their hands in the dirt. As one of the few lingering independent farmers, Hiram took every opportunity to stop by the diner and hold forth. "He said you run off with another man. You're supposed to be long gone."

"That's crazy."

"Not as crazy finding you half-drowned in the creek." He tilted his head. "You get lost on your way to Arizona?"

She lowered her head mournfully. Lost was as a good a word as any for a woman who'd killed the scion of the Givern Valley Spanekers.

"How long have I been here?"

"I found you last night on my way back from town. Lucky thing too. Usually I take route 44, but I came back on the county road last night so I could check on my hay. I saw you half in-and-out of the water, maybe a quarter mile downstream from the railroad bridge. At first I thought you were dead."

"When was the storm? The night before last?"

"Yeah, that would be right."

Her eyes returned to the window. The sound of the stream might have comforted a previous Ellie. No more. She didn't know whether to feel blessed or cursed. "Why am I here?" Westbank had no hospital, but the urgent care clinic would have been adequate for her injuries. She felt like she could walk, if gingerly.

He hesitated before answering. "The way Hiram was going on at the Cup, didn't seem prudent to reach out to the Spanekers. After I got you back here, I went to see your daddy. He asked me to look after you."

The view through the window went silvery and soft. Tears dripped onto her cheeks. Outside, the aspens fluttered through diffuse, watercolor light and the creek flowed, a quiet murmur of water over stone. The breeze breathed through the curtains; the air seemed to expand around her. "Miss? Miss, you okay?" Pastor Sanders voice mingled with the sound of flowing water. "Don't you worry. You're safe, I promise." She blinked, and her vision fell through mist into sapphire. A moment later, she found her voice.

"Why aren't I with my father?"

"He said you'd be safer here. Seems to me you would be in a better position to understand why than me."

She thought of the scissors gleaming orange in the sunset and acid rose in her throat. Pastor Sanders had given no indication he knew what had happened, though he guessed its gravity. But what about her father? Did he know about the scissors? He wanted to hide her, but was he aware of the act that had driven her off the railroad bridge in the storm? She hated to think he might know what she'd done, no matter the reason. And what of this man to whom he'd entrusted her? Her mother had always been the more pious of her parents, but did her father find assurance in the pastor's vocation? If so, it was a faith Ellie didn't share. Reverend Wilburn would have felt her up before turning her over to Hiram.

"So what kind of preacher are you anyway?"

He smiled. "Oh, I'm no preacher. Pastor is my name ... after my daddy."

"Your father's name was Pastor?"

"No, that was his job. Pastor Meeks, of the Little Liver Creek Methodist Church. A white man, though you might not guess it to look at me."

Except for his eyes. "You weren't named in honor of him."

"In honor? No, not exactly." He chuckled. "I think Pastor Meeks figured he had nothing to worry about from some Injun girl, but my mama was someone you crossed at your peril."

"Must have made for interesting Sundays."

"It might have, but Indians didn't attend Little Liver Methodist. We had our own church, so my father didn't have to fret me in the pews Sunday mornings." He waved his hand. "All ancient history. The important thing now is for you to understand you're safe here."

She felt her breath catch in her throat, but after a moment her tension seemed to drain away. Pastor seemed to sense her sudden need to sleep. He smiled and slipped away.

Later, when he brought Ellie's clothes, washed and folded, Pastor Sanders included a set of men's pajamas. "I'm sorry I don't have anything else. Your father is going to collect some things for you, but he wants me to be careful about meeting with him. Doesn't want to draw attention."

"These are fine. Thank you." The pajamas smelled of grass from hanging on the line outside. Most of the time she slept, or gazed out her window at the creek and the aspens on the far bank. Unlike everyone else she knew, Pastor had no television or satellite dish. He didn't even have a phone. The long August days passed by with the breathless expectancy of a ticking clock. Sunlight pressed down on the flowing water and surrounding barley fields like a hot blanket. During trips to the bathroom, she avoided the mirror, afraid to see the damage her fall from the bridge had done. The stiff ache in her ribs and neck told her enough. Each morning, almost as if he could hear her thoughts, Pastor assured her the bruises were fading. During the days, he left her alone with her thoughts while he ventured out to tend to his own chores or work for other valley farmers, returning each evening with the lengthening shadows.

By the third evening she started to feel restless. She dressed and joined him on the back porch, where they sat in a pair of handmade rocking chairs and watched the brown-edged creek flow down valley toward the setting sun. Every so often, Pastor Sanders would refill their iced tea glasses, the only interruption to their companionable silence. Ellie listened to birdsong from the pasture above the yard, to the quiet sounds inside her own body. After days with nothing required of her but rest, she felt she could almost hear her damaged tissues knitting together again. But within her healing flesh lingered a pain she knew would not be cured in a few short days, no matter how comfortable her room or hospitable her caretaker.

As the sun dropped lower, the fields around them awoke with the chirping of crickets. A spider worked under the porch eave, its growing web gleaming in the orange light. Ellie saw the flicker of bats over the aspens, and heard a splash as a trout jumped in the stream.

"Your father wants me to meet him tomorrow to give me your things."

"Can I come? I want to see him."

"He doesn't think it's a good idea. If anyone sees me and him together, we can say it's about work, but you—well, it's too risky."

She sighed. She felt so alone, yet that was nothing new. Even before Luellen left, she'd been alone. But it was a strange and crowded isolation. Someone was always watching over her, making sure she didn't cross unseen and often shifting boundaries. Her mother, Pastor Wilburn, Stuart. They sought to shape her into docile, daunted Lizzie, yet she remained Dark Ellie. She gazed across the rickety porch at Pastor Sanders, rocking gently in his chair, glass of tea in his hands. His eyes were as deep and bold as the waters under the railroad bridge.

"You've done so much already."

"I've done no more than any good Christian would do."

"A lot more than most."

"Not for me to judge." He smiled a comforting, grandfatherly smile. "I'm just glad you're feeling better."

She spent the next day pacing from room to room. Through the windows she looked first out upon Pastor's barley field, then the rising hills, then the creek—and back again. At points during the day she felt certain Hiram would be waiting when Pastor met with her father, would follow him back to her. As the afternoon wore at last into early evening, she found herself staring down the long gravel driveway, her ribs aching and her breath tight in her throat. At last she saw a dust plume rise, and a short time later Pastor's old green pickup drove into view.

He carried a jacket draped over one arm and a small black duffel bag in his hand. Inside were a couple changes of underwear, socks, a bra, a pair of jeans and a shirt, as well as her old sneakers. She blushed at the thought of her father going through her underwear drawer, but felt even more troubled by him in her house at all. Did he see the blood on the kitchen floor? Could he tell what had happened?

Pastor offered her the jacket. Dark blue, with Givern Valley Future Farmers of America stitched across the back.

"Your daddy said Stuart wasn't home." He looked into her eyes. "Maybe Hiram was confused about which of you was long gone."

Was she holding her breath? "He's a long way from long gone."

He led her into the kitchen. She helped him mix a salad and make a couple of sandwiches from leftover meatloaf. They carried the food out to the porch, hoping to catch an evening breeze. Ellie sipped her iced tea, chewed listlessly on her sandwich.

Pastor watched her, his expression solemn.

"Your daddy said Stuart was rough on you, not a proper man. He told me you lost your baby at Stuart's hand."

Ellie's vision went dark and she pressed her hand against her stomach. A moment later, she found herself vomiting over the porch rail. Meatloaf and half-chewed lettuce spilled into the impatiens below. She'd eaten little, and her stomach emptied quickly. "I'm sorry ..." Dry heaves continued to wrack her. "I'm sorry ..." Pastor placed a gentle hand on her back and *shhh'd* quietly. "S'okay. Let it out."

After a few minutes, the contractions subsided and she dropped back into her chair. Pastor brought her a damp washcloth and a glass of water. "Don't drink a lot at first. Just clear the taste from your mouth."

She smiled gratefully and wiped her face. When he took the cloth, she sat back with her eyes closed. A stitch pulsed in her side, but she tried to focus on the creek and the chorus of crickets instead. After a time, her breath returned and her stomach settled enough to speak.

"So important, what you have in your hand."

Ellie looked at the water glass, an old jelly jar. "I don't understand."

"Come and see." He stood and put his hands on the porch railing. After a moment, she joined him. Her stomach still felt loose, but she was steady on her feet. He gestured across the narrow patch of yard to the barley field beyond. The stalks stood almost waist high, a sea of rolling green breaking against the foothills a quarter mile distant. Pastor then pointed back across the creek. There, the terrain was more open and flat, with patches of tall grass and reeds among shallows that stretched across the valley. She knew the far edge of the marshland backed up on her father's fields, and much of it, in fact, had been in Kern hands for generations.

"I don't have a lot, but my barley crop is enough each year to carry me through till spring when work picks up again. I don't own any of the wetlands, but I have good water even in dry years. It helps that I back up on the hills."

Ellie couldn't count the number of times she'd gazed across her own family's land toward these same hills. In the fall her father and brothers would hunt ducks in the marsh. In summer they'd flush chukars and pheasant. Ellie's father tried to include her, but her mother disapproved of such notions. Left to herself, she settled for solitary hikes through the wetlands to see the yellow rails in migration, and sometimes even sandhill cranes.

"It's beautiful."

"It's what Hiram wants."

"For the water."

"Yes, for the water."

She blew air up through her dark bangs. "Why are you telling me this?"

The old man turned and got his tea glass, drank, and shook the melting ice that remained. "Your brother died up to Chiloquin, didn't he?"

She nodded slowly. "Yeah. Rob. He got involved in a fight or something at the casino up there. We never got the whole story."

"And then your other brother—"

"Brett died in Iraq. He joined the Marines after he lost his farm."

"I understand your father tried to buy back the land when it went to auction."

"He didn't have enough cash on hand, and he couldn't swing a loan."

"I imagine it didn't help that Hiram Spaneker was standing there with a cashier's check."

Ellie had no response to that.

"That leaves you and your sister to inherit the Kern land when your father finally passes."

"No one knows where Myra is." There'd been talk of Myra riding, bony and hag dry, with bikers out of Redding, or up in Medford. Even as far off as Yakima.

"Which leaves you sole heir to the best water in Givern Valley, even discounting Brett's parcel already peeled off through bank auction."

"Hiram thinks he can get the land from me? After everything that's happened?"

"Not from you. Stuart."

"But Stuart is—"

Pastor raised his hand. "Right now, Stuart is whatever Hiram says he is. Hiram's interests are better served by you alive and wed to his boy than dead or in jail. Even if he does own half the valley, the last thing he wants is to take a chance your father will hire some smart defense lawyer outa K-Falls or Eugene, or hell, even Portland."

"My father would never hire someone from Portland." But she was thinking of her choices. Go to the police and face up to what she did. Or turn herself over to Hiram. Maybe he wouldn't kill her, but he could make her wish she was dead. And someday, when her father passed and she inherited the land, what then? How long would Hiram hide Stuart's death, if he thought doing so might give him title to the best water in Givern Valley? It would have been better to die in the swollen creek than to fall into his hands.

"What can I do?"

Now Pastor leaned forward. When he spoke, his voice was low, conspiratorial. "You've got to outthink him."

"I don't know how to do that."

"Of course you do. Your daddy told me you're a smart girl."

"How could he say that after everything I've done? This mess—"

Pastor drew himself up. "A woman is entitled to protect herself." His voice snapped like a leather strap and Ellie drew a sharp breath at the sound. But then his eyes softened again. "Now you listen to me. Your daddy says you're to use Hiram's scheming against him."

She let out her breath and ran her hands through her hair. It felt greasy on her fingers. The sensation reminded her of the infection between her legs, of the medicine left behind. She wondered when she would get the chance to see another doctor.

"Your father sent money with your clothes. It's in the zipper pocket inside your coat. It's not much, but it'll get you started."

She'd never been on her own. Her stomach clenched and she felt like she would throw up again. Pastor Sanders reached over and took her hands in his own. She flinched at the touch, but he held on.

"Listen to me." Her eyes filled with tears. "You made a decision the other night, and no one is blaming you. But now you got to see it through. Hiram thinks you'll go to ground, try to hide in familiar haunts. So slip away instead. Go quiet. Then in a month or two, once you're safe, call your father. He's preparing something for you, and he says it will be ready by then."

"Call him?" Her last, tenuous tie to the valley was dissolving. "From where?" Even her father no longer saw a place for her here.

"Wherever you are. Call him when it's safe."

She looked at him sharply. Luellen's words … *when it's safe.* But suddenly Ellie knew what path she might follow. Luellen had led the way, another young woman who fled Givern Valley. Ellie would travel north to Portland and find her old friend.

Pastor Sanders seemed to sense her new resolve. She met his deep eyes and felt a moment of solace. "Okay. I will go."

They drove to Klamath Falls the next afternoon, forty miles down the state road. Their first stop was the Greyhound station. Pastor waited while she bought her ticket, north to find Luellen. From there, who knew? She also bought a card at the newsstand. She wrote Luellen a short note to let her know she was on her way and mailed it in the station.

It was too late for that day's bus to Medford, where she would make the Portland connection. She'd have to go the next morning. Back in the pickup, Pastor drove to a nearby motel. She told him he didn't have to stay with her, but he insisted it was no trouble.

"It'll be a comfort to your daddy to know I've seen you off."

"I don't know how to thank you."

"Stay safe. That's thanks enough."

Once they were settled in their room, Pastor went out to get them some supper. He didn't think it was a good idea for her to be seen in public, as unlikely as it was she'd be recognized this far from Givern. She tried to watch television while she waited, but nothing could distract her. She found herself going to the window again and again, looking out at the parking lot and the street beyond. The sound of the television was shapeless buzz in her ears. Pastor did not return.

Ellie slept poorly, fled the motel early. Though she knew the safest course was to remain in her room until time to catch the bus mid-morning, a boxed-in feeling drove her out. For a while, she walked the empty streets, duffel bag clutched to her chest. There was no sign of Pastor's pickup. She thought about calling her father, but didn't, afraid of who might be listening. After a while she found herself in a bagel shop. She tried to eat, but the food was dry and flavorless; the coffee tasted like ash. She eyed every customer who came through the door, recognized none of them. When an older man with a blue gaze strikingly similar to Pastor's caught her eye she fled the shop. No one followed, near as she could tell. Two hours later, the bus carried her away.

Three Years, Three Months Before

Body Of Elderly Klamath Man Found By State Trooper

BONANZA, OR: An Oregon State Police trooper discovered the body of an elderly man last night in a ditch off W. Langell Valley Road three miles south of Bonanza, according to a state police spokesman. The Klamath County Sheriff's Department was called in to investigate the death.

The victim was identified as Pastor Sanders of Westbank, Oregon. A pickup truck registered to Mister Sanders was also found nearby.

Sgt. Joanne Ellison, a spokeswoman for the Klamath County Sheriff's Department, said the death is being treated as "suspicious in nature," but would provide no further details, pending an investigation.

PART THREE

NOR SET DOWN AUGHT IN MALICE: THEN MUST YOU SPEAK
OF ONE THAT LOVED NOT WISELY BUT TOO WELL

—Othello, Act 5, Scene 2

No One You Want to Fuck With

My front door is locked, something I forget to do more often than not. Susan would have ensured her team took care of such details when they pulled out. They had no way of knowing I'd left my keys in the little drawer of the mail stand next to the front door. I look through the front window from the porch. Everything is neat and tidy, table tops clear, chairs in place, all more orderly than when the cops appeared this morning. Susan would have seen to that too.

I stick my hands in my pockets and turn, stare out at nothing. The street is now quiet, the only sign of the morning's chaos the trampled patch of grass in front of the Bronstein house and the yellow warning tape crisscrossing the porch. A year or so back, Luellen and I traded keys, though I took some convincing. She thought it would be nice if we could look after things for each other, feed the cat and bring in the mail while the other was away. Not that I ever go away, but a spare key with the neighbor would serve as a hedge against moments like this. I guess we didn't anticipate her husband facing off against SERT. I breathe, try to ignore the tightness in my belly. After a moment, I make for the side gate. I can usually pop the spring lock on the back door, assuming I didn't engage the deadbolt.

I'm not a pride-and-joy kind of person, but if I were, the back yard would be mine. The plants are mostly northwest native, climate zone appropriate and selected to attract local birds. With the help of Ruby Jane and Pete I designed the space to have a natural quality, soft-edged and shaggy, full of color in the spring and summer and dark evergreen during the rainy season. The deck is large enough for me and a guest or three when the weather cooperates and my mood is tolerant of invasion. Not a big yard, private and suited to my temperament.

A lot of the birders I know live for the unusual sighting, for the chance to add a check mark to their book. I'm content to sit on the deck and watch the finches work the nyjer thistle feeders or listen to the sparrows bicker over the millet. This late in the year only a few stragglers linger. With the cold now pushing west from the Columbia Gorge, the juncos will soon arrive from the hills, which means the arguments will move from the feeders hanging from the arbor at the back of the yard to those on the ground. By then, I'll settle for watching through the kitchen window. I may possess an Oregonian's inbred tolerance for rain and chill, but even I have my limits.

As I climb up onto the deck, I can still make out the shadow of a blood stain in the wood, evidence of a past act of violence I was lucky enough to miss. Been meaning to get the deck sanded and resealed for almost a year and a half—focused and on task I'm not. I head for the back door, stop when I hear a quiet burble behind me, a soft coo like a pigeon. I turn and see him standing in the ivy at the back of the yard, half among the branches of the maple tree that hang over the fence from the yard next door. He's peering up into the tree, though I can't tell what he's looking for. Danny Bronstein.

"Hey there, little fellow."

He glances my way, but I'm not nearly as interesting as whatever's up in the tree. I jump off the deck, walk over and crouch next to him. He's wearing a Big Bird pajama top and a pair of blue overalls, both damp. He must have been caught out in the rain earlier. At least he's wearing shoes. The afternoon temperature is hovering around sixty, unusual but not unheard of this deep into November. He's not acting as though he's cold.

"You doing okay, Danny?" I still can't tell what he's fixated on in the branches overhead.

"Mister Skin." His voice is a whisper. No surprise there. At his most raucous, Danny is a quiet child.

"What are you doing here, little fellow? Where's your grandpa?"

His expression is blank. I can't tell if he's afraid or at ease. I don't know how he got here. Luellen has brought him over dozens of times. He knows my backyard almost as well as he knows his own. He's helped me fill the feeders and pointed with delight when a flock of bush tits sweeps through. But I can't remember him coming back here on his own. I don't think he's ever crossed the street without his mother.

"Did your grandpa leave you here?"

In response, he looks at me through round, moist eyes, then turns and points at the arbor. "Feed the birds." The hanging feeders are less than half full, and this time of year they don't need replenishment often. But Danny isn't concerned with the details of urban migratory patterns. He wants to pour the seed into the cylindrical feeders. He continues to point until I smile. "Sure, we can feed the birds, but then I think we need to get you to your mommy. Okay?"

"Mommy isn't here."

"We'll find her, little guy." Like I have a clue. But I can make a call, and until Susan tracks Luellen down, she'll keep Danny safe.

He heads across the yard for the garage door. He knows where I keep the seed. I follow and push the door open. Together we fill the feed scoop with black oil sunflower seeds. I let him carry it.

When I step back out into the daylight, I see a figure on my deck, a man. He's tall and broad and crew cut. His brown, leathery face suggests a lot of time out in the sun. He's got one hand stuck in his pocket, the other tucked up under his chin—an odd, strangled gesture. His dark coat is a little heavier than the cool afternoon demands, and his eyes squint against the grey-white dazzle scattered by the thin overcast. I feel Danny press the feed scoop against the back of my leg as he looks up at the big man from behind me.

"Who the hell are you?"

The man's jaw pulses. "No one you want to fuck with." His voice has a mechanical quality, almost metallic. "Bring the boy. We are leaving."

I push back half a pace. "I don't think so."

"Do not argue with me." He lifts his pocketed hand without pulling it free of his coat. For a moment, the image is almost comical, a slapstick robber pretending his finger is a gun. But his face remains hard and cold, draining any humor from the situation. Suddenly I realize why his voice sounds so strange—why he keeps one hand pressed to his throat. He's using an artificial voice box. I can make out the black, cylindrical device between his fingers.

"What do you want?"

"I want you to not give me a reason to take my hand out of my pocket."

A cold, liquid sensation percolates through me. "You realize there are cops all over the place. A team is right across—"

"Shut up." I can see in the weight of his eyelids he knows the lie for what it is. He draws a heavy breath. "I got no time for bullshit."

"Maybe we can talk about this."

"There is nothing to talk about. I will take your phone and any weapon." He lowers the electrolarynx. If I'm going to try something, now is the time. But I realize just as quickly I won't, not with even the chance of a gun in his pocket. Not with Danny here.

He knows it too.

I retrieve my cell phone. "I'm not armed." He lowers his hand and takes my phone, drops it on the deck and crushes it beneath his boot heel. I look down at the cracked plastic and glass, thinking Ruby Jane would say this is my big chance to get the iPhone she's always wanted. The big man pats me down, one-handed.

Danny doesn't take his eyes from the man's hand, seems fascinated by the electronic voice. I'm not fascinated. I once knew a cop who used a voice box after he lost his larynx to cancer. Lifetime smoker, like me. His cancer found his esophagus; mine settled in my bladder. Guess I'm the lucky one, though I'm not feeling too lucky right now. The big man's throat is a tangle of scar tissue. His jaw seems slightly askew, as if broken and poorly set. It's no stretch to realize the injury occurred under circumstances that precluded professional medical care.

He raises the device back to his throat. "We will go out through the gate, walking slowly, two men and a boy. No big deal. You get in the Cadillac out front without a fuss, maybe you live through the day."

"Listen, friend—"

"I am not your friend."

A knife's edge of fear slashes through my belly. I run the odds, and they're not good. My neighbors are all gone, those who don't work having cleared out once the morning's excitement boiled down to mere procedural tedium. No news vans, no helicopters buzzing overhead. And now the cops have left too, which means it's just me standing between Luellen's little boy and this armed mountain of flesh and scar tissue.

He catches my eye, his expression almost thoughtful. "Whatever you are thinking, I am here to tell you, do not try it. If you fuck with me, I will rain hell down on you."

The atonal quality of his mechanical voice only adds to the awful dread hanging in the still air between us. I take the feed scoop from Danny and set it on the deck, then grab his hand and lead him around the corner of the house to the gate. The man follows, enough steps behind to ensure he'll have time to react if I try anything. Not that he has anything to worry about. I'm about fifteen years past trying anything.

Danny and I go through the gate, stop when he tells us to hold up. He takes a quick look around, seems content with what he sees. The one hand remains in his coat pocket. He gestures with his chin and I continue to my empty front yard. No cops, no earnest staring onlookers. There's a frightful calm in the air. Nothing moves now, but it's hard to forget that just a few hours earlier bullets were flying. Mitch's dried blood stands out, stark against the lemon paint on the wall next to his front door. I wonder if Jase will have to scrub it off.

The man points to a battered, land yacht-era Fleetwood of indeterminate color parked across the driveway of the house next door. Any other day my neighbor, a graphic designer with a home office and a deep commitment to his own entitlement, would have been all over it, making phone calls and pitching a public fit.

"Why do you want the boy?"

"Buckle him in the back, then get in next to him." I hesitate. "Do not give me a reason to kill you. It would be too much hassle to deal with your body. But if you cause trouble I might change my mind."

There's a woman in the front seat of the Cadillac, passenger side. She draws hard on a cigarette, then tosses the butt out through her open window. Even when I still smoked I didn't tolerate butts on my walk, but I don't get the impression she'll give a damn about my feelings on the matter. She's sitting hunkered down, like she's afraid of being noticed, and I can see in a glance why. Her sunken cheeks and wild, darting eyes are the hallmark of the committed crank head. She glares our way as the big man urges us across the front lawn. I don't like the darkness in the hungry gaze she fixes on little Danny at my side. I stop, pull Danny against me.

"Keep it moving, mister." He pushes me up to the rear passenger door.

The woman looks up and down the street. Her nerves seem to vibrate in the air around her. From three paces away, I can smell her, a bitter ammonia reek mixed with tobacco and the whiff of rot. She's wearing a stained quilted coat, but I see tattoos lacing out from under the sleeves and from under her collar. They're muddy and dark against her blotchy skin, a tangle of thorns on her hands, unintelligible slashes and cross-hatching on her throat. The artless rendering and smeared color, the blue of a ballpoint pen, tells me she's been incarcerated.

"What's the fucking hold up? Jesus." Her voice is almost as dead and mechanical as the target of her ire.

The big man doesn't bother to respond as he pulls open the door, pushes Danny into the back seat. I don't want him in there alone with the woman, even for a moment, so I slide in quickly after him. Then I turn to the big man before he can close the door behind me.

"Fella, listen—"

The woman spins around in the front seat. "Shut the bloody fuck up!" All I can see are sharp, yellow teeth and fiery red eyes as big as eggs. She swings a bony fist at my jaw. The blow lands like a grenade. Danny starts screaming, but I can't see him. My vision swirls and I taste blood. As I try to blink the tears from my eyes the big man's hand snakes in through the open door. He grabs the woman's wrist just below her filthy coat sleeve. She jerks her hand back, her twitching eyes wide and staring. He points at her across the back of the seat, the gesture buzzing with threat. The moment seems to hang there, a tightening spring, but then she presses herself back against the dashboard and, with an exhalation of foul breath, topples over onto the front seat out of sight. In an instant, Danny quiets, but she starts to sob in his place, a dry noise like wind through a tube.

I turn to the big man, put my hand on his forearm. "There's still time to stop this. No one has to know it ever happened. I'll take the boy back to his mother and you go wherever you want to go."

I'm just pissing him off. He shakes his arm free of my touch and lifts the artificial larynx to his neck.

"His mother is dead."

For a moment, his words don't seem to have meaning, as if he'd declared I have a hat growing out of my ear. But then a sharp, sinking despair falls through me. I reach out blindly, find Danny's hand, clutch it in my own. His skin is cool and dry. I hope he doesn't understand—if he even heard. I look up through the open car door into the big man's squinting eyes. "What did you do?" My voice sounds hollow inside my head.

"You think it was me." The toneless voice offers no clue as to his rectitude. After a moment he shakes his head. For the first time I sense an emotion in him other than cold-blooded resolve. "Some dumb ass boy. I do not even know who he was." From up front, the tweaker continues to wheeze, but more quietly now, as if she senses the weight of the moment. "Right up there on top of the hill." Tilt of his head, in case I don't know which hill he means. "Who can say what really happened?"

That's all he has, this modest disclosure—modest for him, if not for me. He starts to close the car door, ready to move on to whatever he has planned next, when I surprise us both and allow the name to spill from my mouth. "Eager." The name of the boy I've thought about, worried about, for the last three years suddenly feels alien on my tongue.

He stares down at me. His face is flat, his eyes dead as doll's eyes. I drop my gaze, turn and look at Danny. Little Danny, quiet and oblivious to everything around him. I have no idea what will happen to him now, but I know that I won't live to see it. This man beside me—Eager's father, Big Ed Gillespie, has to be—is not going to let me live after such a revelation.

November 18

Shadow Ale

Shadow.

Shadow something. He could see the word shining. The road was dark, no cars, no people. Just the shine. Shadow. Other words, other letters, over the door. Through the window past glowing signs he saw people. A man, a woman. They were speaking, the man on one side of the bar, woman on the other. He didn't see anyone else under the yellow glow of old wall sconces. The woman sipped from a tall glass, and suddenly Shadow felt the need to slip inside. He'd grown tired of the scrunch of one footstep after another on the gravel shoulder of the road.

The door stuck for a second, then popped open. The man and woman both turned at the sharp sound. Warm air rushed through the doorway, smelling faintly of a wood fire. Inside, the low ceiling was held up by sawn posts, polished and dark like the paneled walls. A line of booths ran along one long wall, each adorned with its own mounted animal head, glassy-eyed elk and antelope. The wall behind the bar was covered with liquor bottles and fishing trophies.

"Where'd you come from, pal? I didn't hear your car." The man leaned across the bar, his forearms resting on wood, his hands clasped together. His head stood tall on wide shoulders and he looked at Shadow through grey eyes. He was smiling. The woman looked at him and she smiled too. "Long way from nowhere."

Shadow opened his mouth, tried to form the word. It wouldn't quite come. Half a letter, tip of his tongue. The man's smile dropped, became flatter, less friendly. One eyebrow lifted the width of an eyelash. Shadow knew he needed to say it, but he couldn't. He curled his lips, made the shape of the letter. "... W ..." Nothing more. No sound.

"You okay, mister?" The woman's voice had a ring to, a rising lilt, as though she'd learned to speak by listening to the radio.

He looked at her, clenched his teeth. Tried to smile. "S ... s ..."

"Hey, it's cool." The man behind the bar again. "No need to stress out."

Stress out. He could say that, and with the realization the word he sought presented itself like a treasure. "Strolling." Then he found his smile as well. The woman laughed, the sound like bells, and the man shook his head. "Okay, you say so. Long way to stroll though. You walk out from West Linn?"

He nodded, unaware of what West Linn was. "Strolling."

"What can I get you?"

He knew what he wanted. *Something.* Something to eat. He smelled it in the air. He couldn't remember last when he last ate, not clearly. How to say it though, that he remembered. "Supper."

"Grill's closed, but I can make you a sandwich."

He nodded. "Sandwich."

"Sure. No problem. Roast beef, turkey, ham, or smoked salmon."

Pick the easy one. Not the other stuff, no. "Smoke salmon." Easy. Saying the words made him want to laugh, but he held his grin. The man pulled a stained white apron over his head and went through a swinging door at the end of the bar. The woman patted the stool next to her, tilted her head, fixed him with a gaze. "Take a load off. Wherever you come from, it had to be a long frakking walk. Not that you need me to tell you that."

He sat down. She was looking him over, but he didn't want to look back. Her stare made him uncomfortable. Stare. *Staring.*

Stop.

"You'll love the smoked salmon. Todd gets it from some Indians, right from the source, you know."

Salmon from Indians. The words sounded a tone in his head, a familiar note. He didn't say anything. He wouldn't know how.

"They fish down below the falls, smoke it themselves. The old way, you know."

He shrugged. It was a word he knew.

"You're not from around here."

He stole a look her way. She had a long face, red-cheeked and warm, framed by curly brown hair. Her expression was direct, but soft. Not angry. Maybe curious. Did he know that word? After a moment, he shook his head. A way to talk without speaking.

She laughed. "Shy one, aren't you?"

"Shy."

That seemed to satisfy her. She turned back to her drink, something brown with bubbles. He waited, silent. Music was playing, soft, a voice going on about a lost dog. He laughed a bit, a quiet snicker, and the woman looked at him. "Song."

"Yeah, that old crap on the jukebox. Todd hasn't changed anything in fifteen years. Have you, Todd?"

The bartender came back through the door from the kitchen. "Not a damned thing." He set a plate down in front of Shadow, the sandwich and some chips, a pickle wedge. "Hope sourdough is okay. I'm getting ready to close, and that's all I have left."

Shadow nodded, salivating.

"Anything to drink?"

He didn't like the questions, but he liked the the taste of the sandwich. He wolfed down half of it before the bartender asked again.

"Nothing?"

"Shadow …" He didn't mean to say it. Didn't want to say it. Didn't want them to know. But all the talking, all the questions, they made him skittish. And the word over the door. *Shadow*. It came out before he could stop himself.

"Sure. No problem." The man went down the counter, grabbed a glass from below. Stopped at a tall wooden rod, smooth, with a brass cap embossed with the word. Shadow.

The word in lights, the word on the rod. A handle. He recognized it. A handle, a tap. The man filled the glass with brown foamy liquid from the tap.

"Here you go. Shadow Ale. Best amber around."

"Sure, not that Todd's an impartial observer." The woman leaned toward Shadow and winked.

"Hey, it took gold last year at Brewfest."

He took the glass, lifted it and tasted. Shadow Ale. It tasted like night, like smoke. Like who he was. It was a strange flavor, but strangely familiar, like a long forgotten memory. He drank the glass down, set it on the bar. Surprised himself and the others with his belch. Todd laughed and the woman clapped him on the shoulder. "Good stuff, isn't it?"

He nodded. "Shadow."

"You want another with your sandwich? Hell, I'll charge you the happy hour price if you do."

He didn't know what happy hour price was. But he did know the Shadow tasted sweet, satisfying. He nodded his head, an unconscious act.

The woman reached out across the bar and put her hand on the man's forearm. Their eyes locked and Shadow felt disquiet settle over him. She turned her gaze to him, her eyes focused.

"Todd, I'm thinking maybe you should be sure he can pay happy hour prices before you set him up again."

"Dawn …" But he didn't finish. He leaned against the bar top, and his lips screwed up tight. Shadow felt their suspicion like pressure against the back of his eyes. The word formed in his throat, collected against the back of his tongue. He slid off the stool, felt his hands fall to his sides.

"Suspicion."

Todd pulled himself to his full height. Tall, wiry, taut muscles hinted at under his shirt. "Now, fella, no need for anything untoward. But Dawn's got a good point. We just need to know you can pay for your meal." He paused, flexed his hands on the edge of the bar. "You do have some money, don't you?"

Money. The word meant something to him. He couldn't form it in his mouth, but he knew what the man was asking for. Sheets of folded paper, green and grey. He'd found some the night before, driven by an urge he couldn't understand. Money. Green money.

"S-s—" He couldn't say it. He wanted to say it. He wanted them to like him again, like they had when he came in. He wanted to taste the Shadow again, to finish his sandwich and feel warm. It had been so long.

"S-s-s … m—"

It wasn't there.

"Mister, maybe you should be on your way." The woman slid off her own stool, backed away a step. Shadow pulled a memory out of a box in the back of his head, an old man, throat popping like an apple under a boot heel.

"Shadow."

"I hear you, but we don't want no trouble."

He slapped his pants and Todd backed away, feeling behind him. He was reaching for something. Something … Shadow thrust his hands into his pockets and found the sheets of green and grey. He pulled them out, dropped them on the bar. Looked from Todd to Dawn to Todd again.

"Simoleons."

The moment hung between them, then suddenly Dawn laughed. The sound was round and throaty and in an instant all tension melted away. Todd's shoulders dropped and his hands came forward, empty. He took Shadow's glass and filled it from the tap. Dawn moved back onto her stool, her eyes still fixed on him, but now softer.

"Mister ... are you okay?"

She stole a look at Todd, who offered a half shrug. He sorted through the simoleons on the bar, set most aside, took some and turned to the cash register on the counter back of the bar. Buttons and bells, the drawer popped open and simoleons went inside. He took some coins from the drawer, closed it, and turned back to the bar. Set the coins with the remaining simoleons. Silver and sheets of green and grey.

"Your change."

Shadow tried another smile, another word he knew he could say. "Sure." Then he took the glass and sipped. The Shadow wasn't quite as good, had a bitter edge he hadn't noticed before. Or maybe it was him. He felt tired, awash in disquiet. But the room was warm and he liked the feeling of a full stomach. He sipped the Shadow again, and the taste was a little better.

Todd folded his arms on the bar top. "Mister, what are you up to anyway?" He motioned with his head toward the door. "Out this far, at night, on foot."

He knew it was a question, but he couldn't find the meaning in the words. He looked at them, tall Todd and kindly Dawn. Something happened to his tongue with that thought. He opened his mouth. "Tall Todd. Kindly Dawn." As the words spilled out, he grinned.

"Well, that's nice of your to say. But I still gotta wonder. What are you doing out here on this road alone?"

The words made more sense this time. He swallowed the Shadow and let them roll around back of his eyes. The answer hid back there somewhere, he knew it did. But he couldn't quite fix on it. All he could think was Tall Todd, Kindly Dawn, a kind of sing-song his mind. *Tall Todd, Kindly Dawn ... Tall Todd, Kindly Dawn.* Then something else spilled out, a song.

"Todd and Dawn, sitting in a tree, K-I-S-S-I-N-G ..."

Dawn's eyes got big and round. Then she sat back and laughed. Todd shook his head and reached out for the glass. "Okay, okay. I think that's enough beer for you. Cripes." Shadow didn't resist, so taken with the sound of the song on his tongue. He sang it again, and again.

"Todd and Dawn, sitting in a tree, K-I-S-S-I-N-G ... Todd and Dawn, sitting in a tree, K-I-S-S-I-N-G ..."

He slid off the stool, smiled and spun, feeling silly and stupid and sunny. He left the simoleons, spun toward the door. Singing, singing.

"Hey, wait. Where you going?" It was Todd, or Dawn. It didn't matter. He stopped at the door and looked back. Startled faces. The sight made him laugh. He pulled open the door, found the answer as he exited into the night, stomach full, mind swimming.

Singing. "Searching ... searching ..."

Know Nothing of Deserves

Big Ed drives east and north, making his way to 60th and up to Belmont, and then around to the north entrance of Mount Tabor Park. The woman next to him stares ahead, her head trembling on her neck, a fiendish bobblehead. She breathes aloud through her mouth. A miasma of acrid sweat and stale tobacco fills the passenger compartment. Her head snaps my way sharply at intervals, as if she wants to turn around, but the power of Big Ed behind the wheel seems to hold her in check. I don't know who she is, what she represents in this situation, but I'd rather face the back of her head than the back of her hand.

Danny sits quietly beside me and stares out the window. I try to hold his hand, but he pulls it free. He's never been a touchy-feely kid. Big Ed stops in the upper lot on the north side of the park. There are a half dozen cars present, but no one in sight. The weather is iffy enough that only the most committed will be out today, the serious runners and bikers, and the Portland stalwarts who wear the chill air and threat of rain like another layer atop their Gore-Tex. That's good, I suppose, but bad too. There's no one who can call for help. There's also no one to catch an errant bullet if Big Ed starts shooting.

Big Ed turns to face me. "Silence."

I meet his stare, don't blink. That seems to satisfy him. He pulls out his cell phone and speed dials, waits, eyes fixed on mine. "It is me ... yes, I have good news ... exactly. He led us right to him ... a long day, yes." His eyes flick quickly to Danny, then back to me. "I understand ... What time then? ... Okay, we will be there." He snaps the phone shut and turns to the woman. "It is all set, but it will be a while. We cannot wait here."

"So? Is that my problem?"

He closes his eyes for a moment. "We will not sit here where people come and go all the time. There is a bolt cutter in the trunk. Go cut the lock on the gate over there. After I drive through, close the gate and try to make it look like it's latched. We do not want it to be obvious someone has driven through."

"Why do I have to do it?"

"Because I do not want you alone in the car with the boy."

She faces him, her jaw tight and working. No honor among thieves. I'm almost reassured by the hostility between them. I have no idea what the plan is, but I can see he doesn't trust her any more than I do. I don't trust him either, but I'll take Big Ed and his cold deliberation over the rabid instability of a tweaker any day.

Big Ed shifts his weight in his seat. "Myra, get out of the car. Take care of the gate."

"You do it, asshole."

A muscle twitches in his gnarled neck. I can feel the heat rise between them, and I slide toward Danny. Their eyes meet across the long bench seat. Her thin dry lips pull away from her teeth, then she suddenly drops her gaze.

"Fine. Fine. *Fine.*" Her voice rises to almost a shriek. She bangs the car door open and throws herself out, slams the door shut behind her. The tension fades like a passing shadow as she lurches to the rear of the car. Big Ed pops the trunk latch. I hear her rooting around behind us, then a second later she stalks over to the white steel gate that blocks access to the upper Reservoir Loop Drive. The drive runs along the west face of Mount Tabor above the soap box derby track and then dips through trees past the south reservoir, only to loop back north between the two big reservoirs on the 60th Avenue side of the park. Normally it's reserved for park maintenance and official vehicles, but Big Ed obviously isn't a rules kinda guy.

I lean forward in my seat. "Listen, we need to talk about this."

"There is nothing to say."

"You can't put a child at risk like this. You used to be a cop, for chrissakes."

He fixes me with his cold gaze. "How do you know that?"

"I used to be a cop too, homicide. Right here." It's a dangerous admission, but near as I can tell, I'm already dead. My only hope is to reset whatever he has planned by convincing him it can't work, even if I have to lie. "Listen, there's already a BOLO out for this kid, Amber Alert by now too. Cops in three states are looking for him. Think about it."

He turns his head, watches as Myra tries to make sense of the gate latch. For a moment he taps the electrolarynx against his cheek, as if he's considering my words. When he speaks, I realize he was considering only his own. "I carried a badge, maybe. I drove a car, pulled over speeders, responded to calls. But I was never a cop." He emits a harsh, strangled laugh. "I just played one on TV."

I sit back. Outside, the gate latch pops. Myra swings the long arm of the gate wide. Big Ed backs out of the parking space, drives through. Behind me, I can hear Myra swearing. I don't need to know her history to see she's been on the crystal for a long time. Her motor skills are a distant memory. Finally she gets the gate closed and comes back to the car, slams the door as she sits down. "Mother fucking bullshit."

"There is no need to swear in front of the boy."

"Fuck you, Ed."

He clenches his teeth and drives. Just past the soap box derby track he turns right onto a narrow dirt track that climbs a spur looking west toward downtown and the river. The path is steep, no wider than the old Fleetwood as it grinds upward between massive fir trees. At the top of the spur, he stops in a shallow depression filled with fir needles and moss. The car is far enough off the loop drive that we won't be seen unless someone climbs the spur. There's no guarantee someone won't. I've walked up here more than once myself to take in the view. Big Ed doesn't seem concerned. Far below, a jogger runs along the lower loop drive. In the distance, a pair of determined tennis players trade volleys on the courts at the far end of the reservoir. A spit of rain dots the windshield as if to punctuate our isolation.

"Now we wait." Big Ed turns and for a moment catches my eye, a quick warning, then hands something across the back of the seat to Danny. A small portable DVD viewer. Danny takes it without comment, instantly curious. Ed presses a button and it starts to play. He hands me a pair of headphones. "Help him."

Childhood's most formidable mesmer. I don't know how well Big Ed knows kids, but he's at least foreseen that a four-year-old is likely to get restless sitting in the back seat of an unmoving car. I don't want to make it easy for him, and hesitate. He can see the defiance in my face and gestures at the player without speaking. His eyes are hard, but it's the tangle of scar tissue on his neck that breaks my nerve. I take the headphones.

"Here, buddy, put these on. You want to hear the show, don't you?" The screen displays a *Spongebob* cartoon collection. It takes me a moment to figure out the player's controls, but finally I manage to highlight Play All and hit Enter.

"Guess you couldn't be bothered getting a TV for all of us." Myra manages more childish petulance in one phrase than I've heard in all the time I've known Danny.

Big Ed gives her a long stare in response. At first she returns it, but she quickly gets fidgety under his gaze. "Jesus, Ed, it was just a joke."

"I think you are overdue for a smoke."

She lifts her chin and for a moment I think she's going to start screaming at him. Veins pulse at her temple and her eyes look ready to pop out of their sockets. But then she slumps, riding a crest-and-crash cycle measured in minutes.

"Fuck. Fuck fuck *fuck*." She gets out of the car and stomps farther up the spur. I see her fish a pack of Parliaments out of her coat and fire one up. She draws hard and snaps the cigarette out of her mouth, spews smoke like spit-up. Her movements have a herky-jerky quality and I wonder when she last used. I don't think she's tweaking right now, which can only mean she's anxious for a hit.

"What's with that woman?"

"It is not your concern."

"Listen, I get it that you're a big bad fellow, but you don't seem crazy. Whatever is going on, you gotta get that woman away from Danny."

"You might have noticed she is out there and he is in here."

"You know what I'm talking about."

"I know, and I have nothing to say to you."

"What are we waiting for?"

He is silent for a moment. "You are a man who likes to live dangerously."

"Jesus, Ed, look at me. I'm past my sell-by date. But this boy, he doesn't deserve to be part of whatever you've got go—"

He turns on me suddenly, his mouth working furiously. All I hear is a strange hiss. Then he remembers the electrolarynx, presses it to his neck. "You know nothing of deserves."

I sit back. Danny's focus is on the screen in front of him, and I'm glad he doesn't notice the anger in Ed's face, his voice.

"We are meeting people. But not yet. So we will wait until they are ready for us. Then I will take the boy up to the summit and finish what I have started, and you will be quiet. I do not want to kill you, but I will not let you interfere."

I believe him, at least about not letting me interfere. I'm less convinced about the killing. I could try making a run for it, but between Ed and his tweaker bitch, I won't get far. And I won't leave without Danny anyway. All I can do is wait, and hope. Danny sits beside me, quiet, fixated. *Spongebob* is an endless mystery to me, but he seems to like it. Outside, Myra smokes one cigarette, then another. She can't stop moving, and I can't take my eyes off of her. I don't want her to get back into the car.

"I've got a question for you."

"Do not ask it."

"It's not about any of this."

He closes his eyes, shakes his head, but doesn't tell me to shut up again.

"You were married to Charm?"

He tenses. "How do you know Charm?"

"I interviewed her the day after you showed up at her place looking for action three years back."

"Why did you interview her?"

"You know why." The Tabor Doe hadn't been too far from here. We were on familiar ground for Big Ed Gillespie.

I hear him breathe through his nose. "And the boy? What did you do with him?"

"Not a thing. I always figured you for the shooter."

He's quiet for a long time. I see no reason to get into the details of the investigation. I also don't want to discuss what happened in front of my house this morning, or my worries about where Eager is now. I want to put him at ease while Myra is out of position to poison the air around us.

"Why do you ask about Charm?"

"Just curious is all."

"About what?"

"Was she always that way?"

He stares out the windshield for a long moment. Then he shrugs. "Mmm-hmm."

The cartoon flickers in the corner of my eye, and I can hear the high-pitched trill of Spongebob's voice from the headphones. It occurs to me I should turn the volume down. Don't want Danny to hurt his ears. But Big Ed takes that moment to return the larynx to his throat. "She used to be better looking."

I chuckle.

"It is true. She had legs from here to the ground and tits that could put a man's eye out. But she stole money from me. I figured the cash was long gone, but my employer found her and got her to agree to repay it on her back. Did not plan on her getting knocked up. Knowing what I know now, I can tell you it was not worth it."

He understands my thinking better than I expected. He settles back in his seat and leans his head against the door post, closes his eyes. Outside, Myra continues pacing, continues smoking. She moves like the ground is on fire beneath her feet. Beside me, Spongebob's voice grows louder. I turn to Danny. He's still staring at the little video player, but he's taken off the headphones. The light from the video screen shines on his round cheeks.

"What's up, little guy? Don't you want to listen?"

He looks up at me. "My ears are sore." His mouth hangs partway open, and a little bubble of spit has gathered on the bulb of his lower lip. I don't know if I should wipe it off or leave him alone. I'm not good at this sort of thing, despite all the times he stayed with me while Luellen ran errands. We kept it simple. Mostly I let him do whatever he wanted. Fortunately, it was never much. Watch the birds, pretend to sweep the deck. Drink grape juice. Run Hot Wheels around on the floor. I wouldn't have known what to do if he'd tried to drive my car or set fire to the couch. The price of reaching my senior years without siring offspring.

"I never smoked."

Ed's voice startles me. At first I don't realize he's speaking to me. He's looking out the window, watching Myra pace.

"You see guys like me, talking with a machine, and they are almost always someone who chain-smoked three packs a days for thirty years, or kept their cheek stuffed full of chew. I have inhaled my share of secondhand smoke, mostly Charm's. But I never lit up myself."

"I see."

"You are a smoker, right?"

"Yeah." I hesitate a moment. "I quit, but yeah. For upwards of forty years."

"Why did you quit?"

"The usual reason, I guess."

"Cancer, or fear of cancer."

"Little of both. I'm in remission."

He nods.

"I was always proud of myself for not smoking, like I was flipping off the Devil himself and nothing he could do about it. But only a fool tests Old Scratch. Because now I know he put my own gun into my son's hands and gave him cause to pull the trigger. There is no escape."

I draw a breath. "Ed, listen to me. It doesn't have to be like that. Okay? Let me take Danny and walk away."

"That is not possible."

"I'm not a cop anymore. You let us go, I won't tell anyone I even saw you. I won't say anything. I just want Danny to be safe."

"It is out of my control."

"Please—" The car door opens beside me. I turn, catch a blast of Myra's toxic breath in my face.

"What the fuck, Ed. Following dicklips all over hell today wasn't enough for you? Now you gotta sit here jawing with him while the sun sets? I'm getting cold. Ain't it about fucking time?"

I push away from her, feel Ed grip my arm. He doesn't speak, just grunts an affirmation from the bottom of his throat. I quickly see why. He's dropped the larynx so he can grab my other arm too and press my forearms together. Myra leans through the open door and twists a length of clothesline around my wrists. My eyes water in the stench that boils off of her. I struggle, but Ed is too strong. He holds my bound wrists in one big hand, takes the clothesline in the other and yanks my hands across the seat back. He pulls the rope tight, then ties it off as Myra thrusts her arm under the front seat from the back, finds the free end of the rope. I kick with both feet, stomp her arm and she squeals. Ed pops me in the cheek. In the instant I'm dazed, she pulls the rope around my ankles, too fast for me to writhe free. She knots it tight, then pulls back. Her face is red with rage.

"Did you see what that fucker did to me?"

Ed checks the tension on the clothesline. I'm trussed hands and feet, unable to move. The more I pull on my bonds, the tighter they become. Already my hands are starting to grow numb. His eyes are empty as he raises the electrolarynx.

"I am sorry if I gave you the idea we had become friends."

Miss Safe Sex Klamath County

In the Victory Chapel, there was only the cross. No graven images, no images of the Apostles. The Bible picture books in the Sunday School rooms showed no illustrations of Moses, Abraham or the Savior. Such were deemed idolatry and thus forbidden. The fallen churches may defy the second Commandment—the Catholics and Lutherans and Presbyterians—but not the Victory Chapel. On this matter, as with many others, doctrine was firm. It didn't stop Ellie's mother from keeping a framed print of Jesus. The picture hung in the hallway at the top of the stairs. Jesus among family pictures: Brett and Rob in their Little League uniforms, Myra and Ellie in school pictures. Second grade, no front teeth. Tenth grade, first FFA ribbon. Grandparents, cousins, some of the pictures as old as photography itself, some of them as new as one-hour digital printing from Wal-Mart. Among them was a faded shot of the original homestead, her three-greats grandfather and grandmother standing in front of a sod-topped house, peering blankly into the camera. Hasting Kern, the oldest stone in the family plot, his wife Marybell next to him. And Jesus, there in the midst of them all. Ellie would sometimes catch her mother at the top of the stairs, gazing at the print, her expression blank as Marybell Kern's. Ellie never knew if the picture offered her comfort, if or it hung there as an act of defiance, a holdover from her life before she found the Victory Chapel. Her mother's past was never discussed, but it wasn't a secret she was raised a mainline Christian. An idolater.

In the moment Ellie reached Mount Tabor's summit and saw the statue of Harvey Scott for the first time, she thought of her mother's forbidden print. The statue stood a dozen feet high, eyes smoldering, right arm pointing west. Guiding, or commanding—Ellie couldn't tell. She pulled up short, a trickle of understanding springing up within her. Perhaps her mother's print served as an anchor to her life before she became a Kern. Perhaps she didn't see Jesus when she looked at the picture, but rather a glimpse of her own history. And what did Luellen see when she looked up at this stern figure? Did she find a similar anchor in Harvey Scott's graven image, or did it mean something else to her; a link to a new history in a new land, worlds away from Givern Valley?

A woman sat on a concrete bench below the statue, her back to Ellie. Her dark hair was tied in a knot at her neck. With one pale hand she gently pushed a stroller back and forth in front of her. Ellie moved closer. She heard the woman's quiet voice singing a wordless lullaby, a tune she faintly recalled across the years from her own childhood, something her mother might have sang to her, or to Myra. She couldn't name it, but the sound brought up a swelling ache in her chest. She paused and pressed her hand to her breast as if she could force the pain back down again. For a moment she stood there, until the sight of footie-clad baby feet kicking in the stroller, tiny pink hands waving, drew her forward. Trying not to make a sound, Ellie climbed a set of narrow steps from the roadway up to the grassy area at the foot of the statue. A twig snapped under her foot. The woman turned her head. Ellie drew a sharp breath.

"Lu—?"

She stood and smiled, her hand still resting on the stroller's handle. "Hi, Ellie."

For a moment Ellie's sight blurred. "I didn't know if I would ever find you."

"I'm glad you made it."

Ellie felt as though she was standing in a dream. A breeze rushed up the hill behind her, carrying with it the scent of fir resin and water. Somewhere inside her a clock seemed to be ticking down the seconds since she'd fled Hiram through Stuart's corn. With Luellen's appearance, unexpected yet hoped for, it ran down to zero and stopped. She lost all strength in her legs, started to slide sideways. Luellen moved quickly to take hold of her, led her to the concrete bench and helped her sit. Her hands fell into her lap. Luellen's arm curled across her shoulders and pulled her in tight. Ellie lowered her head and leaned against Luellen's shoulder. She'd made it, Givern to Portland, a step ahead of the storm.

They sat together for a long time without speaking. The only sounds were of the winds pushing through Douglas-fir trees above their heads, the footsteps of runners and dog walkers passing on the summit drive. Ellie listened to the casual chatter of strangers in the park, felt the cool concrete bench against her bottom. After a while, the breeze lifted her hair off her face and she opened her eyes.

"Your note didn't say much."

"I was afraid someone would read it." From the stroller, the baby looked up at her through round, dark eyes. "I just wanted you to know I was coming."

"Interesting choice of a place to meet."

"I remembered it from one of your letters."

"That's right. I told you how I like this place." Luellen paused, turned to face Ellie. Her eyebrows gathered together between her eyes. "What happened? Why did you come here?"

Ellie had planned to tell Luellen everything. With Pastor Sanders, she might avoid an outright admission, but Luellen was different. Luellen was her friend, the only island of security in the deep, turbulent sea of her life in Givern Valley. But as she gazed at the baby, she hesitated. She thought about the many brief notes Luellen had sent from Portland, snippets of information appearing almost at random ... *rented a mail box ... I've moved again ... started a new job ... rented a room in a house near the park ...* Taken together, the notes might fill a page or two. None had mentioned a baby.

"Luellen, who is this?"

"His name is Danny." She licked her lips and shifted on the bench. "He's my son."

"Your son."

"You know," Ellie felt Luellen's arm slide off her shoulders, "I haven't checked that mail box in over a month."

"You never told me."

"They called me to tell me I had mail." As she spoke, her fingers knotted and unknotted in her lap. "They've never done that."

That boy with the strange name. "Raajit."

"Yeah, that's right." Luellen shrugged. "I assumed he was calling because the box was jammed with junk mail and they wanted me to clear it out. But all that was there were your two notes."

"That was very thoughtful of him."

"A world first from that place."

"Lu, why didn't you tell me about your baby?"

Luellen leaned forward and brushed a wisp of hair off the baby's forehead. He squirmed at her touch. Danny, she'd called him. Ellie tried to remember the name of Luellen's college boyfriend, the one who presented nicer than he turned out to be. Not Dan.

"It's complicated."

"Complicated how? You think I don't understand that people don't always have their children when they want to?"

"Ellie, please—"

"I get it, Luellen." Her fingers dug into her palms. "I'm not some backwoods hayseed."

"I didn't mean to suggest you were."

"Then what do you mean?"

Luellen put her hands to her temples. For a moment she held them there, her eyes closed. Then her eyes snapped open and she dropped her hands back in her lap.

"After I got to Portland, one of the first things I did was make an appointment at Planned Parenthood. I wanted to get it out of me." She stole a glance into Ellie's eyes. "I suppose that's a shock to you."

"I'm not my family, Luellen. I'm not the Little Liver Creek Victory Chapel."

"I shouldn't have said that."

An uneasy silence fell between them. Ellie gazed out over the city to the east. She looked for Mount Hood in the distance, but low clouds clung to the horizon, a reflection of her dark mood.

"How did this happen? You always were the one who said we should pay attention to Lady Latex."

Luellen attempted a laugh, the sound rueful and tired. "Remember when my mom cornered me on my sixteenth birthday to give me that box of condoms? I thought I would die."

Ellie managed a wistful smile. Luellen's mother had always been kind to her, the poor farm girl living among superstitious cavemen without the benefits of civilization. Mrs. Granger often seemed surprised if Ellie said something to indicate the Kerns had running water or electricity.

"You know what's worse? At my appointment I found out I had chlamydia. Go figure, huh? Me, Miss Safe Sex Klamath County, not just knocked up, but infected."

"Chlamydia?" The air seemed to evacuate from around her.

"When I heard, a switch must have flipped in my brain. I'd been impregnated, infected, had my life turned upside down. As I sat there in that exam room I decided to hell with him. It was my life and it would be my baby. I told the doctor I wanted to treat the infection and keep the baby."

"Chlamydia."

"Like I said. Complicated."

"Lu, where's that clinic? Can anyone go?"

"What do you mean?"

"I lost my prescription when I left the house. I couldn't go back for it. It wasn't safe."

"Ellie—"

Ellie's mind flashed back to the sitting room, the scent of moldy bread, the slap of Stuart's worm against her cheeks. The clam dip. "He has Stuart's eyes." Spoken softly. She reached out and stroked the fat baby cheeks. "Big and round and dark. Danny."

Luellen went stiff. She seemed to have stopped breathing. Then she sagged. "He started showing up after you lost the baby. He felt guilty, and sad. Angry with his father." She shook her head. "I should have made him go away. I didn't mean for any of this to happen."

Ellie felt suddenly cold. She lifted her head, saw the clouds had moved closer from the east, heavier and darker. She wrapped her arms around herself and stared at Luellen's baby. Stuart's baby.

"I don't expect you to forgive me."

"Stuart finds his own way." Her words carried the flat inflection of a machine voice. "He moves with the same drive that sends salmon upstream to spawn, and with just about the same self-reflection."

"I should have known better."

"You always liked him."

"That's no excuse."

Ellie had no response. It was true. But after everything else that had happened, Luellen's betrayal seemed almost trifling. And Stuart, … Stuart got what he wanted, if only he'd known. And where would she be if he had? Who would she be, which new Ellie? She didn't know whether to feel angry or devastated or … relieved.

"Ellie, I know what you must be thinking—"

"How could you ever begin to guess what I think?"

"You're right. I can't. Not really."

"It doesn't matter anyway." She wondered how much of Stuart survived in his son. "He's dead. I killed him."

Luellen gasped and her hand leapt to her mouth, but before she could speak, a sound drew their attention. A harsh voice.

"Well, look at that. Stuart's bitch and another one of Stuart's bitches. A two-for-one special."

Deputy G strode out from behind the statue of Harvey Scott, his big round face smug and leering. His hands were in his jacket pockets, but when Ellie met his eyes he grinned. Pulled a revolver out of his right pocket. He let the gun hang there for a moment, then raised it and pointed between Ellie's eyes. "You thinking of rabbiting, dollface, think again. I lost whatever patience I might have had down at the bottom of the hill."

November 19 - 4:21 pm

Man Comes Out of the Trees

Big Ed and Myra don't seem too worried someone might come along and see me all trussed up in the back seat of the Caddy. I guess I should be grateful they haven't gagged and blindfolded me—or put bullet in my brain. Ed gets out of the car, stretches his arms over his head. His mouth moves. "Long day." Silent, but I can see the shapes of the words on his lips.

"Ed, I'm asking you one more time—"

Myra twists around in the front seat, her face a mask of wrath. "You can just shut the fuck up!"

But Big Ed is less fervent. He smiles sadly and shakes his head, seems to think a moment. Juggles the electrolarynx in his hand before pocketing it. Then he shuts the door and comes around to my side. He checks the cord on my wrists and feet, satisfies himself I'm not going anywhere. As if his crank-addled crone in the front seat isn't enough. I'm thinking I need at least ten minutes to get loose, but Myra shows no signs of joining him. He shuts my door, goes around to Danny's side, motions him out.

"Danny, don't go. Stay here with me."

Myra slaps me. "Christ, Ed. Just kill the fucker!" I glare at her.

Big Ed looks me over like he's considering it, but then he shakes a finger and sorta laughs, the sound a moist jangle. I wonder if he resists the idea only because she suggested it, so palpable is his ambivalence toward her. He lifts the larynx.

"A body is the last thing we need. You know the rules. He will keep till we are done, then he will not matter anymore." He hands her his cell phone. "We will call you when it is over." With that, he leans through the open car door over Danny and cracks me, hard, across the jaw. The little guy makes a noise, a startled chirp, as I collapse. The pain is a swarm of black gnats churned up before my eyes. I tilt my head, try to speak, but my tongue fills my mouth like a wet rag. Ed hits me again. I taste metal and the swarm fills my vision until all I see is a curtain of dark points.

I feel rather than see him take Danny out of the car. The sound of my breath thunders in my ears, but I hear other sounds as well. Myra wheezing, Ed and Danny's footsteps outside the car, the splat of saliva from my mouth onto the leather seat. I blink and the swarm vaporizes. I manage to focus on my bound wrists for a long moment. "Ed … *goddamn* it … please." I'm not sure if I've spoken aloud or only in my mind.

The car doors are closed, windows up. I'm trapped in a cage with a creature possessed of all the wiry strength and fury of a longtime meth addict. Through the half-fogged glass I see him walking away, Danny's tiny hand engulfed in his great paw. I sag, helpless. *Susan, find me.* Or, hell, not me. I don't matter. Find Danny. My mind fills with a sudden image of Ruby Jane, her hair smelling of apples, her blue eyes gazing at me across the table at Uncommon Cup. *You can call me tonight.* I know I will never see her again, will never get to finish what we started in the glimmer of the fish tank. Myra glowers at me across the back of the seat. Her cheeks are sunken and dark, her teeth cracked and brown behind her thin, chapped lips. Her face tells me the only reason I'm alive is because Big Ed is still within earshot.

Down the hill, I glimpse a flash of color, blue against evergreen and bark. Myra's head pivots with my own. A man comes out of the trees a dozen paces from Big Ed and the boy. I pull against my bonds, press against the window. The light is steely and grey, colors shifting and uncertain, but I feel like I recognize him. Red-brown hair, blue pants and jacket. He crosses the path, stops in front of Big Ed. Myra gasps, and I steal a glance her way. She slaps both hands against the window, and her mouth is working, working. "Can't be, can't be, can't be." I turn back to Ed and the stranger, wondering what she sees, what she knows. The two are a study in contrasts, Ed a side of beef, the stranger muscular but small, almost child-like. They both hesitate and I wonder if this is the person Ed is here to see. Yet the encounter has the feel of happenstance, Ed's posture uncertain after an afternoon of unrelenting determination. He starts to lift his electrolarynx, but at that moment the man reaches up and grabs him on either side of the head. Ed releases Danny's hand and lunges backward, without effect. Myra shrieks as the man yanks and twists and throws Ed face-first to the ground. I can see the effort in Ed's taut arms and straining back, but it's as if he has no strength, as if he's the one with the stature of a boy. Danny backs away from the struggle. Ed flails, tries to push himself up on his hands. Myra slaps at the door, the car window, her ululating cries impotent. As I watch, the stranger in blue drops with all his weight, slams his knee into the back of Ed's neck. I can almost hear the pop. Ed's limbs flop. Even from here, a hundred feet away, I can see the unnatural twist of his neck.

The stranger stands with apparent deliberation, his gaze fixed on Ed's unmoving form. He doesn't seem to notice as Danny runs off. At that moment, I find my voice, my real voice, or maybe I found it earlier. All I know is now I can hear myself screaming, as loud or louder than Myra. Beating my bound hands against the seat back in front of me. The man turns to face the car and in a heartbeat I go quiet.

For a moment he's motionless, his gaze fixed on me, or Myra, or the car, or—I don't know. I feel like I should know him, but I don't want to know him. I want him to go away, to never have been. I don't know where Big Ed was taking Danny, who he was taking him to, but while I'm sure it was not for Danny's benefit, this is not the way I would have interrupted Ed's plan. This stranger out of the trees, dressed in dusty, mud-stained blue, eyes deep points of shadow in a slack, incurious face. He looks around, his head swiveling on his neck like an owl's. As he rotates his gaze around to his left, I see a strange darkness on the right side of his head. It takes me moment before I realize a divot is missing from his skull, an oval as deep as my fist.

"Oh, Jesus …" He moves up the slope. In the front seat, Myra turns and crawls toward the driver's side door. For an instant she tangles herself in the loop of my bonds, jerking me forward against the seat back. But then she pops the door latch and falls out of the car, staggers to her feet and runs. I yank on the ropes, but don't have time to free myself. Big Ed tied them too well. By the time the stranger reaches the car door beside me, my hands have lost all sensation. I push myself away from the door as he pulls it open, ducks his head. Looks in at me.

My ass tightens, a hot, wet pucker.

"Silly, silly." His voice is soft. He looks me up and down, two eyes rolling independent of one another. He reaches out and touches my face, my neck, my arms. The rope on my wrists. He traces it with his fingertips.

"Stuck." His mouth curls, a strange and alarming smile. "S … s … s—ahhhh." I can't take my eyes off the cavity in his head. It's as if a section of skull and brain have been gouged out. A thin down grows from the skin in the depression. I force my gaze away from the hole, meet his misaligned eyes. In that moment I recognize him. From earlier today, outside my house among all the chaos of Mitch's porch front fiasco. A figure in blue with a dirty white cloth wrapped around his head, staring up at Tabor summit. Now the cloth is gone, revealing too clearly what it hid.

"Stupid." He runs his hands back down the rope to my wrists, feeling the tension in the cord. I jerk and pull and hear the mewling inside my head. Suddenly he grips my arm with fingers like steel springs. I can't pull away, can't move. There's a scent on the air like electricity and acid. For a second I fear my bowels will let go, but he raises his finger to his lips. A glimmer of light from the setting sun glints off his wet, rolling eyes. "Shhhh …," the whisper is just at the threshold of sound, "… stop."

I stop.

He holds my wrists for a long moment, eyeballs a pair of loose marbles. His breath smells of licorice, his skin of leaf mold. I can see his shirt under the open denim jacket, see stitched lettering on the left chest. *Upper Basin Center for Cognitive Medicine.* No shit. He jerks suddenly and the rope tears through the seat back. Then he stands and laughs into the wind.

"Skedaddle!"

Sliding Rocks and Runoff

B ig Ed moved up the north stairway toward the summit of Mount Tabor Park. Eager spotted him from the steep path that rose from the playground west of the stairs. Only the shoulder of the grassy slope and a few trees shielded him from his old man's view. Eager scurried behind the trunk of a Douglas fir. Big Ed climbed slowly, pausing every few steps to look around, to cock his head and listen. All Eager could hear was the wind in the tree tops. Overhead, clouds had dropped low and dark over the park. He knew it would start raining soon. Moms in the playground were already scooping up their kids when Eager ran past.

Once Big Ed was out of sight, Eager headed south along the grain of the hillside, skateboard tucked under his arm. Soon he came to another path, which forked upward. As he moved up the exposed west face of the hill, he felt the feathery touch of drizzle wet his cheeks. Far below, people fled ahead of the rain to cars parked along Reservoir Loop Drive. In the distance, mist cloaked the West Hills.

At that moment, the sky opened.

Within seconds, dozens of rivulets poured through the grass and scrub and over the path. Raindrops struck his head and neck like falling walnuts. He ran along the exposed hillside, checking above for signs of Big Ed. The path dipped when it reached the trees and forked again, the trail right descending to the southwest, leftward curling around to a short flight of concrete steps up to the top. There, at the south end of the long tree-covered oval stood the statue flanked by a pair of concrete benches. The sodden ground alternately pulled at his shoes and gave way beneath his feet.

In the rain, the trail down the steep south side of Mount Tabor functioned as a long sluice cleared by sliding rocks and runoff. Climbing through the torrent, he heard the shouting before he saw anyone. He gripped his skateboard in both hands and pushed upward through rain and flowing mud.

"For Christ's sake, girl, stop with the bawling already."

"No no *no no no*—"

Eager sidled sideways up the path, carving his heels into the muck to keep from slipping back down. When he reached the steps, he paused to catch his breath and peer over the rim of the summit drive. Across the roadway, his girl and another stood next to the statue, both dark-haired and shivering. A baby stroller beside them. Big Ed was pointing a gun at his girl. He recognized the FFA jacket.

Eager hadn't realized his old man had a gun.

A spring seemed to constrict across his chest. He no longer felt the rain. He dropped down below the lip of the hilltop. If he tried to cross the road in the open, he'd be seen. No way to call for help. His mother refused to pay for him to have a cell phone, and his last stolen burner had run out of minutes weeks ago; he'd tossed it. That left him, here now, the only thing between his girl and his old man.

Eager stole another glance at the trio. Still shouting. His girl seemed almost to be begging. The other woman held the baby. Eager could hear it crying. In his mind, Eager pictured himself rushing up through the trees, the rain breaking as he crossed the road. His old man would look up, surprised, frightened at his fury. *Here I come, bastard!* He could picture himself beating the old man down. He would save his girl and her friend, save the baby. She'd adore him for it.

But Eager wasn't stupid. He might imagine himself something greater than he was; that didn't make it so. His only hope was to take the old man by surprise.

Eager slid back down the hill. He moved through the trees until he reached a narrow trail that curved around and climbed up the east face, now a running stream that threatened to wash him back down the hill. To make any headway, he had to push through the lengthy grass at the path's edge. He slipped more than once, almost lost his board in the deluge, but finally he scrambled across the summit drive and into a stand of Doulas firs clustered behind the statue. The rain subsided to a drizzle under the dense trees.

Aside from Big Ed and the two girls, the hilltop was empty. As Eager moved through the trees, trunk to trunk, he could feel his heartbeat in every nerve. He held his skateboard in both hands, clutched like a bat. His girl now kneeled on the ground, her friend beside her. Big Ed had hold of the jacket, the FFA coat, yanking. Eager's girl pulled away, left the big man with the jacket in his hand. He threw the jacket at her and shouted, but Eager could no longer hear him. The thrum of his heart was too loud in his ears. Heat boiled up from his core and turned the world hazy and red. For an instant, as he slipped into the shadow of the statue, Eager hesitated. His old man, his father. Big Ed Gillespie. The man was a giant, a mountain of flesh and bone. And the gun. But then Eager thought of his girl held by the neck against the auto shop fence, remembered her soft warm kiss under the hawthorn tree.

He charged and swung the skateboard. His feet slid half a step on the wet grass, but the board found the back of the big man's skull.

Big Ed grunted and dropped to one knee. As he turned, Eager hit him again, the hard edge of the deck thumping the meaty muscle between his shoulder and neck. The gun went off. Eager flinched as Big Ed drove his fist from the shoulder. The blow glanced off Eager's cheek and he fell onto his ass. For an instant he sat there, stunned less by the force of the blow than how little it bothered him. As Big Ed loomed over him again, he felt his body flood with a wild exhilaration. "Here I come, bastard!" He jumped back to his feet and swung once more. A sharp crack snapped through the air as the edge of the board struck Big Ed's forearm. The gun spun off in the shadows behind the statue. The old man howled.

"You fuck … you cockbite little *fuck*!"

Eager had never been too keen on Charm's life lessons, but there was one that he'd absorbed through his skin: "You're not done till you're done." She was usually talking about washing dishes or folding laundry, but it was a lesson that had once given Eager enough focus to escape with a driver side airbag when a front porch light came on suddenly at three o'clock in the morning. And now it told Eager to hit the fucker one more time. A strange power seemed to sing in his ears as he cocked the board back and let fly, swinging now like he was swinging a bat. Swinging for the fences. The deck connected with the side of Big Ed's head. The big man seemed to hang in the air for an instant, then he toppled over. Eager stared at him, open mouthed, as he lay face down in the mud. Then, suddenly, his whole body shook and he pushed himself up with his intact arm. Growling in fury or pain, he fled. Didn't look back. Staggered across the road through the rain and vanished over the rim of the summit.

"That's right, mother fucker. Run!" Eager's voice seemed to chase Big Ed's fading howl down the hill, until he was left only with the patter of the falling rain.

But as the quiet descended, Eager turned. Something was wrong. A baby stroller lay on its side in the grass, his girl's FFA jacket tangled in the wheels. The baby was gone, the mother too. But Eager's girl was there. She lay on the ground, face down in the grass on the far side of the statue. Unmoving. Breath thick in his throat, he knelt down beside her, pressed his fingertips to her shoulder. She didn't move. Blood mixed with rainwater and ran through the grass. Her face was embedded in the too-soft earth.

Eager managed to turn his head before he puked.

When he lifted his head again, he saw the gun in the grass in back of the statue. Black metal and mud. Eager looked around. Rain this heavy drove even the most determined park visitors off the summit. He listened, but all he could hear was the sound of rain in the trees.

He didn't know what to do … no, he knew exactly what to do. He picked up the gun.

It was heavier than he expected, dense and solid in his hand. He turned and circled the statue. He looked down at his girl, her dark hair tangled and matted with mud. The flowing blood.

Eager stumbled away through haze raised by the rain, wet to the bone, unaware of the cold. His eyes were fixed on the spot where Big Ed vanished. Pavement, curb, grass, slope. He crossed the summit drive. Rain water rushed along the curb and over his shoes. He slipped on the grass, caught himself with his free hand. Moved downward. His skin hot and alive. Rain steamed as it struck. He blinked away tears as the form materialized among the trees, tall and round. Big Ed. But Eager didn't see his father. He saw the man who shot his girl. Killer.

Big Ed held his broken arm against his chest. He reached out with the other. "Give me the gun, kid—"

Eager didn't stop to think. He raised the gun and squeezed the trigger.

The bullet struck Big Ed in the neck. His mouth opened, a dark gap visible through the pouring rain. Eager squeezed the trigger one more time and the bastard dropped. A sack of gravel falling off the back a truck.

"Eat that."

But then his stomach lurched again. He turned, managed a couple of short steps before falling onto his butt, gun in his hand beside him. So wet he didn't feel the mud soak into his pants. The heat drained out of him. Through the rain came a snuffling sound, a cough. His old man. His father. His father killed the girl and her kiss, and he'd killed his father. He puked into his own lap. The warmth of the vomit felt good on his thighs. He heard laughter, recognized it as his own. The rain fell and his old man sounded like a percolator against a backdrop of popping corn. Eager gazed through mist at his father's form. The big man's eyes were open. He turned his head an inch toward Eager, worked his mouth, but the only sound was a bubbling gasp. Eager looked at him, knew he'd never speak again.

"Why?" Eager's jaw popped as he spoke.

Big Ed's eyes widened for a second, then relaxed. A cold, black fear settled over Eager and he started crying. Big Ed was a cop. You shoot a cop, no matter how dirty he was, they'd kill you. He slumped onto his side and wept.

The girl with the baby. He could hear it, crying in the rain. Strange thoughts: too damned wet and cold to be outside with a baby. The girl spoke to him, her voice quiet but insistent.

"Shhh, listen to me. You need to leave. Please, hurry."

"I … I—"

"Give me that. Give me the gun." He felt her peel the revolver out of his hand. "You have to get out of here. You don't know about these people. You can't be found here."

Eager tried to look at her, but all he could see was water. Rain falling, grey clouds, and water. Her voice was like a mountain stream. He could hear the baby crying.

"We have to go."

"He was a cop." Eager's voice rose in pitch with each word. "Why did he shoot her if he was a cop?"

"You don't know these people."

She pulled at his hand, dragged him to his feet. He struggled against her at first, but the rain fell even harder and he found no traction. And then he was following her blindly under into the trees. The slope dropped away from them, and Eager fell onto his ass. "Get out of here." Her voice was quiet, but insistent.

"Wait. Who—?"

"No one ..." He couldn't see her, tears and rain. "Listen, I'll find you later if I can, when it's safe. Just go now." She squeezed his arm and was gone. He stood and waited, unmoving, wanting her to return, wanting his girl to get up out of the mud and run to him. Then he thought he heard another voice. A voice calling his name. "Eager!" Maybe it was the wind through the fir trees. He ran back up the hill, his feet pulling against the sucking mud. She called to him, her voice growing fainter and fainter. His girl, her voice. He was sure of it. The baby crying too, fainter. Muted by the rain. He scrambled back up through the trees and found the roadway. The body was there, but no one else. He looked from side to side, but there was no one. He started running, this time away from the trees, along the road as it curled around the summit. Ran headlong into the grill of a car as it rolled slowly up the roadway from below. A moment later, the words burst from his mouth as he looked into the face of a cop. Another fucking cop. Jesus. He was dead.

November 19 - 4:29 pm

Balance of Power

The smart choice is to head for the nearest telephone and call for the cavalry. But at my best pace, I'm ten minutes from even the closest houses at the edge of the park. And then I have to hope I catch someone at home and willing to open the door to a man raving about meth heads and mad-eyed apparitions in the park. By the time the troops arrive, anything could happen to Danny. I don't like the possibilities simmering behind Myra's dark eyes.

I pat down Big Ed's body, can't decide to laugh or cry when I find no gun. The fucker snookered me. But there's no time for recriminations. I leave him to serve as a cry for help and head down to the loop drive in the direction I saw Danny run.

The rain starts as I head up the path from the soap box track, the direction I think Danny may have gone. I'm gasping before I've run a hundred feet, but I don't let myself slow down. The path curls up Tabor's south face into a thick stand of Douglas firs, a dirt-and-gravel track favored by mountain bikers and dog walkers. The cold rain soaks to my skin and my feet slip on the slickening mud as I climb, but I keep moving. One foot in front of the other. Between gulps of air, I call out. "Danny! Come out, Danny!" My voice sounds dull in my ears.

A kid on a bike, college-age, rolls down the path toward me. I wave my arms. He skids past me, wheels throwing up a fan of mud, almost wipes out.

"Jesus Christ, old man!"

"Did you see a little boy? Maybe a woman chasing him up the hill?"

He doesn't seem to hear me, flips me off.

"Call 9-1-1—!" But he's already rolling off through the rain. I see him cut left down the grassy slope above the south reservoir short of Big Ed's body. I turn, continue uphill.

I've walked through the park on a sunny summer day, six o'clock, unable to spit without wetting someone. But on a chilly November evening in the rain as the sun sets, the park is shadowed by a forbidding emptiness. With each step, I feel more and more certain I've made the wrong choice. There are a thousand places Danny can hide in the park. And, my luck being what it is, I'm sure whoever Ed was meeting—Grandpa, I assume—will find him first. I'm unarmed, gasping for air, frozen and wet. What the fuck do I think I can do, except add myself to the body count?

The rain tip-taps among the firs and tilting maples on the slope around me. The glow of the city stretched out below provides no illumination. The darkness under the trees is almost total, the only light the remnants of sunset suffusing the cloud cover to the west. I stop at a tree to catch my breath. "Danny!" Nothing. My stomach burns and water runs in my eyes. I wipe my face.

A cough pulls me around and I gape into the black for its source. Another cough, and I see him. Eager Gillespie sits on the ground at the foot of a tree, a dozen feet off the path. I move over to him, kneel down. "Eager, Jesus, what the hell is going on?"

I wish the light was better, but up close I can see his face, ash pale and tinted by the blood that flows, thick and slow as syrup, from his bulging red eye. He looks up at me, his expression blank. When he opens his mouth, his thick tongue presses against his teeth.

"Skin, dude, wha' up?"

"What up? What the hell *up*?" He makes a choking noise and for an instant I feel a hot panic in my chest until I realize he's laughing. Still, it's a sick, dangerous sound. "You need to be in a hospital."

He shakes his head. "No can do, dude. I'm busy."

"Busy hell. You need to get to the emergency room. Where's your cell phone?"

"Made a funny sound, stopped working." He gestures and I look, see the phone on the wet fir needles at his side. I grab it, but it drips water. Dead.

"Come on then, let me help you." I grab his arm, wonder if I can help him to his feet, if the two of us can hobble down the hill together to find help.

"No, no. I'm the ace. I'm the card up the sleeve." He shifts against the tree and I see he's got his other hand stuffed in the pocket of his zip-up hoodie. He sees where I'm looking and pulls out a gun, sloppy grin on his face.

"Where did you get that?"

But I know. Not an S&W 500, not a Python. Big enough though, a .357, late of Mitch and Luellen's kitchen, I've no doubt. I reach out to take it from him, but he holds on with surprising strength. "No. Got a job. I'm the ace."

"Eager, I don't know what you're talking about—" He swivels his head, peers up the hill through the shadows. Voices trickle down from above, the sound broken by trees and falling rain.

"They're bad."

"Who?"

"I gotta stop 'em."

"Eager, don't be ridiculous. We need to get the police."

He shakes his head, tries to lift the gun again. "No time."

I don't want to, but I believe him. I've seen too much already; Myra, Big Ed, the stranger with the hole in his head. I can't make out the words from above, but the anger is unmistakable. I guess they're at the top, south end of the summit near the Harvey Scott statue. Not far from where Michael Masliah found Eager and the Tabor Doe three years earlier.

"Who's up there, Eager?"

He rolls his head, tries to look. He coughs. The gun slips out of his hand. Someone shouts, someone else screams. A man, a woman, I can't be sure. "Is it Luellen?"

His head yaws. "Yeah. Luellen."

"And Danny's grandfather?"

"Grandpa and some dude with a gun. They want Danny."

"Danny ran away."

The crazy grin fades and he closes his eyes. His swollen orb won't quite shut. A red bubble seems to press against his eyelid. "She's still okay only as long as they don't got Danny."

"What do you think you're going to do, Eager?"

He pushes the gun toward me. "S'prise them. They don't know about me. I'm the ace."

I try to make sense of what I'm hearing. The ace in the hole? … Eager? He comes out of the woods with the gun, unexpected, and changes the balance of power. At least, that's what he thinks he's gonna do, though whether or not he can would be an open question even if he wasn't crumpled half-dead at the foot of a tree.

"Eager, you can't just walk up to a man and shoot him."

"Have to. You fucked it up. Now I gotta fix it."

"Eager, damn it …"

"You supposed to take care of her, protect her. That's why I told her to buy the house, cuz you would make sure she was okay."

"Jesus." I press my fingers to my eyes.

"You thought I was casing the joint. But I never went in for house prowls." He laughs again. "You were supposed to protect her. Now I gotta. But I can't lift the gun."

"Eager—"

"They're bad people."

Up the hill, the shouting continues as the rain falls and my feet sink into the mud. Eager pushes the gun toward me and I pick it up. Heavy. It's been a while since I held a gun.

"Eager, how long have you known Luellen?"

"A while."

"How long?"

"Whole time, I guess. Since the day she got to town."

"And when was that, exactly?"

He rolls his head downhill. His next words are mumbled.

"Speak up, Eager."

"You know."

I have no idea what's going on, but there's already a man face down in mud, a boy lost in the woods, and too many questions without answers. If Luellen is up there, if the stranger with the brain injury is up there, if there really is a man who'll kill for a little boy, what are my choices?

Eager stares at me, bulging eye like a boil.

"Remember that day we met, Skin?"

"Eager, come on."

"Seriously. Remember it?"

I sigh. I have to figure out a way to get help, find Danny. It's all bigger than I am. "Of course. Crazy day."

He moves his head side-to-side, a slow-motion negation. "Not that day."

It takes me a moment to realize what day he means. "Out in front of my house. You were on your board, I was putting out the recycling."

"I was lookin' for you. Found you. Now you found me." He laughs his strangled laugh. "Full circle, my girl would say."

"We have to get the police, Eager."

"No." His voice finds sudden strength "Can't be any police." I know why Eager doesn't want cops, and not just because he's a thief and a scammer. *He was a cop.* I wonder if it would matter if he knew about Big Ed down the hill. Probably not. Other thoughts are bouncing around in Eager's mind, clanking pinballs of certainty. There is too much I don't know, too much Eager couldn't explain even if he was able to form a coherent thought.

Yet here under the trees in the rain and the dark he's been trying to make me understand. The house across the street. Mitch and Luellen's house. I was supposed to protect her, he said. It's with a dull shock I finally recognize the bridge of trust Eager tried to build between us. Not just a punk messing with the head of the cop too dumb to catch him, but a kid who looked at me and somehow saw a man who would do the thing he was unable to do.

Is it possible to fail at a task you didn't know was yours to begin with? Looking into Eager's focusless eyes and blood-drained flesh, I see the answer. I've grown blind and bitter, congratulating myself for babysitting a four-year-old, all the while unaware his mother looked to me as her guardian. And where is Danny now? Lost in the woods, hunted by a savage tweaker and faceless figures out of the inscrutable past of a girl who, unbeknownst to me, put her faith in me.

I lean back on my haunches. I'd like to believe it wasn't always like this. I'd like to believe Ruby Jane saw something greater in me when she accepted, for the briefest moment, my fumbling advance. Can I become a Skin who doesn't fear his own imagined irrelevance? Accept the charge given to me by Eager Gillespie, dipshit stray, enigma, man-child with a gun? Can I find my way out of the dark?

The voices above flicker through the trees, bitter motes and fear and rage. I grasp Eager's icy shoulder, and for a second his focus clears.

"Someone's coming." His good eye blinks.

"Who?"

He breathes, a gasp. I don't think he has many more in him. "It's time, dude. Don't worry about me. Help my girl."

"Eager, please hang in there."

But he slumps. The last thing he says to me is a faint whisper. "The only problem with being dead is it lasts such a fucking long time."

The young bastard has become who I wish I could be before my eyes.

November 19 - 4:42 pm

Wade into the Storm

This is what I must do: acknowledge who I can never be again, accept what I am. Older than dried shit, sick as last month's soup. Hanging by a thread in an empty house, working in a coffee shop to make rent after a life behind a badge. In love with a woman young enough to be my daughter, wise enough to by my mother. Every joint hurts. Every nerve is a frayed wire. I'm out of time and fading fast, with nowhere to go but down. Fresh out of illusions.

The bodies are piling up. I can smell Eager's blood and vomit along with mud and wet fir needles. A little boy is lost in the dark. Luellen is up the hill, her and others. Grandpa, his man, maybe Myra. I look up through the trees into the amber glow of dusk and dream I have one last gasp in me. Maybe, just maybe, I can get to my feet, climb up out of the shreds of my life, and do something worth remembering.

Did you kiss me because of how you feel about me, or because you've lost faith in who you are?

I draw a breath, heave myself upright.

Breathe …

      breathe …

            breathe.

"Ruby Jane." I speak to the weighty, indifferent clouds. Streaks of red vein the sky at the horizon. "I hope I've found the way past myself."

I wade into the storm.

Sheath of Overdeveloped Contractile Tissue

Big Ed remembered three things from his last visit to Mount Tabor: pulling the trigger, falling to the ground with his arm flapping like a roadhouse skank's tongue, and seeing the girl run off through the trees with the baby. Somewhere in there he lost the gun. Somewhere in there the skate punk picked it up and then— Christ in a Cheeto—shot him like some kinda of vermin.

Grasping his numb throat, he'd staggered off, somehow convinced he could still finish the assignment. Along the hillside through the rain-soaked trees. Then he heard shouting, saw the flashing lights. Fucking cops arrived before anyone could even know what went down. His bearings lost, he climbed as best he could until he came out at the road that circled the summit. The light was viscous and grey, but he could make out the form of the cop and the kid on the ground in front of the patrol car. The boy sat silent and staring at the girl on the ground in front of the statue, face down and unmoving. Big Ed's gun, who knew where the fuck.

Only two pieces of good news in the whole goddamn mess. He was still alive and the gun couldn't be traced to him. Maybe it shot one person, maybe it shot two. Maybe it shot a dozen before Big Ed took it off that toothless lemon dropper. Didn't matter. No longer his problem. He stumbled back into the trees until he found a path down to the parking area. Soaked to the skin by the time he reached his car, but that was all right. Rain meant no one had seen him shoot the girl, and no one would see him when he got into his car, drove straight to the highway, and set his compass south. He could tell any story he wanted.

Once behind the wheel, he turned the rearview mirror to check out his neck. Blood and jagged flaps of skin, a sucking sound he hadn't noticed over the *rat-a-tat* of falling rain. He probed the damage with his bloody fingertips. The punk had hurt him bad. But it would be days before he'd learn he would never speak with his own voice again.

Three years ago.

Some things don't change, some change a lot. Hawthorne Avenue looked much the same as he remembered it. There were small differences, places gone he couldn't quite remember, places new he didn't recognize. But the obvious landmarks were still there. The movie theatre with the pub, the tchotchke stores and granola-muncher restaurants. The Ship Shop was a UPS Store now, but the coffee house was still there, joined by a new one just a few blocks up the street. First thing when he got to town he stopped in, ordered himself a latte. Hiram would give him shit if he knew, but the soreness had never left his throat, and warm milk soothed on the way down. Wasn't like Westbank didn't have its own espresso shop. He'd enjoyed his latte, then found the Bronsteins, right where Myra said they'd be.

Big Ed no longer worked out like he had back in his playing days. Been a long time since he'd hit the gym five days a week, run every morning, and played pick-up basketball in between—good for agility, basketball, especially for a big man. But if those days were long past, Big Ed still deserved the name. If Hiram needed you to throw hay, you threw hay. If he needed you to beat down some puffed-up beaner who thought he could organize the day laborers, you beat down a beaner. He hadn't run in years, but between Hiram's business and the free weights in his apartment, Ed had maintained most of his bulk and all of his strength. Layers of muscle protected his cervical spine. When the blue-clad man appeared from among the tree and pulled him to the ground, he'd failed to crack Big Ed's neck by dint of a sheath of overdeveloped contractile tissue. A smaller man, a weaker man, a man more soft fat than dense muscle might be paralyzed now. Or dead.

He wasn't dead, but he almost wished he was. He awoke face down in a river of mud. For a moment he thought nothing was wrong. He felt no pain, just a chill in his hands and feet and a wet itch up and down his legs. A good itch. He knew where the man's knee had struck and he knew what such a blow could do. The itch and the chill meant he still had intact nerve fibers between his brain and limbs.

Then he tried to lift his head. Pain speared up his back and reached around to grab him by the jaw. He tried to scream, but managed only a huff, hardly a sound at all. His head dropped back into the muck. Silty fluid flowed over his teeth and into his nose and he spluttered. He couldn't close his mouth, something fucked about his jaw.

When the pain receded, fire to molten earth, he tried rolling rather than pushing. Got onto his side, watched the rain flow past as he gathered his strength for another attempt. He pressed his hand into the mud, gulped sodden air as the spear pierced his back once more. Somewhere behind him he heard a clatter of stones like running footsteps. Fear of his attacker fueled a surge onto his hands and knees, then to his feet. He turned in a slow circle. He saw the Caddy above on the spur, doors standing open and interior lights on, no sign of Myra or the babysitter. No sign of the leverage. No sign of the man in blue.

How did he get here, four hundred miles from a lock-down ward in a zombie asylum? Near as anyone could tell the bastard didn't even think actual thoughts. All he did was hiss, drool, and piss himself. And yet, somehow, he'd strolled out of the woods here on Mount Tabor and all but killed Big Ed in his tracks.

He ran a hand over his bristly hair, wincing. There was only one thing for it now—they had to get away. Leave Portland, return to Givern Valley and ride out whatever storm happened to chase them south. Everything had gone wrong. Same as always. Big Ed had been given a simple task, had nearly blown it when the leverage escaped the car this morning. He'd redeemed himself, he thought, when he followed the babysitter into the man's back yard. All fucking day he followed him, Myra bitching the whole time, but he found the boy. Then this, right out of the woods. And now Myra was gone, their leverage fled. If he were another man, Big Ed might attempt to flee himself. Follow Myra's lead and run like hell. He didn't know how long he'd been out, but the failing light told him the leverage had plenty of time to get away. Which left him with the choice of facing Hiram's wrath or going to ground, all six-foot-*scarred-throat-robot-talking*-five of him. Yeah, that would work. Big Ed would be lucky to live out the week.

Still.

What else could he do? He'd been Hiram's man for so long he didn't know how to be anything else. And maybe he could make the old man understand one more time.

For fuck's sake, Hiram, has the goddamn party started yet?

His legs didn't want to cooperate, but somehow he picked up one foot, then the other. The rain followed him downslope. At the loop drive, he stopped and gazed across the derby track to the reservoir. The water reflected the mustard glow of the lampposts and light from houses along the edge of the park. The little boy might be in any one of those houses by now, awaiting the arrival of cops. *He wandered out of the park, Officer, wet and alone.* Big Ed would never escape Hiram so easily.

He crossed the road and climbed, winding up the hill as darkness thickened around him. The forested slopes chattered with falling rain. He flinched at every movement, the sway of a branch, the glint of city glow on rainwater tumbling through the undergrowth. His neck and back were a lattice of pain, his feet throbbed and his thighs raged against every step. The hillside seemed to groan around him, or perhaps he heard only his own nerves strained to their tensile limits inside his head. He shuddered and pushed on, only realized he was nearing the top when he spied the gleam of a lamppost ahead. He topped a rocky shoulder and found himself on a broad natural terrace sloping up to a steep, grassy bank. At the top, he could see a concrete curb illuminated by the lamppost. A short flight of steps, a dozen or fewer, climbed from the muddy terrace to the road bounding the summit. Hiram would be just beyond, waiting near the statue. Expecting his leverage.

Big Ed paused. His tongue felt swollen in his hanging jaw. How could he face the old man, having failed yet again? How could he tell Hiram of the one who'd appeared like a ghost from the trees to unravel all their plans?

A voice cried out above, the girl—had to be. Stuart's bitch. A deeper voice answered, gravelly and edged with menace. Hiram. Big Ed could only imagine the conversation, the pleading and the threats. Ed knew they were waiting for him, anger and fear thickening in the air around them like soup. Still, he couldn't bring himself to take the last few steps. He hung poised on a blade's edge, unable to fall to either side, wanting to be cut in half. Then he heard a grunt and turned his head.

The ugly ex-cop was moving along the bank in the shadows midway between two lampposts. Big Ed inhaled through his gaping mouth, felt his chest and neck swell. The old guy paused, his head level with the curb. He cocked his head, listening maybe, a hesitation long enough for Big Ed to close the distance. At the last moment, he seemed to sense the approaching presence and turned. Too late. Big Ed drove a fist between his shoulder blades. The force of the blow sent a stab of pain through Ed's back and neck. The ex-cop dropped, groaning, and tried to crawl away. Big Ed hit him again, this time aiming for the kidney. Then Ed grasped him below the collar and tossed him up the bank. The old man flopped over, no heavier than a wet towel. Lift, *slam*, lift, *slam*. Each time the bastard's body struck the bank, wind rushed out of him. Despite his own snarling agony, Big Ed wanted to laugh. Felt so damn good to whale on the mouthy fucker.

When the cop finally stopped wriggling around, Ed pawed though his clothes. Found a .357 revolver, almost familiar in its heft. The gun surprised him, but also filled him with a crazy euphoria. A gun, *now*, after everything. Where the fucker found it between the Cadillac and this hilltop Ed had no idea. But it only added to the sudden power he felt. He tucked the gun into his belt and grabbed the old man's collar again. He was gonna enjoy explaining to *Mister You-Don't-Have-To-Do-This* the way the world really worked. Hiram Spaneker awaited his due. Ex-pork belly didn't want to tell them where to look for the kid, the no-bodies rule was out the fucking door.

He dragged the old man up the bank and across the curb, digging for the larynx in his belt pouch, then each coat pocket. He felt the gun, felt Myra's car keys. He stopped on the edge of the pavement, patting himself like a man trying to put out a fire. Across the summit drive he saw the statue, recognized the trio gathered in its shadow. His steely glee deflated. The electrolarynx was gone. George the Flea wasn't.

November 19 - 4:49 pm

Harvey Scott Watches

HARVEY SCOTT
1838 - 1910

PIONEER
EDITOR
PUBLISHER

MOLDER OF OPINION
IN OREGON
AND THE NATION

After nightfall, Mount Tabor's summit is lit by faux-antique lampposts at intervals along the encircling oval drive. Their fulvous glow casts oily shadows of the Douglas-firs across the asphalt to the central knoll. The wet pavement absorbs more light than it reflects.

At the southern tip of the oval, Harvey Scott stands atop his six-foot stone pedestal, his tarnished bronze effigy invisible in the darkness; the light from the nearest lampposts reveals only a suggestion of the pedestal itself. I can make out the trio gathered next to the statue only because one of them holds a flashlight. The beam points at the ground, shining fitfully. One hunched figure sits on one of the concrete benches flanking the statue. The other two stand. Beyond the trio, the faint gleam of the flashlight is swallowed by the rain-drenched grass and trees.

I crouch on the embankment that drops down from the summit drive. Luellen is the only one I recognize: the figure on the bench. Head down, hands in her lap, I see her only in profile. Even at this distance I recognize the posture of a woman who's lost hope. The old man in front of her holds the flashlight. Grandpa, I assume. Tall and thin, dressed in jeans and a heavy jacket, steel hair slicked back. He's propped up on a crutch, resting all his weight on one leg. The other is bandaged at the thigh. The bullet in the kitchen wall. Through the watery light I can see in his malevolent expression that the world would be a better place if the bullet had gone through his forehead instead.

The third figure stands behind Grandpa. Six feet and easily three hundred pounds of meat and gristle, head shaved, long beard, body clad in leather—Big Ed is gaunt in comparison. Grandpa has brought himself a bodyguard. I can't make out details, but I see a motorcycle club patch on his jacket. If he's local, he's most likely Free Souls. If the old man imported him, could be anything. Whatever his colors, I know trouble when I see it. I also know he won't be relying on his substantial brawn. A gun hangs in his hand at his side, huge and nickel-plated, gleaming in the guttering light. Semi-auto, big slide. Jase could tell me manufacturer and model. I don't need to know. The gun has heft to match the man holding it, capable of producing enough kinetic energy to blow me and Luellen both into next week.

At least Danny isn't here, nor Big Ed's tweaker girlfriend. I can only pray the little fellow ran downhill rather than up, got clear of

Myra and found his way into one of the many yards backing up to the park. With him out of the picture, I can focus on helping Luellen—which means focusing on the mountain of meat. Unlike Eager, I don't see myself charging the hilltop, gun blazing. The ace in the hole. But if I can get the drop on them, maybe I can end this thing without having to fire a shot.

Yeah, right. A boy can dream, I suppose, but in the black hole I call a mind a little voice tells me not to fool myself. I'm gonna have to shoot the big fucker.

Eager's .357 is heavier than the Baby Glock I carried when I was still working. I'd be worried about how the difference might influence my aim if I'd ever been a decent shot to begin with. My only chance is to get close enough it won't matter. Not a sure bet, but the falling rain should cover the sound of my footsteps and the darkness may hide me until I get close. The flashlight, even flickering, works in my favor. Their night vision has to be for shit. The best approach, I decide, is to work my way to the right below the drive and come up from the east. From that approach, the biker will have his back to me and the statue's base will shield Luellen should the world skid out from beneath my feet.

Jesus. When did I become a man who could shoot another without a second thought?

Desire for Ruby Jane suddenly threads through me, tendrils of need entwining tendrils of doubt. I picture my cell phone shattered on the deck, try to imagine what she's doing as I stand here contemplating murder. All three Uncommon Cup locations are closed by now. She might be working in one of the offices, making the schedule for next week or closing out the day's books. I'm not sure what time it is. Maybe she's home already in her converted warehouse apartment behind the shop on Sandy. There's a bathtub in the middle of the living room, legacy of a time when the space was split into smaller studios. She enjoys soaking in the tub after a long day, loud music rattling the rafters. If she's not in the tub, maybe she's shooting baskets in the hoop at one end of the high-beamed room, or sitting on one of her big soft couches reading. I wonder if she's tried to call me, or if she's rethinking the things she said to me earlier. I want to be there with her. I want to talk to her about all that's happened. I want to ask her what she would do in my shoes.

I know what she would say. Protect Danny, help Luellen.

Even if it means putting a bullet in a man's back?

I close my eyes, picture myself among the fish. Ruby Jane is watching me; I'm a flash of silver and coral. A comforting illusion, a soothing delusion. It changes nothing. I've seen too much already between Big Ed and Myra, between Mitch and Eager to hesitate now. I have no real idea what's going on. The words of a lovesick teenaged boy only confuse a situation already a muddle. All I know is I'm here, now. Whatever is going down feels like something I need to stop. I can apologize to Susan later, beg Ruby Jane to understand how narrow the way seems through the darkness. Assuming I live through the next few minutes.

I stick the gun in my jacket pocket and move through the long grass on the slope below the summit. Luellen and Grandpa are talking, but I'm too far away to hear. I scoot lower down the slope to avoid the circle of light from the lamppost at the southern tip of the summit oval. For a moment the statue and the trio are out of sight. I move maybe a dozen paces then stop, alerted by an unfamiliar sound, a sucking pop behind me. Despite its urban setting, Mount Tabor harbors all manner of wildlife. Juncos, sparrows, hawks, and owls. Squirrels, raccoons, and opossums. Feral cats, stray dogs. Even the occasional coyote. Anything could be moving in the dark. I turn, but see nothing the darkness under the trees. Wait the length of a dozen heartbeats. Nothing. I'm wound tight, my every nerve on full alert.

It's not good enough.

Something hard slams between my shoulder blades, pitching me forward into the grass. Another blow strikes the soft spot below my floating ribs as I swallow mud and choke. Then I feel myself yanked off the ground by my collar. Arms flailing, I try to gain purchase on the slick hillside. My assailant slams me back into the ground, once, twice. Then he drops me and I slump into the mud, too little breath left in my lungs to even groan.

He flips me onto my back. Silhouetted by the lamp above us, I can just make out Big Ed's profile. His jaw hangs at an odd angle, seems to move of its own accord. His head tilts to one side as well. As he pats me down, I can hear his labored breathing. He's hurting. Doesn't stop him from finding Eager's gun. He tucks it into his waistband then spends a moment feeling through his own pockets. The larynx, I guess, but he doesn't find it. I don't know how he expects to talk anyway, the way his jaw is sagging. Frustration seems to have him bound in knots. He grabs me roughly by the jacket front, pulls me up the hill. My ribs protest, but all I can do is grunt with each jolt. The dark sky above swims with flickering lights. They must be inside my own eyeballs. Part of me wants to struggle, but I'm too dazed by the sudden assault, or by the shock of seeing Big Ed upright and walking.

Grandpa jumps and nearly loses his grip on the crutch when Ed throws me at the base of the statue. "Jesus Christ, Ed, you scared the shit outa me." He looks down at me like I'm a piece of rotten meat. "What the hell's this? Where's the kid?" The biker glances down at me too, but Luellen doesn't seem to notice, is perhaps beyond noticing. Her dark hair hangs loose over her forehead, hiding her eyes.

Big Ed indicates his throat and shakes his head, then points down the hill. He's trying to mouth words. Grandpa shakes his head as Ed slaps the side of his head and wheezes, his gestures increasingly frantic. His chin shuffles side to side with each gesticulation, a loose flap. He's got something to say, but no way to say it.

"You want something to write with?" No missing the ice in Grandpa's voice.

Big Ed knots his fists and closes his eyes for a second, exasperated. Then he draws a breath and nods.

"Didn't know you could read and write." His expression is one of mock regret. "Hey, George, I don't suppose you got a spare voice-a-ma-jig, do ya? I think Ed here done lost his."

The biker, George, taps the gun against his thigh. "'Fraid not, boss."

Grandpa shrugs at Big Ed. "The Flea can't help ya, I can't help ya. You're shit outa luck."

I could help if I wanted to. From Big Ed's gestures and urgency the message he's trying to convey is obvious. He wants Grandpa to know about the man with the hole in his head. Even as the thought crosses my mind, Big Ed reaches the same conclusion. He points at me, tosses his head Grandpa's direction. I have no intention of clearing things up for him. He bends over and prods me in the ear with the knuckle of his middle finger, but I just clench my teeth.

Grandpa waves him off. "Forget it. Don't know who this guy is. I surely don't see how I'm gonna get any leverage out of him." He glances toward Luellen. "How about it, sweetheart? You give a damn about this lame fuck?"

Luellen lifts her head and looks at me. In the darkness of her eyes, I see the resignation I guessed at from across the road. "He's …" She swallows. "He's my friend."

"I don't recall giving you permission to have friends." He laughs, harsh and sadistic, then turns back to Big Ed. His gaze is now laced with pity, no more genuine than an email promise of easy wealth or natural male enhancement. "Well, Big Ed, this whole day has been one fucking mess and then some, don'tcha think?" He doesn't expect Big Ed to respond. "Fortunately there is one piece of good news."

Tension flickers through Big Ed's eyes, asking the question his throat can't.

"George the Flea grabbed your hog leg outa the Suburban." He gestures to the biker and his big gun. "Shoot 'em both."

November 19 - 4:54 pm

Civil Twilight

He floats in and out of consciousness. His head has the weight of a stone on the end of his neck. It's jammed into the crook of two twisted roots. A knot digs into his back. Not a pain exactly; an awareness, a sensitivity. Rain falls through the branches of the tree above him and he blinks as drops strike his eyes, swallows when they fall into his open mouth. The drops fail to slake his thirst. He wants to move, find a spot more comfortable, a place with more flowing water. No strength. He tries to move his arms, but he has no arms. No legs. All he has is a head and a knot in the back. The rain pitters and patters against the soft fall of fir needles around him and he's just a head with a bullet in it.

He remembers another place, somewhere far away. Stern faces and latex gloves. "Let me look at your eye. What happened?" He can't recall what he told them. He can't remember if he said anything at all. All he remembers is needing to get away. He's the ace in the hole. But everything has gotten so mixed up.

A snap draws his attention, brings him back to the moment. The rain. Another snap, a footstep in the darkness. It isn't all dark. The sun has set, the clouds closed in, but a faint glow still filters through the trees from the west. Skin had once told him what it was called, a word. Two words. Skin used to try to teach him things, stupid shit like you learn in school. Stupid, but more interesting coming from Skin. Like, the waning light after sunset is called civil twilight. That's it. In the fading civil twilight someone is walking, *snap-crack* through the trees. He can't turn his head. No arms or legs. He blinks and swallows rain and listens to the *crack-snap* in the civil twilight, and then a form materializes out of the shadows.

A head. But not a head. Something is wrong with it. Misshapen, distorted. He swallows and tries to speak.

"Civil twilight."

A man. He recognizes a man. White face, staring eyes, shaggy hair. But something wrong. The head.

"Your head."

Round on the one side, caved in on the other. Like someone scooped out the right side of his skull with an ice cream scoop. The fellow doesn't seem to care. He smiles a haphazard smile and one eye rolls around all on its own.

"Your head …"

"S-s-s-shhhh …"

Eager thinks the fellow might say more, but at that moment a shot rings out from up above, then another. Eager hears shouting and screaming and he knows it all went wrong. She's screaming. He tries to move, but the roots hold his head in place and the knot digs into his back and he has no arms and legs. He feels the fear, though. The fear bubbles through him and rain falls into his eyes as he strains against the inexorable pressure of gravity.

And he fails. He looks at the stranger, and in that strange, sloppy gaze he feels a moment of hope. Maybe this fellow, head awonk, can do something. Save her. "You … she—" But the man reaches out, strokes Eager's cheek. He shakes his half-head and grins, eyes sad in the civil twilight under the trees. Eager feels himself start to fall away. He can do nothing. Skin can do nothing. She's screaming, yet the man strokes his face until his fear slides away. He closes his eyes and swallows rain and listens for the pitter-pat under the trees. But all he hears now is the stranger's voice.

"S-s-s-sleep."

Long Past Time

George the Flea's face cracks wide with a nasty leer as he lifts the gleaming handgun. Big Ed stumbles backward, scrabbling at his belt. I raise one knee, slip, and catch myself on my hands. I don't know what I think I'm going to do, but it doesn't matter anyway. The gunshot drowns out Luellen's rising scream, tears at my ear drums like shrapnel. A warm, metallic spray of arterial blood douses my face and neck as I scramble to find purchase on the sodden ground.

I don't hear the second shot, just catch a spark off the stone pedestal. For an instant I think he's missed, but then something kicks me in the gut. I hang in space the length of a heartbeat before my strength rushes out through my hands and feet and I collapse.

For a moment, I'm wrapped in a sensation like a hot, rushing wind. Voices scatter through my mind, whispering: *you're fine—it's nothing ... nothing.* I hear Luellen scream through the white noise, pitched like it's coming from the end of a tube. There's more behind it, a wail, high-pitched and strangely familiar. I blink through tears, unaware of any pain. Or maybe the wail is the pain, fire shrieking up every nerve and coalescing in my brain as sound. She's sobbing now, "No no no …," and I know the whispers mean nothing. I'm a long way from fine. A piercing note like an eruption of flame bursts from my belly. Bullet or fragment of Harvey Scott's stone base, doesn't matter. I'm gut-shot.

I roll my head side to side. The old man leans into his crutch, sneering. Flashlight swings from his hand and throws light into the trees, briefly illuminating a haggard face. I recognize her from the stench. Myra. She pushes Danny before her, and her fingers are digging in to his thin shoulder. I can tell it hurts. His face is damp and his lips twisted with fear or pain. But he's quiet, as always. Quiet Danny. I know him well enough to know how scared he is. He doesn't notice Luellen on the bench in the darkness, but when he sees me, he twists out of Myra's grip and runs toward me. George thrusts out a big meaty paw and snags him mid-stride. As Danny struggles, he points the gun at me, ready to finish me off.

But Grandpa throws up his free hand, hobbles toward the biker. "For chrissakes, don't be shooting that damn thing around the kid."

"You said—"

"Just stand there. We got this. That fucker ain't going nowhere."

I can hear Myra's voice, strident through Luellen's sobs, but I can't make out the words. She glares at me, her eyes big black marbles, cracked lips twisted with feral glee. Somehow she's scored a hit or three of crank since she fled the Caddy. Maybe had it with her all along. Her nostrils are flaking caverns and the cords in her neck stretch tight as she grabs Danny by both shoulders and presses him against her legs. Her hands look like talons in the thin light.

To me, she's a horror. Luellen shrivels at the sight of her. But Grandpa is pleased. "Damn, girl, right on fucking time." He cackles and turns his attention to Luellen. "So, Lizzie, time you and me got down to business, don'tcha think?"

But Myra interrupts him. "Hiram. Something you need to know. We ain't alone …"

I don't want to hear any more. I've failed. Eager's faith in me was misplaced. I shoulda stayed down in the flats. Now where am I? Sinking into the soft earth. No one pays me or Big Ed any heed. We might as well be tree limbs brought down by a storm. I can see him beside me, eyes open and staring, and I wonder if he's looking back at me thinking the same thoughts. I've no doubt he's dead, which can only mean I am too. The prospect leaves me indifferent, even if the fire in my belly gives me a pretty good idea of my next stop. But then I feel a rush of misgiving, as though I've left something important undone. Stove on, iron plugged in. Can't be the coffee maker—I sent Mr. Coffee to Goodwill when Ruby Jane gave me my French press. A birthday present months before my birthday. "Long past time you learned to make a proper cup of coffee, Skin." I still don't have the method down to her satisfaction. As my blood mixes with rain and mud, I fear I never will.

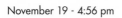

S-s-s-shadow

Whation are you telling me? What the *fuck* ... are *you* ... *telling* me?"

Grandpa leans into his crutch, eyes aquiver, a single greased spear of metallic hair bobbing forward on each barked syllable.

"I saw him. He messed up Ed and sent the kid running." Myra clutches Danny like a piece of flotsam at sea, her teeth bared. He struggles, but her tweaker strength is too much for him.

Grandpa looks like he wants to hit her. "How do you even know what he looks like now?"

Already a withered crone, she seems to shrink in the face of his rage. "I went to see him is all. After I heard my dad talking to Lizzie on the phone about the land and about the boy—"

"Went to see him *how*? His own goddamn *mother* doesn't even know where is."

"Everyone knows where you keep him. I just thought I'd tell him about his son."

"There's *nothing there to tell anything to.* He's a fucking potato, you stupid bitch."

I'm not really listening. My stomach feels like an overfilled tire ready to pop, and my mind keeps drifting off to a day deep in my past, the summer before I enlisted, only seventeen years old. My friend Tommy and I took a road trip, drove his cherry '61 Chevy Impala up to B.C. He knew a guy who knew a guy whose parents owned a cabin near Whistler. Tommy finagled us an invite for a week of hell-raising, claimed girls would be there. About that he was right. He also said everyone would be so hammered even I could get laid. About that I knew he was blowing smoke up my ass. But I figured it would be fun anyway. What neither of us anticipated was his car getting totaled by a moose.

It happened the afternoon we arrived. Tommy and I were hanging out on the porch with some guy we'd just met, one of the other guests. Drinking Molson's and smoking a little pot and considering the nature of the sky above the deep green haze of the forest. As we looked on, a moose appeared from among the resinous fir trees and strolled across Tommy's Impala. Sheet metal squealed and buckled, the roof took on the shape of the front bench seat. The engine appeared from under an abrupt fold in the hood. And then the moose stopped, stood there and gazed up at us, eyes serene.

The other guy—Marvin? Morvin?—muttered something about never having seen a moose before. "Cool." Tommy made a little sound somewhere down in the bore of his throat and dropped his joint. We were poor enough in those days that I remember hoping we could find it; didn't want good dope going to waste. I opened my mouth to say something, but Tommy was already moving. Jumped down off the porch in a single bound and charged across the wide gravel driveway. He threw his beer bottle as he ran. It bounced off the moose's shaggy flank and fell among the rocks and lichens that lined the ditch below the parking turn-out. "Get off ... get off *get off!*" The moose shrugged and turned, shattering safety glass and collapsing the trunk. Tommy pulled up, realizing perhaps his impotence against a half ton of indifferent ruminant. At forest's edge, the moose looked back over its shoulder at Tommy, expression fathomless, then vanished in a swoosh of verdant fir branches.

Something about the way the man with the divot in his head comes out of the shadows beyond the statue reminds me of that moose. Maybe I'm a little delirious; my blood has to be draining at a pace I can't long sustain. I might be the first to notice him. I'm certainly the first to recognize him for who he is. He stared up at this very spot from the street in front of my house, and he broke Big Ed like he was made of balsa wood. And now he moves with aloof indifference across the grass and unceremoniously grabs George's head and twists. For all his great mass, the Flea's neck is less sturdy than Big Ed's. He drops like a log, dead before he hits the ground. The fellow leans over him, eyes wide and curious.

"Snap."

No one moves. Myra and Grandpa stare at the biker's body in stunned silence. Luellen's face is milk-white. She recognizes the man with the hole in his head—they all do. But for Luellen, he holds some special meaning. She looks like she's about to break in half. The stranger steps over the body, puts a finger to Grandpa's lips. "S-s-shhh." The old fellow's eyes bulge, but he doesn't speak. The stranger turns to Luellen, who sits quivering, face wet with tears and rain.

"No, please." Her voice sounds like tearing fabric. "Please, no more."

But he reaches out and touches her on the cheek, wipes away the tears. He grins, sloppy and wide, as he puts his finger in his mouth. "S-s-s …" His lolling, glassy eye loses focus for a moment. A potato.

Luellen puts her face in her hands. "No more." Her voice is an echo of the wind and rain.

"S-s-s …" He runs the back of his hand across his lips, slicking his wrist with glistening spit. "S-s-s—" Then he gulps air and closes his eyes. When he opens them again his eyes are clear, his voice strong.

"Ellie."

I open my mouth, afraid to make a sound. Afraid to draw attention to myself. Under the statue, her arms clasped around her breasts like a shield, Luellen begins to sob. I roll onto my side, bite back a whimper at the pain. Danny notices the movement or sound and lunges toward me. Myra digs her fingers into his shoulders. A chirrup emits from his lips, a sound faint enough it could easily be missed. In my ears, he might as well be screaming. I struggle to push myself up, but my life is leaking out of me. I can feel it in the coldness in my feet and hands, in the shadows swimming before my eyes. I have no strength. Grandpa, Myra, Luellen, none of them are looking at me. The stranger consumes them. Beside me, Big Ed lies in the wet grass. His eyes stare, lifeless. His mouth hangs open as if he's calling out. I reach toward him with my free arm.

The gun is still tucked in his belt. Eager's gun. My gun. Two pounds of murder, too much for me to lift as my blood dribbles into the mud beneath me. But Danny is whimpering and frantic murmurs spill from Luellen's lips, *no more.* Beyond Big Ed's bulk, I see a mark on Harvey Scott's pedestal. EG®, Sharpie-etched on marble. Eager looking over my shoulder hardens my resolve. It's down to me, the ace in the hole. Big Ed is dead, the old man's Flea is dead. I raise the gun, like lifting a boulder. I've got one chance, one shot at most. If I don't make it count, the next shot will be the one that puts me down for good. George's gun is closer to them than me.

Grandpa, sharp eyes wide, reaches out to the stranger. Myra pulls away from them all, yanking Danny along with her. Luellen catches Myra's movement and lurches off the bench toward her little boy, thinking or not thinking, I don't know. Reacting. But Myra, cranked wide, is too quick for her. She pushes Danny down into the mud and rakes her claws across Luellen's face. Danny comes to life, not just screaming in my head, but screaming for all to hear.

Everyone freezes, stunned, perhaps, by the sound he's making, a keening wail only a terrorized child can make. His shriek awakens the last shred of strength left to me. I bring the gun up, that big ol' .357, ace in the hole. Myra catches something in the corner of her tweaked eye, the movement of my arm. Turns.

That's when I put the bullet in her ear.

November 19 - 5:01 pm

Lucy-Loo

Her name is Luellen Bronstein. When she orders a hot dog at Zach's Shack and they ask her name for the ticket, she tells them, "Luellen." When someone calls from Franklin High School to find out why Jase isn't in class for the fifth day running, they ask for her by name. Her Discover Card is embossed LUELLEN BRONSTEIN. Her friends call her Lu. When he's got the sillies, Mister Kadash across the street calls her Lucy-Loo. Luellen. It's her name. It's been her name all her life.

What she doesn't like to acknowledge is her life began three years before on the summit of Mount Tabor amid falling rain and gunfire. The latest of many resets, a string of women and girls stretching back to Opal Kern's crowded womb. Crazy Lizzie. Penitent Ellie. Stuart's Ellie. Clam Dip Ellie, Scissors Ellie. Waiting and Watching Ellie. Heartbroken Ellie … Danny's Mother Ellie. *Luellen*. It's her secret—only two people even know. Neither, she believes, will ever tell, though if they do she's already rehearsed the explanation. "Someone had to look after the baby. Ellie was in no state to do that. It had to be Luellen. I wanted us to be safe. I thought we *were* safe." She hoped to never have to explain. If only she kept her head down, everything would be fine.

And then, so many safe years later, she found Hiram Spaneker in her Luellen Bronstein kitchen at six-thirty on a school day. Now she's here where life began, where Luellen's life fell in ruins at her feet. Givern Valley arisen from the darkness like one of those creatures in the movies Jase likes so much. It will never let her go.

She has no strength to move. She watches, helpless, as Stuart gently extracts the gun from Mister Kadash's hand. He struggles to speak, pushes out words she cannot hear. For a long moment, he gazes at the gun like he's examining an alien artifact. Then he draws a breath through his nose and turns to Hiram. The old man hobbles toward him, one hand raised, whether to take the gun or reach out to his son Ellie doesn't know. "Boy—" Stuart shakes his head.

"Stop."

Hiram stops.

Stuart's head rolls around on his neck as loose as a top, searching. After a moment it finds its target. Danny. He holds the gun aimed uncertainly at Hiram's feet as he moves toward the little boy. She reaches out to stop him. Stuart ignores her, brushing past. He looks down at Danny, a broad grin splitting his face.

She doesn't know what to do. Everything has gone so wrong. She only ever had one goal, all this short life. Take care of the boy. Luellen's baby. Thoughts of her previous lives flood through her, memories of the damage done throughout her many histories by the elemental force within her, and by this other standing with her. Stuart. But not Stuart. Something else, something larger than Stuart.

Hiram Spaneker.

It had always been Hiram. Stuart was his creature from the start, a creature made of anger and need and desperation. He'd come to her in the darkness outside the Victory Chapel and claimed her as his own, but at his father's behest. Hiram Spaneker, lord of a petty fiefdom in out-of-the-way Givern Valley. He took what he wanted, and used whoever he needed to take it. Stuart. Myra. The man who'd pursued her years before and again today. Many others. She was an inconsequential obstacle between him and the Kern water.

But maybe not so inconsequential, because now here they are on the top of a faraway mountain in a city that couldn't be more disconnected from all her lost history. Hiram, Stuart, and Danny. Luellen's boy. Stuart's—

"Son, we need to get you back to the hospital, okay?" Hiram's tone is solicitous. She recognizes the feigned concern. "We're a long way from home, don'tcha think?" She knows he cares about no one except himself. But Stuart stares his father down. "Silence." Then he turns to Danny again, smiles again.

"Son." He pats the little boy on the head, a familiar gesture, as if he's known Danny all his life. For an instant, his expression grows troubled, as if he's come to some realization there on the hilltop. But how could he? Half his brain is gone.

When he looks up at her at last, eyes loose, he has one last thing to say.

"S-s-sorry … Ellie. Sorry." With that, he grabs Hiram by the neck and drags him thrashing and shouting into the darkness.

November 19 - 5:09 pm

Forgotten

Grandpa and the stranger have left, but we're not alone. Big Ed sprawls beside me, dead eyes unblinking in the rain. George looks away, his body twisted into an unlikely pose. Myra is somewhere off in the shadows under the firs. Maybe I can make out her spindly legs, maybe that's her blood on the stone pedestal where Harvey Scott perches. I can feel them all in the darkness, a stillness like pressure in the base of my skull. My own blood collects in my belly. Slowly, but fast enough. Danny and Luellen, at least, are still alive.

Luellen dials 9-1-1 on her cell phone. I can only make out bits and pieces of what she's saying. "… a shooting … I'm not sure … bad." I might offer my own interpretation of my condition. Gunshot wound to the abdomen, musta missed the spleen, liver, pancreas, kidneys, aorta—I'm still alive, after all. Possible tamponade is slowing blood loss, but not enough they should dawdle. "… Mount Tabor near the statue … a retired police officer, Skin Kadash … please, hurry." She closes the phone, drops it in the grass. They won't like that back at the 9-1-1 call center. They want you to stay on the line, answer a million questions. But they'll send someone to check it out. Luellen leads Danny to the concrete bench next to Harvey, sits him down with her coat draped over his shoulders and a kiss on his little cheek. Then she joins me on the wet ground below the statue and cradles my head in her lap. My gaze takes in the night. It hurts to even shift my eyeballs side to side. He's a shadow above us, old Harvey, though I can make out his arm pointing toward the horizon as a silhouette against the blue-black sky. In grade school he's presented as an Oregon treasure. I suppose he is, but from my angle at the foot of the statue, he strikes me as a sinister old bastard. If not for him and his goddamn pedestal, maybe my blood wouldn't be pooling in my abdomen right now. On the other hand, better a ricochet than a direct hit from George's goddamn hand cannon.

Danny shivers on the bench. Luellen looks back at him, her face worried. Luellen. Or—?

"You've always reminded me of someone I used to know, another man who helped me. Pastor Sanders." I've never been mistaken for a holy man before. "You probably have a lot of questions."

I could write a book. "You don't need to stay with me. Someone will come."

She continues to gaze at Danny. He rubs his cheek and sighs. "Where else would I go?"

Somewhere rattling around behind the pain is the thought that I want her to be away from here before the police arrive, Danny with her. This mess will take a year to sort out, and I don't want her to be tangled up in it.

"Who …?"

I hesitate. Maybe I don't want to get into this. Maybe I want to let her be who she is. Danny is safe now, the man who came to take him is gone. Eager is dead, of that I'm sure. Maybe what I want is to let things drift backward a bit, back to a time when all I knew about her was that her name was Luellen Bronstein and she was the young mother of a good little boy who called me Mister Skin. I can't go back too far, because nothing I can do or say will unshoot Mitch Bronstein's gun. But maybe that doesn't matter anyway. His path will be veering off on its own no matter who the girl beside me really is. And mine as well. The pain in my gut is a credible augury of my own fate. Every passing moment brings me a little bit closer to too late.

Luellen strokes my forehead. "When I was a little girl, I wanted to grow my hair out and wear it like a dress."

The grass is cold against my wet ass. I lick my lips. Wince.

"Yes, I know what it sounds like. But I was young. What did I know?"

I think of Danny finding his way into my backyard. Looking for a place he thought was safe. No way he could know about Big Ed. He knew about the birds, though. "Maybe you knew more than you realize." My voice is a whisper.

"The thing is, I remember thinking it. I remember telling my family. I even remember my mother getting angry at me about it. I can picture it all in my mind. But I can't remember what it felt like. That little girl who wanted to dress in hair is gone. She's just a snapshot in my mind, faded and cracked. Everything else is gone. Forgotten."

I don't have the strength to respond, but Luellen doesn't need my encouragement.

"I miss her."

She's so young. I want to explain to her how as you grow older you leave behind a whole long history of shed skins. The girl she misses is just one of many, one who will never be truly gone. I have my own long history of the forgotten, the men and boys I once was. My newest iteration formed bare days before when I let my feelings for another young woman overcome reason. And before him was the Shiftless Skin, retired and without purpose, a man with nowhere to go, only places he'd been. Going back, the Skins I'd shed pile up like discarded clothes. Detective Skins, first Property, then Person Crimes. Eventually Homicide. Officer Skins, schools and traffic and patrol. Skin the student. Skin the enlisted man, Vietnam MP. Teenaged Skin with the ugly mug and oft-bloodied fists. I miss all of them, a little. Glad I've left them behind too, a little. And kept them all close by. A little. But how am I going to explain to this girl, this lost girl who stepped into another's skin in order to protect something important? How can I get her to understand that what she's lost, what she's forgotten, is just a piece of what it means to be alive?

I close my eyes. I want her to get away. The way the bodies are piled up around us, it's hard to imagine another threat, but I still know too little about what's been going on to be sure. Big Ed, the grandfather, the crazy tweaker. The man with the divot in his head. It's all a jumble in my head, stirred into a roiling soup by the fire of my wound. I draw a breath, feel my whole body tremble with the pain.

Luellen strokes my forehead again. "This is all my fault, you know."

I find that hard to believe. "What did you do?"

"Besides try to kill my husband?"

I attempt a wry smile. Probably comes off as a grimace. "Mitch does inspire a certain—"

"Not Mitch. Mitch has always been kind to me. Kinder than I deserve." She sighs and shakes her head. "No, the man who came, the man ..." Her voice trails off, and I realize she speaking of the stranger.

"The man with the injury to his head."

"My husband. His name is Stuart."

"But—?"

"Yes." She breathes, long and slow. "I guess I can now add bigamist to my list of crimes."

"You didn't know until tonight he was still alive."

"The last time I saw him, I jammed a pair of scissors into his head."

"Why?" A shadow passes over her face and I regret the question. I know a host of reasons a young woman like Luellen might need to stab her husband. "You don't have to answer."

She smiles, tight and bitter. "Just seemed like a good idea at the time." She strokes my forehead, a mother's gesture. "It's all so complicated."

Isn't everything?

"Mitch came home from work with something his firm was doing. Pro bono work for an environmental advocacy group. It was no big deal. He does a lot of that sort of thing and usually I don't pay much attention. But he left a stack of papers sitting on the kitchen table and something caught my eye. My father's name."

"What did your father have to do with environmental advocacy?"

"My family has a lot of land, thousands of acres in Givern Valley, a lot of it wetlands. One of the things Mitch's client did was facilitate land swaps between private owners and the Bureau of Land Management, or with the Nature Conservancy, groups like that. The goal is to move threatened habitat into protection. My father's name was on a memo, one of a list of people who had been approached by this organization. Federal policy has been shifting in recent years to be more favorable to private land owners and I guess environmental groups are trying to get more land under protection before policy makes it too difficult to arrange affordable deals. I don't know the specifics, but this group had approached my father and made an offer for his wetlands, but he wasn't interested. According to the memo, they were working on better offers for the listed land owners who resisted their initial overtures."

"And you called him about it."

"How did you know?"

"That woman, she was your sister, right? She said she heard her father talking to you about Danny."

Her expression darkens, a confirmation. I wait, too weak to push her on the matter. She doesn't make me wait long.

"I was calling him to tell him I would make the deal."

"I don't understand."

"When I left, he gave me the land. Everything, to protect it."

"And no one knows."

She nods. "If anyone looks hard enough, they can find out. Officially he sold the land to a holding company with layers of lawyers to hide my interest, and then leased it back. The details aren't important. The point is he couldn't make any deals without my signature. So I called to tell him it was okay. He should take whatever they offered so long as it was enough for him to retire. If there was anything left for Danny, that was fine. But the point was I didn't care about the land. I live here now. I have a new life. I'm married to a man whose values are very different from the values of the place I came from. I wanted to be free."

"How did your father feel about it?"

"He hated the idea of the Kern homestead going to dirt worshippers."

"But you told him to sell anyway."

"The whole world is changing around us. If I can't save the life my father lives, maybe I can at least keep Hiram Spaneker from taking it away from him."

From what little I'd seen of him, it was hard to argue. I force a nod past the pain. "But Myra had an opinion on the matter."

"You've seen her." She gestures toward the body. "One of the reasons my father gave it all to me was to keep it out of her hands." She looks away from me, her eyes welling up. "She killed him, I believe. Someone did. I saw a news story online a day or so after the last time he and I spoke."

That's easy to believe. If not her, then Big Ed with her help.

"What was supposed to happen up here?"

"Hiram said he would trade Danny for the Kern land." She draws a breath. "I knew better than that though."

"You were going to kill him."

"The threat against my family needed to end."

I'm not sure what to make of this young woman beside me. For all her evident regret, she exudes a degree of conviction I've never known myself. I have no way of comprehending what she's been through to bring her to this end. So determined, so focused. Danny, a boy who wasn't even her blood, yet who she would protect unto death.

She turns to me. "What are you going to tell the police?"

"I plan to die during questioning."

"I wouldn't blame you if you turned me in. And so long as Danny is safe, I don't care."

I take my time responding. In one sense, I've already answered. I answered when I took the gun from Eager, when I waded into the storm. I answered when I put Myra down like a rabid dog. I answered when I let the stranger take the gun and leave. After all that, was I going to up and turn over this young woman for the crime of protecting the child she loves?

"Near as I could see, Lu, that old fellow and his henchman were trying to steal your boy. The police might take issue with you going solo, but they'll get over it. As far as I'm concerned, you've done nothing wrong."

She drops her head. I feel the heavy shake of her sobs. I try to raise an arm to comfort her. After a moment, she speaks into my jacket. "Do you think he'll be okay?"

"Who?"

"Eager."

I don't want to tell her what I'm sure is true.

"I told him to go to the hospital, but he wouldn't and I was too focused on Danny to insist."

"Eager wouldn't have listened if you had."

"He got hurt because of me. And now he's dead, isn't he?"

A shadow seems to cross over her face. I wish there was some comfort I could offer her. All I have feels like thin gruel. "He wanted to protect you."

"He always has, since the day we met."

"Three years ago."

"At first, he thought I was the one who died up here that day. A couple of weeks later, when he saw me with Danny, I realized what I had to do. Who I had to be."

"And he helped you."

"Do you think he'll be okay?"

I'm not sure what she's asking me. I'm not a religious man, and if she is herself, it's a side of her I've never seen. Mitch's religion always seemed to be the Church of Mitch, but there was obviously more at work in that house across from my own than I've ever understood. I stare into the darkness, uncertain and in pain. Afraid I don't know the right thing to say. Ruby Jane would know. My Ruby Jane. But she isn't here, and it's just me, battered and gut-shot, and now a felon in my own right. Am I being asked to judge whether Eager will find his way to heaven or hell? How can I even know? But I understand now all he cared about was Luellen. Ellie. This young woman. "He loved you." My voice sounds more hesitant than my intent, but I can see in her eyes her recognition of the truth in my words. "I think he's fine, Luellen. Maybe for the first time in years."

Fresh tears fall, joining the rain on her cheeks and flashing blue and red in the darkness. For a moment the sight confuses me, and I think it's a trick of my own fading consciousness. What's next, a tunnel of light? I chuckle, surprised it doesn't hurt too bad. One more sign I'm dying, I guess. I look into the sky, which has grown brighter. The branches of the fir trees and Harvey's Scott's arm stand out in stark relief against a breathing grey flood. Through shreds in the clouds I catch a glimpse of Orion's Belt. The cold flutters against my face like tatters of lace. An unlikely snow in Portland in November. Yet I know the snow sometimes kisses the hilltops while down in the flats below we are granted only the numbing, indifferent rain. The lights continue to flash and I rotate my head, slowly, weakly, then laugh again. Not the tunnel of light after all.

Just a patrol car.

November 19 - 5:22 pm

Find What You Find

Swirling faces in the blue and red light, some I recognize, many I don't. Michael Masliah, Sergeant Kuhl. EMTs swarm over me like flies. Masliah gazes down at me with sad-eyed pity before he gently leads Luellen and Danny to his car. Kuhl looks like he wants to spit on me, as if a button in the belly is less than I deserve. Maybe he's right. The pain in my stomach is so great I feel nothing when they insert the IV. I do feel something when the first compress is packed into my wound. "Can you hear me, sir? Can you hear me?" *Jesus, yes.* "Can you hear me?" *Yes, goddammit.* But I'm talking only in my head. "Sir, sir?" A light flashes in my eyes. "What? I hear you." Then there's Susan. I don't see her arrive. "Okay, sir, we're going to lift you, okay?" She's just there, materialized like a phantom, stalking at the perimeter of the scene, scowling at the bodies. She doesn't even know who these people are yet, Myra the tweaker, George the Flea. Only the name Big Ed Gillespie will mean anything to her, though knowing it won't help her frame of mind. But her expression softens when she gets to Luellen, who sits clutching Danny against her chest in the back of Masliah's car.

Then she sees me.

The EMTs heave me onto a gurney. I want to scream, hold it back. They're prepping me for transport. Straps and tubes, blood pressure cuff on my arm. I hear a sound, beeping, and wonder about Mitch. Somewhere inside I know there's little time to waste. I tell them I need to talk to Susan. "Sir, there's no time. We need to get you moving." Susan steps forward, promises to make it quick. One of them argues but I cut him short. "If I die en route to the hospital, I'll be really pissed if you didn't let me talk to the lieutenant." I think they've given me something for the pain, or maybe Susan is surrounded by some locus of lucidity.

"Take too long and you will die."

I believe him. My legs are cold and my hands tingling. I don't care. "Susan, you need to understand something. Luellen was only thinking about Danny. Okay? It was all about making sure Danny was safe."

"I don't even know what that means." Her voice is cold and far away.

"Just believe her when you talk to her, okay?"

"Believe *her*? What about you? You're Batman now? What the hell were you thinking?"

The beep continues, all in one ear. Blue and red light flashes to my right. Alcohol vapor stings my nostrils. I don't have time, or energy, to explain about finding Danny in the yard, about Big Ed's appearance. "It all went sideways. I did my best."

She's pressing her lips tight against her teeth. Her hair is damp with rain. "We found Eager."

"Is he—?"

"Yes." She shakes her head. "Jesus, Skin."

"I would have called you if I could. Check my back deck. You'll find my phone, smashed. Big Ed's doing."

"What would I find if I had Justin Marcille check you for gunshot residue?"

There's no good answer for a question like that. The fact she's asking at all tells me she knows exactly what she'd find. "A lot of crazy shit was going down. I guess you'll find what you find."

"How about the gun? Will I ever find that?"

Not something I'd want to bet on, either way. If the man with the hole in his head gets away, maybe not. But someone in his condition? Maybe a uniform will come across him, or his body, halfway down the hill or halfway across the state, gun in hand, roaming eye rolling.

She retrieves a pack of Marlboros from her coat pocket. Sometime during the day she crossed a line. Will the cigarettes make it home with her, or will she do what I did for months before I finally quit—buy a pack, smoke one, toss the rest with a pledge to never buy another? Expensive. She throws a sour, defensive look my way as she lights up and jets smoke upward like she wants to obscure the sky. "What are the chances I'll ever find out what happened up here?"

"A young woman recovered her child, unharmed, from a would-be kidnapper. A psychotic tweaker and a couple of brutal thugs are dead. Fuck it. It's a win all around for the good guys."

She's not happy. In her shoes I wouldn't be either. The way things developed today, everything that could go wrong for her has. Just as well I'm one foot in the grave. It's no matter to me enough confusion was wrought even Mitch Bronstein—a man who drew down on a street full of cops—may walk without ever being charged. To the extent justice has been served here atop Mount Tabor, it's vigilante justice—something no good cop ever wants. A bunch of bad guys are dead and a mother and child are safe, and that's all well and good, but the whole situation stinks from Susan's perspective. And me in the middle of it. Former cop, former partner. Batman indeed. I'm supposed to know better than to get hip deep in the shit. But even Susan had to admit sometimes you take what you can get, be it verdict reached at trial or fondue fork in the eye.

I hear her sigh. The energy required for thought is suddenly more than I have. I close my eyes, against my will. I feel myself moving.

"Susan?" I turn my head and blink, but she isn't there. I look from side to side, see only grim-faced paramedics. Hear the tip-tap of the rain. And Charm. Charm Gillespie. Hutchison. Whatever her name is. There she is, rising up out of the darkness into the red and blue light of the patrol cars and the ambulances. When did I speak to her husband? Six hours earlier? She must have driven like her ass was on fire to get here in that time.

She heads right toward me, indifferent to the tubes in my arms and the blood on my shirt. "Where's my son?"

One of the paramedics tries to front her. I lift my head, the weight of a stone.

"Mrs. Gillespie—"

An arm appears and slows Charm's advance. "Susan …" I can't remember why I should feel grateful she would try to protect me. But Susan isn't interested in me. I don't even know if she can see me. "Mrs. Gillespie, you need to understand—"

Charm throws off Susan's arm. "Damn it, bitch, I know he's dead. I don't need any soft focus bullshit out of you. Just take me to him."

Susan's shoulders drop, a capitulation built of weariness. I'm sorry for my part in it. She gestures toward the trees rising on the north slope. Charm diverts mid-stride, Susan beside her. Before either take more than a few steps, I croak Charm's name, try to wave with my IV-stabbed arm. The EMTs are pissed, but I croak again and Charm turns and looks at me.

"Charm."

Her expression is the familiar sneer she's worn as long as I've known her. "You gonna die too, Detective?"

Probably. It hurts too much to shrug. "How'd you know to come here?"

She just shakes her head like I'm a fucking idiot. "Where the hell else would he be?"

I Can Do This

I t was the kind of unexpected warm, sunny day that sometimes crops up in late February, a cruel tease before a long, damp spring. The clear air reminded her of the air that blew across her father's barley in June, and for a moment a cloud seemed to pass in front of the sun. She brushed a loose hair off her face and drew a breath.

I can do this.

She stood on the porch of the new house. *Our house,* she thought, though the idea seemed foreign to her still. Being part of an *our.* Mitch claimed the porch would need paint, probably the whole house, and he'd complained about a squeaky board. She walked the porch from end to end, pausing to look through the broad front window into the still empty living room, but all she heard was her own soft footfalls and the high breeze through the trees behind the house across the street. She went to the rail, brushed the cool wood with her fingertips. *Our porch rail.* Then she felt a presence at her back, and before she could turn, heard Mitch's voice. "You're singing again."

As soon as he spoke, she heard the music in the back of her throat, the song Luellen had hummed over Danny's stroller that day under Harvey Scott's dour gaze. She flushed and looked at her hands.

"What are you thinking about, sweets?"

"Nothing."

"Sure you are. You always sing like that when you think."

"I had no idea."

But she did. She'd caught herself humming the tune over Danny's crib at night, and as he fussed in his stroller when she was first learning his habits. Eager noticed it too.

"Well, does this belong to you?"

She turned. Mitch stood in the wide front doorway, a wiggling Danny in his arms.

"I'm not sure. Does he have a name tag?"

"No, but he keeps saying Da. Could that be a name?"

"He might just be agreeable. Where did you find him?"

"Crawling through the kitchen cupboards."

She held out her arms and Danny reached for her as if she'd always been his. She took him from Mitch and hugged him tight. "You're so big. Do you belong to me?"

"Da."

"I think I'll keep you then."

Mitch crossed the porch and planted his hands on the rail next to her. It creaked under his weight.

"See?"

"It's fine."

"The porch is fine, maybe, but of the ten thousand houses we looked at, why'd you have to pick the one with a dump across the street?"

She hitched Danny onto her hip. The house across the street wasn't much to look at. Grey siding overdue for paint, a slight slouch to the porch. No doubt the boards squeaked underfoot. The houses on either side were much nicer, with crisp-edged landscaping, clearer colors, sharper lines. Clean windows, hanging baskets. She knew she didn't have to explain herself. Mitch understood the situation. She was doing her part, looking after his son, holding the family together, meeting his needs from basement to bedroom. His part was simple enough, and Lord knew he was no Stuart.

She looked back to the grey house. In the dirt below the slumping porch, she saw a purple flash, spring's first crocuses at least a month earlier than she ever saw them back in Givern Valley.

"It's not that bad. Eager says the man who lives there is a police officer, a good man."

"Thank god we relied of the broad experience of Eager Gillespie Realty."

"Mitch, please." She didn't want to argue with him. It wasn't something she was used to, not yet. The whole pose, wife and mother. *Our fight.*

"I suppose if there's one thing Eager knows, it's cops."

"He's been through a lot more than you realize."

"Yeah, yeah. I know." Mitch looked at the house again. "Whatever. Maybe we won't get robbed, at least."

She closed her eyes and counted backwards, five to one. It used to be more. Ten to one, twenty to one. A hundred. She was learning.

"Oy. I know that look. Hey, babe, we're moving in, right?"

"Thank you, Mitch." She turned and leaned into him, kissed him lightly on the cheek. He smelled faintly of shaving cream and hazelnuts. "You know I appreciate it."

"One of these days you gotta explain—" He stopped, pursed his lips briefly. He was learning too.

Across the street, the front door opened. The man who emerged was no one to inspire confidence. He was of medium height, lumpy, with shaggy grey hair and a wrinkled brown suit jacket over tan pants. She wasn't sure what she expected, but this wasn't it. He grabbed his newspaper and went back inside without appearing to notice he was being observed.

This is who you sent me to?

She took a breath and turned to Mitch. "I'm going over to say hello."

"To the cop?"

"Yes."

"What about the rest of the neighbors? The ones who've painted their houses some time in the last decade."

"You need to be nicer to me."

"Okay, okay." He rolled his eyes. "Take Danny with you. The movers will be here any minute, and I'm trying to get Jase off his ass in the remote hope we'll be ready for them."

"I know there's a lot to do. I won't be long."

Mitch headed into the house. She counted his steps until they faded away, then bounced Danny on her hip. "Ready to go meet Eager's friend?"

Danny squirmed in response. There was a big empty house behind them. He wanted down, wanted to go explore.

"You can climb all over the place and get filthy later."

"Da."

She crossed the street and went up the front walk, Danny bouncing on her hip. But as she climbed the stoop and stepped onto the porch—*squeak*—her courage failed her. An image of Eager in Common Grounds Coffee House flashed through her mind.

"When he says his name is Skin and sticks his neck out at you, roll with it. He's just trying to freak you out."

"Do you really think this is a good idea?"

"Don't worry. He's all right. He's not fucking afraid of Big Ed, that's for sure."

She thought of her father's inability to stand up to her mother, how he never took her on the hunting trips through the marsh, how he wouldn't stand up for her when she wanted to cancel the wedding to Stuart. He only found his courage when it was almost too late. She remembered talking to him on the phone that first time after she made her way back to Luellen's little apartment, guided by an electric bill she found in Danny's diaper bag. Her father described how Hiram showed up at the house suggesting that for all anyone knew she might be dead on a faraway hilltop. She lay on the floor next to Danny's crib afterwards, crying for Pastor Sanders, for her fucked-up brothers, even for Myra. And Luellen. Especially for Luellen. She tried to imagine a different Ellie, one who drowned in the creek, or one who floated downstream for miles and days from creek to river, river to shore. Maybe a different Ellie floated out to the deep sea where no one would ever be harmed by her passage again. But that wasn't the Ellie who stood here now, who'd crawled off that hilltop. Who found a way to be mother to Stuart's child, because it was Luellen's child too. She owed Luellen that much.

Some choices, once made, never stop being who you are.

The door opened and he appeared. The cop. Skin. He must have heard her on the porch. Maybe having squeaky boards wasn't such a bad thing. Or maybe he heard her humming Luellen's lullaby.

"Help you?" His voice was rough and smoky. He stood with one shoulder back so the red patch on his neck was mostly hidden.

She found a smile somewhere inside. "Hi, we're moving in across the street and I came to introduce myself."

"Oh." He looked across at the house. Their house. It was as if he was seeing it for the first time. "I remember the For Sale sign going up, but I didn't realize anyone had bought it." He looked back at her, and at Danny on her hip. The little fellow met his gaze, his round Stuart eyes clear and unwavering beneath his shaggy bangs.

"Da."

The cop's gaze went soft. "And who might this be?"

"His name's Danny, and I'm ... my name is Luellen."

The cop raised his eyes back to hers but kept his head tilted—if anything, he was trying to hide the red patch on his neck. "Well, you might as well call me Skin. Everyone else does."

November 19 - late

The Moose Comes Out of the Trees

My thoughts swim, rainbows of flame filtered through antique glass. Floating on a raft of air. Images, observations ... my whole life is a sequence of observations, randomly ordered and clouded by sensation. A loose, fluid sound, cold and damp. I blink and discover the light, warm to the sound of a needle piercing my neck. It feels like water flowing uphill. Floating among bubbles. Voices through the end of a tube, recordings on wax cylinders. The moose comes out of the trees. I blink again, and swallow. My throat opens and emits a red, round sound. I taste hot pepper.

"Tell ..."

The voices, distant. I can't feel them, can't see them.

"Please."

A face, sudden focus from out of the dark, out of the light. A shaft of forehead, an eye shaped like wind, the rattle of a drum. "Take it easy, Mister Kadash." I understand the words. "We're rolling now, okay?" They smell like apples. Words shaped like apples. A dash of salt with the cayenne.

"We're rolling ..."

"Please." I think it's my voice. "Please tell Ruby Jane … find her. Tell her …"

I float away, raft of air, unable to remember what.

November 22

Police Seek Help Identifying Man
Found Dead On Green Springs Highway

KLAMATH FALLS, OR: Local police are seeking help from
the public in identifying the body of a man found dead
on Green Springs Highway late Tuesday night. The man
appears to have suffered a gunshot wound to the chest,
though the official cause of death has not been announced,
pending autopsy.

The victim is described as six feet tall, in his early fifties,
with short, steel-grey hair and a medium build. He was
discovered in the ditch by a group of teenagers driving
along the road shortly after midnight. No identification was
found on the body.

Police theorize the man was the victim of a robbery. He
was found without cash, keys, cell phone, wallet or other
identifying items. A statewide alert has been issued.

Acknowledgements

Writing is often seen as a solitary act, and there's no doubt writers spend plenty of time inside their own heads. Even those, like me, who write in public—the coffee shop, the library, the nearest pub—spend an inordinate amount of time focused on the keyboard and on the hermitic act of creation. Despite that, I find the collaborative aspects of writing to be among the most rewarding. Interactions with readers, other writers, friends, and colleagues keep me as sane as I am likely to ever be. Sometimes it's kicking around ideas, sometimes it's commiserating, but mostly it's just sharing a love of the written word.

I'm not sure what I'd do without my friends, fellow writers Brett Battles and Rob Browne. Daily IM buddies, and drinking buddies on those too rare occasions when we find ourselves in the same city. They're never more than an email or a phone call away when I need them. And not to be overlooked are Tasha Alexander, Kelli Stanley, JT Ellison, and Eric Stone—confederates and confidants all!

On the research front, I owe a huge debt of gratitude to Dr. Steven Seres, who coached me on acute trauma care, particularly the effects of gunshot wounds. Whatever I managed to get right on the medical front is thanks to him. Whatever I got wrong is all on me.

Thanks as always go out to Janet Reid for her hard work on my behalf and for her deadly shark's teeth, perhaps not so sharp as she might like us all to believe. Thank you also to Tyrus Books publisher Ben LeRoy and editor (and Sheriff) Alison Janssen for being smart and delightfully nerdy, and for their vision and risk-taking. I am humbled to be part of the of Tyrus family.

I thank my good friends and fellow writers Candace Clark, Andy Fort, Corissa Neufeldt, and Theresa Snyder, who beta-read *Day One* and offered invaluable critiques.

And last, but not least, I thank my lovely wife Jill, who puts up with my tics and weirdnesses and gets mad when I kill off her favorite characters, but who manages to love me nonetheless.

BILL CAMERON lives with his wife and a menagerie of critters in Portland, Oregon. His stories have appeared in *Spinetingler, Killer Year, Portland Noir,* and the forthcoming *First Thrills.* He is a member of Friends of Mystery, International Thriller Writers, Sisters-in-Crime and Mystery Writers of America. Visit www.bill cameronmysteries.com for more information.